T

Cocktail Bar

Isabella May

CROOKED
CAT

Discover us online:
www.crookedcatbooks.com

Join us on facebook:
www.facebook.com/crookedcat

Tweet a photo of yourself holding
this book to **@crookedcatbooks**
and something nice will happen.

This novel is dedicated to all of
those in need of magic.

Open your eyes; it was
there all along…

About the Author

Isabella May lives in (mostly) sunny Andalucia, Spain with her husband, daughter and son, creatively inspired by the sea and the mountains. When she isn't having her cake and eating it, sampling a new cocktail on the beach, or ferrying her children to after school activities, she is usually writing.

As a Co-founder and a former contributing writer for the popular online women's magazine, The Glass House Girls - **www.theglasshousegirls.com** - she has also been lucky enough to subject the digital world to her other favourite pastimes, travel and the Law of Attraction.

The Cocktail Bar is her second novel. Oh! What a Pavlova is her first.

Acknowledgements

Sophie Partridge comes in at top of this list. Little did she know how her Florida Cocktail Trip of 2016 would plant the champagne bubble that became this book, but those pictures she shared on Facebook were something else and inspired me to get scribbling immediately. So thank you, Soph. I owe you one mahoosive Key West Cooler next time we meet!

Alas, there are so many cocktail companions to list. Old and new, remembered and (eek) forgotten. So here is my attempt at doing just a little bit of that:

Sarah Hill and Laura Moore: I pray to God we never experiment with a drinks cabinet containing Jack Daniels ever again. Caroline Stacey: here's hoping neither of us will ever be led once more into Mad Dog 20/20, or Diamond White, or neat Cinzano, or Pernod and Black temptation...

Tracy Hails, Jon Davies, Collis Boucher, Peter Mitchelmore,

Rich Ellis and Alan Patmore: If my memory serves me correctly, we partook in many a jug of whatever-Happy-Hour-wanted-to-dispense-of at one Las Iguanas in Bristol... overlooking the night that I mistook the kitchen for the Ladies' room. My curiosity as to the magical notes of mixology could only have grown from there.

Collis: on the Key West Cooler front, maybe eight in a row should be the limit though... especially when one is gracing Covent Garden on a Saturday afternoon!

Book Fair Buddies: Vicky Bostock, Louise Viveiros, Cristina Galimberti, Selena Johnstone, Ruth Owen. Thank you for not raising either eyebrow as I uncouthly supped cocktails with my meal (whilst everybody else politely glugged down their wine). You have all helped to shape my kooky drinking habits.

And Cristina, I shall be ever grateful to you for introducing me to a proper Campari and Orange – with blood orange. If a mixer is to be mixed, it's to be mixed meticulously.

My husband really cannot be overlooked in all of this either. How patiently he sits and awaits my cocktail verdict (especially if it's a brand new one I'm trying) wherever we go. He also knocks up the meanest of White Russians.

Mum: I have you to thank for treating me to my first proper Piña Colada – Waldorf Astoria style.

Emma Wilson and Natali Drake: You both added fuel to the cocktail fire that burned within when we collectively began to write about our favourite tipples for a certain magazine.

Ailsa Abraham and Vanessa Couchman, I am indebted to you for the fabulous creations you have kindly donated to The Cocktail Bar, courtesy of the online launch party competition for my first novel. The recipes for both of these magical glasses of elixir can be found at the end of the book. Make sure you patent them: you're going to sell millions!

Huge gratitude, as ever, to Crooked Cat Books for confirming I am not a One Trick Pony (or kitten). It means the world to me to get another story out there.

And thank you billions to all who have so passionately supported my first novel, only adding to the momentum that is this one:

My family - particularly my dad who tore a knee ligament in the process of carrying out Book Fairy drops! - my mum and my sister, my cousin and my aunt for their constant and fabulous promotion of 'Pavlova' all over Somerset – there's no way I'd have generated such a pre-sales buzz without you. And I cannot forget my niece, who even hiked up Glastonbury Tor for her auntie. Thanks also goes out to my friends (especially Natali Drake for her unparalleled support and beautiful photography, and my old school friends: wow, just wow!), my former colleagues, my current colleagues: the amazing CATS whose knowledge, advice, tips and excitement has been monumental. Then there is my lovely Editor Maureen Vincent-Northam, my Spanish friends, all the fabulous book bloggers… especially the one and only Karlita from Heartale Fix, all the fantastic Facebook book groups… especially the wonderful Wendy Clarke's (where I 'just happened' to meet Jennifer Gilmour), and Helen Boyce's TBC Reviewer Request Group (well… perhaps with the exception of THAT 2 star review!). The Book Fairies in London and Bristol have also been amazingly helpful with all of the exciting and inspired book drops they voluntarily carried out.

An extra special thank you to Emma Mitchell for everything she has done to help both books shine extra brightly, too.

And an extra, extra special thank you to the Lovely Loomies

and Emma Gibbard who kindly let me promote the book for the day, leading to one Jeremy Clarkson being knocked off the top spot in Hot New Releases for Food and Travel Writing on Amazon. Magic!

Last but definitely not least: Bryony Curtis, THANK YOU for introducing me to the marmalade magic of Aperol Spritz at the time of writing these acknowledgements. Where had it been hiding all my life?

The Cocktail Bar

"Cocktails: Because no great story ever started with someone eating a salad."

Source Unknown

Chapter One
RIVER

River Jackson didn't care that the words Glastonbury and Piña Colada hardly belonged in the same paragraph. He had to go back. Instinct told him he had unfinished business. Besides which, he had a duty to a certain Mexican bottle, one which thankfully wasn't yet adorning the bar. Since the day he realised he'd stopped raising either eyebrow at his mother for "becoming a goddess," logic was an alien notion anyway.

It was something he was at least half questioning now though. His matted pony tail reeked of sticky Kahlua. Blake could have elected to slam dunk his head into a puddle of something cheaper. But River's balaclava-attired attacker had reached for the three closest bottles to hand, sliding them along the length of the fully stocked shelf as if it were his xylophone finale in a requiem. Splinters of glass flew across River's business opportunity, until they became a broken mirror, glistening their danger warning to a thirty-four-year-old who'd gotten way too ahead of himself. The Cointreau doused the freshly laid wooden floor, the Peach Schnapps' heady scent coated the tables and chairs, and the Kahlua re-painted the bar's counter creamy beige – alongside River's twisted head, right shoulder and part of his torso.

He knew it was Blake as soon as the daylight dissolved the silhouette that had entered the bar. It was all in the eyes; the left green, the right hazel. Too tempestuously thick for his own good, nothing much had changed there. Neither had Lee's role as passive observer; River detected that teenage nervousness was still part of his physique, emanating like a leaky tap he'd never got round to fixing. Lee shuffled from foot to foot in front of the bay window's enormous blind – which he'd made

3

a cack-handed attempt to pull over their intrusion; a stray tuft of flame red peeped from beneath the seam of his head gear.

"You're lucky you picked on me," said River, swallowing hard to stifle a fit of ill-timed giggles, despite the fact nothing about this was the modern definition of hilarious. "Don't give up the day jobs just yet though. Probably best you don't start raiding the bank—"

"Zip it, fucker," said Blake. He yanked off his head gear and stooped to look River in the eye, excited spittle flying in all directions, "who the frick do you think you are waltzing back into town as if you own the joint?"

River felt his old school friend's wrath anew through the thin black gloves, whose role of safeguarding identity revealing fingerprints, was equally laughable. Blake pressed River's face harder onto the counter; further acknowledgement of his fresh burst of fury. Then all remained hauntingly calm, until he decided to spit his disdain at River's forehead, before pulling himself away as if he'd come to his senses.

"You're not wanted here. Isn't that right, mate?" he said across the hazy bar to Lee's ghostly shape.

The outline nodded in agreement and continued to transfer its weight from foot to foot.

River hoped the height of the action was over but didn't dare move a fraction. His teenage years with Blake were reminder enough of his tendency to come back with a sudden and unexpected vengeance.

"Hey, beanpole," said Blake, seemingly forgetful of their attempt at anonymity, and reminding River why his former friend was so shit at *Cluedo* as a kid. "Well? Don't just stand there like a lanky moron, help me get rid of the evidence." He beckoned Lee's willowy figure over from the doorway.

Poor Lee, as much as he'd grown up, he'd obviously never managed to outgrow his moniker.

"Look, there's no need, guys," said River, somehow barely moving his lips for fear of reprisal. "Just leave it to me, yeah? It's not like I'd totally finished decorating anyway. It's cool, really. Least I can do—"

"And did I ask for your opinion?" Blake stood with

authority, turning a triangular piece of glass over and over between comic book villain fingers as if contemplating its edges' many uses. "It's just that last time I made that mistake; last time I called you because I thought you were a mate... someone who gave a crap about my life when it was dangling by a thread... you were thousands of miles away on a stage in California." He sniffed hard and tossed the glass behind him. A tinkle of destruction pierced the air.

"I know. I've been rubbish. Going to make up for lost time now though. It's one of the reasons I'm back."

"Did you hear that?" said Blake to his sidekick who was busying himself kicking shards of glass into a pile. "He thinks he can swan off with his F list entourage, jet around the world making millions with his two-a-penny voice, drummer and guitarist, forget about us until the novelty wears off, and then we'll be waiting here with open arms."

"Don't work like that," Lee finally found his voice although his gaze remained fixed to the drama decorating the floor.

"The kid's right for once in his life; it doesn't work like that," said Blake with a menacing smile as he rubbed his hands together. "'Cos not only have you flounced back to Glastonbury, but you've also been dense enough to buy the pub where my old man, my very own flesh and blood, used to enjoy his one and only pleasure in life after my bitch of a mother did the dirty on him."

Shit, how could River have forgotten the importance of the skittles? It was the life force of men of a certain era and ilk. Not just here but in towns dotted all over Somerset. No, he genuinely hadn't thought any of this through.

River's heart pounded like it was backstage at his last gig in Guadalajara all over again. He knew Blake's body language intimately. Too many high school science lessons exchanging secret looks before one or the other of them unleashed the stink bomb behind a gaggle of girls, 'accidentally' dropped the box of iron filings, or pestered Miss Willoughby with questions of 'genuine concern' about the correct application of condoms and all things reproductive.

"Remember that game we used to play at Tor Fair every September?"

"Um," River began and then cleared his throat to buy some guessing time. "Hook the duck, the darts?"

Damn, why did he have to go and mention yet another pub game whose tradition was about as far removed from a cocktail bar as it got?

"River," said Blake with the addition of several tuts and an unexpected kick to his private parts. "How could you forget?"

River yelped. It had been at least a decade since anybody had attacked him there (notwithstanding the ending of last year's fling with the Parisian model). He breathed in deeply, whistling through clenched teeth, hoping to avoid a delayed reaction of effeminate cries.

"I'm uh, I'm sure it'll come back to me... if you uh... if you jog my memory."

"Is there anything you remember about your roots, Jackson? Or were there too many drugs on the road?" Blake sniffed at his empty palm in a pitiful attempt to imitate a coke head. "You're just a traitor through and through. Back here to bleed the place dry selling Sex on the Beach to eighteen-year-olds now forty is on your horizon and the paparazzi are making a beeline for the younger models. Unless of course, you'd been smart enough to do the indie band shebang like HRH Chris Martin, which you most definitely haven't." He shook his greying head with more than a striking resemblance of Miss Willoughby on detention duty.

"No, man, no, it's nothing like that. I promise." He hissed inwardly at the mere mention of the paps, the local rag was already on his case, and he was praying he'd got away without attracting the lens of the tabloids. "It's me, the real me. The River you know and love. And I'm back for good this time. I've turned my back on all that fame and fake crap. It's meaningless, especially the money."

"See, that, my man, is where you are very much mistaken." Blake lowered his posture again so River was in no doubt he had something very serious to say – and that he really was sporting an interesting cluster of badger streaks. "You are not back for good." He grabbed roughly at the day-old stubble on River's chin, "neither are you wanted here," and then released it.

He spat again at the floor, an impediment which appeared to be carrying him from the football field as a teenager and on into adult life. River held his breath wondering what was coming next as Blake began to pace around the bar, stopping here and there to mimic somebody admiring the portraits in an art gallery. One glove was removed now and he dipped his index finger into the Schnapps' sticky river, swirling it thoughtfully as if it were the blood of his prey. He lifted it to his lips, the alcohol re-painting an evil grin.

"Peachy... but then you'd know all about that... because you weren't just satisfied with obliterating a skittles team—"

"But I couldn't stop The Ring O'Bells being sold, that wasn't my fault. If I hadn't bought it, somebody else would—"

"Shut it," Blake yelled. "I'm doing the talking," he continued softly.

"Now where was I? Oh yes, peaches... ripe juicy peaches, none more so than Alice's rump." He paused to laugh. Lee's echo joined in a few seconds later, the double entendre catching on.

River's pulse quickened as he too connected the dots.

"A *derriere* so pert and delicious, that not only did you steal an old man's pastime, but you swiped my woman while you were at it too—"

"But that was years ago, man... a... a... one night stand," River gulped. "It meant nothing... to either of us."

"Nothing?" Blake cackled. "The love of my life meant nothing?"

He was a tornado of rage again. His face contorted with revenge as he reached for the chair behind him, slamming it into the wall. The legs buckled, debris scattered. Even Lee looked terrified this time.

The haunting silence returned, offering up a brief interlude until Blake decided he was ready to speak.

"Oh, incidentally," he said, stooping once more to look deep into the pools of River's eyes, "the fairground game I

7

was referring to is called the Whack-a-Mole."

River nodded. It seemed all words were probably best left to Blake now.

"It's a game where this annoying little pillock," he paused, and River sensed the direction of Blake's thoughts before his attacker had chance to process them for himself, "hand me that bottle, Lee…" Blake pointed to a shelf that River had mistakenly thought was concealed to the customer's side of the bar.

Holy shit: Not the Mexican elixir.

But Lee was a soldier, under sergeant's command. His hands moved along the line of bottles, feeling for the most suitable weapon.

River tore his eyes away, praying silently that Lee would pick out any other bottle.

"As I was saying," said Blake, "the annoying son of a bitch mole pokes its head up… uninvited," he ran his hand along River's jawline in a bizarre caress, "and so… what you do to this irritating excuse for a creature," he beckoned to Lee who passed him a bottle in perfectly choreographed timing, "is you whack it back down into the hole again as hard as you can with a mallet."

"Yeah, I re—"

But Blake's fingertip welded River's lips firmly together.

"Just a polite warning, buddy: you're the mole, I'm the mallet; the steel mallet," he raised the bottle high and smashed it, mercifully, against the counter as opposed to the skull, "and I will come back again and again with a vengeance to destroy this place, and its proprietor," he paused and closed his eyes as if deep in thought, searching for his next words, "ex pop star or not, until I drive them to the brink of insanity and back to the city of angels where they belong."

Chapter Two
RIVER

Two twenty-two am; that had to be a sign. If it wasn't eleven-eleven it was two twenty-two, whenever and wherever River was, he always seemed to look at a timepiece at either of these precise moments – day or night. Now was decidedly night. He shivered and pulled his soiled denim jacket over his chest, curled as he was in the foetal position on the comfiest drinking couch in the bar.

The late afternoon's events were a blur, namely because he'd chosen to numb their existence with one and a half cheap bottles of Prosecco. But bit by bit the scene replayed itself, making him shudder and retch, hardly helped along by Blake's reference to the tacky innuendo cocktails he most definitely wouldn't be serving up, as well as his audacity to label him a pop star.

Then again he had always been a lightweight when it came to the bubbles.

Thank god Lee had chosen the Drambuie though – which had only been right next to the Mexican tipple – whatever it was the mystical vessel contained. River still hadn't the foggiest of its alcoholic composition, despite its mission nearing completion. As soon as Blake and Lee had fled, he'd hidden it in a cubbyhole in the backyard's former skittle alley, swaddled in blankets to keep it at room temperature, then returned to the bar's sink, studded as it was with broken glass and ethanol in all of its guises, to wash the stench of coffee liquor from his hair.

He rubbed his eyes and scoured the contents of his investment. He was as good as back to square one on the decorating front, but money was no object, he'd soon call in the professionals to set it straight. And hopefully Blake wouldn't follow through with his threat.

"You haven't seen the last of me by a long shot," was his parting gesture.

"No, nor me," Lee had put in his two pennies worth moments later, clawing at the door Blake had slammed with an almighty bang.

He couldn't really blame him. He'd had it hard these past few years. River had heard about Blake's parents' on-off relationship courtesy of his own mum filling him in on the town's gossip. And then if he was honest with himself, despite the haze of teenage marijuana-filled days when they used to cycle down to the moors and the secret hideaway under the bridge straddling the River Brue, he did recall the way he used to stare at Alice as they fell about in fits of stoned laughter. But the two of them being an item; he wasn't sure if that part was lost somewhere in the recesses of his imagination, or a mere figment of Blake's. Either way, it had to smart if he'd never truly moved on, seeing her date American actor after American actor; the rosebud of his indie rock band – well, former indie rock band, once *Avalonia* hit the big time, Alice had never looked back at any of her vanilla college boys.

River stretched his arms wide and rose slowly, desperately trying to ignore his sore head. He tiptoed between the piles and lone shards of glass – a kid playing the don't-step-on-the-cracks-in-the-pavement game. The floor behind the bar was surprisingly clear of Blake's aftermath, with most of the debris having landed on the counter, making an easy pathway to The Bible. He lodged it under his arm and navigated his way back to the couch. His fingers traced the cover and the echoes of Varadero beach in Cuba beckoned, a rum so pure it rivalled even the best Haiti had to offer, a sand so white that after a spectacularly heavy session, you wondered whether you really had died and gone to heaven.

He had to get some air. The negative energy of Blake's tirade still permeated the bar. He re-positioned the book under his arm. It was hefty and definitely not inconspicuous. But the chances of anybody loafing around town at this time of night on a Tuesday were slim to say the least, and soon he was powerwalking his way up to Bove Town and beyond, his mind and the rest of his body following his feet.

That was until his phone started to vibrate against his thigh, rudely interrupting his stride. He retrieved it from his pocket without thinking, the innocent looking number momentarily deceiving him.

"Hello?"

"It's Lennie," the caller said, adding a chain of heavy breaths. "Don't hang up. I say don't hang up. Come on, lad, we really need to talk. You can't just leave me dangling by a thread like—"

Goddamnit.

River cut him off and shoved the phone back in his pocket. He needed to be sharper than this, one hundred per cent on the ball at all times. He'd change his number tomorrow. That would soon put paid to future conversation with his ex-manager. He was his own boss now. Besides, he'd made a promise to Mercedes. Okay, maybe only in his head, half an hour into that flight back from Guadalajara to Heathrow. But she knew he was committed, of that much he was sure.

His steps soon became meditative and purposeful again, brushing aside the internal chatter. And within an hour he was sat atop the Ancient Isle of Avalon, a solitary figure in the archway of Glastonbury Tor waiting for sunrise.

***

River woke to fingers of light dancing on his cheek and the warble and crimson flash of a pair of male robins flitting overhead in May's cool morning air. He unpeeled the layers of his sleeping bag – he'd been crashing out at the bar during the renovations and had instinctively stuffed it into his backpack to keep him warm, wherever he should end up laying his head – but strangely he'd no recollection of drifting off to sleep.

And shit. Where had he put the book?

No sooner had the fear of a decade and a bit of lost cocktail recipes clutched at his breath, than he pulled back the hood of

11

his sleeping bag to see he'd been using it as a pillow.

He exhaled and watched as his clouds of relief filtered through the archway like smoke from a beacon, as the Tor was sometimes used for special ceremonies. Something dug into his side and he pulled out his mobile once more from his trouser pocket, half tempted to fling it down the hillside while he was at it. There were a string of missed calls and messages from Heather, his mum, who would insist that he use her first name once he turned sixteen, as if it were some kind of spiritual coming of age ritual. He remembered to acquiesce when he could, especially when he needed a favour.

"Paps have been hanging around outside on the street all night, Riv. I don't feel safe to leave the house. I told you I have a transcendental meditation class to teach at 11am!"

Hadn't they anything better to do? At this rate he was going to have to live up here on this mound to avoid the madness that had become his life. He wasn't in the limelight any more. It was high time they respected that.

He randomly opened the book, making a mental note to reimburse Heather for today's lost earnings. The page was littered with scribbles and sketches from his discoveries in New York: The Manhattan, too obvious a choice perhaps, but it was River's cocktail bar and he couldn't think of a better entrée for his yet to be created menu; bold bracing Bourbon, Sweet Vermouth and a dash of Angostura bitters. A theatrical performance going off with a bang, the stage curtain lifted on a procession of liquid masterpieces. In fact, he'd put the whole thing together like this, by intuitively opening up his Bible and choosing between left page and right. Heather would definitely approve.

He knew he'd upset Blake, and Lee besides, but his quest was more important than that. He'd been entrusted in a way the unenlightened simply couldn't understand. And anyway, he could make it up to him, if he could somehow get Blake to be one of the three, although he knew that tampering with destiny was strictly off the cards, and other than another episode of destruction, he had no idea how he would physically get him into the bar in a social capacity.

A whirr of activity snapped him out of his daydream. A black and white terrier yapped and bounded, streaking comet-like around his former sanctuary. The robins scarpered in protest. And the dog growled at the foot of River's sleeping bag, deeply disturbed at what it had uncovered in a territory it clearly knew as its own at six am.

"Do you always have this effect on women?"

A vision of red cheeks, bobble hat, and wild brown hair came to the fore. The dog, taking its attempt at conversation as a green light, jumped on River's lap and sniffed somewhat embarrassingly at his groin.

"Oh my god, get out of here, it's you!" she said.

"Excuse me? Do I know you?"

River rubbed his eyes with his fists, breaking the terrier's new fascination with licking his face.

"It's me, Georgina. Well, George. But I'm Georgina nowadays. Reinvented myself, like Lady Gaga," she said with a wink.

"George? Georgie George? As in Blake's little sister, Georgie George?"

"Georgina," she shouted with a massive grin, so there was no doubt as to her new identity as it reverberated inside the tower, spilling out and rolling down the Tor's dewy slopes and onto the patchwork quilt of the Somerset Levels beyond.

"Crikey, I should think you have reinvented yourself." River couldn't help but whistle as he looked her up and down. She was about as far removed from the shell suit-betrothed teen with the bob, dot-to-dot acne, and tram track braces to match, as could be. How had this transformation happened?

"Oh purlease," Georgina's cheeks were ever so slightly more berry-stained than they'd appeared on her arrival.

"I heard you were back," she said, pausing briefly to summon new breath. "Rumour mill's hard to escape in this town. Here, girl." She called the dog back to her side and clipped on its lead. "Sorry about that, she's always been a bit of a case, and well, at this time of day we rarely bump into anybody else up here."

"You used to be more of a night owl as I recall. What

13

happened?"

"Reality bit some of us. We weren't all as lucky as you," she said removing her hat to further reveal the extent of her beauty, despite a trace of contempt in her watery green eyes.

"Yeah, I was sorry to hear about your parents finally calling it a day," River lowered his head. "Must have hit you both hard." He rubbed a couple of loose stones together, unsure whether it was safe to resume eye contact with the Tom Boy turned Vixen. "And um, I kind of bumped into your brother last night too."

"Really? Where? He never mentioned it." Her reply came in one quick and breathless succession.

"Oh, he just popped his head into the bar to say hello, as you do. Lee came too, always good to catch up with old friends." He cursed himself silently for letting out a nervous laugh.

"Hmm, yes, well I did hear about you buying up Dad's drinking and skittles den. Tut tut. Not exactly the subtlest move in the book."

"Maybe not but it spares you all from another shop full of crystals and crap."

Nice one, River. Despite the lack of sleep and the mother of all hangovers, you're on surprisingly good form this morning.

"Touché," she said, clearly agreeing with him whilst rubbing and bending the double jointed tips of her digits into the warmth of her fingerless gloves, "but in all honesty it's hit Dad hard. The pub was his haven, not just for the ale and the opportunity to knock down a few pins twice a week. It's the company he misses, the friendships. Men of his generation, they don't do the coffee and cake thing like the women." She paused to study River with the kind of just-got-out-of-bed-hair that makes a man want to bury his face in it, taking in the remnants of last night's perfume before a quick round of second helpings.

He pushed the very idea to the back of his mind and pondered his defence, but she was simply too fast to keep up with, her youth giving her quick quips an unfair advantage.

"So that's what you've effectively done, you see, ripped a community apart at its very heart," she carried on with her crusade.

"Oh come on, surely that's a tad extreme," he said, trying to soften the lead of those words, "nothing stays the same forever."

He clocked those utterly kissable lips beginning to curve into the slightest of smiles. She was damn well enjoying this, bordering on flirting with him. He'd even go as far as to say the challenge was beginning to turn him on, too.

"Okay, I get it, I get it. I've put my foot in things good and proper. But don't knock me down before you've given the bar a try."

Will you just give it up already with the flaming skittles references!

"Even your dad might find he likes it."

"Ha, so sure of yourself, aren't you? All those years of stardom have clearly inflated your ego to some wuthering heights. But these are cider drinkers we're talking about, loyal only to purveyors of the finest Scrumpy. No amount of 'Sex on the Beach' is going to lead them astray."

Why was everyone so hell-bent on stereotyping a mixologist's repertoire? This conversation was in dire need of a change of direction.

"So, how is life treating you? And why in the heck are you up here of all places so early?"

"I could ask the same of you? Haven't you got a bed to sleep in?" Her cheekiness batted back her reply.

"I uh, I had a late one decorating the bar last night... yeah. And Mum, Heather, she needed her kip... got some kind of meditation class to give today at that new centre near the Chalice Well."

"I see." She raised her eyebrows, and if River wasn't mistaken, he could detect – just for a fleeting moment – that quirky little Blake's sibling trait of hers: calculation. And then like a puff of smoke it was gone, as if it had never been.

"Me?" she asked, the cogs in her brain having evidently resumed their usual pattern. "I'm doing a bit of everything at the moment. Dog walking and sitting, hence being up here at this ungodly hour, some waitressing, cleaning and shopping for a few of the elderly neighbours, you know, that sort of thing. Pays the bills, helps Dad out with the mortgage after *she* ditched us for the fourth time and ran off to Benidorm to be with that utter tosser for ever. At twenty-nine it's hardly the way I saw my life panning out." Georgina sighed, "But I'm the woman of the house now, somebody's got to look after the men."

"Well you're looking good on it... really good," said River with a smile, hoping in futile hindsight that she wouldn't interpret it as anything more than the hung-over compliment it was; the hung-over compliment he should have kept to himself, for she would always be the younger out-of-bounds sister of his childhood best friend. Some things were simply never meant to be explored.

"And what's this?" she changed the subject, not before raising those perfect brows once more, then sitting by his side, dog now (thankfully) already in a semi-slumber.

"Nothing, just a scrapbook of junk." He tried in vain not to sound protective as he attempted to cocoon The Bible in the hood of his sleeping bag.

But she snatched it off him, resuming the role of annoying brat like it was some kind of lifelong prerogative.

"I'd rather you didn't, Georgie."

"Georgina," she corrected him.

"It's precious actually."

"Oh, now he says it's precious all of a sudden," she smirked.

"Years of notes and stuff." A trickle of heat began to cover his body as he made a pathetic tackle to grab it back and she childishly tugged it further away. "But they wouldn't mean anything to anyone else."

"I'll be the judge of that," she said. "Blue Lagoon," she softly traced the outline of the highball glass in which River had sketched the liquid swimming pool and its disc of lime, "very tropical." She leafed through the pages again, a provocative smile, quite different to anything he remembered adorning her teenage face, curled her lips.

"Can you make me one of these?" She looked at him, a coquettish glint in her eyes, something he fast realised was not his mind playing tricks on him since she was now also biting gently at the corner of her lip.

"When the bar's redecorated, up and running in a few weeks, yeah?"

"I've always had a thing for you, you know." Georgina put the book down slowly as if to back up her declaration with only the most sensual of movements. River swallowed. Despite their banter, he had not been expecting the dialogue to take him quite so far in this direction. Georgina smiled as she removed her gloves, careful not to take her eyes off him. And then she straddled River's still swaddled legs and to his utter astonishment began to undress. He found he could do no more than swallow yet again as one by one the layers unpeeled themselves, and he let her take his rough hands in hers, directing them to a pair of superbly pert breasts as she sighed deeply.

"I um, I don't think this is a good idea. Like, what about Blake?"

River forced the memory of the navy and red shell-suited keepy-uppy obsessed *Take That* fan into his head, willing it to stay put. But the football bounced off, and the George of yesteryear faded fast. There was just no escaping the fact that 2017's version of Georgina was a vision and a temptress all at once. He knew he shouldn't. This was the ultimate treason but god he was so horny he didn't care. And he realised, somehow rolling back the months in his mind as she parted his lips with her tongue and pressed her body urgently against him, that he couldn't even remember the last time he'd gotten laid. The thrill of getting caught in the act by an early morning passer-by only added to his hunger, but she'd catch her death like this. Spring or not, this was Somerset.

He unzipped the side of his sleeping bag, inviting her in. They fumbled and twisted, slipped and slid, and before common sense got a look in, he was deep inside her, groaning and bucking in pleasure.

"Still want to try that Blue Lagoon?" he found himself whispering into her ear.

"I want you to line up every cocktail on the bar, she stopped to softly bite his lip, "so I can drink it dry before you strip naked and take me... over and over."

"And over?" he said with a suggestive smile, their eyes locking so that phase two was inevitable.

"But... mmm," she panted as he grinded, hands possessing her backside, "I get the feeling my favourite tipple will be the Screaming Orgasm." She kissed him greedily, as if unleashing the pent-up lust of a starved adolescence and the fantasy of bedding a rock star.

"You've got yourself a job," he said, coming up for air, blinking Blake and his warning away, as well as Georgina's cringe worthy suggestion that he'd serve up anything so seedy and classless. "Just so happens I'm looking for bar staff... and I think you'll find I pay rather well."

Chapter Three
GEORGINA

It couldn't have been simpler. She wouldn't deny that she hadn't enjoyed herself. He was definitely as experienced as she'd hoped, and his willingness to bend so easily to her spontaneous behaviour had certainly helped turn her on.

But then Georgina would do anything for her boys; her dad and Blake were her world.

Of course there was the not so small matter of pre-empting Blake finding out about the sudden career change. But it turned out that was nothing but a minor kink to which she could turn her expert hand at manipulation.

"You are not working for him in that bell-end of a bar. For crying out loud, George, have some dignity."

"Blake, can't you see, I'm doing this for you. What's that saying? Keep your friends close and your enemies even closer? I just know I can get you something out of this; a long overdue upper hand to make up for his betrayal." She paused and transported herself and her steaming coffee mug to the window for effect. "Think of all the dirty secrets I can extract about his rock star days," she said gazing trance-like at the earthy mounds where her dad had sewn his cauliflowers in haste before summer made a mockery of his efforts. Her father's depression had notably eased since the promise of *eau de* sweet pea, backyard barbecues and Georgina's shabby apple crumble. Things were on the up now for all of them. She could sense it.

And if nothing else, River was paying her more (significantly more) than all her odd jobs put together, meaning she could wave sweet farewell to bathing oldies and their unsavoury bits, her clothes stinking of hideous wet dog fur, and an organic café full of shitty 'cultured' tourists and their yawn worthy complaints, backchat and measly tips.

She turned to her brother who had just finished his night shift stacking shelves at the local supermarket, and by all accounts looked ready to drop into an early grave.

"Please. Just trust me on this, I'm almost thirty. I know what I'm getting myself into. River wouldn't dare try anything on with me, if that's what you're thinking."

Blake's laugh was a snort. He grabbed the TV guide from the nest of tables, positioned himself along the length of the sofa and started flicking through its pages.

"Course he wouldn't. He's hardly going to be interested in a local after all the international beauties he's bedded. You wouldn't as much as get a look in. No offence, Sis."

I wouldn't be so certain about that.

"No, of course not," she said, smirking to herself as she caught the image of the Tor rising in the top left hand window pane, high above the rooftops. She took a sip of strong coffee, enjoying the bitterness and heat as she replayed her role of dominatrix last week. "None taken, Bro."

If there was one thing nowadays that was rocket fuel to Georgina and her aspirations, particularly when it came to getting the attention of the opposite sex, it was her family's reluctance to acknowledge her metamorphosis from Ugly Duckling to Elegant Swan. In Blake's eyes, in her dad's eyes, she was still climbing trees and knocking a football about in the garden. And if she wasn't still doing that she was scurrying into Blake's bedroom to steal his Bristol City football stickers for her 'secret' album, or hashing out a riff on his drum kit before he was back from footie practise, before it was mobbed by the bailiffs that fateful year when both her parents had lost their jobs and they'd had to start all over again.

Not that she'd particularly want either of them to be cooing over her physique; flawless skin, or choice of attire for a Friday night pub crawl – that would be freaky. But still. It would be nice, just for once, if they could get with the times, open their eyes to the sexy creature who'd blossomed before them, stop insinuating she was nothing but gamine.

And then there was the envelope. Obviously Blake hadn't a clue about that either. In truth neither had Georgina, for she'd only loosely translated the letter inside.

Last Wednesday's shenanigans had evidently left River a little jaded. When Georgina had spied the rectangular manila shape falling from his cocktail book as they'd finally stood to descend the Tor's symmetrical terraces, and had wasted no time stuffing it into the back pocket of her jeans, remarkably, he hadn't noticed a thing.

"Damn," she'd said as she'd opened it carefully with a cheese knife once she was sure she had the house to herself. "I should have known it was too good to be true."

She'd guessed it contained money, or something juicy and confidential about the band, in return for which *OK Magazine* or *The Daily Mail* would reward her handsomely.

She'd stared at the senseless Spanish words; that much she could tell about their etymology. Probably some hippie-dippy saying, like you get on those pathetically whimsical memes doing the rounds on Facebook; or the artificial 'Dance like nobody's watching' style tableaus adorning just about every home in the UK. Even her former boss at the café had fallen prey to them. Well, at least she wouldn't have to stare at 'I cook with wine…' the word 'organic' added to it in red marker pen '… sometimes I even add it to the food,' anymore as she offloaded empties in the kitchen. All hail one W.C Fields for that cruddy attempt at humour.

But she was also smart enough to realise this was no Spanish shopping list of cocktail ingredients. Chances were it was a couple of lines of highly inconsequential nothingness. That's why it took her so long to get the note translated. But then one day indifference could distract her no longer and she headed online to the *Google Translate* site. She was well aware of the pitfalls of not doing things the old-fashioned way with the aid of a dictionary, but she was also switched on enough to fill in the missing gaps, to spot any words whose context was questionable.

"Remember not to tamper with fate. You are entrusted with the destiny of this bottle, with the blessing of the Toltex

Indians. Let the three Chosen Ones come to you. Do not chase them. And then watch the magic unfold. Ten drops exactly. No more, no less. Repeat as and when a new destination calls."

She bit down hard on her lip in excitement, so hard she almost drew blood.

"There's a little bit more to this coming back and setting up a cocktail bar gig than meets the eye, it would seem," she gasped, her eyes bulging out of their sockets as she frantically scribbled the copy down, stashing the original paper and its English meaning into the note compartment of her purse.

So now the million dollar question was: How to dig deeper, and more specifically, without River noticing?

Although, when it came to the latter, he'd already more than proven himself a prize-winning numpty. She'd just have to get good – very good – at encouraging him to let his guard down. She'd build up the trust and then bingo... she could really root around. But for now not a word would she utter to Blake. It would only complicate things. No point in him rushing in all guns blazing, patience had never been his strong point. She'd be the one searching for this elusive bottle, and she'd be searching for it alone.

Chapter Four
RIVER

"What am I trying to prove, Mum?"

It had been a week since the local paper's photographer, Cath Deacon, had unceremoniously burst onto the re-decorated premises. Her sneaky shot of River's infamous self, dry shaking a Pisco Sour in its new role as cocktail bartender gracing the front page for all and sundry to debate its sheer arrogance at "attempting to spice up a former working men's pub with Mai Tais and Moscow Mules." The matching headline: *Fallen Rock Star Returns to cause a Rumble,* making it very clear where the local media's loyalties lay. But the sneaky jobs worth hadn't stopped there. Oh no. Taking in the empty tables and chairs, she'd gone on a full blown front page rampage detailing his apparent failure in the business world, selective hearing filtering out River's plain English reminder that it was still a couple of weeks before he officially opened the bar.

"That you're following your heart, not giving a rip about the naysayers," said Heather.

She flung her yarn out across the length of the floor, revealing a psychedelic rainbow-hued 'red carpet', hardly luring in the kind of punters River wished to attract. She nudged her specs higher up the ridge of her nose, took a deep breath and began counting stitches in a manner which suggested she had always known this would be par for the course.

"Maybe I should have stuck with what I knew, fizzled out into obscurity like an Adam Ant or a Sting—"

"Don't you go knocking Sting; he's still going strong, bless his chakras. You've got to have a loyalty to Sting somewhere in your heart." She stopped stitching briefly, eyes fixed high above on the mock gold of the elaborate coving. "Remember the day he filmed the *If I Ever Lose my Faith in you* video up on Glastonbury Tor? Oh, was your Aunt Sheba's tarot reading ever right. She predicted I'd be entranced by a tall blonde stranger on a mound that very week. And what do you know; next day there I was following the film crew – you on my coattails, but still…"

A group of hippies peered into the doorway, pondered the offerings of the blackboard and gingerly climbed the steps, purple and green dreadlocks swinging like pendulums in perfect timing with the light jazz playing behind the bar.

"Heather, not now, looks like we've got our first customers —"

"Nah, you're alright," said the tallest in a loud voice, popping hope like a pin to a balloon. "Was just thinking," he scratched his tangled head, "didn't this used to be a pub? Run by some geezer who could get discounted weed?"

"It was the Ring O'Bells formerly, yes," said River. "Slightly more refined these days," he added under his breath as his hands transferred their frustration to the shiny steel cocktail shaker. "As for the hash supplies, I really wouldn't know about that. Can I tempt you to a Tom Collins while you're here? We're ten minutes into Happy Hour. Not that I advertise it. Looks cheap, attracts the teenagers."

"Defo not a Tom, mate. I'm thinking he might have been a Pete though. Yeah, that's right, he was… and as for his last name, I ain't got the foggiest. Swift transaction then we was always quick to get out of here, like… in case the pigs should be hovering."

"How about a Daiquiri then, I've just blended up a fresh batch of watermelon."

"You're beginning to sound a little desperate, mate. I've already told you, we're not here for your fancy shit with umbrellas… although I might have made an exception if you were serving up an Avalon Amber or a Tor in the Mist."

River was speechless, Heather not so.

"Scarper and hop it," she yelled uncharacteristically,

pointing yarn needles as if she were a water dowser, an additional string to her bohemian bow which totally wouldn't have surprised. "Do you have any idea how much work my son's put into this place?"

"Well, dudes and dudettes," Head Hippie ignored her and turned back to his gang, "it's high time," he paused for a laugh, which his entourage echoed back at him, "we tracked down the Lurve Bus and headed on down to Sir Michael of Eavis's fest. Hash cakes for supper!"

"Fine, your loss, and don't bother coming back," said River.

Glastonbury bloody Festival. That was about right.

River had forgotten it started at the weekend, unbelievable really when he considered how many Junes he'd spent there himself. Especially the June that had changed his and Alice's lives; the June when Blake and Lee would go one way to watch Fat Boy Slim's much coveted 'final performance before retirement' in the navy and custard striped circus tent, the June when River and Alice would opt for the earthiness of The Levellers on the pyramid stage, the June when they were destined to meet two complete strangers from London in the crowd... strangers from London who soon became friends, friends who soon became band mates.

The June when Blake would return at ten to midnight only to find River and Alice entwined in his very own tent.

River stopped his vigorous shaking, bringing himself and his regrets back to the present: to trade or not to trade?

Anyone in their business-savvy mind would have assumed this was the best week in the year for making money if you were a local establishment. Except Pilton, the village where the festival actually took place was several miles away, luring potential punters like the Pied Piper. So that all that remained in the town were The Miffed, who had either been unable to obtain tickets and were mightily pissed off, or The Troublemakers, who – November's carnival aside – patiently stored their pent-up testosterone for seven months, ready to let loose on The Outsiders. Both groups screamed Blake. And that was not good.

25

"Maybe we should close this week, Heather?"

"And why would you want to do that?"

"I just sense trouble on the horizon, you know, all these non-locals," River stuck his two index fingers either side of his head for emphasis and wiggled them up and down, "invading the town."

"Are you sure you're not still harbouring a grudge because the big Mr Michael Eavis CBE never invited you and Avalonia to play at Glastonbury... not even on one of the fringe stages?" Heather picked at her yarn, head cocked to one side.

"Of course I'm not, no. I got over that like years ago." River flicked at an ice shaving as if he were playing his favourite childhood game of Tiddlywinks.

"I'm glad to hear it, love. Anger is a bitter swine of a pill," she said, making a concertina of her work and then resting it and needles on top of the nearest table to the bar. "Not that I've ever condoned the lack of an invitation, mind you. If he could give the time of day to that other local band... what are they called, Reeves...?" she furrowed her brow.

"Reef," spat River, much as he was a clandestine fan.

"Well, whatever, the point is he should have jolly well acknowledged your musical talents too. You, Alice, Bear and Alex, you were ten times better." She stopped to smile encouragingly. "But hey, you don't need that kind of recognition anymore. Just look at you. You're an artist across genres now—"

"Yeah, that's my mind made up," River changed the subject. "We'll open officially when the festival is over and people are looking for something to cheer themselves up with. Gut instinct tells me this is not divine timing."

"The festival brings yin and the festival brings yang," said Heather. "Good and bad," her words lingered.

"What do you mean, Mum? Did you have a dodgy hash cake supper there back in the day that you forgot to tell me about?" He added a timely chuckle thinking of the many hearty specimens he himself had regrettably consumed. "I hope that's what that bunch of eejits get for their supper anyway."

26

On the other hand, those eejits had not only given him a couple of new cocktail names that he fully intended to smuggle behind the bar (every cloud), but an injection of hope… that things were finally dying down on the camouflage front. If you'd had a taste of the fame game, this ambivalent town was the best one in the world to come back to. It's why Nicholas Cage had a house here, why Johnny Depp and the ilk were often shuffling around country houses on the outskirts, looking for somewhere to call home, somewhere to call incognito. Nobody batted an eyelid at you if you were dressed as a faery here, or a Goth with a steampunk top hat. All of this was just normal for a town called Glastonbury, where nobody stood out.

"It's nothing, forget I mentioned it," Heather snapped out of her trance. "Aw, River," she skipped over to him and smothered her son in a hug, "I'm bursting with pride to call you mine. You really have got a little of me in there somewhere. This will all blow over quickly enough. People are being momentarily resentful, that's all. They'll soon change their tune once they hear how delicious your creations are. Just you wait and see."

"I hope you're right, I really do." He let out the deepest of breaths.

Because at this rate, River couldn't see how anybody would ever make it past page one of the menu. Let alone reach the magic of page fifty-nine. And now he'd been and promised Georgina a job, starting Monday night.

Heather bundled wool and needles in her bag, went home to get ready for her kundalini yoga class, and left him to his thoughts.

He poured himself a Pisco Sour. It was fast becoming his favourite feature of the menu, but he made a mental note to add just a hint more brandy on his next attempt. A couple of sips and soon his memories were flickering once again like fire licking at kindling, this time carrying him back to Mexico.

The final gig had been perfection; one of those seamless sets that flowed with synchronicity: song, rapturous applause, song, rapturous applause. Okay, he couldn't pretend the way the crowd held their lighters aloft like a flock of sheep didn't nark him right off. Alicia Keays and her ode to New York had a lot to answer for when it came to that tragic mainstream nod at enlightenment. But other than that, the gruelling weeks touring Latin America had ended on a high; a high that, try as he might, River couldn't quite seem to find a cocktail in the city to match.

Next morning he'd pulled back the curtains to reveal a Guadalajara sunrise which further revealed Avalonia's band members strewn across the penthouse suite of the hotel; a domino rally that had gone badly wrong. Alex, the guitarist, had evidently pulled again. River rubbed his eyes so he could focus on the local beauty whose naked thigh entrapped his Egyptian cotton-cocooned friend. Alex's height never seemed to restrict his magnetism when it came to the ladies; it was as if his guitar was the musical equivalent to the Mercedes SLK, driven by many a pint-sized male. And just behind this aftermath of lust lay Bear (or Edward to his parents). He definitely hadn't been as lucky. His light snores brushed over the top of the empty bottle of Jack Daniels balancing in the palm of his right hand, creating something almost Peruvian as a backdrop to the scene. Still, it made a somewhat refreshing change to see he'd traded drugs for liqueur last night. For some reason he'd never matured past chemical experimentation, unlike the others. River was finding it increasingly hard to wrap his head around that – and the fact that nobody else shared his passion for a fine cocktail.

This snapshot in time, minus Alice, who'd taken on a penthouse suite of her own as per usual, wasn't all that different to every other session of partying after a final show. But for some reason this morning it looked more desperate than ever. In six years they'd practically be forty for crying out loud. At some point life had to get more sophisticated, reveal some kind of meaning.

He showered and dressed then beachcombed the squalor amidst the luxury for his wallet, and made for the streets, even though they were the last place he wanted to be. Mexico's fourth largest city was strangely cleansing. True, it was a

Sunday which accounted for less bodies but something else was different out here too. He felt he had a journey to take. The breeze seemed to whisper it, but coffee first.

River followed a group of locals to a café opposite the train station. Small chirpy birds covered one of the few remaining empty tables, pecking at crumbs on a thoroughly unwashed surface until he interrupted them by pulling out a chair. But he was too entranced by the conversation he was already eavesdropping in on to care.

"*A que hora sale el tren por Tequila*?" a voice from the neighbouring table asked of somebody in its group.

Of course, Guadalajara was practically down the road from Tequila.

Tequila!

How could he not catch the next train there and take up the opportunity for a quick mooch around? He'd buy some interesting varieties, ask the locals if they'd be happy to impart their wisdom on all things mixology, maybe visit a smallholding and get to do a bit of tasting straight from source.

"*Sale a las dos*," came the reply.

Two o'clock, too late.

The waitress came and went with his order, swiftly followed by a strong shot of coffee, not a dash of milk in sight. The oozing cheese of his breakfast *burrito* cut through the bitterness and as he sank his teeth into a most surprisingly hot *jalapeño*, forcing the words "*leche por favor*" somewhat embarrassingly into the air, he found last night's dream sailing back to him in a strange mosaic he couldn't piece together: a child with long, dark braids finished off with bright red bows, a row of gleaming blue and green bottles, and a small, sky blue hut.

He shook his head, unable to fathom it out, wrapped the remnants of the burrito in a napkin, stuffed it into his backpack, visited the toilets – holding his breath, pinching his nose – and then headed out of the city towards the two-lane highway.

He decided to walk to Tequila instead. It was only thirty miles away, he'd hitch a lift; the heat wasn't so intense at this time of year. And if he couldn't catch a ride with someone, well, he'd walk fast – and he'd spend the night there too. The band weren't flying back to London for another couple of days. He'd earned his down time.

Two hours later and he'd barely made a dent in his journey. The sun was relentless too; something he'd grossly underestimated the power of. He resorted to sticking his thumb out and resigning himself to a very long wait. But within minutes a pickup truck had stopped. A *vaquero*, sombrero-clad, leaned out of the window and asked him where he was headed.

"*Tequila, hombre… por favor*," River replied.

The driver nodded in agreement and opened the door to provide relief to River's aching limbs. They drove in silence broken only by the interruption of the can of beer which he tossed to his right. River gratefully caught it and began to sip, taking in the sights of the landscape as the dark shape of the volcano on the horizon loomed ever closer.

"*Vale, tienes que irte aqui, yo voy a la izquierda.*" said the driver some fifteen minutes later as he pulled over into a layby.

Say what? Surely his Spanish wasn't that bad. Had he only imagined he'd asked to be driven to Tequila? This was the middle of nowhere. The driver could have told him he'd be turning off left and couldn't take him all the way to town.

"*Gracias*," said River, depositing himself and his bag back onto concrete before his reflexes could think to question the driver, "*por nada*," he added as the truck sped off down a dirt track as opposed to straight on to the home of the agave plant.

"Great. Now what?"

Emboldened by the dregs of his beer, he continued his dusty walk, passing cacti and bottle-shaped signs of intoxicating goodness, teasing him. So close yet so far away. He stuck out his thumb again in the hope of somebody being good enough to complete his journey. He sensed his despondency glowing around him like the child in the *Ready Brek* adverts all those years ago, warning people away from his strange red-rimmed silhouette.

After what felt like an eternity, in the very far distance on the left hand side of the road, River could just about make out a *choza*. As he approached, he saw the shack was sky blue and corrugated, its undulations rippling and reflecting the late afternoon sun.

He clambered ungracefully over the fence and into the bluish grey of the agave field, careful to keep his tread between the spikey rows, whose musky barrels he could almost smell on the air, if only he could get to a distillery by nightfall. But then something else caught his eye. A row of bottles glistened at the base of the shack and moments later a small child appeared. She stopped for a moment to take in his presence and then a giant beam took over her face and she beckoned to him excitedly with her arms open wide, as if he were her *papa* – or some long lost uncle who'd returned from his travels around the world.

It was at this precise moment that River's blood ran cold. She was the girl from his dream.

Without thinking he marched forward; the sparkle of the bottles rendering him moth-like. He watched as the braided child disappeared inside the small hut, overcome with a curiosity he couldn't put words to. Moments later as he walked closer still, an elderly woman emerged from the entrance; her hand shielding the sun from her eyes as she took in River's form, wending its way to her abode.

"It was written in the air," she said, as he stood before her with his hand instinctively reaching out to shake hers. He was too dazed to reply but assumed this would be a culturally acceptable greeting.

"No need to carry on to Tequila. Your journey ends," she smiled to reveal two rows of crooked teeth, "and begins right here. Come inside and let me explain."

His head told him now was the time to do a runner, not that there was exactly anywhere to hide. His heart somehow warmed in an instant to this apparition of a female and her child.

"How do you speak such perfect English?" he said, stunned at his ability to enter into routine chitchat as he also bent to enter the tiny doorway, immediately hit by the pungent smell of ribs, chili and oregano, simmering on a tiny stove.

"Everything is connected," said the woman.

"But, you live here in deepest Mexico. Or did you go to school, college?"

"I'm surrounded by infinite intelligence, why would I ever need to do that?"

She sat on a colourful stool, picked up a bowl and began to peel lima beans, a task she'd evidently made little progress with.

"Okaaay, this is starting to freak me out now."

"You're welcome to stay for supper before you head back to the city." She ignored his confusion.

"I um... I really wanted to check out Tequila actually."

She stopped her peeling for a few seconds, studied his face and then carried on with the job in hand.

"It's just that, well," he turned to look for a seat and she pointed at a similarly Aztec painted stool in the corner of the room, which he tentatively perched on, "I've uh... I've been collecting cocktail recipes from locals on my travels for a few years now, got a book full of them, and as soon as the plane touches down in London in a few days' time – I'm uh... I'm here with my band and we played at the VFG arena last night – that's it, man, I'm outta the music industry, time to move on to ventures new."

He paused briefly to take in the knowing nods of the woman now standing before him. "I've put in a sealed bid for a rundown pub, in the town that I grew up in back home," he continued, encouraged by her approval, "gonna refurbish it, make it pretty, turn it into a cocktail bar as it happens. Bring my inspiration back to Glastonbury, give her a new lease of life and the locals a hangout to put a smile on their faces."

"All of this I know," she said. "Although, I hope you have never been fooled into believing in the legend of Princess Xoctl of Mexico." She giggled a little then paused, her finger and thumb pinching together in the air, as if plucking an invisible idea that had just flown past her. "It was the *cola de gallo* that really leant the cocktail its current name."

32

River knew the former hearsay probably was just that: hearsay. The theories as to the provenance of a cocktail had piled up thick and fast over the years, only adding to the drink's intrigue. But his ears pricked up now as the old woman bread crumbed yet another possible story of the cocktail's origins.

"You probably know it already, of course, but it was the sailors arriving on the Yucatan peninsula, hundreds of years ago, here in my country... it was they who inadvertently gave your future bar its name," she wagged her finger as if to autocorrect any other ideas that had formed in his mind over time. "One day," she patted at her apron for effect, "a certain sailor asked for his usual *drac* in a bar, but the bartender couldn't find his trusty wooden spoon to mix the liquor up with – and it had to be mixed slowly, precisely," she took to wagging her finger again, "that was of utmost importance... so he improvised, used the root of the plant instead. And from that day forward, every sailor coming to shore would visit a bar and ask for a *cola de gallo*, which I'm sure I don't need to tell you translates as 'tail of the cock', cocktail," she finished with a wink.

"But how can you possibly know this? That's insane." (River was no longer referring to the folklore but his future plans.) "I mean, I had a kind of premonition last night, a dream about a place just like this, and the glass bottles, a girl who looked just like your... your *granddaughter?*"

"That she is. You interpret my age well. And yes, the wind sent that intuition your way."

"Ah, man, I mean *lady*. Will you stop talking in these riddles, please? It's messing with my head. I'm as open-minded as it gets, it goes with the territory where I come from. But none of this makes a scrap of sense." River's upturned palms flew to shoulder height as if to demonstrate his confusion. "Am I like stuck in a weird parallel universe or something? What do you want from me? Why did you lead me here?"

"My name is Mercedes," the woman finally introduced herself. "And you... you were chosen long, long ago to be a

Messenger. There are many who have passed this way taking a bottle to their corners of the Earth, River. Your desire is so strong that destiny, the path you have been carving out, has come to fruition, brought you to this point. The spiritual nature of your hometown, your musical calling, your love of liqueur has made you a connoisseur. And now you are ready."

"Ready for what?"

"For this." She picked up her bowl and set it down on her stool, walked over to a wooden shelf and then handed him a bottle containing a clear liquid.

"What is this? Mezcal?"

"*Para todo mal, Mezcal, y para todo bien, tambien,*" she said and started laughing as if enjoying a private joke with herself. "This is no kind of Tequila, River. It's a very special tonic... a tonic without a name."

"Woah there, let's back up a minute. Are you saying... are you honestly saying... you want me to take this back to my bar and serve it up to... to paying customers, without any idea of its composition? Do you think I've totally lost the plot? I can't do that."

"Then that is your choice and I respect you for it. However, think for a minute, my child: why did you wake up with such a longing and pull to trek this very road this morning? Why did you hitch a lift which just happened to appear the moment you required a set of wheels... wheels which took you as far as my *choza pequeña*? The universe delivered you to me. This was always meant to be. And now, if you decide to accept the mission, if you decide to commit, then the lives of three people will change, for the better, forever. And that's just in your first bar."

"Okay. You've lost me completely now. How's that going to change the world?"

"Never underestimate the power of three. It's a magic number. The ripples of joy this chosen trio will generate is going to envelope your town – and beyond – in something never seen before. Magic catches like that, it's wildfire," her eyes became lanterns, as if to convince him, "breathing new life into the saddest and darkest of corners."

"Can't I have a glass of this... this whatever-it-is... or a shot of something, anything? Maybe that will stop me feeling like I'm having an out of body experience."

River couldn't believe he was even half going along with this claptrap. It was as if his actual self was watching a duplicated version of him from afar on one of those old-fashioned film projectors, powerless to intervene and talk some sense.

"Well of course, my child, you had only to ask. But it will have no effect on you," she tutted at the very idea, "why you are just The Messenger, remember."

"All the same, if you're expecting me to even contemplate serving it to this *trio of customers*, as you put it... a mixologist does have ethics, you know."

"You've heard of the genie in the bottle, no?" said Mercedes as she fulfilled his request, pouring a trickle of the clear liquid into a shot glass, as well as a small measure of local Tequila in another.

"From Aladdin you mean?"

"Yes, the genie from the fairy tale."

"Keep talking."

"Well, just ten drops of this will have the same effect."

River questioned his sanity again as he cautiously brought the thimble to his lips, swirled it, sniffed it and poured a little onto the tip of his tongue.

"But it's completely tasteless."

"Except unlike the genie granting only three wishes," Mercedes continued with her story, "this magic potion will grant three people endless wishes. But only wishes for good; therein lies the beauty. The genie couldn't say no to anything... a bit like The Law of Attraction that everybody is raving about these days, even though it's as ancient as gravity," her chuckle spoke a thousand words, all leaning toward the naivety of ninety-nine per cent of humanity. "This liquid on the other hand, is discerning; blessed by a deity during the time of the Toltex Indians. Its composition has remained a secret, even to me." She raised her brow and the deep furrows of her wrinkles became the crests of ragged waves.

"Right," River screwed up his face as if trying to wake himself from a nightmare. "Okay," he opened his eyes again to see that it hadn't worked, and Mercedes was once again tending to her beans. "So, I have never met you before… and I am supposed to just go with this legend, burying my head in the sand that actually, it might be a bottle of poison with which you are really intending to wipe out the UK's population?"

"Oh, River, you really aren't an easy *nuez* to crack," Mercedes almost spat out her words as she abandoned her beans once again, putting him in mind of a Flamenco dancer about to take to the stage to display her *duende* at the unnecessary struggle he was inflicting upon her.

She picked up the bottle and returned it to him as if it were now his responsibility regardless, and walked out of the hut clutching an intricately patterned fan which she flapped fiercely, unable to hide her exasperation.

The child eyed River curiously.

"What?" he said. "*Que*? What am I supposed to make of all of this? It's a bit far-fetched, grant me that much."

She smiled and continued to play with her spinning top.

He slammed back his Tequila, basking in its purity, negating the need for salt and a lime wedge to temper the burn; a tick in the box as far as helping to convince him the mystery bottle might be kosher after all, and stood to join Mercedes outside in the field, the elixir tucked under his arm.

"It's hard for me, you know," she said with her back to him as he stepped outside the hut. She continued staring off into the mountainous hinterland and he slowly joined her, two strangers they may have been, yet he was already beginning to feel as if he'd somehow known her a lifetime – perhaps just a very different lifetime. "I never asked to be entrusted with this. But that's what my family signed up for all those centuries ago. We have our supply, we pass it down the generations, and when the time is right, we set the intention; we call in a Messenger and off goes a bottle to another part of the world. Today it's you. Tomorrow, next week, next month, next year, it's another. It's just the design. Slowly but surely," she turned

36

now to face him, her face pure and somehow loving, "when humanity has reached a certain level of understanding, evil will be wiped out, non-existent, leaving only good. Until then, a few people here, a few people there will have the ability to scatter non-stop joy."

"And what's in all of this for me, if I'm not one of the three?"

"You will return to find the missing pieces to your own puzzle."

"But nothing's missing from my life," he said, kicking lightly at the dusty ground. "I've already decided to take a new direction with the bar... *the one bar*... I'm not sure why you're referring to it as 'my first' as if I'm the Donald bloody Trump of the brewery industry." He waved his hands like that might help reassure her. "I'm sorry, I didn't mean to use the expletive there, but don't presume to know more about me than I do about myself."

"Take the bottle... and this," she clung to her convictions, handing him a pale brown envelope which he hadn't previously noticed folded into her apron strings, "but don't open it until you are much closer to your home and you've made your final decision." She held her arms out wide to embrace him firmly. "Felix, my nephew, is waiting. He will take you back to the city now."

She pointed to a pickup truck which looked suspiciously like the same one that had so ungracefully deposited River in the middle of nowhere.

"Goodbye, River and good luck... que *sera, sera*," she said with the trace of a laugh. And with that she turned, walked back to the entrance of the shack, gave him one final wave and disappeared inside.

He was glued to the spot for several seconds, until a loud horn from the highway made its intentions clear and River found himself with little option but to head over to it. Halfway to the fence he was certain that if he turned to look at the little blue hut, it would evaporate into a hot mist, a mirage in the desert, fuzzing at the edges until it was but a dot on the horizon. But there it stood, real as could be. The truck sounded

37

its horn again, and River pivoted, then marched quickly, careful not to shake the contents of the bottle as Felix and his giant cigar became clearer and clearer. Felix nodded at him as he rounded the bonnet of the vehicle to climb into the passenger side, and didn't stop nodding until River lodged his backpack in-between his feet, hugging the bottle to his chest.

"*Cual es tu hotel, hombre?*"

"The new five star place in the *centro, El Paraiso*," said River, thinking that surely Felix should intuitively know.

He started to ponder the so-called piece of his life puzzle that was 'missing' as his chauffeur drove silently, puffing great rings of smoke out of the window and into the sultry air, the bi-polar and chilled out opposite of his previous bout of impatience, until Felix flicked on the stereo and hummed along lightly to the mariachi music which soon filled the cabin, lulling River into a light but much needed sleep.

Forty-two minutes later and the city's traffic jerked him awake with a start. Felix switched off the stereo and pulled over to the side of the road.

"*El hotel esta al fin del calle*," he said.

River had never seen the street of his hotel from this perspective before, but took Felix's word for it that he'd reached his final destination. He thanked his driver, a little more gratefully this time, jumped down from the top step of the cabin, and held his hand aloft for a brief and silent farewell, as he knew was now the norm. But then Felix took him by surprise.

"*Una cosa más*," he said, before adding his sudden grasp of the English language, "just one more thing…"

"Yes?" said River. "What is it?"

"Belief is everything."

"What do you mean?"

But Felix's foot was already on the throttle. River could only watch, fascinated, as he did a masterful three point turn – for which the stream of traffic obediently, biblically, parted – and returned to wherever it was that he'd first come from, knowing full well that just like Mercedes, he would never see him again.

***

"Where the heck have you been? You missed this afternoon's interview with the local press and the others have had to go on and film that drinks commercial I was telling you about without you."

Lennie was waiting for River as he entered reception, shades strapped to his brooding face, New York Yankees cap concealing his dusting of a Mr Whippy hairdo as he paced manically with his mobile attached to his ear. "You can forget all about your cut, was a tidy little number you'd have pocketed for it, too."

"Sorry, it won't happen again." River made for the elevator, avoiding eye contact with his manager, swinging his backpack around to his chest as if he were protecting a baby in a sling, double checking he really had placed the bottle and envelope inside, impressed with himself for his short but sweet and un-scripted double entendre.

"Make sure you're back down here by eight sharp. We've got a taxi booked and a reservation for dinner at *Taberna Frederico* with no less than the stars of one of Mexico's most famous sitcoms. And for god's sake take a shower and blitz yourself with aftershave... got more dust on you than the Sahara... you never know who you might get to bring back for dessert if you play your cards right," Lennie yelled after him.

With the lift to himself, River wasted no time in pressing the button to his floor, but then, taking in the poster of the hotel cocktail bar and the promise of a half-decent Martini, he thought better of playing his boss's game and opted for floor twenty-two instead.

***

River stared down at the wonder of the city sprawling out before him, seated at the thin glass bar with its panoramic view that seemed to extend to the very heart of Tequila itself. Pushing the influence of Heather's eccentricities aside, and his childhood upbringing on the ley lines of a mystical town, as bizarre as the afternoon had been, somehow it had also made perfect sense. And he was even more reassured when he acknowledged the fact that he was still physically standing, feeling absolutely fine, that the liquid must have been all that Mercedes promised it was and more.

The Martini mellowed him into blissful oblivion as to the evening's pre-requisite and pre-scripted 'it goes with the territory' duties. Lennie could swivel quite frankly, the others too – even Alice. He was done with the industry and its schmoozing.

Lack of food sent the alcohol straight to his head but he ordered a fresh Martini anyway, whittling away an hour, or two, who knew, who cared? Lennie's agenda just didn't bother him anymore. They'd filmed the stupid thumbs-up-to-aspartame soft drinks ad without him earlier that afternoon, and they could carry on producing records without him too. Christ, they'd hardly be the first band to change its line-up, some with more success than others admittedly, but the remainder of Avalonia were definitely no *Atomic Kitten*.

The punch of his first sip sent him into a world of his own once again, following the zigzags, curves and bends of the city's streets, scanning the skyscrapers, grand colonial buildings illuminated in all their glory, as well as the leafy green parks. He let his two favourite V's do their liquid thing, warming the hunger pangs of his stomach, as he nibbled away at the small bowl of peanuts for added effect. Once he was sure the others had left for dinner, he'd take himself out there and get lost in Guadalajara's legendary street markets, feasting on the equally legendary *Tortas Ahogadas* as he bumbled along the wide boulevards with nothing but his thoughts about this exciting new fork in his own road for company. Yes, a 'drowned sandwich' full of fire and salsa would be a fitting tribute to the end of his music career.

He knocked back the last of his drink, rustled around in his wallet for some pesos, counting them out and adding a few extra coins for a tip, looked up to catch the eye of the waiter, but found himself catching the belligerent eye of Lennie instead, hands upon hips, trademark baseball cap pulled down, but shades removed, undoubtedly his nod at etiquette, since he was being mindful of his surroundings. River's pulse quickened and his eyes quickly scoured the room for a second exit point.

Phew, his luck was in.

Just to the left side of the toilets, at the opposite end of the room to where Lennie was imitating the statue of a dictator, he could either make a very sharp escape, his flagship shot at official independence… or toe Lennie's managerial line, lapping up the evening's formalities one last time. Another exotic woman whose face would fade into a distant memory the moment room service banged on his door with coffee and croissants… and she fled before her naked size eight frame gave in to yet more temptation.

He signalled to the waiter to take his money as Lennie paced forward, swung his backpack onto his shoulder, and ran faster than he'd ever done in his life.

Chapter Five
RIVER

River peeped through the spyhole, an unnecessary action given that Heather's description of 'man in a black cap with an N and a Y on it, bulbous nose, searching emerald eyes and naff gold medallion, accompanied by an aura... or on second thoughts, perhaps it's just a huddle of bodies behind him' painted the picture of band manager and entire line-up.

"You're wasting your time, guys," he shouted at the door and its peeling claret paint, heart thudding so loudly he was sure they could all hear its drum beat outside. "There's nothing you can say to make me change my mind. It's over. You'll easily find a replacement for me. Just switch on *The Voice* and pilfer one of the rejects. They're all pretty good these days."

"River: Open up and stop being childish, you owe me an explanation," Lennie echoed back. "You can't play hide and seek for ever. If you don't talk to me soon, it'll only be the paps that end up cornering you... your choice, but I know what I'd prefer in your shoes."

"Yeah," chimed in a band member whose voice he couldn't put a face to through the wood, though it definitely wasn't Alice.

"Let them in, love," said Heather, placing a heavily bejewelled hand on her son's shoulder. "You were going to have to face the music... oops, 'scuse the pun," she paused and closed her eyes at her careless remark, "at some point. I'll brew up some catnip tea. It'll help calm you all down so you can come to some sort of arrangement and move on."

"There's nothing to discuss, Mum." River uncurled her fingers and shook himself free. "My mind was made up a long time ago, you know that. There's more to life than getting out of our heads on the road, no idea of where we are, who we've slept with or what day of the week it is."

"Look, son," Lennie said in that manner of his that River was more than accustomed to. He imagined him squaring his jaw against the door, just like he had all those times when Bear and Alex had refused to open their hotel door for a rehearsal, and River and Lennie had paced the corridor, facepalming foreheads as to how the evening's gig could even happen.

"Look, son," he said it again as River let out a deep breath and scratched at the shoddy paintwork. "You're under contract and all."

"I think you're forgetting the slightly important fact that we didn't actually renew the contract last—"

"Horses for courses…yada yada yada… you can't just walk away mid tour, or mid anything. This is business. Have you any idea how much money, not to mention credibility, you're costing me… I mean *us*?"

"Wanker."

That was definitely Alex. A fitting reply too. Well, too bad, rules were there to be broken.

"I told all of you to pipe down, leave this to me," Lennie's words trailed behind him. "This is delicate business," he added in a stern whisper, oblivious to the fact that River and Heather could hear everything.

"Would you like me to pass you a tray of catnip through the kitchen window?" Heather said to the door. "I've got some freshly baked root ginger biscuits too, perfect for grounding the body."

"You what?" said Lennie.

"Catnip tea," said Heather. "It's a soother, and if I can get River to drink a little too, well, who knows, maybe you can come to some sort of agreement."

"Mother, *Heather*, just stay out of this please."

"Sounds delectable," said Lennie, and even through the shield of the front door, River knew he was embarking on his Condescending Charade.

"Tell you what, you bring it round to the kitchen window, sweetheart, and I'll meet you there for a sip or two. Don't fret, these hangers-on will be firmly *root gingered here*, to the spot," he could be heard to shout the latter behind himself.

"You're a fool if you trust a word that comes out of his mouth," said River. "Once the window's up, he can easily force his way in."

Lennie's hot and recent, but frankly quite pointless (owing to the size of his paunch) pursuit popped into his head. River saw himself sliding down the banister once again, all the way to the ground floor of their Mexican hotel and the haven of the busy streets, in a bid to beat his manager who'd no doubt have opted for the lift, which at that time of night would have stopped at just about every floor, carrying diners to the first floor restaurant for all things à la carte.

The guy was an avarice stopping at nothing if he thought he was in danger of losing money.

"And here was me thinking I'd brought you up to see the positives in people." Heather shook her head in her hallmark what-are-we-going-to-do-with-you way.

River shrugged as if he didn't know the answer himself, and retreated to his old bedroom, not that Heather had ever really done anything with it since his exodus from the West Country anyway. It was clear she'd always expected the rock bubble to burst; for him to come running back to his roots. You can take the boy out of Somerset but you can't take Somerset out of the boy.

Jim Morrison was the first to challenge his loyalty as he flopped onto his bed. Their eyes met above the headboard in a moment which seemed to scream now or never. Funny, River had never noticed The Doors' lead singer look at him like that before. He sat up, crawled over to his pillow and smiled pitifully at him.

"Yeah? Look what all of this did to you, mate."

Jim was ripped briskly from the wall and River proceeded to do the same to Bowie, Gary Stringer from the local band Reef, (who the media loved to portray as their pedestal rival), The White Stripes, and finally the members of Muse, whose curious Mona Lisa-esque gazes all seemed to follow wherever he placed himself in the tiny room. The bare walls strangely soothed; a cathartic symbol of a fresh beginning. River drew in his breath through his nose, enlarging his navel, bringing his shoulders up high as he'd seen Heather do before meditation and yoga, and exhaled slowly through his mouth, letting out the burden and baggage of twelve years of musical institution.

He dimmed the light and crept to the window, peeling back the mock velvet curtains and their mouldy linings which Heather never seemed to get round to washing, to reveal two shifty looking former band mates – and the angelic Alice – crunching gravel on the front path below. They reminded him of the trick-or-treaters who used to gather in their garden for pranks. Although Heather never opened the door at Halloween given her Pagan roots, she and River would snoop on the hullaballoo below from his bedroom window, praying there wouldn't be a re-enactment this year of the gate being wrenched from its brackets and flung into the hedge – or too many eggs and bags of flour pelted at the kitchen window.

Alice, Bear and Alex, they may have been furious now, but in all honesty, Alice was evidently more enamoured with all things L.A., hot-blooded, swanky and size zero, and Bear and Alex had been getting lazier by the day. At the very least, the trio beneath him needed time out themselves. By which time they'd either recognise that one of them could easily take over on the lyrics front, making the spanner River had thrown into the works even easier to resolve, hiring a new guitarist or drummer; a piece of musical cake. Alice, yes, their paths were sure to cross again when she came back to visit her parents, but as for the other two London lads, what had they ever really had in common with River besides a chance meeting at a festival anyway?

Naff all.

But it was no use trying to distract himself, he just had to listen in on the downstairs proceedings. He opened the door to his room so it was just ajar, and instantly heard the unmistakable sound of the lower kitchen window's eerie creak along with an accompanying tray of clinking china.

"Thanks, darling, appreciate it," he could hear Lennie

saying to his mum.

"It's the least I can do," she replied. "So where are you all staying? There's not a lot of accommodation in town at the moment, what with the festival in full swing."

"Don't you go worrying about that; we've got an RV with all the mod cons parked down the end of the road. It's just a quick visit anyways."

River could no longer contain his curiosity and tiptoed down the stairs to spy on their dialogue behind the kitchen door, where the narrow crack in the hinges revealed Lennie's brown-nosing mug talking to Heather.

"I know you from somewhere, doll. I'm sure of it. Your face is ever so familiar," he said unexpectedly, looking at Heather in earnest, offering her a distasteful but light flutter of his translucent eyelashes as she strained leaves into her small green hand-painted teacup.

"I really don't think so." Heather furrowed her brow. "Here, take some tea," she added without looking at him. "Perhaps I can coax him down in a minute."

Lennie took off his baseball cap, hanging it on the edge of Heather's window box, resplendent with its flurries of marjoram and dill. He poured some ombre-coloured liquid into his own teacup, which, whilst the same size as Heather's, suddenly became an accessory from a doll's house, lifted it to his lips with sausage fingers and took a polite sip. As Heather did the same, and their eyes met properly, minus his Yankees' peak, she began to tremble. There was no mistaking her reaction. Even from afar. Something unspoken passed between them. What, River had no idea. But it was circuitry enough for Heather to push tray, china and root ginger biscuits outside, somehow also lunging at the window frame in the same sudden movement. And then she pulled the lower half of the frame down in blind panic, secured the lock, drew the peacock feather print curtains together tightly and grappled at the window sill, taking several shallow breaths.

"Mum! What's up? Did he try to hurt you? I heard a right commotion just then."

River waited a few seconds for authenticity before bursting

into the kitchen.

"It's nothing, nothing," she hyperventilated, "just… just one of my panic attacks – that's all. It'll pass… in a while," she added finally, steadying herself. "See… if we've got… some brown bags in the top… drawer there." She pointed to the cupboard next to the cooker. "I'll try… that… that technique to slow down… my breathing."

River quickly found her a paper bag, stood to watch her slowly regain control, protective hand on her shoulder as her chest puffed in and out, and then made for the front door.

"He won't be back, Mum, but don't answer the door to anybody… just in case. Not that there will be a just-in-case, but you know what I mean. Stay here and stay safe. I'm going to have to give him a piece of my mind, put an end to this shit for once and for all. He's got to accept that it's over and stop hounding me. I'll get the police involved if I have to."

It had crossed his mind to tuck his teenage baseball bat, still lying beneath his bed, under his arm while he was at it, but then he thought better of it, remembering his naturally peaceful nature; the very reason he must have been reeled in by Mercedes all along.

"River, no!"

But Heather's delayed protest became a whisper as he stormed out of the house.

Outside in the damp summer evening air, he pounded the pavements near and far for the last traces of Lennie's RV, a screech of tyres perhaps, a whiff of diesel maybe; the hum of a distant engine.

Lennie and the band may have long gone. But River's mind burned with curiosity. What in the hell was that sequence of events at the kitchen window really all about?

Chapter Six
GEORGINA

If it wasn't for his celebrity status she'd have been utterly humiliated. Six people turned up for the official opening night.

Just six!

And one of those was Heather. It was like a sketch out of a very bad comedy.

"There will be one rule in this bar and one rule only," River announced. "I'll never serve you more than two cocktails of an evening." A flurry of muffled voices ensued. "Why?" he paused until he'd regained their attention, "because the cocktail is to be savoured, not devoured. The construction of a cocktail is a work of art; the degustation of a cocktail is an evening at the theatre. You wouldn't eat a three course meal during the *Phantom of the Opera*; in the same way, you won't drink three courses of cocktails in this bar."

Fabulous, there went all of Georgina's future tips every time a starry-eyed customer thought he was in with a chance with her. What a stuck up thing to say. People knew their limits when it came to drink. You might get away with this in some swanky speakeasy in the capital, the kind of place 'the other half' visited before their *soiree* in a plummy theatre, but in a small town like this, it was an insult that would only drive away footfall. He should have run this past her first. She'd soon have persuaded him to up it to four. Two cocktails did not comprise a night out. This was beyond ludicrous.

She gave him a conspiratorial nod to keep up the charade anyway. What else could she do?

Yes, her own reputation in this gossip-rife town might be at stake now, but she was doing this for Blake – and her dad. She just had to stick with it. There was still time to turn things around. If nothing else, the hearsay that wended its way out of here tonight was going to prick up so many only-too-willing-ears to put his outlandish theory to the test.

The gathered ensemble clearly didn't know whether to huddle at one table to avoid the mortifyingly, socially embarrassing phenomenon of rattling around at a party, or to do just that, flinging themselves far and wide to create the illusion of roaring success. How the first floor of the bar would ever be populated, she had no idea.

Georgina needed a tipple to deal with this herself, but instead she held her head high, remembering beauty's power to take the edge off disappointment. Ever the hospitality pro, she sashayed over to a couple of decidedly middle-aged ladies who had evidently just finished work, dressed as they were in their hideous High Street travel agents' regalia.

"What can I get you, girls?" she prompted, notebook at the ready. River had asked her to try to memorise cocktail names, said it looked more authentic that way, but it was hardly going to make or break business if she did jot them down, and besides, it was still early days as far as her own training went, some of these creations had some unnecessarily complicated titles.

"We just can't decide," said the older one. "What does your sexy bartender over there recommend?" the ever-so-slightly younger one chimed in, unable to tear her besotted eyes off River as he needlessly demonstrated his showy pouring skills in the background, only adding to their collective pool of drool.

Georgina felt her hackles rise, and a twinge of a distant relative to jealousy stir in the pit of her stomach. Was this what she was going to have to contend with every night? He was hers, *all hers*, and as much as that was simply part of a revenge-fuelled plan, she was not used to sharing her treats with anybody, and not about to start.

"Why don't I ask him to surprise you then? Yes, what a great idea," she said, catching River's eye in a moment of perfect synchronicity and walking back to the bar before they had chance to protest.

"They've asked for two Earthquakes," she said, slapping her notebook down on the counter and letting her pen catch up with her mischief.

"But that's not even on the menu," said River, clearly alarmed at the strength of their choice.

"Well, these ladies do seem very experienced when it comes to their spirits. Best give them what they've asked for. I'm just as surprised as you are, but we can't be discerning or sexist when it comes to serving up Absinthe. There's a very good reason they let it back into the States in 2007."

"I'm impressed, George... Georgina, *Georgina*."

She scowled.

"You are a little powerhouse of knowledge, aren't you?" he winked, and then heard the laughter coming from the travel agents' table which clearly helped to back up their letting-their-hair-down choice of drink. "Hopefully they've both got a day off tomorrow."

He turned to find a couple of Champagne coupe glasses and Georgina breathed an imaginary sigh of relief. This was going to be entertaining all right.

While she waited for River to prep their drinks, she made for the table nearest the window quickly realising she'd committed the ultimate faux pas by tending to local resident, Lord Rigby-Chandler's order, only second. Why hadn't she noticed him sooner wearing his trademark bowler hat and hideous silk dandelion yellow scarf, whose reflection gave him a complexion to rival *The Incredible Hulk*?

Naturally, her charm would make up for that.

"So wonderful to see you here this evening with your charmingly dressed wife, my Lord." She stooped to air kiss Lady Rigby-Chandler first, spinning on her heel and smiling sweetly at her husband – who no doubt wished he was several years younger, minus the girth, double chin and doormat eyebrows, and cocktailing now alone. He took her hand and shook it eagerly, reluctant to let go, also no doubt imagining what her young silken paws were capable of doing to his anatomy.

Disgusting creature, she could read him like a book.

She took their orders anyway and Heather chimed in with hers as she made her way back to the bar: "a Ginger Rabbit, please for me, Georgina love."

She couldn't help but laugh inwardly at that. River had told her all about his mother's penchant for the 'grounding properties of ginger', which is why he'd had no choice but to feature at least one cocktail in the menu granting it the leading role. Ginger, star anise, bourbon, Crème Yvette – whatever in god's name that was – black tea-infused syrup, angostura bitters and lemon peel? No thank you. That was one creation she definitely wouldn't be sampling.

"Lord Pervert over there has ordered a Trafalgar Punch – something I wouldn't mind giving him the honour of myself, and her Ladyship requests a Kir Royale; poor woman having to wake up to *that* in the morning."

"Do you mean to tell me we have actual aristocracy in here on opening night? Oh. My. God. Had I known I'd have asked him to do the honours and cut the red ribbon… just don't tell my mum… I mean, she did a grand job and all – well, with the exception of picking up that blunt pair of kitchen scissors and you having to help her hack at the material midway through the deed – but he could have got us into the paper… and beyond, for all the right reasons this time."

River's lack of loyalty to his family was astounding. Okay, so Heather had made a complete mess of the 'ceremony', and he had grown up never knowing his dad. But still, his mother had been his biggest fan since the bar's conception; he didn't know how lucky he was to have her as a constant in his life. What a jerk putting strangers before blood.

"So now there's just the woman from next door's bakery and I think I'm up-to-date," Georgina let her own agenda take priority.

"Nice job," he said, "really nice job," the twinkle in his eyes telling her just how well her plan was starting to take shape. He was falling for her all right, no two ways about it. "I'll show you how much it means to me later," he added.

She tried to stop her cheeks colouring to candy floss but they had a cotton wool mind of their own. And, well, the sex was pretty amazing... and luckily she didn't 'do' emotion, so she was as safe as houses when it came to the question of reciprocation. She coughed and added a stern "erhem" reminding him there was a time and a place, a quick seductive pout – definitely not of the tragic trout pout variety – thrown in for good measure. Then over she sashayed again (for it was the second best thing to her standard elongated stride which left men trailing in her wake) to their next-door neighbour in trade.

She'll be a B52. In and out, five short but powerful sips from a shot glass, a pleasantry or two at the 'housewarming' and that's the last we'll ever see of her in here.

"Hi there, thanks," her final customer greeted her with a friendly grin as she played with the corners of her coaster.

"It should be me thanking you," Georgina heard herself croon. "What can I get you and I'm so very sorry for the short delay. Needless to say, this will be on the house."

"No really, no need to apologise at all, and I'm more than happy to pay my way. I um... I can see you've been," she paused, "rushed off your feet," she whispered.

They laughed in unison, the joke very much understood between them.

"I'm in a bit of a rush as it happens, got to prep for tomorrow before locking up so the bakers have all they need for the early morning start – I'm Zara by the way. So I'll make it a quick, but much-needed B52 for a little energy burst."

"Perfect choice, he makes the best for miles," Georgina nodded toward the bar, glowing at how in tune she was with her customers. "And I'm Georgina, pleased to meet you. I will definitely be calling in for some goodies, especially if I'm working a late shift."

"Please do, that would be wonderful. It'll be good to have some female company next door, pop in any time, won't you?"

Something told Georgina this was the beginning of a rather beneficial alliance.

***

One hour later saw the bar in danger of Demolition Revisited.

"Georgina, I need you to try to prise a mobile off one of them," said River, shaking his hands like palm leaves caught up in a hurricane. "I don't think I should be man-handling a pair of fifty year old women – much as it might make their days – and we can't leave them to the fate of a taxi without speaking to their other halves, being sure about their addresses."

"No worries, leave it to me," she said, tutting at their lack of responsibility, especially when they were so publicly advertising their workplace.

The ever-so-slightly-younger one was a heap on the floor, sitting in a puddle of her own vomit, as the elder of the two now looked double her age, face creased with laughter at her colleague's inability to hold down her drink.

Heather was equally less than impressed.

"I can't believe you've served them up Absinthe." She stood hands on hips, incredulous as to the disaster before them both. "This really doesn't bode well for the reputation of the bar. Your only saving grace is the fact hardly anybody turned up tonight."

"I tried to warn him, Heather, really I did," said Georgina, shaking her head at the pitiful scene as she asked the eldest travel agent for their addresses in the neighbouring town, to avoid her having to go through their personal belongings. "It wouldn't have been half as bad if they'd not followed those Earthquakes up with a couple of Kamikazes."

"This is no time at all for dilly-dallying about," Lady Rigby-Chandler barged past them both, hauling the younger woman up from the floor and dumping her onto a nearby couch. "I'll be billing you for these, too," she took in the extent of her broken ruby shellac nails, flashed them at River who stood behind the bar, and shouted, "my husband and I were super excited to learn of a proper cocktail establishment opening its doors in Somerset, you've had a lot of backlash in the press, but we were only too happy to buck that trend, prove all the Negative Nellies wrong about their reluctance to get past their anally retentive traditions. But I fear they had a point all along."

Lord Rigby-Chandler rose from his seat, as if on cue, and took his bowler hat off in a gesture to back up the sentiments of his wife.

"My Lady's right. The evening's proceedings really have got quite – hic – out of hand," he flumped back into his chair and started to resemble a Tory backbencher falling into a post liquid lunch slumber.

"Give me their bags," said Lady Rigby-Chandler to Heather and Georgina.

Heather managed to extract one from the chair back of the travel agent turned hyena, Georgina had a slight battle with the other when Hyena's laugh became paranoia and the elder dove onto the shoulder bag of her friend, grappling momentarily with its bulk until the contents spilled across the floor and she surrendered to her next round of giggles.

"Righty-ho, I will hunt for the numbers of their next-of-kin and inform them of the situation, requesting they call us back once these women are safely deposited to their husbands – one presumes they are married to men anyway. Do they have rings?"

Heather and Georgina were cardboard cutouts.

"Well? Help me out, dears, for goodness sake," she sighed. "Both of you have been about as much use as a chocolate teapot so far."

Oh, Georgina really needed that drink now, to think she'd even felt sorry for this Hooray Henrietta and her marital status moments earlier!

How dare this Snotty Toff look down her snout at them, at *her*, like this? Notwithstanding the conveniently overlooked fact this was all Georgina's own doing in the first place. Thank goodness Zara had left half an hour ago, although, even then things were getting louder in the volume department. One thing was for sure: next time a semi-attractive woman hinted at dalliance with her bartender, a subtler method was required.

"Once I have done the honours, Mr Jackson, you will call a cab and we'll wait until we get the call from the uh…

husbands, or partners, or whatever. I do hope neither of them resides alone. Goodness gracious, they might well choke in their sleep tonight."

***

"There was a flippin' good reason behind the prohibition of Absinthe in America in 1915, River," Heather shook her head in disbelief. "How could you be so irresponsible as to keep a bottle behind the bar?"

"It's long been OK'd, that's how." He stared at her, mimicking the frost on one of his glasses as she swirled at the remnants of her Ginger Rabbit. She was still only on her first drink.

Just as well really. Georgina felt she'd seen enough of this kind of drama for one night, and was now looking forward to a little hanky-panky in the hotel to help River put it all behind him. They'd been 'together' just six weeks, a secret to the outside world, all bar the receptionist at the nicest of Glastonbury's two hotels, anyway. River, despite having his box room at home, had more than enough money besides to block book the 'penthouse suite' of the Hotel Guinevere for a six month stretch, at which point he planned to have found the perfect house of his own.

"Your mum has been a star this evening. Don't take it out on her. It's just one of those things, and we can all thank our own lucky stars it happened on a quiet night. It's only going to get busier from now on."

This was slightly optimistic given that Lady Rigby-Chandler had warned them in her inimitable style:

"I will have my beady little eye on the antics of this place. Oh yes. I will be in here at the most select of times, according to my social schedule, much like those hideously infuriating undercover diners. Naturally, Lord R.C here will accompany me; naturally since one and one's husband are such esteemed members of aristocracy, one will not be paying for this evening's toddies... or any future refreshments."

"Heather," Georgina warded off a shudder and turned to

the woman she was all too aware could be her future mother-in-law, like if she *wanted* her to be, which she most categorically did not, "why don't we call you a taxi now, too? We'll clean up here and handle this and you go home and chill out. You were never meant to have got involved in the commotion. An early night and everything will look good as new in the morning – we'll be ready to start afresh."

After I have ridden your son senseless this evening; drawing him ever deeper under my spell on that king-sized bed.

Chapter Seven
ALICE

There was nowhere quite like Somerset. Many were those who would 'search for themselves' in every conceivable dot on the globe, the further away, supposedly the more of their inner being they'd come to discover. Alice had seen them leave only to return sure as boomerangs. And now, just like everybody else who thought life would be better far away from the privilege of grass green roots, no matter where she found herself unpacking her ever-growing collection of suitcases, she yearned to go home. Glastonbury was calling; the earth wire in her veins, willing her to plug herself back into all that was familiar, that tactile earth of the cowslip-dotted Levels, September's plump blackberry hedgerows and her beloved stables; grounded at last, able to breathe.

She needn't ever have left this world. That was perhaps the only thing life in London – and beyond – had taught her. Just like the young boy, Santiago, in Paulo Coelho's *The Alchemist*, she'd had everything she'd ever needed – not only inside her, but overflowing from her cup and into her small West Country universe all along. For all her love conquests won, for all her red carpet appearances attached to the arm of a leading man, and for all the boxer shorts catapulted at her on the stage, here in Glastonbury she'd never stopped being the centre of attention anyway.

Butterflies circled her stomach as the bus bound from Bristol rounded the corner and began its slight descent into her home town's High Street. She knew his bar was next to the bakery, but it had been so long since she'd been back to pay a visit, that she'd actually forgotten what side of the road the fat, greasy Lardy Cakes and Death By Chocolate slabs lined the windows. She needn't have fretted, 'The Cocktail Bar', as it was unimaginatively, perhaps even ingeniously titled; glistened enticingly on the right, overshadowing anything the now trendy, overhauled, and all things organic-looking bakery had to offer. But it was decidedly closed. Bang went her plan to surprise River.

The number 376 pulled over next to the bus stop opposite the town hall, and on the doorstep of her favourite pizzeria in the whole world. She glanced up at the giant clock on the friendly building across the road, momentarily reminiscing on her roller boot disco days. Those iron hands were notorious for not being wound forward or back with the changing of the hours, but the aroma wrapping around her in a vortex of deliciousness, told her all she needed to know: *Cagnola's* was open, it had to be lunchtime.

She pulled her case behind her, weary from lack of food since the plastic-tasting veggie breakfast platter on her flight into London, stopped to re-check her dark shades masked the equally dark circles under her eyes and went inside, asking for a table for one, as far away from the other diners as possible.

She mulled over the menu, as reassuring as ever, Cagnola's stuck with what they knew. Perhaps her own life wouldn't be in such confusing tatters had she done the same. She scanned the pizzas, quickly deciding carbs were the only way forward, ordered a Margarita and a Coke – scowling at herself for the crime that was the latter, but sometimes even Clean Eaters needed a dirty weekend – and called River, failing miserably to get through.

Shoot. So now what?

She could only guess he'd changed his number because of Lennie.

Eugh – the power of two unsuspecting syllables to make a girl wince.

Was there ever a name so synonymous with slime – excusing his excellence of the Kravitz variety, of course? Dodging him, not to mention the local press, was going to be a daily occurrence. Thank god she didn't live in London. At least there was less chance of a 'newsworthier' photographer flooring it down the M4 to take a picture when they could kill several 'birds' with the same stone from Kensington and Chelsea to Islington.

But how else was she going to get hold of River? She didn't want to turn up unannounced at his mum's house, not after the charade with the band several weeks ago when they'd flown over to the UK for the premier of the new movie their lyrics were providing the soundtrack for – she'd already forgotten its name – and Lennie had insisted they accompany him to Somerset to track down The Boy Gone AWOL. Luckily it was Friday, the bar was sure to be open to see in the weekend at some point today, but in all seriousness, how many hours could she spend picking at pizza and gelato? She barely had an appetite at the best of times. And then her jetlagged brain kicked into gear: Facebook and Twitter (a private message on both, of course). He must still be connected to his social media.

Lunch came and lunch went, the waiter did his best to flirt his way into an autograph, but Alice wasn't even up for friendly small talk today. Still there was no sign of contact. She sighed, wondering what to do now. It wasn't that her parents wouldn't have her back at the farm in Butleigh, one of the quaint villages that fringed the town she'd always really called home. She just didn't want them to know she'd 'come to her senses', not quite yet, they'd never been enamoured by her 'alternative lifestyle' and she had to be ready for the inevitable point scoring that would ensue.

"But you have a place in the Great Britain equestrian team, darling. Daddy's pulled strings the likes of which you simply cannot imagine to grant you this privilege. Are you out of your mind throwing away that honour of representing Queen and country… for… for… for a place in one of those scruffy grunge bands? Oh, the shame with which you're tarnishing the family!"

Alice had reduced her mother to a sherry-fuelled stammer several Christmases ago. But on January the second, she'd hopped on that National Express coach with River all the same, a new life awaiting them both in the Big Smoke.

Relations had improved somewhat over the years, of course. Her parents were not the type to hold a grudge by the scruff of its neck, but still, there the elephant in the room stayed before them. And she missed her horses too, both of which had long since been sold, her decision the nail in the coffin to the question of Folly Farm ever breeding again.

She began to run through the drinks menu once more, breaking yet again with orthorexic tradition – well it was technically the weekend, and if she did manage to find River later, she could hardly decline quintessential cocktail etiquette when she visited his bar. A Negroni – that would fill another hour here, especially if it came with a stirrer; and then perhaps a coffee, followed by a mineral water, diluting the toxins and hopefully taking her up to six pm. By which time the bar just had to be open. This wasn't London after all, people hit on the booze here at five pm sharp, especially on a Friday; always on a Friday.

The jingle of the little gold bell at the restaurant door sounded too good to be true, but she lifted her head anyway, heart bizarrely pounding in a way it had certainly never done before at the sight of him, wondering how he was going to take this. Would he even trust her? She couldn't blame him if he thought Lennie had sent her out undercover. If the shoe was on the other foot, she'd certainly suspect the same.

"Al, what are you doing here?" he said. "I just got your Facebook message and didn't even stop to reply, just had to get here to see you as quickly as I could."

The pull to his chest was like sinking into a freshly plumped up pillow that made everything suddenly very all right again. If only she'd seen that when they'd fooled around that night at the festival, how much heartache and drama she'd have spared herself, how many narcissistic idiots she'd have spurned.

"This is all so surreal." He released her and stood back, as if to examine the cracks of seven albums.

"It's a long story but it's probably very similar to yours," she said, signalling to the overenthusiastic waiter to take their drinks order, suddenly feeling twenty times more justified, C list celeb (well, according to the press that had been her official ranking), or not.

"I'll have a Negroni," she said, resuming her seated position, beckoning to River to join her. "And you?"

"Yeah… yeah… make that two," River said, lowering his body onto the chair, his incessant goofball stare making her stomach repeat those butterflies, except now they were all simultaneously competing in the Olympic figure skating final.

She tore her own gaze away, embarrassed at her lack of emotional control. They'd known each other forever and a day, this was ridiculous, first date ridiculous. When she finally did lift her eyelids to resume communication, she sensed they were both utterly grateful for their on-the-ball *cameriere,* tray held high in his right hand, showcasing two gleaming amber tumblers topped with lemon slices mimicking surfboards – and token stirrers. This would take the edge off her unfathomable teenage persona, yet something told her she shouldn't down it too quickly either.

River initiated the drinking, Alice followed suit.

"Are you heading back to your parents, or?" He put down his glass and clasped his hands together, easing them midway across the table, something like a prayer, something like a businessman on the cusp of sealing a deal.

"Well, that's the thing. You remember how they reacted all those years ago when we set off for London…? I'm not sure I can face the 'we-told-you-so' routine just yet," she tugged awkwardly at her hair, "but on the other hand, if I'm back, I'm back. I don't want to play stowaway until I die."

"Do you want me to help? I can." He reached further across the table now and reassuringly placed that clasp on her hands, drawing them together until she wondered if he was about to play that one-potato-two-potato game Daddy refused to relinquish until way into her teens.

She inhaled deeply, fighting back the tears, knowing full well that once she started, she'd never stop. But the tenderness of skin upon skin lingered, even moments after his hands were gripping his glass again, a trace of electricity surging back into

61

her own body, as if there it had always belonged. This was crazy, why had she never felt like this with him before? All she knew is she had definitely never felt this way with any of the others, not a single Beverly Hills residing, *Armani* toting, *Nobu* dining one of them.

On the other hand, it could just be the jetlag, east to west was the worst. And yes, she'd experienced it before, but normally she'd have a chauffeur driven limo waiting to pick her up and take her somewhere like The Dorchester, or her sister Tamara's spare Notting Hill pad. This time was different though. She and Tamara had fallen out over her last choice of boyfriend and his shoe fiasco; Glenn had only gone and stepped out in crocodile skin loafers, red rag to the staunchest of animal rights bulls. Which had had nothing to do with Alice, she was hardly his personal dresser, she'd been in Guadalajara at the time, he at an award ceremony in Palm Springs. Sodding typical that Tamara had stumbled across the pictures in the society pages at the rear end of *Hello*. As for her parents, they'd long ago withheld regular payment into her trust fund; the trust fund she'd found herself equally regularly dipping into to top up her fifty-per-cent-less-for-being-a-female salary that came with the band.

And then there was the not so small matter of Lennie blocking her credit card since she was in breach of contract.

In short she was destitute and homeless. But she couldn't land all of this on River today, not until she'd told him the news that would shake *his* world.

"I'm okay, I'm fine, it'll be…," she cut off to blow her nose, eyes scanning the premises moments later in case anybody was sneakily filming her sad demise on their mobile phone.

"You're not okay." He shook his head at her. "But you will be, everything will fall into place, I promise. There is life out here after the band, you know? Look at me."

She smiled a wobbly smile. He'd done amazingly for himself, especially when she considered his somewhat off-kilter single parent upbringing. The quirky Heather; Alice had always had a soft spot for her, in fact Heather and her veggie lentil hotpot were the very reason she'd stopped eating meat herself.

"I've got nowhere to—"

"Shh." He put his finger to his lips. "You'll stay in my penthouse at the Hotel Guinevere, at least for tonight. I'm fine with my old room at Mum's. After that we'll find you a nice apartment, or maybe the hotel has another large room going free. Either way, the last thing I am going to do is abandon you. We started this adventure together... we'll finish it together... in style."

He lifted his tumbler to suggest a toast. Alice's hand trembled as she did the same, not so much through lack of sleep, but the unshakable feeling that River Jackson was in fact, the love of her life.

Chapter Eight
GEORGINA

Some people never really get over their first love. Blake was one of those people. For all her edginess, for all her Fierce Warrior nature, Georgina had long ago excused her brother for being a sopping Wet Blanket.

In part, she realised this was because he'd taken the concept of Alice and blown it up into an inflatable woman of a doll who embodied everything about the female psyche. There was no doubt that his feelings for Alice were more than lingering teenage lust, although even Georgina had to acknowledge that her natural white blonde curls and cobalt eyes on porcelain skin, not to mention the legs that went on for miles and miles, were enough to make any sister's veins course with envy.

But Blake's fascination with this ethereal creature happened to happen the exact Monday after their mother had scarpered back to Benidorm to 'start a new life' with one Miguel, aka. the fling from her best (and in those days, super late to the altar) friend's week long hen do. Which was the precise Monday Georgina's role in the household changed too; aged just nine or not, she had assumed the position of Mama Bear-stroke-one of the lads, unnaturally nonplussed by her mother's hiatus for ever and ever Amen to warmer climes. Something inside her had always known this would be the turn of events. That way it came as no surprise when the love she carried for her big brother – and her father – became the unconditional love a mother is *supposed* to carry for her child. Overnight.

Blake had spurned every female opportunity for his Happy Ever After over the years. Women, including his ex-wife and the child they had created – the nephew Georgina would never get chance to play Auntie to – had come and gone, all because of River. The fact could not be disputed: had he not led Alice astray into the badass world of 'rock 'n' roll', Blake would have moved on with his life. He'd have watched with a strange kind of satisfaction from the sidelines as she'd settled down with another local guy, granted they'd still have a better career than he could ever dream of, an estate agent perhaps or a solicitor, but they certainly wouldn't be publicity hungry, Brad Pitt cloned gazillionaires. She'd have popped out two point four children, lost her mojo and her looks because there was no longer a damned thing to prove in the small town comfort zone, and they all would have lived happily ever after.

But oh no, River's determination to secure her a place in that wretched band had resulted in one thing and one thing only: Blake putting her on an even higher pedestal, this one made of gold, encrusted with diamonds, and ever more out of his reach. Her antics haunted him everywhere he went. Especially the staff canteen where she'd 'grace' the tabloids emerging from a tropical Barbadian beach hand in hand with her latest bit of stuff, or dazzling the crowds in a figure-hugging ball gown on a red carpet in La-La Land, a sharp kick to the stomach as he tucked into his bacon butty.

That was why it was time for revenge, and what sweeter way for revenge to play itself out than between the sheets.

"So what excuse did you make up this time?" said River, breaking her stream of consciousness, a narrative she was rather enjoying along with the subtle dapple of daylight which was nicely warming up her pillow.

Georgina yawned and stretched her arms out of her side of the deluxe bed she'd grown all too accustomed to, a cat about to lick her paws. Last night's activity had been epic.

"They think I'm overnighting at one of my former clients' houses," she said, opening her sleepy eyes and rolling over to face her lover, "there in the middle of the night to accompany him to the bathroom for a pee." She circled River's navel with her fingertip, "And there in the morning to shower him and make him breakfast." She turned over to the bedside table, lifted the half-filled flute of Bolly and faced him again to bring the glass to his lips. River raised his eyebrows as he sipped and she took this as her opportunity to dive in for a luxurious (if slightly flat) bubble-fuelled kiss.

"Good. That is good," he said when they came up for air.

He'd come clean with her last night about what had really happened during Blake's visit, every bead of Champagne seemingly teasing out the smallest of details. She'd feigned her shock well, revelling in the amount of trust he was prepared to bestow on her so quickly.

Blake had mentioned he and Lee had called by with a 'friendly warning', that was the real reason she knew River was back on the scene just hours before *Torgate*, her path crossing with her brother's as they'd met on their own garden path; one heading out to walk the neighbour's feisty terrier, one about to flunk out on the couch with a breakfast of leftover cottage pie. But despite Blake's hint, she hadn't been at all prepared for the slightly bigger picture River had painted. She'd even started to feel sorry for River last night. Just for a couple of seconds anyway.

"I can't believe it," she'd finally said.

"Well, straight up, babe, it's the truth," River had downed his champers from the bottle before adding, "the irony being it was actually your dad and a couple of other painters and decorators who patched the bar back up again – a great job they did too – although thankfully he didn't recognise me... or if he did, he did a very good job of playing dumb anyway."

"Geez, yes," she'd gasped. "That does explain the recent spell of contract work he was going on about." She'd propped her head up with her elbow, unable to hide the legitimate worry that had wrinkled her face. "I mean, I know Blake can get flighty, that he's not happy in that dead-end job, that he misses Ethan... who's got to be going on for like eight now. But going to those lengths and dragging poor Lee along for the ride...?" she'd paused, puffing air from her cheeks like a dragon, "...all I can say is I am really sorry. This is not going to happen again. I can't confront him, obviously—"

"No, do not even go there. He made it more than quartz

66

crystal clear this wasn't his last visit… maybe this was all too big a risk you working for me? What if he does come back when you're in the bar… or one of his friends spots you as they walk past the window?"

Georgina couldn't believe how dense River could be at times. She lay in bed reflecting on their recent dialogue, in awe of those fabulously muscular buttocks which never seemed to get a workout, other than when parked on a mattress, and shook her head at last night's naïve remark as he pulled on his boxer shorts.

"a) Blake doesn't have any friends, they're just workmates," she'd said, "well, except for Lee, who's hardly contender of the year for Iron Man, b) Blake drinks at The Pear Tree to avoid seeing Dad's sorry face prop up the bar at the Ring O'Bells… okay, what *was* the Ring O'Bells…," she'd swallowed, she'd really not intended to keep labouring that point. "So I wouldn't worry about him putting in an appearance at the bar any time soon to switch pints for piña coladas – either alone or with a baseball bat armed group of drinking buddies." She'd stopped to sigh at the tragedy of it all, taking in River's face, intent and hooked on her revelation. "In fact, he's Dad's mirror image at *his* pub, face melded to the head of his beer, his only communication a quick gawp at the barmaid's cleavage, or a head nod to the landlord… such a sorry state of affairs." Georgina had broken off again. "Now, where was I, oh yes… point c)… both Dad and Blake know I wear the trousers. I will tell them I'm working *with* you," how she'd enjoyed the lingering of that four letter word, "but when the moment is right."

And with that he'd pulled her on top of him, just as he was doing now, tempting her libido out of its daydream, despite him being fully dressed.

What could she say? She was yet to meet a woman who operated smoother than she did.

Chapter Nine
RIVER

"Do you like it like this?" River beamed at Georgina as she bent over to reveal a sneaky peek of her black lace thong beneath her increasingly short peplum skirt. "Or would Sir prefer it a little higher," she said, sliding the poster advertising 'BOOK CLUB NIGHT' further up the window with her right hand, and the hem of her skirt further up her body with her left, leaving very little to the imagination.

"Definitely higher," he replied, arms wrapped around her now, oblivious to the fact the blinds too were rolled up, so their frolicking was on full-on display to a rain-soaked and windswept High Street.

"So, do you think it will work?" he asked, and she span round to reward him with a speedy peck on the lips, before hopping off the windowsill with the grace of a dainty sparrow.

"You've nothing to lose, but in all honesty, a book club... in a cocktail bar... in Glastonbury? It's ever so slightly bonkers."

"Well cheers for the vote of confidence." He came at her again with that embrace.

"Hey, I never said it was impossible but, Riv, I think you've forgotten what this town is all about." She pulled away and started to get animated with Latino-style hand movements. "Look around you. We're surrounded by bongo drum shops, tarot cards and incense. It's not London or Manchester. It's not some quaint little Devonshire village either. And then there are the townies... and they're hardly anyone's definition of literati."

"Ah c'mon, people still read here." He found himself throwing his arms wide open like Pavarotti now, too.

"Yeah, *Fifty Shades of Grey* and the ilk, or *The Encyclopedia of Faeries and Goddesses* at the other end of the spectrum – no offence to your mum – but it's nothing worthy of analysis and debate."

"Okay then, let's make this interesting." He marched to the other side of the bar, slammed two Tequila shot glasses onto the counter and began to encrust their rims with pink Himalayan salt, an act that would have the masters of his trade more up in arms than a cocktail battle. "Since we're on the subject... I will make love to you... dressed up as a...a... well," he brought his fist to his chin deep in thought, sensing the intrigue lighting up those sexy eyes, "as a superhero, yes, a caped crusader... of madam's choice... depending of course on what *Amazon* have got in stock... if at least five people – non-family or friends, honorary human beings – show up."

She threw her head back and let out a wild Cruella De Ville cackle, to which he simply shook his head in response, filled their glasses, and then nudged hers across the bar.

"I don't want you to lose, babe... and I can't deny the thought of you coming to my rescue totes turns me on," she said through her pout when she was finally able to compose herself, glass clinking against his, where there she let it rest just a second or two before swinging it operatically to her lips, her defiant emblem of him almost succeeding in having his fill. "But lose you will."

***

One week later...

"Well, I think it's a truly fantabulous idea. Just what this town needs." A willowy multiple-layered Jane Austen Bourdaloue-skirted bespectacled women of senior years fluttered her spidery, cartoon, violet eyelashes at River as she attempted in vain to perch herself on a bar stool.

"It took me no time at all to round up my four ladies and I can assure you, darling, we'll be a regular fixture every fortnight, come rain, shine or even snow; such a marvellous venue in which to discuss our bi-monthly literary pickings –

with a tipple of the exotic or two and a view of one thoroughly dashing gentleman, of course."

River didn't know whether to laugh or cry, especially as Georgina had clocked on early for her shift, no doubt hoping to point score and prove his optimism wrong. He chewed on his smile as he imagined what he was going to do to her later – not that she'd revealed her choice of costume yet. She was too good to be true; no strings, adventurous sex on tap, a friend to have a laugh with. Just the tonic he needed to ease him back into local life, to almost take his mind off the impending mission, and the kitchen window 'thing', as well as the constant urge to look over his shoulder for hedge-hiding photographers. Miraculously, it appeared Blake was also completely unfazed by her new employment – none the wiser as to what she was getting up to in somebody else's bed besides.

He let his smile have his way with him in a bid to select some appropriate preamble. "This is exactly the positive reaction I hoped my idea would have. I'm a passionate bibliophile myself. Just wish I had more time to indulge in the written word. A bar full of highly educated – and equally classy women," he stopped to swallow his deceitful words away, "it not only sends my heart a flutter, but eases my own lack of reading time guilt."

"Darling, you're too kind." Jane Austen extended her hand and River's stomach catapulted, wondering whether this was an invite to brush it with his lips – he did anyway, cursing himself for being so two-faced, careful to avoid her *Twiglet* fingers, should they snap in half.

"Now then, what can I get you all to drink? These are paid for by the way."

"Oh, sweetheart, you really shouldn't but we'll gratefully oblige."

She swivelled and put two fingers – whose apparent fragility belied their strength – to her over-painted coral lips producing an enviable whistle to attract the attention of the rest of her group.

"Open your menus, girls. Mr Jackson is granting us our

first drinks on the house."

A hubble bubble of cheer brewed at the corner table as the realisation illuminated faces, thankfully not all as heavily made-up.

Jane Austen's elongated fingers reached for one of the menus lying on the bar and she began to flick through its pages in reverse. River, who had taken to polishing glasses in a bid to divert her adoration, almost dropped the tumbler he was buffing.

For crying out loud, no; it's not meant to be you, anybody but you. Start at the front, lady!

He gulped as she immediately ceased fingering the twenty-something blank pages and flipped the menu to its front cover. Heather was right. He did have a knack for telepathy. And thank god. He knew, as he flashed back again to Mercedes in her agave-studded field where she stood waving him off with the bottle, that none of this was up to him; he was simply The Messenger. Whoever chose the elixir chose it. But it didn't stop River being judgmental. Surely there were better candidates to have their life, as they knew it, changed for ever?

"So what is your favourite book, my good man, when you do get time to read?"

Back off lady, less of the *my*.

"See that's a question that always has me torn." He smiled becomingly. "With so many worthy authors in the world, how can we possibly choo—"

"For me it's quite simple, anything about cats, starring cats, cats walking past in the background, a hint of a feline title; an author with cat in their name, matters not a jot," she said.

"Okay… I see you're fond of… err… cats then?"

"Fond of them, she's stark raving bonkers about them, twenty-six of the things in her house and the surrounding fields, at last count any rate," said her friend, looping her arm in Jane Austen's and pulling her back to the table. "Come along now, dear, we're waiting for you to get proceedings started. Everybody's champing at the bit to share their reviews on *A Street Cat Named Bob*."

"You do attract them," said Georgina, propping herself

71

most foxily across the bar, almost making him jump.

"Yeah, well, let's just hope this group grows significantly to dilute the madness," said River, distracting himself from her provocative pose with the realisation that he'd not checked in on Alice for twenty-four hours.

She was still staying at his mum's, apart from the first couple of nights after her arrival, when he'd managed to dampen Georgina and her appetite, sneaking Alice into his penthouse, trading his relative luxury for an unplanned return to his now loud and tie-dye print bedecked bedroom, courtesy of Heather's makeover idea. The hotel would only have a larger room available as of the weekend, so Heather had kindly agreed to Alice's temporary move into River's back bedroom. He was sure she was glad of the company anyway. Since The Lennie Thing, something she had declined to talk about whenever he brought the subject up, she either seemed to want to constantly surround herself with other people, or throw herself into her latest definition of art.

"Listen, can you manage here for ten minutes? I'll be back… quick call to make, that's all."

"Yeah, course," she said. "I'll go see what the bookworms would like to drink."

He patted himself down to check he had his mobile, wandered halfway down to the double gates of the backyard, a quick pit stop at the skittle alley to check up on the bottle in the cupboard, careful to look over his shoulder in case Georgina should be anywhere in sight. But there it lay, reassuringly so, just as it had every time he had thought to look in on it, snuggled beneath the heavy tartan blankets he'd taken from Heather's ottoman. He peeped his head to the left and right outside the rickety door, and then left once again as would a child learning the Green Cross Code, exited the alley and paced confidently to the back gates, his eyes now surveying the car park for passers-by instead. The town's market may have finished at midday but he couldn't get too lax about anything when Lennie – and heck, even Bear and Alex – could be on the prowl. And then there was the press. A lone C-list band member sailing off into the sunset was one thing, he could already sense his five minutes of fame fading into delicious obscurity. But two members, male and female, the latter heroin to the camera's lens, that made for a very different scenario indeed; the juiciest of stories, Sambuca to Lennie's fury.

The truth was he had two obligations now: The Holy Grail and Alice.

Chapter Ten
ALICE

Alice finally moved into The Guinevere on a Sunday morning, the sun throwing a spotlight of new beginnings on her slender frame as she hopped out of River's retro *Citroen 2CV* and onto the doorstep of her new home.

"Tell me something, Riv: why did you never treat yourself much when you were in the band? I mean, that's your old car parked out by the pavement, from the days before we got famous. Didn't you ever think of upgrading it, going for something a little more swish or reliable?"

She found River such a curiosity in that way. Obviously, Heather's matriarch and flower power influence helped to keep him down to Earth, but to all intents and purposes, the bar was his biggest luxury after all those years earning all that money. He put her in mind of one of those hoarders who won the lottery, yet still carried on working at the local D.I.Y superstore, still holidayed in Blackpool every August, only splashing out on a slightly upgraded Skoda – oh, and a new garden shed. If you couldn't enjoy what you had, what was the point? That elusive Rainy Day might never ever come.

"There's just one very small thing I need you to be aware of," said River, completely disregarding the interrogation as he helped her with her case up the stairs, the lift having allegedly broken for the seventh time that week. "I hadn't mentioned it before because, well, it didn't seem relevant." He strained to haul the case's heavy bulk onto the final step and rolled up his sleeves before attempting it again, like that might make all the difference to the power of his biceps. "Georgina will be flitting about."

"And why would I have an issue with that?"

Alice wasn't even completely certain who this apparently infamous Georgina was. Sure, River had inserted her name into conversation here and there, paper clipping her like a convenient accessory. And sure she had also noted the spare toothbrush and girlie-packaged shower gel adorning the bathroom in River's hotel room when he'd let her stay there, giving more than a hint that 'love was in the air'. She knew that Georgina was working in his bar, and gathered she was the attractive younger sister of Brooding Blake, the guy whose pubescent and constantly ogling eyes used to freak her out – especially the one and only time she was stupid enough to take that LSD tablet – his desperate face having swum around her 'trip' all night. But try as she might, she could not remember him having a sibling. That's what also freaked her out, the extent of her gruelling years on the road, boozing, schmoozing and light recreational drug dabbling at parties, meant that now she was back, all those faces from her past morphed into remnants of a dream, so that she half-remembered one person, and only vaguely recalled another.

"But from your perspective, it's probably best to keep a low profile anyway… what with photographers, reporters, and I hate to say it… *him*, Lennie." River's insistent tone brought her back to the present. "Just for the time being, I haven't mentioned to Georgina that you're back yet, you see. Not that there's anything going on between you and I… or me and her, I mean we're all just good friends… you and I," he scratched at his beard, "and she and I."

"River, you don't owe me a rundown of your private life," said Alice impatiently, inserting her key into the lock and entering the front door to her new home, for however long that might be. After the headache-inducing décor of River's bedroom (how had he ever coped with the assault of that luminous pink tie-dye?), her 'penthouse' at The Guinevere was positively paradise. Completely incomparable to the kind of pampering she'd grown used to elsewhere, of course, but a Shangri-La all the same – and all paid for by River. Would any of the excuses for men in her past have gone to such lengths? She doubted it. Unless they'd netted themselves a golden handshake in the process, or a tennis match on the helipad of the *Burj Al Arab* with Federer, or a free *Lamborghini Huracán*. One gave to receive in the world she'd just left behind, and quite often one simply did the taking. The man stood beside her now couldn't be more different, even in spite of his stretch in the limelight.

"I made a pig's ear of explaining that," said River, hiding his face in his hands.

Alice threw him a stern look, momentarily forgetting how much she adored him.

"Sorry, not the right terminology... how could I forget you're a veggie? What I mean is, Georgina might pop up to my room from time to time, but it's nothing serious, she just needs a place to escape from her brother... and her dad and his depression; a bit of downtime since she's turned into the mother figure of the house."

"Like I said, your private life is just that: private. Mine too... not that I'm going to be remotely interested in men for a very long time." She peeled back the voile draping the windows and realised she was going to like this view a lot. What better way to reacquaint herself with this ditzy little town than via a spot of people watching?

Though the seed of possibility of 'them' tainted the vista, consuming her body in a dull aching thud, Alice was smart enough to know there was indeed something going on. This man was protesting way too much. Yet she also knew – better perhaps than River knew himself – that he didn't sound remotely enamoured. And as much as she wasn't here to stir things up, as much as she'd come back because this was her home and ironically she sensed that Glastonbury would re-birth her, help her come to know the Alice she truly was beneath the layers of *Dior* and *De Beers*; if that journey rewarded her with requited longing from a former band mate, then tough luck, Georgina.

***

At two pm Alice returned from Fishers Hill park, where

she had whiled away an hour, a small box of sushi on the swings, contained in her own frazzled mind behind navy blue *Prada* sunnies.

There was much to ponder, her possible new lives all branching out before her like the giant oak whose breadth and beauty she drank in with every soar in the air on the red plastic seat. She counted herself lucky not to have developed those child-rearing hips that most women of her age were now sporting like it was the fashion. How they missed out on great moments like this, only re-enacting them through their offspring, never truly feeling the exhilaration that came from being a five year old girl in a polka dot dress at a birthday party, without a care, agenda, or responsibility in the world.

Now back in her room that feeling had faded fast. She needed to talk, craved some company. But was she brave enough to get chatting with the woman on reception? Was it even a wise move given that anybody could be loitering about downstairs, waiting for that perfect snap, not to mention the possibility that she might be as broke as Alice, with little choice but to cash in her chips, calling the paps for a game of cat and mouse in return for a few thousand to pay off her overdraft? She threw her expensive *Loewe* pashmina around her shoulders anyway; the last gift Glenn had bestowed upon her, the lightest memento of their relationship, symbolic in every sense of the word, and crept down the stairs like a child checking whether Santa was in residence. But from the upper steps, instinct told her to peer down on the ever-descending spiral before her, where she caught a glimpse of a brunette, so cocksure of herself that the sentiment reverberated through the building and into the stratosphere. This was no regular guest. In fact, she had Georgina written all over her. Alice tiptoed quickly back to her room, pulled the door to, leaving but a hairline crack through which she could assess her rival.

Not that she was back to play tug of war over a heart, she reminded herself. It was just sensible, prudent, and wise to know what one was dealing with when it came to the unpredictable affection of the male of the species.

The flash of confidence strode past her door. It flicked its hair, it stopped for a moment outside the main penthouse door to re-apply its cheap High Street lippy (Alice couldn't help but notice this girl was no *Chanel Mademoiselle*), it even caught its breath in its cupped hand, sniffed at it, rifled through its bag for freshener, sprayed minty vapour into its mouth, and then proceeded to douse itself in equally cheap eau de toilette (again, Alice knew this wasn't sandalwood or Sicilian lemon, for its paint stripping smell had assaulted her nasal passage within seconds), before putting its very own key in the door.

Just how vulgar could a woman get?

"Hey babe," she could hear River greet his 'friend', "I've missed you."

Clunk.

The door shut and for a moment Alice wondered what had happened to her rank and profile in this world, how had it come to this, that she'd been reduced to rubble, gawping desperately like some pervert of a Peeping Tom?

But then she assessed not just her outer, but her inner beauty in the bathroom mirror. The real Alice was in there somewhere, she was starting to shine back at her, a glint here and a twinkle there. She just needed time, patience, and understanding, as well as a healthy dose of forgiveness. Yes, forgiveness; for beating up on herself, for disappointing her family. Because if this wasn't her own life to live, then what the flaming hell was anybody's birth onto this crazy planet all about?

Her recent visit to her parents, just a couple of days ago, had backfired badly. Mummy had evidently hidden Daddy away in the study, the muffling of voices and slamming of doors completely dismissed as she air kissed Alice on the front porch.

"Alice, darling, how simply lovely to see you, yes I did receive your voicemail, Mummy regrets she didn't have time to return your call." Alice's mother had unfathomably never stopped addressing herself in third person. "However, now really isn't an appropriate time, darling, why I'm about to host a very important Somerset Ladies' Luncheon in just half an hour... and I've yet to even add strawberries to my Pimm's...

or de-crust the cucumber sandwiches. Please excuse me."

Clunk.

Another door shut in her face.

River had gone out of his way to drive her there before the bar had opened that day, sacrificing pre-slicing of his citrus fruit for what? So she'd get her own heart sliced in two.

Next she'd called Tamara, pointless really, given her parents and sister had always sided with one another, no matter how trivial and banal the issue – from the CDs Tamara 'hadn't stolen' from Alice's music collection to the hot pants Tamara 'hadn't pilfered and dyed British racing green'. This, it seemed, was the moment in life Tamara had always been waiting for. Revenge is, as they quite rightly say, a dish best served cold, and from her sister, it couldn't have come any icier.

"Al, sweetheart, I've told you, I'm not your bank. Now you made your choice. Daddy gave you the world, the Milky Way and the universe besides on a silver platter but you rejected him – you've no idea how deep that cut, his youngest angel shunning his love. Yes, you were twenty-two and naïve, god knows we've all been there, but it's no use running to me now your life's gone down shit creek without a paddle. I've acted as Chief Advisor to you for long enough. I've my own family to think about now: Harry and I must put our own children first. If I'm handing out charity to you, why that's thousands taken from Sienna, Allegra, Margot and Humphrey's trust funds, something we simply cannot do. If you ever make it to motherhood, something one seriously doubts given the way you've wasted your life thus far, you'll understand that one day."

And with that Tamara had put down the phone, an act which had dissolved their bond for eternity. Alice would never make the mistake of calling her a sister again. She'd imagined Tamara happy dancing her squeaky clean chequered hallway in sweet victory, telephone script tossed over her shoulder as Harry and the nannies uncorked the *Moët*.

Vain Alice may not have been, but the gift of her physical appearance in contrast with that of her older sister's, as well as

79

her mother's fading looks, was definitely not lost on her. Tamara had clearly waited all those long and bitter years to stick the knife in where it would hurt, and generally, in Alice's family's posh circles, if you didn't have a face to grace *Vogue*, never you mind, sweetie, you had money, nerve, self-importance, and an upturned nose with high cheekbones that gave the world the impression you were the human equivalent of a Faberge egg anyway. Stick a *Cartier* pendant around your neck and who'd be any the wiser?

Somebody knocked on her hotel door at six pm Sunday night. She put down her novel, double checked she no longer resembled a panda, cleared the streaky black crumpled tissues from her bed, and hoped that if it was River, it was River on his own. She was not in the mood for making new friends tonight.

"Have you made any plans for uh… dinner?" he said, all too obviously trying not to get flustered at the sight of her in ivory silk spaghetti strap pyjamas. Once she'd returned from the swings and unpacked her few belongings, all she'd wanted to do was laze on the bed, cry and catch up with the queue of novels on her Kindle. Plus it was hot; heat really did rise in a boutique hotel with non-existent air conditioning, it turned out – as opposed to the instant gratification style suites with remote controls coming out of every orifice that she was more accustomed to.

"We're usually closed then, at the uh," his eyes flitted moth-like, "at the erm… bar, but I want to make sure you're eating properly. It's all too easy to turn into a waif."

Evidently Georgina had left the building then.

"I can't say food is the first thing on my mind at the moment," her short term memory flashed back to the half-eaten sushi she'd binned at the park's gates, "but yes please, that would be lovely. I still haven't seen the inside of this famous bar after all."

"It's hardly that… although yeah, it's certainly gotten itself into the papers a few too many times already. Why don't I call for you in a couple of hours?"

"It's a date." Oops, she hadn't meant to say that.

80

"It is a date," he replied.

"Well, not a *date*-date... I um, I totally didn't mean that kind of a rendezvous," she tried in vain to shake the image of The Vulture in the corridor from earlier out of her head, "you're a taken man—"

"No, course not that kind of a date, just friends, good friends and food and equally good cocktails... but I told you before, Georgina isn't my girlfriend. We're just, you know, having fun. That's it. She knows the score too, she wouldn't tell you any different, but anyway, enough about her. Tonight's about us, and well, making plans for your future."

"That sounds a bit hard core."

"I mean getting you out of here at some point soon, as glam for Glastonbury as it is, The Guinevere is hardly anyone's definition of a long-term home, mine included."

His words circled her head as she showered, spritzed herself – sparingly - in the slightly more upmarket *Guerlain,* ever mindful of the fact that less was more, mystique everything when it came to captivating a man. Not that she was attempting to do that this evening, of course. Still, she couldn't help but wonder how the conversation would flow, especially after a couple of drinks. They'd never spent much time alone since the mayhem of the music world. They were about to enter brand new territory.

***

Precisely two hours after his earlier rap at her door, he chaperoned her down the High Street to his bar, unlocked the door, pulled down the blinds, and dimmed the lights to reveal a table sparkling with candles, fairy lights, and just about everything that stereotypically encapsulated the Danish – and now British borrowed – word *hygge*, plus a couple of takeaway pizza boxes.

"Wow, is all this for me?"

"Yes for you, you deserve it. Take a seat." He patted down the fluffy cushions on the pew Alice had slithered herself onto. "Look, I know that it's pizza again, but it's Cagnola's Special

Margarita… not a carnivorous morsel in sight… plus I don't have an oven here… but I do have one of these," he said excitedly, passing her the cocktail menu.

"Oh my god, where to start?" she said, turning the pages as if she were regarding a treasure in a museum wearing her finest kid gloves. "This is mind blowing, and you've put it together so beautifully… I'm no cocktail connoisseur but in all my travels, even in the likes of Hollywood, I've never seen a menu quite as fancy as this."

"I like to think I've given things a twist."

"That you have," she said. "It really is up there with the masters."

"I'm not sure I'd go as far as to say that. I mean I'm self-taught after all, no formal credentials other than absorbing the methods of many a bartender, but hopefully it's not your bog standard excuse for a cocktail bar either, if I've pulled that much off I'll be happy."

"Why all these blank pages at the end though?" Alice threw him an equally blank expression.

He raised his head behind the bar, looking more than a little unsure of himself.

"Oh, you know, it's kind of a trend nowadays." The bottles he was moving from station to station clinked like church bells interrupting his flow. "Especially in the London bars… I guess… I guess it's my attempt at re-creating the mystery, the evocative nature of the speakeasy… people used to pen one another messages over a cocktail, did you know that?"

"No, I can't say I—"

"Either at the same table," he cut her off, "or to a stranger who had caught their eye across the hazy bar. Maybe they'll use my blank pages in a similar way." Her stomach flipped then, was it just her or did it feel like his eyes had an agenda of their very own as he muttered those words? "I did think of laying out Post-It notes as coasters," he continued, unaware that Alice had floated off with her imagination, "but sometimes you can take the whole concept of minimalist a little too far, don't you think?"

She said nothing, he'd rendered her spellbound, and she

didn't even know it.

"Alice?"

"Oh yes, it's a cute idea, a bit like those cafés with blackboards in London… in everywhere… where small children can entertain themselves with chalks and pastels." Alice thumbed through the empty pages again in a bid to come back down to Earth and stay there, wondering who would end up getting together in this place.

River seemed inexplicably nervous again, keen to take her order.

"It's going to have to be a White Russian," she said, second-guessing his eagerness to change the subject, "a little heavy with a pizza maybe, and totally un-Italian, but I'm curious as to whether you'll make it like the guy in that bar in —"

"Sammy's in New Orleans," he finished her sentence and slapped at the counter in recognition of the blast from the past. "Ah, we did have some awesome times on tour, didn't we? Saw some right eye-opening sights."

"Yeah, not all of them of the good eye-opening variety either."

They both laughed, the movie reel of yesteryear felt so tangible amidst this atmosphere, she just wanted to stay here forever, soaking up the best bits, like a competitor in *The Great British Bake Off* before their eviction from the tent, conveniently skipping over the near-misses, collapses, downright disasters, and Paul Hollywood's condescending turquoise-eyed glares.

"That's what I want now, to hold on to the good stuff," she swore he could read her mind, "the parts that have enriched my life," said River, jug of ice cold milk in hand.

"You're doing a great job of that so far." Alice smiled.

Tonight was definitely not an opportune moment to break the bad news she was bearer of, well, as far as news went, she was pretty damn sure River wouldn't take it too well anyway.

"I've got something to show you while you're waiting… look beneath the cushions to your right."

She didn't look there straightaway but at him, quizzically

instead.

"Go on. Haven't you ever wondered where and how I got the inspiration for this place?"

"What is this? It's exquisite." She lifted a heavy book onto her lap and felt the smooth cover, embellished in parts with a mishmash of materials and textures from who knew where, but evidently from River's travels.

"Look inside, it gets better," he shouted over his receptacle shaking.

"This is magic. Just magic," she said. "So everywhere you went, you either nabbed a recipe, or drank something and memorised the taste so you could recreate it? And these sketches... I always knew you were a bit arty-farty at school, but these are like illustrations in a proper book. I'm so impressed. It was a no-brainer for you to turn your back on Avalonia when this has been for ever stirring in your soul. You were born to do this, it's your calling."

"Just go careful when you get to the back, there's a pocket with an envelope in it."

"Oh, okay, no worries," she said continuing to soak up every detail as if she was reading the plaques in a museum, something that used to infuriate Tamara on their annual trip to London when they'd be hauled around the Tate or The V and A, but never Alice who'd always revelled in the finer detail.

"Here you go." He placed her drink in front of her. "And don't let the pizza get too cold either, these were delivered about half an hour ago... in which case they probably are stone cold already."

Alice laughed. "Luckily I adore cold pizza."

River held her there then, the undoubted object of his attention. It was a moment she wanted to frame, to sneak into his penthouse suite and hang it at the foot of his bed so he couldn't, wouldn't waste any more time with that despicable Money Grabber of a Gold Digger. Yes, that's what she was. It was totally unfair to be so judgmental, perhaps, but Alice had sussed Georgina out already. And she was more than prepared to harbour *her* River with the same fierceness with which he was protecting her.

"So I've been thinking… and you don't have to give me your answer right away, just hear me out, sleep on it, perhaps."

Please ask me to move into a house share with you; please ask me to, *please…*

"How about working with me?"

Oh.

"Not for me… that's what Georgina does, with me. It would be a great way to get you back on your feet again, out of the hotel, mingling with people, taking your mind off the band and your parents… and that sister of yours."

"No offence, River."

"Oh okay then, I see, none taken." His face fell, expressing itself in a way she couldn't recall that it ever had.

"It's just not really what I had in mind," she said, swallowing hard on the urge to take him in her arms and kiss him passionately to make up for upsetting him. "Waitressing, playing barmaid, it would feel ever so slightly like I'd taken several hundred steps backwards. I mean yes, I'm back, and I don't want the celebrity lifestyle any more than you do, but if life takes on any proper meaning now, then that meaning has to be following my passion too. And that's horses. I know my parents sold mine, but there are so many villages and riding centres surrounding us here that for sure I have to be able to find something, even if that's a stable hand, or a live-in position on a farm. I'm not fussy. All I want is not so much a foot up the ladder as a foot in the saddle. I'm young, I'm fit and active, and the time is now. If not now, when?" She raised the cold glass to her lips and took her first sip of creamy vodka coffee goodness. "Oh god this is incredible. Way better than New Orleans, way better… How do you do it, River?"

"I see, and I totally support you," he ignored her praise, evidently still more than a little disappointed that she hadn't snapped his arm off for the opportunity. "That's the way I felt about the bar, it's a good sign when it sets you on fire like that. Well, you know I'm here to help you in any way I can, even if it's just driving you to an interview. We'll get you riding again. Before you know it, you'll be competing again too, just like you used to."

"One trot at a time," she laughed, and then downgraded to a smile of relief as she realised he was – at least trying – to be genuinely happy for her decision.

"Oh, and by the way, what was that envelope you mentioned earlier? I checked in the pocket at the back of the book," she put her glass down and picked the giant cocktail book up to demonstrate. "But it's empty; no trace of an envelope anywhere."

Her words cast River to stone.

"I'm guessing it was pretty important, huh?"

"Shit," said River finally. "Oh Shit."

Chapter Eleven
RIVER

"Well? What can I get you? A tall drink, a classic, mostly spirits, something exotic?"

"I don't usually go in for this type of stuff – as you may well remember," said Lee, eyes blinking left and right, not quite able to match River's inquiry. "To tell you the truth, I'm uh… I'm what you might call a Cocktail Virgin."

River couldn't have been more surprised when one Saturday afternoon, a short and undeniable – yet curiously interesting with it – Plain Jane, lugged a befuddled Lee into the bar. He whistled car salesman-style, as if Lee's revelation was going to cost him dearly.

"It's about time we made up for lost time then," said River, passing him the menu, hoping today wouldn't be the day Lee cut his teeth on anything Mexican.

Not because he didn't deserve it, despite his part in smashing up the bar, River knew Lee's heart had never truly been involved in the massacre. It was a sad thing to see a grown man unable to shake off the school playground ringleader. He could only feel sorry for someone with such a lack of self-esteem. Rather, River didn't feel ready to witness the unravelling of the alchemy, not quite yet anyway; the bar had only been open a couple of months, and with the envelope still mysteriously missing, he didn't trust himself to remember Mercedes' written instructions; despite the fact he had committed them to memory, despite the fact their English translation was simply a re-cap of the words she had spoken to him in Mexico. He could only hope his confidence would somehow be bolstered between now and the revelation of Chosen One Number One.

"Help me out," said Lee, eyes bulging widely. "I mean, what am I meant to choose? I've finally got myself a bird." He turned nervously to look back at his girlfriend who was engrossed in her own menu. "What's an acceptable drink for a male? Last thing I want to do is make a complete tit of myself. Oh, and before I forget, I'm err... sorry... for my part in it all... I genuinely had no idea Blake was going to go so off the rails that day... but you ain't seen me here, right...? George isn't working tonight, is she? Please tell me no."

"Apology accepted. But you do realise you can do better than that, surely?"

"Are you trying to run down my woman already?" Lee's back became ruler straight.

River laughed. "Not your lady, no, course not, she seems pukka... although, I don't see any wings; best cut the bird reference out. Chicks don't like that." His eyes danced with merriment.

"Yeah, cheers for the tip."

"Lee, mate, what I mean is Blake's not going to have some neighbourhood watch patrol burst in here any minute. Besides, your life is your own... But tell me, how did you find out about Georgina?"

"Through Blake of course."

River's blood ran cold, so cold he had to stop himself from straining tea-coloured liquid into the glass of his current order for fear of drowning the cocktail. He exhaled deeply, eyes closed in a bid to compose himself.

"He definitely knows? And he's okay with it?"

"I wouldn't say *okay* with it... but he doesn't seem to be as angry about it as he was when you shelled out for this joint. So that's gotta be a good sign, right? For you, I mean. Hopefully no more re-decorating for a while." Lee's voice was tinged with nervousness, tossing River's emotional state back to him like a hot potato.

"So then what's it to be?" said River, unsure as to what the hidden meaning behind any of that implied. It was pretty obvious that when Blake did let Lee in on Georgina's professional news, he'd done so with a loaded sting in the tail of his sentence. As was typical with Lee though, that part had been more than lost in translation. "Actually, don't bother looking. I've just had a brainwave."

"Great."

River headed for his Bible, under pleasant sedation at the idea of introducing Lee to his very first cocktail, and concurrently cursing himself for *still* keeping his treasured book in public view. Yet what else was he supposed to do? He could hardly keep running off to the skittle alley for a furtive glance. Yes, he should have kept the envelope somewhere safer once he'd read those words and sealed it for a second time. But he operated on trust, he had to, especially given the amount Mercedes had instilled in him. If he changed his stance now, the mission would never get started, let alone completed. In any case, her Spanish words would read as complete and utter tosh to anyone who understood them, or bothered to get them translated.

Of course, his first thought was the culprit might be Georgina, but there was no way it could have been her. She thought the world of him… *already*, a visible fact which slightly freaked him out, for at some point he knew he would have to let her fall. He was far from in love with her. If that kind of magic was going to happen, it would have happened already. So then his next thought had been this was an act of the Rigby-Chandlers. But Lord Pervert was too sloth-like to operate covertly, and as for Her Ladyship, the notion of her putting herself in such a lower class position as to be stood behind a bar was utterly preposterous. And so for the moment he could only draw a blank.

"Don't go being scared of the cocktail," he said, throwing his words over his shoulder and back to Lee at the bar, the serving of a brand new customer sweet salvation to the chaos in his mind. "It's all in the mixology… not only what I'm doing stood here, but what your body is asking to drink. And I think I have just the thing for it today, The Woodstock."

"Sounds strong." Lee began to rifle through the pages of the menu.

"Nah, it's really not. Gin, vodka and rum are the least

hangover-inducing of the spirits, but you won't find it in there, this one's a little bit special."

River turned to see Lee's eyes bulging out of their sockets again, this time with terror. "Ha bleedin' ha... I think," he said finally.

"Do you honestly think I'd have a licence if I meddled all three of those together and served it up to you in a glass?" River knew anybody else but Lee could reel off endless cocktail varieties containing that particular combo as their base, but therein lay the beauty of his school buddy's naivety. "Geez, you really are clueless. But it does have a kick. Perfect tipple to get you acquainted with good taste. Before you know it your pint of cider will be a thing of the past and your girlfriend – what's her name?"

"Jonie."

"Jonie will be declaring her undying love and making you an honest man."

"Chance'll be a fine thing," said Lee. "Cupid's never taken much notice of me before, why should it be any different this time?"

And there it was. That was the moment.

River saw it like he'd never seen anything before. Lee was going to be one of the three, his fate sealed, just like that bloody envelope should be. And when Mercedes' voice whispered 'yes' into River's ear, a tickle on the breeze quite from nowhere as he cruelly jazzed his friend's inaugural cocktail up with the Full Monty décor of swizzle sticks, umbrellas and star fruit slices, he was sure of it.

With Lee now back at his table and glued to Jonie's conversation, and Georgina on a break, he made his way excitedly to the lovebirds, laden with a tray that produced 'oohs' and 'ahs' from fellow drinkers, whilst its smitten recipient hadn't the foggiest of how embarrassed he was about to get.

River served Jonie her somewhat solemn in comparison Mai Tai first, then turned to Lee, who still hadn't noticed he was expected to imbibe a Rio Carnival of a spectacle, slap bang in the centre of the bar's main window, for the entire

High Street to see.

"You really are a toss—"

"Etiquette," said Jonie, cutting Lee's undoubted expletive off before it was airborne. "Thank you, these look stunning... mmm..." She took a first sip through her straw and encouraged Lee with her spare hand to do the same through his completely unnecessary four pink stripy straws.

"Get used to the high life," River couldn't resist dropping Lee an early hint, "you're going to love it."

Chapter Twelve
GEORGINA

Georgina almost dropped her tray laden with Pimm's and glasses, but not because of its weight. The perks of this job meant her biceps were firming up nicely, thank you very much, not in a weird female bodybuilder type way – and thank god for that – but she was definitely keeping those blessed bingo wings at bay for at least a decade by her reckoning. And her arms didn't almost give way through lack of nourishment either; Georgina was lucky in that respect, she'd always been able to eat more or less what she wanted, Zara's Organic Raspberry Tartlets seeing her through until clock off time (she'd treated herself to two from the bakery next door, figuring that if she was 'acting as if' on the floozie front in real life, she may as well do it with her food as well). No, the reason she almost covered herself in sticky liquid strawberry, cucumber and mint leaves was the sight of her father walking in through the front door of the bar.

Of course she'd told him about the job, and he'd fessed up to her about the DIY in exchange, (she hadn't the heart to tell him he was, in fact, clearing up after the destruction of his very own son).

"I left some paintbrushes here all those weeks ago, thought I'd call in to pick them up before they get pilfered," said Terry, adding a wink as he approached River.

"Mate, great to see you... and I'm so sorry, I did notice them, had put them away in the cupboard in the backyard... where I erm... where I keep my other bits and bobs, was intending to get them back to you via Georgina... I um... I just wasn't sure if you knew who I was at the time when you were patching up for me... it's not like we did ever properly introduce ourselves."

"Well I didn't know then but I do now, courtesy of Georgie."

Georgina cringed. Thanks, Dad, for making me sound like I'm crouching in the tree house again with my bow and arrow, just the kind of image to take me back to first base with River. Blithering idiot! She'd lost count of the number of times she'd instructed him to address her by her full name in public.

"Just wait there a minute, Terry. I won't be long," said River before turning to Georgina and adding, "Gee, will you ask him what he wants to drink?"

Gee?

No, no, no, no, no. She did not 'do' Gee. Nor George, or Georgie, but definitely not bloody Gee. She'd be having more than a word with him later about that – on or off the mattress.

"C'mon, Dad, stay for one why don't you?" she asked obediently anyway.

And then her short term memory caught up with River's recent flurry of words. Hang on a minute; hadn't he mentioned a 'backyard cupboard' just then, and hadn't he spectacularly faltered and bumbled in the process? Hmm, intriguing, her dad's paintbrushes clearly weren't the only things he was storing down there.

"Aw no, this isn't really my cuppa in here," said her dad with that wistful look in his eyes, the one she was hoping had now been firmly relegated to the past.

"Terry," said River, a tinge of exasperation in his voice, "now that's not strictly true and you know it... go on... tell Georgina what I fixed you and the others up with that afternoon when you'd finished the painting."

"Oh, I can't remember the posh name of it," said Terry, face flushing since he'd been rumbled, "t'weren't too bad though, I'll give you that, lad, no, t'weren't too bad at all."

"Well then, perhaps it's time for another," said Heather, appearing from absolutely nowhere and draping her arm around Terry's waist as if she were the tinsel decorating a Christmas tree.

Christ, tonight's Ginger Rabbit was taking effect a little too

93

quickly, poor Dad.

"Another G.R for me when you're ready, sweetheart." She nodded at Georgina before turning her attention back to Terry. "Long time no see, Terence. How the devil are you? I'm pretty sure the last time our paths crossed, despite our geographic proximity in this town, was at the Year Twelve parents' evening... both of us solo and navigating the regimented Yes Men – and Women – of academia."

"Heather Jackson," Terry stood back then to make room for the vision that was River's mother, "well I'll be damned, fancy seeing you here. Then again, tis your lad's pub... I mean bar... after all, hasn't he done well for himself? Wish I could the say the same for my two, then again, they're earning their keep, that's the main—"

"Nice to know I've done you proud, thanks, Dad," said Georgina, pivoting to deposit drinks to the group at the corner table.

"Georgie, that's not what I—" Terry gripped at her arm and she very nearly did let go of her tray.

"Actually," said River, who still hadn't managed to venture outside, "I have a little something for you, and it seems like now is the perfect moment." He pulled a letter from his blazer pocket, a letter whose pale brown hued envelope threw Georgina momentarily, hardly helped by everybody's undivided attention, and her concern that they could all see the English translation about those Toltex Indians and their sacred Mexican bottle inscribed across her transparent face.

"What is it?"

"Open it and see."

Holy shit, he *had* found her out, somehow retrieved his weird Spanish text and its meaning from her purse. So that's why her dad – and now Heather – were here to enjoy the moment, her axe from the bar, back to grovelling for work in another minimum wage per hour café, back to serving up Meals on Wheels, back to five am starts, whining toy dogs and the collecting of their stinking poop in see-through bags.

She put the tray on an empty table, holding her breath as the liquid in the jug took on the ferocity of stormy ocean waves, took the envelope from River's hands and tried to suppress her tears, hands trembling as she started to read the letter, silently first, and then aloud.

"*MIXOLOGY AND COCKTAIL COURSE LEVEL 1: LONDON'S ESMERALDA HOTEL, AUGUST 30th-31st 2017*

Dear Miss Hopkins

We hereby confirm your place on the coveted Brunswick Mixology and Cocktail course..."

But before she could read any further, the saline was embarrassingly trickling.

"Oh, come here, love," said Terry, wrapping his daughter in his arms. "I am beyond proud of you for helping hold the fort together, you know that, and as for this," he took the paper from her hand and pulled out his old and sellotaped together NHS glasses from the top pocket of his boiler suit to skim read the rest of it, "this is proof of the pudding of your worth. You're off to London, darling, the Big Smoke... somewhere your Pops hasn't ever been, that's for sure. From one generation to the next, you see, things are moving on."

She buried her head in his paint-fumed chest mortified at the scene she had created, as well as the fact the entire bar was now au-fait with the alarming fact that at twenty-nine, she still hadn't visited the capital of her own country. This was so not like her; she was categorically not one for empathy and cupcakes. She wasn't sure what had come over her but she would not, could not, let her guard down like this again.

"Stay for a drink. Go on, Terry. It's the very first travel group meet-up here tonight, an idea I believe that was instigated by your very own daughter to help rustle up more custom."

She winced at Heather's appalling chat-up line.

"Get on, then," her dad replied. "Just for the one mind, I've gotta be up early for work tomorrow morning."

Their toe-curling chat gave Georgina the chance to come to her senses and she straightened herself up with a sniffle: "I'll just nip to the powder room, sort out my face, and take a deep breath or two. But thank you, River. Thank you so much for putting all of your trust in me." Oh, the irony of that remark, as she felt this prissy little girlie façade fade and the real Georgina kick back into gear.

Backyard and cupboard: never had two unassuming words been more alluring. She wasn't sure when and she wasn't sure how, but she was sure – prestigious mixology course and sugar-coated pleasantries aside – she would soon get to find out exactly what they were all about.

Chapter Thirteen
RIVER

Book club night had proven a roaring success with the fortnightly travel group thankfully lagging not far behind it. As River was becoming increasingly aware, outsmarting Georgina – whose idea the latter fixture had been – went down about as well as a Rusty Nail on top of a Screwdriver.

Tonight's crowd almost filled the downstairs part of the bar, just four empty tables remained. It was a record since he'd started trading, but a painful reminder too that Alice hadn't miraculously changed her mind about his offer of employment. And things were getting way too busy to carry on with just two members of staff, that much was certain.

Alice.

He was beginning to wish his mind would adopt the nonplussed sentiment of Smokie's lead singer in their eponymous *Living Next Door to Alice* song, but unfortunately, River knew all too well who the eff the Alice in his life was. She was the one who infiltrated his dreams, yes, even – especially – the nights when Georgina lay by his side, running her fingers through his hair as if it was her god given right, edging ever closer to that fine line between lovers and beloved.

The notion of anything more than friendship with Alice was insane, presumptuous at best, but how he longed to cradle her in his arms, and hell, there was no point denying it, he wanted to do a damn sight more with her besides. But it wouldn't be like it was with Georgina, lust masking lack, an action to fill a deep void. For the first time in his life, this felt different, it felt real.

He'd tried over the years, as a male does when he needs to

'relieve' himself, to re-play their forbidden tryst under the black velvet sky (and Blake's canvas) that starry festival night. But the strange thing was: he couldn't remember it, not her touch, or her moves, or the way she encouraged him to do the little things that turned her on, gently guiding his hand to her erogenous zones. Sure, it was a long time ago, and a one night stand, but lately, ever since her return to be more precise, he was starting to question whether it had really happened at all. Perhaps it had been *Much ado about Nothing*, a Chinese whisper intercepted by a sulky bewitched teen, who knew not really what he'd witnessed himself, drunk as he would have been, doped up on joints as he also could have been – the Mr Innocent charade Blake had the audacity to transmit when it came to his past use of recreational drugs, didn't wash with River, who knew full well he'd certainly inhaled his fill of marijuana with the rest of them back in the day.

Maybe he should just confront Alice? Perhaps that would somehow help them both move on with their lives, unpeeling the Band Aid, giving air to the wound that was imperceptibly holding them back from their destinies. Could it be that was what Mercedes had alluded to when she'd spoken of missing puzzle pieces? But if that was one piece, where was the other?

Jane Austen brought him back to the present like the pique from a bee's sting.

"I'm going to go for it tonight. The time is right. I think I'm as ready as I'll ever be."

"You know my rule, Cassandra," (now she was a regular every fourteen nights, River had of course learnt of her real name), "no more than two cocktails of an evening, pace yourself." He added a wink.

"Oh yes, but I'm only intending to drink *the one*… whilst we dissect Catherine Cookson's *Feathers in the Fire*. I'm going to savour it you see. Such an idyllic sounding cocktail deserves only the fullest of my taste buds' attention."

She needn't have continued, or placed her intonation on the number of beverages she'd be consuming that evening. River was looking at The Chosen One Numero Uno. And in case he wasn't clear on the duty he was bound to, Mercedes' double marched past the window, peering inside to make direct eye contact with him at the very table he was serving in the process, rendering him absolutely speechless and dizzy all in one fell swoop. He tried to disguise his stunned expression and lack of coordination with a coughing fit.

"Are you all right, dear boy?" said Cassandra.

"Fine," the word finally rolled off the tip of his tongue before he could think to keep his disdain in check. But Cassandra was too entranced by the drink's description to notice:

"The Magical Mañana," she whispered. "Ooh, it sounds like an affirmation of good times to come... and just look at the ingredients, all my favourite liquid sensations, all blended into one drink. Why hadn't I spotted this before? How very queer: what's it doing playing hide and seek in the middle of the menu?"

"Print error," River managed to compose himself, firing out the two words he'd long ago decided could be the only explanation he'd give when somebody did stumble across the hidden cocktail, whilst the real temptation *was* to spit feathers... in the fire. How bloody apt was that read! "And the rest of you lovely ladies?" he couldn't wait to look at somebody, anybody else, palpitations at the dozen in the terrifying realisation that he now had to remember just how to construct the mystical drink.

"We'll stay traditional and go for a quartet... not each... that would break your rules on a school night." They all laughed then, as irritatingly in tune with one another as the London Philharmonic. River offered a half smile, too narked off to care if it looked false. "No, I mean we'll each of us have a Brandy Alexander... just like two weeks ago, four weeks ago, and six; so four of those in total." Cassandra's friend looked expectantly at River who was now supposed to flatter them with what had become the trademark line:

"But you look too young, even for a Brandy Alexander, why... are you sure your parents know you're out gallivanting at this hour?"

A 'one-liner' whose meaning would only be understood if

you were a woman of a certain age, who liked to be reminded she was merely twenty-one again, or a geek of a bartender who knew the social history of every cocktail in the book, and how it got its name.

***

Shutting up shop could not have come sooner. He was famished, tired and just needed to get his head straight. But before he could rewind the evening in his head as he began his short trudge up the High Street from bar to hotel, he spotted Georgina in the next door bakery, leaning across the counter, in that hypnotic way of hers, this time talking to Zara. Both were completely unaware of his presence as he cupped his hands against the bakery's window pane like makeshift binoculars to block out the sun's fading rays, their backs were turned, shoulders slumped and hunched over what looked like reading material on the counter. Probably a copy of *OK Magazine* – that would be about right. Georgina was spending way too many of her increasingly frequent breaks gawping at the lives of the rich and famous, camped outside in the backyard on a stray bar stool. An image which was as big a turn off as a supermarket can of Singapore Sling.

He smiled anyway and left them to it. So nice to see Georgina was making a friend. She was a little bit of an oddball in that way, since they'd started 'seeing one another' she'd made no mention of female mates; all a bit peculiar for somebody who'd spent their life in this town, ex spitfire or not.

It took a lot to spook him out, but the way Mercedes' twin had walked past the window at the exact same moment he was taking Jane Austen's order; that was freaky, inexplicable, even to somebody as spiritually in tune as his mother – and there was no way he was ever going to divulge any of this crazy tale to her. Heather had mellowed of late after the bizarre incident with Lennie, and he didn't wish to encourage her otherwise. That 'date' of sorts with Terry had seemingly grounded her more than an entire batch of her ginger biscuits. Whilst

Georgina had reported Heather having the opposite effect on Terry:

"But in a good way," she'd reassured River who could sense the apology mixed with alarm colouring his face. "For a man who's never left the country, Dad happening to walk in for his paintbrushes on travel group night was a very fortunate thing. At first I thought it was just the hangover talking," she'd paused to roll her eyes dramatically, "but even days later he was full of it, couldn't stop gassing about the first group planned excursion to the Prague Christmas market and all the things he wants to buy there. He's even working some extra days to put some money by... I don't think I ever recall him beaming like that from ear to ear. Not that the idea of my dad and your mum doesn't make me want to reach for a bucket... But, as a friend, a companion, she's certainly bringing him out of his shell. Of course we haven't said anything to Blake yet..."

Blake.

He was a mystery all by himself, a little too quiet for River to feel comfortable, a little too accepting of his sister's job for it to be believable. And as for his mum, befriending Terry so readily; yes, he was pleased for her if it was genuine. But what if she was doing it out of some strange subconscious psychological need to feel buffered from Lennie? A goddess she may have been, still he sensed she was on the hunt for a half-decent man to play bodyguard. But River filed both Blake and Heather away in the back of his mind, they could be revisited later, he'd more pressing issues going on right now.

Mercedes' apparition was kind of oddly reassuring too though. Now the assignment really had begun and he was curious to see what would happen to Cassandra. He must start thinking of Jane Austen as Cassandra from this moment on, he decided. One of these days he was going to put his foot in it, ask her to sign a copy of *Sense and Sensibility,* crack a joke about Mr Darcy or something equally silly.

Anyway, Cassandra had seemed to enjoy the rich base notes of Tequila, Sherry and orange. As far as cocktails went, it was one heady concoction, and sexist as it may seem, a little strong for a lady, those ten pipette drops of Mexican elixir presumably only enhancing the taste sensation and upping the throttle. River wished he could go there himself, but it was against the rules for him to partake, even in a sip, Mercedes hadn't needed to spell that out. His head had berated him as he'd prepped the mix, sneakily disappearing to the skittle alley's cupboard where he'd dropped ten beaded globules into a tiny ink-sized bottle, stuffed that into his trouser pocket and then returned again to the bar to add it to the base and give everything an almighty shake.

What would happen next? Where would the story take Cassandra? Where would it take him?

His questions trailed behind him like the potent exhaust fumes of his car as he pushed open the door of The Guinevere, acknowledged the receptionist with a nod, took in the sight of the gent hidden behind *The Times* in the red velvet chair by the redundant fireplace, and made for the stairs.

The paper crackled as his right foot made contact with the bottom step.

"Mr Jackson," said a familiar voice in its disturbingly unique blend of Cockney crossed with The Bronx, "I've been expecting you…"

Chapter Fourteen
ALICE

Unfortunately, Alice knew her current career was very much position filled the exact moment River suggested a role in the bar. It made sense, it was money coming in, and it would get her out of the 'boutique' hotel room that was now driving her crazy – funny how one soon got used to the banality of one's new trying-to-be-original-like-everybody-else IKEA furnished surroundings, conveniently forgetting the hideous tie-dye clad room one had come from. Plus she didn't want to sound ungrateful in retrospect, or to hurt River's feelings, not when her own emotions seemed to be increasingly dependent on them.

But it was an undeniable risk. For by spending more time with the man who, try as she might, she could not wash out of her hair, she would have to face the harsh reality that was Georgina, see the whole hideousness of her flirtation play out in the bar, night after night after night; followed of course, by the inevitable music making, echoing down the corridor at her, the screams of his name torturing her till dawn.

It was a chance she had little option but to take. Not only for the money but because the growing fear ebbed and flowed at her like the tide: Georgina was a scavenging, backstabbing opportunist. She wouldn't be at all surprised if this missing envelope and whatever it contained within was the exclusive work of his mistress. She hadn't even come face to face with River's Alluring Charmer yet, but the other thing about growing up on the ley lines, is you never question your intuition. That was an insight Heather had passed on to her all those years ago when she'd inspired her vegetarian shape shift, and she'd strangely reiterated it days ago too, as she'd packed her bags for her Goddess convention tour, bound for Stonehenge.

"It's a feeling you just can't shrug off, Alice. When something is right, your gut will let you know, it takes its communication from the solar plexus." She'd let her hand hover over her own stomach by means of a demo. "It's no coincidence that particular chakra lies so close to your belly. And vice versa of course too… when something feels off, or out of kilter, your stomach will give you a sign. Always listen to that signal, even over and above your head."

Shame River wasn't taking note. Then again, Alice supposed it was all too easy to get caught up in somebody's web of deceit when they were buttering you up this way and that, hell, she'd fallen for it enough times over the years when it came to men.

But not only was this an opportunity to save up some money, with which to chase her own dreams, getting any further with her parents would require a degree in Anthropology, and so it was that she accepted the premise: a little hard graft and sacrifice in return for a future paddock.

Alice gingerly opened the hotel door; the sudden and inexplicable commotion downstairs luring her to the staircase, where she peered down at the ever-decreasing snail's shell of spirals trying to make head or tail of the noise which had invaded her thoughts.

"In slightly the wrong position to play whizzing down the banister now, boy," a familiar voice laughed sadistically, echoing higher and higher. "We're going to stay here until we sort this out."

Shit, Lennie!

How did he know River would be here? How could they have been so gullible as to think he'd never return? The cushioning of rural life had lulled them both into a pathetically naïve sense of security. Here in Somerset it was ten times easier to track someone down than in the mazes and labyrinths of London, L.A., or New York.

"Has he paid you or something?"

That was River, and there was no doubt he was directing

his question at the receptionist, whose silence spoke louder than words, a facsimile of Alice's previous thoughts as to her loyalty.

But there was no time to run down to his defence. The sound of a very distinctive pair of footsteps on the stairs, heading ever closer and upwards, told her all she needed to know. Georgina was in residence.

As Alice hot footed it as quietly as possible back to her room, and sank to the floor behind the safety of the door, the questions flapped and flew at her just like the pigeons had done in St Mark's Square when they'd kicked off with their very first Italian show in Venice. Why had Georgina said nothing? How could she pretend to be a random guest, leaving River there to fend for himself, after all he'd evidently done for her? How could the receptionist sell her soul so easily even if Alice had second-guessed she would? What if River caved in… told Lennie she was hiding upstairs? What if Lennie already knew that and was just going to hang about until Alice turned herself in, or died of starvation?

One thing was for sure: staying at The Guinevere was clearly no longer an option.

Chapter Fifteen
GEORGINA

"And pray tell me what in the hell is this?"

Georgina froze at the photo stuck to the fridge with the Llanfairpwllgwyngyllgogerychwyrndrobwllllantysiliogogogoch souvenir magnet. She was going to have to think, and she was going to have to think epically fast.

A glossy snap of herself and River in the rain-spattered front window of The Cocktail Bar stared back at her accusatorially; his arms around her waist, indicating she was very much his possession, her ridiculously short skirt almost showing her knicker line as she slid that stupid book club night poster higher up the window pane.

"Look, I was going to tell you sooner, I promise." Her heart pounded in disbelief that she'd been found out. "I just didn't want you jumping to the wrong conclusion, Blakey," she continued without turning to face her brother, whose presence loomed larger than life in the doorway behind her.

"Do not Blakey me, and I have asked you a question, to which I expect a bloody fantastical answer. What are you playing at? You're showing the family up… and with him of all people, he who hath screwed up my life!"

"Oh give me some credit, will you." She turned ready to fight fire with fire, if that's what it was going to take. "I have, as it happens, reason to believe he is up to no good again, no good for his customers this time, no good for this town. But what did I tell you about the enemy, Blake? Keep your friends close and your enemies even clo—"

"So you take that as carte blanche to jump in his bed!"

"It's not like that."

"Then what is it like? Because from where I'm standing,

106

your options look rather limited, shall we say?"

"I need a key, okay… a key to access a certain something. And if I can't get a key, then I need to do something else, something drastic, something *massive*… to get him found out… all of which obviously requires an intimate knowledge of his daily life, movements, and his complete and utter trust. Then… once the job is done, and he's paid me – *us* – for his silence, he is out of this town, out of our lives… everything can get back to normal. Justice prevailed."

"I'm surprised you didn't see me," Blake seemed unnaturally satisfied, calm in an instant. "I was crouching behind a car boot on the opposite side of the street. Perfect shot, don't you think? Maybe I'm in the wrong profession?"

And with that he disappeared upstairs.

Georgina exhaled deeply. What a sneak.

And yet part of her admired him for it. There was no mistaking they were siblings through and through.

She ripped the photo into tiny pieces, binned it and berated that small part of herself whose heart pined for River's touch. They'd been damned fools with that little charade. Clearly anybody could have been watching – even in bad weather. And why couldn't it have been the media who'd spotted them? Now that kind of coverage could have done her all sorts of favours… leading to a stint on *Big Brother* or *Gogglebox* perhaps. Oh, make no bones about it, she loathed these ridiculous lowlife shows, but you had to be cold, business-like about the opportunity to make a quick fortune. In and out, five minutes of fame, blending neatly back into mainstream obscurity but living a lavish life as the claim-to-fame-fix for the locals. What could be better for a girl's self-esteem? That magical feeling of turning out the lights one by one, just like on Paddy McGuiness's hellish show, all of the local men wanting a piece of Gorgeous Georgina, none of them succeeding.

And it turned out 'Gorgeous Georgina' was more than a smooth operator in the bedroom, or just with men. Women too, whom she had long kept at arm's length thanks to her mother abusing her trust, were equally easy to manipulate.

For weeks now she'd been calling into Zara's bakery, a couple of Cornish Pasties to take home for Dad and Blake's tea/breakfast (organic of course, she was getting good at playing the Earth Mama game); a piece of carrot cake here, a pumpernickel bread there (yuk, she would not be making the mistake of buying that loaf of dried corrugated cardboard again), and Zara was almost in her pocket. Georgina was also supplying her with free cocktails on a Friday, smuggled over the backyard wall whenever River was meticulously building an operatic creation. That seemed to suit Zara well; she could waltz down her own backyard after she'd got everything ready for her early morning bakers, sip at her leisure and return the empty glass. Any trace of guilt Georgina momentarily felt for coaxing this unlikely friendship into bloom evaporated in a haze when she thought of all the pounds she was saving her, and all the moments of pure Caribbean-tinged relaxation she was providing her – with the exception of the deckchair, that was Zara's own accessory.

Then one August evening after the bombardment of the book club brigade, when River suggested she go back to the penthouse early, for an evening of movies and takeaway because he was too exhausted for anything else, Georgina knew it was time to up the tempo. One: because something was clearly on his mind, and two: because if she procrastinated any longer, she'd start going down Lover's Lane, a destination she was not prepared to travel to, despite the fact he'd recently started referring to their bedroom antics as 'making love', despite the fact every time she heard those words fly out of his mouth, it made her belly all warm and gooey inside.

"Hey Zed," she'd greeted Zara, who was sorting out stale baguettes to drop off at one of the homeless charities nearby.

"Georgina, how's it going? You look cream crackered, that's gotta be a good thing, right? You're certainly getting more customers than you were when we first met not so many moons ago!"

"Am I ever, and I shouldn't complain, but my feet are ever-so-slightly killing me. I only wish River would put on a PJ and slippers themed night."

"Well, why don't you run it past him? He seems open to the weird and the whacky... talking of which, Heather was in here earlier buying me out of root ginger biscuits for the second time in a fortnight."

"Oh don't, the woman's obsessed with that spice."

"But not as obsessed it seems as she is with your dad." Zara flashed Georgina a toothy grin. "A baker is like a taxi driver... or even a receptionist, you know. Oh yes, we hear all the little and not so little secrets of our customers, they all come voluntarily spilling out when there's no-one in earshot. There's something about the sight of cake," she ran her hands along the bakery counter, "the smell of fresh bread besides, that makes grown men and women forget themselves, think of us as their Agony Aunts," she laughed.

"Well you've got to spill the pinto beans now," said Georgina, wishing she hadn't made mention of those hideous 'legumes' Zara took it upon herself to unnecessarily stuff in her chocolate cakes. "Come on, talk about a carrot cake dangle."

"All right, all right, all I know is she is 'simply too busy to bake the weekly root ginger grounders'." They both sniggered.

"That makes sense. Dad is claiming to be taking on more work to pay for this Prague Christmas market trip thingy organised by the travel group – I invented that idea." She smiled at her own intelligence. "But now you're telling me this, I'm half wondering if he's doing something else with those extra hours he claims to be working instead."

"I wouldn't be at all surprised if we are talking about another type of spice, going on the look of lurve in her eyes, at any rate."

"Oh great, I'm beginning to think I preferred Dad when he'd lost his swagger."

"Well, I think it's great, not only is the bar making money and introducing the town to a taste of the exotic, but it's spreading the love bug too, what could be better? I only wish some of it would rub off on me. There doesn't seem to be a half-decent man left in this town... with the exception of River, of course."

"While we're on the subject of bean spilling," Georgina briskly redirected the conversation drumming her beautifully French polished nails on the counter to create something of a build-up effect, "I have a little secret of my own." She quit the tapping and pulled a paper from her wallet, wishing she'd secured Zara's word before she displayed the evidence. "But I need you to take an oath."

"Can I think about it for five minutes?"

"Um, okay then... but I was kind of hoping we were friends, as well as me being your star customer... not to mention almost your personal *travel agent*." Zara cracked up at this point, Georgina grinned too, her narcissistic self in complete and utter egotistical adoration of her wit and timing.

"Oh, what a story that was about those two from round the corner. Why did I have to leave the bar so early that night? Do you know, I might well book my next holiday the old fashioned way rather than through my regular airbnb, just to sit in front of them in their shop and drop several hundred hints that the rumours about their behaviour have done the Glasto rounds... Oh dear, what a place we live in, hey? Sorry, Georgina, that was rude of me to interrupt, you were saying?"

"Nothing much really, just that I was assuming I wouldn't even need to ask you to volunteer to be sworn to secrecy."

"Of course you don't, kiddo. I was only messing with you, spill away."

***

So that was that. Zara was officially on board. Not only a fully-fledged member of Team Georgina, but keeper of a very beneficial secret herself; a secret way sweeter than any of her organic stevia and chia seed stuffed pastries put together.

Georgina simply couldn't hide her grin as she exited the bakery, made her way back to The Guinevere for her insipid movie night with River, wondering what takeaway decision they'd debate tonight. He always wanted a Chinese or a Thai, something stinky, garlicky and spicy to pong out the room, while she'd opt for a sweeter smelling pizza or chips. Travel to far-flung places and jumping on the *Waitrose*-foodie-bandwagon-express had never been her thing, no man on Earth was going to change that now. Not even River.

She paused to check her purse was zipped shut, saw that the paper translation was poking out enticingly, buried it deeper into her bag and pushed open the door to walk in on quite the scene.

"In slightly the wrong position to play whizzing down the banister now, boy," said a monstrous looking figure as he rose from the throne next to the fireplace, slapped his broadsheet down on the table, and followed his statement up with a beastly chuckle. "We're going to stay here until we sort this out."

"Excuse me, love," he muttered under his breath.

Oh, she did indeed love that commandeering effect that her presence cast on males like him: priceless.

She was quick enough to do the maths. This was some 'acquaintance' of River's and now was not the time to pledge her allegiance to her beau. So she blanked him completely, acknowledging instead the stranger who un-capped his frizz of a hair-do, as if she were The Queen, walking on imaginary red carpet, and marched right past him and on up the stairs, leaving the fragments of their conversation to dissipate in a haze behind her, echoes of "Has he paid you or something?" rebounding in the reception's hallway.

It was at this point that she realised she was not alone on the stairs. Someone else, it seemed, had been listening in on the debauchery below. A snappy burst of tumbling strawberry blonde curls, an expensive china doll face, one of those haughty-taughty posh shawls draped around her size zero frame, and then she was gone, the only clue of her presence a door closing gently overhead. Georgina wondered if she was half asleep. The day had been long after all, the scheming with Zara had clearly over-stimulated her senses. Maybe a film was just the tonic to calm her livewires? The words "press", "paps" and "contract" pinged through the air as she hunted in her bag for her key, shutting the door on the madness. River would free himself soon enough, congratulate her for playing dumb, not giving their relationship status away.

Unless of course, the very reason Mr Hideous down below had been put on her path was to mesh with her plan? And now those cogs in her brain really started turning.

Chapter Sixteen
RIVER

"Rules don't apply to me, I've told you before. Now just move on, switch some band members around, shuffle things up, recruit a couple of eager new faces, and be done with it," said River to Lennie, swivelling promptly thereafter to face the hotel's receptionist, "and as for you... how could you, you two-faced little—?"

"I'm so sorry," she blurted, her heavy sniffs turning immediately to loud guttural sobs as she grabbed her bag and ran out of the building.

He turned back to Lennie: "Wow, you really are a conniving son of a—"

"Now that's no way to talk about your..." but Lennie stopped himself going further. "And hark at you thinking you're above the ts and cs of a legally binding document... I don't think so."

"Legally binding nothing, Lennie! For the gazillionth time, you forgot to renew it. So bring it on. All you'll do is stress yourself out and keel over with a heart attack, take my advice, find a replacement, it'll be easier on the arteries that way."

"Ha!" Lennie nodded, rocking his head back and forth like one of those moving toy dogs people stick on the parcel shelf of their cars. "You're hilarious, you. Slight problem there though, River. Not only did you go AWOL, but you encouraged Alice to go AWOL too."

"That had nothing to do with me." River let his eyes bore into Lennie's, willing him to know it was the truth.

"Oh come on, you must think I was born yesterday, thick as thieves you two."

"Really it didn't, I had no idea until she turned—"

113

Damn him. Lennie always had that irksome way about him that made River say more than he'd intended to.

"Aha, so you don't deny you know of her whereabouts."

"I never said that."

"I rather think you'll find you just did."

"Look, you've done enough damage already by bribing the receptionist, now kindly go."

"Are you kidding? I won't kindly anything, I haven't even got started. Gonna get my money's worth now I'm staying here at The Guinevere... indefinitely." He disappeared behind his former throne to wheel out a giant leopard print suitcase.

"Fine, then I'm moving out."

"River, think about it," Lennie's voice softened, but River was no fool to this customary tactic. "I'm prepared to let you go... in return for Alice. Hand her over, it's obvious she's here... or at your mother's... I've already spoken with the lovely Tamara, such an accommodating filly she is, shame about the clock face." He drew a circle around his own face with one of his pork chipolatas and let out another of his monstrous laughs. "You wouldn't want me pestering Heather again now, would you... talking of 'accommodating fillies'." He whistled between the gaps of cemented together teeth.

"Don't even think about it." Rage consumed River and his mouth contorted at the very implication.

"Bit late for that," Lennie chuckled.

"And what's that supposed to mean?"

"For all your musical gifts you never were the sharpest note." Lennie shook his head pitifully. "Forget it. I'm messing with you, too long a story anyway. Now then: back to business. What's it to be, your good self or Alice?"

"Um, that would be neither of us; I think I've made that pretty clear." River felt the anger burning in his throat now, wishing it would convert to fire so he could douse the putrid specimen stood in front of him for once and for all.

"Fair dos, son, fair dos. I've tried to play nicely, really I have." Lennie's hand twitched at the handle of his case, firm grip and release, firm grip and release, as if he were a chess piece trying to work out his next move.

114

"So what are you going to do now?" River challenged him with an arch of his eyebrows.

"That's for me to know and you to find out."

"No," River smirked and shook his head at the supposed riddle. "No, no, no. I'll tell you what you're going to do now: you're going to accept our decisions as final." He put his hands on his hips as if to back up his words with some authority, "You're going to realise that this happens to every manager in the music industry at some point, even the likes of Simon Sodding Cowell. And you are going to go back, talk to the members of Avalonia who still want to keep the band alive and kicking, ask them what they want to do, organise some auditions and recruit two new members. It couldn't be simpler. Now, have a happy rest of your life and excuse me while I get on with mine."

"Nice try, River." Lennie flipped open the lid of his mobile, pressed some buttons, and stared menacingly at him, breathing deeply as he waited. "Yeah, taxi please… central London."

"Good. Now stay there." River headed up the stairs, shaking his head again in disbelief, ready to relay the whole episode to Georgina, not before slipping a note under the door to Alice. Fortunately, he had the order book he'd pilfered from Georgina for the umpteenth time, lodged into his back pocket; he took it out, and the biro attached to it:

"*Stay in your room until further notice. Tonight will be our last night here at The Guinevere! I'll sort out new accommodation for both of us tomorrow… not Mum's and the shitty pink tie-dye, don't worry. Oh, and we'll be together, promise. Riv xx.*"

He paced the corridor, unsure whether to go back downstairs and check up on Lennie's current status, or play bouncer to Alice's room. Just in case. The heavy creak of the door and trundling of wheels onto the steps outside, followed by a slam, marking the end of a chapter – as far as he was concerned anyway – told him all he needed to know. Alice would be fine now; the scumbag had taken the hint. Time to rekindle whatever it was that he had left with Georgina.

"I just cannot believe the audacity of that loser," he said as he opened the door to his room. "Thanks for not letting on that we're sort of an item."

But there was no reply. Funny, unless his mind was completely messing with him, he swore he'd seen her walk into reception and up the stairs.

"Georgina? George?" He went to the bathroom, even swiping at the shower curtain, in case she should be there in a Psycho-inspired bloodbath; please god no.

Chapter Seventeen
ALICE

River banged frantically on the door. "Have you seen her? She's not even answering her phone?"

"Who are you looking for?" Alice said to the rather serious looking fire escape map, mentally erasing the immediate past.

Great, just when she was beginning to think his affection was wearing thin. Alice opened the door with a feigned look of interest, her heart sinking lower as she took in the genuine concern on River's face, the kind of concern only displayed when emotions are at stake.

"It's Georgina, she's missing."

"Yeah, I gathered already. But it's a bit difficult for me to help when I don't even know what she looks like, you haven't introduced us yet, Riv, remember?"

"I know, I know. But no time for that now, Lennie knows we're here by the way."

"I did get the note." She fanned it in front of him since she was still holding it in her right hand. "You're flustered, come in, calm down, you're not going to find anyone in this state."

"No, it's not us I'm worried about anymore," his words were sparking up in all directions, offshoots from a Catherine Wheel at an amateur firework show, "although we do need to get out of here sharpish. I could have sworn Georgina walked past me when I was in reception, I know I'm not imagining it. Then again, I was slightly stunned at him tracking us down like that, not to mention the freakin' receptionist tipping him off, utter nerve of that woman… and god only knows who else besides."

"I wouldn't panic. From everything you've told me about Georgina already, she sounds as street wise as they come. Are you positive that you saw her walk in though? Couldn't it have been another female guest?"

Alice couldn't believe she was practically lying to him. She'd heard those trademark footsteps, after all. Nobody else lived on the top floor. As for the disloyal woman behind the front desk, she was beginning to realise just how these things happened when someone was down on their luck, her own funds like dregs at the bottom of a petrol tank. What choice had she ever had? Lennie had certainly charmed Alice into all sorts of scenarios her logical mind wouldn't usually have said yes to.

"I'm useless at thinking straight in situations like this, what should we do?"

"Well, I think for one thing, let's leave it until the end of the day before sending out a search party. How long has it been? She's probably just gone home, nothing more sinister than that."

"Half an hour, forty minutes, I don't know." River scratched at his half-formed beard and paced the hallway. "I definitely can't call her there. Blake won't have started work yet. Something tells me she won't be at home anyway. There's something darker going on, I can sense it."

"Lennie's probably just trying to scare you, us, but beneath that façade he's just a…" Alice realised she couldn't finish her sentence, since she had zero belief in the lexicon which was randomly flying out of her mouth to try to make him, them, feel better. "Why don't you come inside and wait here? Or we could scour the streets together?"

"Not safe." River shook his head as if that were the most appalling idea anyone could ever come up with and she immediately wished she could retract it. "Lennie's making out he's heading back to London, quick fake call on his mobile downstairs for a taxi… I'm not stupid… five minutes earlier he claimed to be staying here at the hotel indefinitely. He's out there, still at large, throwing all sorts of possibilities around to try and confuse me."

"I'm at a loss as to what else to suggest." Alice shrugged and held her hand out to pull him inside. "Vigilante at the window?"

"Pack your things," River exclaimed in a bizarre Eureka-esque moment. "I can't promise it'll be immediate, I'll have to talk her round, but sometime next week I'll have cracked her for sure: we're moving into Aunt Sheba's."

Chapter Eighteen
GEORGINA

"What the flamin' hell is she doing here?"

"Excuse me? I could well ask the same of you. Where the eff have you been? We've been worried sick," said River, clearly stunned at Georgina's nonchalance over her recent disappearing act. "Two days and not a word from you, and now you just swan into the bar as if nothing happened."

"Those days were mine to do with as I pleased... holiday days... or had you forgotten to check the diary? Oh, I see, you had. If you must have an explanation, I decided to decline your kind invite for a movie and stinky grub, and walked straight home after my last shift instead."

Georgina also declined to reveal that shortly before this decision, she had slunk out the fire exit on the third floor of the hotel, shimmied down the drainpipe since the outdoors stairs were covered in ivy, moss and cardboard boxes full of who only knew what, loitered on the High Street for fifteen minutes, spotted Lennie waiting at the town's one and only taxi rank, and swiftly traversed the street to introduce herself.

"You are unbelievable," said River, approaching her for a hug, relief flooding his face. "I was beyond worried, and I could hardly call you on the landline. I could only guess that the fact the local rag and radio station hadn't reported on the disappearance of a stunning twenty-nine year old brunette, meant you just wanted some time out."

"Something like that," she said, basking for a few seconds in his public adoration, smoothing down her hair which was much longer than Alice's – ha; flicking it over her shoulder to signal time out from her rant was most definitely up.

"I took myself off to a boutique hotel in Bath if you must

know, bit of pampering and TLC. But backtracking to my initial question, pray what is *this* all about?" She looked Alice up and down, recycling the words Blake had recently spat at her, eyes purposely scanning her opponent for defects, of which of course, there were none. But ha again, she was older. She would always be older than Georgina. That was match point nailed as far as she was concerned.

"Alice meet Georgina, Georgina meet Alice," said River.

Ooh, how dare he say her name first?

"See, I really should remember you," said Alice holding out her hand to shake Georgina's, which remained welded to her hip, but the face doesn't ring a bell at all. You're Blake's lil' sis I understand?"

"Yes, I'm well aware of who she is but that hasn't answered my question, babe," Georgina ignored Alice's question, throwing a stern look at River coupled with a counterfeit smile, relegating his former band member to the status of spectre. "And why is she waiting on tables? Am I suddenly not good enough? Did you not think to run this past me first, seeing as we were, the last time I checked anyway, a team of just two?"

"She's quit the band – well, done a bit of a runner following in my footsteps." They smiled a mutual smile which spoke of the places they'd been and the people they'd seen; a mutual smile which dropped a big fat bomb on Georgina's perfectly scripted plans.

"Yeah, please don't talk to Riv like that," said Alice. "He's been my Guardian Angel and rock all rolled into one these past couple of weeks, stowing me away while Lennie and the media have been hot on my trail. People like you haven't a clue what that feels like."

"People. Like. Me? Well excuse the rest of us for being common as muck."

"That came out all wrong, I'm sorry, it's not at all what I was implying. It's just, well, it's been stressful, listen, let's start all over again, shall we?" Alice went in for another handshake and Georgina stood firm in her decision not to accept it.

121

"Talk to the hand, lady," Georgina removed her right one from her hip and put it flat in front of her, swiftly breaking the dialogue, flung her bag across the bar and onto the floor with her left hand and then caught River by the edge of his collar, summonsing him to the backyard.

"I can't believe you've hired her!" she said once she'd slammed down the latch on the bar's back door. "She doesn't need the money, surely? And as for not telling me she was back... and... and hiding her away... I'm not even going to ask where, because now I know who that posh totty running up and down The Guinevere's staircase was... eugh! So she was just down the corridor from us while we were *at it*... I'm surprised you didn't invite her in for a threesome."

"Actually she does need the money," said River, his naivety not catching on in the same way as it had with Georgina as to the hideous picture that he was painting with regards to her last few words. "Her cut in the band was significantly less than mine, less than everyone's."

"So? She's not your responsibility."

"She's a mate. We go back years. Mates look after one another."

"Yeah, Blake filled me in pretty well when it comes to exactly what *mates* do... funnily enough."

"We're just good friends, Georgina," he moved closer to her, stroking her cheek, something about his words feeling like a double entendre, which, intentional or not, applied to their own relationship and she knew it. "That's it," he went on, "nothing more, nothing less." And there it was again.

"Hmm, I s'pose."

"Don't you think that if there was some sort of magnetism between us, it would have transpired by now? Twelve years in a band, on tour all over the world, drink... mostly drink... put up in places ten times more glamorous than our kinky love nest at The Guinevere. Actually, make that former love nest... we've had to move out."

A question mark of a silence hung in the air.

"You s'pose right," he added finally. "Besides, it's not like you and I are an *item*-item, now is it? We've always been clear

122

about that. Nothing's changed in that respect for me, me luvver." He grinned at his piss poor attempt at a Somerset accent and moved in for a kiss.

Georgina obliged, quickly drawing away for effect as his hand travelled down her back.

"Well no, obviously, of course not for me either," she said.

"And so your problem is?"

"I just don't want her comeback to affect my brother, that's all."

"Oh man." River closed his eyes and took a deep breath. "Blake has to move on, yeah? For heaven's sake, it's not natural to hold someone who was clearly always unobtainable as your object of attention for twenty years. Especially not when you've been married, had a child."

That was it. That was the straw that broke *her* back, the sting in the tail, the salt in the wound and just about every other cringe worthy cliché besides.

How dare he pin all of this on Blake's 'warped imagination'? What happened in the teenage years left you scarred, haunted; it ate away at the mind, not to mention the soul in an irretractable act of injustice. Any psychologist could tell you that.

This was all River's fault, every last drop of it. And now she had her blossoming friendship with Zara right where she wanted it, and a band manager almost eating from the palm of her hand, Georgina would ensure the ever turning wheels of karma would be set in motion, very quickly indeed.

Chapter Nineteen
RIVER

There had been nothing else for it but to try his luck with Aunt Sheba. His mother and her sister may not have exchanged a word since the evening Sting had wrapped up his music video filming on the Tor all those years back, Sheba being completely miffed that Heather had 'cashed in' on her wisdom without bothering to invite her along to be a groupie too. But River was her nephew, and with no children of her own, he knew he'd soon melt her heart and be granted a free caravan in such a dire situation – even in the height of peak season.

"You couldn't make it up," said Alice, as River recounted the tale of her resentment towards Heather, and pulled the car into the driveway which would take them to the sales office of the 'Baa Caravan Park' on the outskirts of town – so named because it was housed on the land of a former sheepskin factory.

"You're not kidding me." River cringed, as he drove them slowly past the sign – complete with its token sheep jumping over a rainbow, hurdled the speed bump and looked for a parking space. If this were a romantic trip away, he'd have failed miserably. Despite both of their lack of morals that early spring morning, he couldn't see Georgina standing for the idea of intimacy here, not when she'd got a little too used to The Guinevere's comparatively luxurious surroundings.

"I can't believe you've put her first, sacrificing our special place, what a cop-out, do I mean nothing to you?" Georgina had screamed when the realisation had finally tumbled down upon her a few days ago in the bar's backyard, that actually, "we've had to move out", did not mean he'd found the house of his dreams where they could shack up together. And the royal 'we' referred to himself and Alice, Georgina not as much as figuring in the equation.

It was becoming more and more of a question to ponder: *did* she mean anything to him, after all? He opened another filing cabinet in his head and stored away another conundrum. Puzzles: instead of solving them, all he seemed to be doing was creating new ones lately, piling them up in an overflowing in-tray inside a head that felt it might spontaneously combust. If it wasn't Blake and his reticence then it was Georgina and her jet stream versus cold front forecasts, and if not brother and sister, then it was his mother and her censorship as to the episode at the windowsill with Lennie. Never mind Heather fleeing to the Goddess convention for a little mindfulness, River was beginning to feel that he should have traded places and gone there himself.

Aunt Sheba, sitting at her desk by the window, leafing through paperwork and donning her half-moon glasses, raised her hand to indicate she'd be with them shortly. River parked the car, stretched his arms as if he'd been five hours on the motorway and finally reached the service station for a cuppa, stepped out of his mustard tin on wheels, and ran to the passenger door to play chauffeur.

"Honestly, Riv, there's no need, I'm not Geor—"Alice stopped herself and pressed her lips together so they were almost invisible, like an old lady before she'd lodged in her false teeth, a little too late to take back her blunder. "What I meant to say was I'm not posh… anymore."

That was a kick and a half. But then he remembered the thriftiness was his choice; little did Alice know his grander plans, well, not quite yet.

"We've met each other in the middle." He found himself responding in the kind of deep and meaningful dialogue that usually comes from sitting around a drunken campfire, guitar strumming a rendition of *Hotel California*, goose bumps on T-shirted arms on some Cornish beach where woes are a million miles away.

"You're right. I think we have. Wanna know something hilarious?"

"I'm listening." He raised his eyebrows expectantly.

"This is the first time I've ever... like *ever* set foot on a caravan park. Lennie's RV hardly counts," she giggled. "I'm actually really looking forward to it. How cosy it's going to be!"

The difference between the two women in his life, in this bizarre circle which seemed to be running rings around him of its own accord, a circle in danger of turning into a triangle like some tragic ménage a trois, could not have been clearer right then.

Sheba practically flew out to greet them, her approval of Alice only backing up River's growing realisation.

"Oh my darlings." She threw herself at them both in a warming group hug, as if she'd known Alice her entire life. "You cannot imagine how long I have waited for this day... Heather to one side, of course." She suddenly released them, as if the uncalled for mention of her sister couldn't possibly collude with an embrace.

"Now, now, Auntie," said River. "We did say Mum was a word to be strictly prohibited."

"Yes, yes, slap me on the wrist several hundred times now, I'll try to refrain from another slip up, but you know how easy these things are." She sighed. "Losing that once in a lifetime opportunity to see Sting, not so much on tour but *on the Tor*." She shook her hands and screwed her eyes tightly shut in this spiel that was clearly oh-so-over-rehearsed, "well, that was a hard cross to bear for me, I'm afraid. You'll never meet a bigger fan of his."

"I know what you mean," said Alice. "I've long been enamoured by his music: *The Police*, right through to the modern day, such a skilled artist, he's really stood the test of time."

"Never ever," Sheba added, still in a trance hanging on her very own words.

"Anyways," said River, poking Alice gently in the ribs to indicate his preferred direction of future dialogue. "Would it be okay for us to take our things to the caravan now, get settled in and unpacked?"

"Why yes, of course." Sheba mutated to business-woman all over again, half-moons now folding back random parts of her fringe atop her crown, so her forehead resembled the keys on a piano. "Walk this way."

They followed her along the winding path which opened out onto a play area and sandpit complete with squealing toddlers and watchful parents, and then became more neat and orderly; static homes and caravans facing one another off as if in hierarchical battle, a stony path slicing between them dotted with children on bikes, and walkers pretending to be mountaineering with their Nordic poles. People sat outside reading, eating on their wooden chalet style balconies, enjoying the great outdoors, raising their heads a fraction to give Sheba an acknowledgement style nod, good-afternoon-ing the three of them as they carried their worldly possessions to their latest abode.

"So here we are then," Sheba announced. "I've saved the best for last, literally. I'm not going to make your eyes water by telling you the price this one should be rented out for per week at this time of year."

Which was so clearly an invite to enquire, leading River to remind his Aunt that:

"I am prepared to foot the bill for this, you know."

"Oh no, I couldn't." Sheba pursed her lips together as if about to wolf whistle. "Family is family."

"In that case, maybe one evening, we could invite Mum round for supper... and you could come down to join us?"

"Righty-ho." Sheba tapped her finger on the laminated instructions and welcome pack lying on the draining board. "If there's anything else you need, you know where I am."

"Thank you so much, for everything," Alice shouted to her as she dramatically scooted out of the caravan and closed the door on the two of them, as well as River's proposition.

"I had to try." He shrugged.

"This is just incredible. I don't know how to repay you."

"You don't have to."

"But I owe you so much. You haven't let me open my purse since I've been back."

"Do you, really? I tempted you… away to a land that was meaningless, at a time in your life when you had the world at your feet, the love of two parents – that's something I'll never know, not to mention a place in the Olympics. And now look at you… holed up in a peasant's holiday camp."

"River, no." She put her arms around him, giving his back a long languorous rub; which he sensed that she sensed was all of a sudden the height of inappropriate, and so began the descent to a pat on the back. "This is hardly *Butlins*… which I hear is actually very upmarket these days… I made my choice back then, and I made it by myself. I had a tongue and a voice besides, and you know what? I will never regret Avalonia, the places it took me, the lessons I've learned along the way. Don't you ever let me hear you say that again, okay?"

He didn't answer and so she withdrew from her embrace, looked him in the eye. "Okay?"

"Okay," he said the word.

But it wasn't okay. Not until he'd made it up to her. Set her back on her path. All he could do right now was trust that Mercedes actually did somehow know more about his life. The idea that anybody else could have better tabs on his destiny than him; that was something that used to frighten him, the reason he had never been into the notion of a 'God'. And yet, perhaps this very hut without wheels – albeit a brand spanking new one with every home comfort required – was another small puzzle piece slotting into a bigger picture, the one that wise old Mexican woman had hinted at?

Much later at supper, as Alice insisted on trying for the second time to cook them scrambled egg and beans on toast without burning anything, a skill she'd clearly never had thrust upon her as a basic mode of survival in her teens unlike the majority of those who grew up in the early 90s, he started to get a glimpse of what that completed puzzle might look like.

Chapter Twenty
RIVER

"Nah ah, cheapest ingredient first, if you build it wrong you've cost me less money."

River winked playfully, although he was semi-serious. This was the third time they'd had to start from scratch on Lord Rigby-Chandler's order. How hard could it honestly be to make The Smoking Geisha? Okay, it was as barbaric as it got to even contemplate drinking said cocktail outside of autumn, but constructing this tipple was hardly rocket science.

The wink was not reciprocated. In fact he noticed something about Georgina's demeanour sharpen right then; a bond unravelled, the disappointing taste of flat Champagne, whose cork would never recapture the bubbles.

He was training her up, slowly, *patiently* to help him out behind the bar. He'd thought Georgina's not-so-distant future title of mixologist (she was off to London that very weekend) could only ease Alice's much needed transition into their lives.

It was funny really how she had appeared at just the right moment, business had more than tripled and an extra pair of hands was essential now. He'd even increased Georgina's salary in a bid to soften the apparent but mystifying blow that was his friend. Sure, Alice possessed a beauty that was simply mesmerising, sure, they were sharing a caravan (although it was eight birth, in many ways giving them more distance at night than The Guinevere had ever done), but beneath all of that, her inner beauty was even more compelling. So why couldn't Georgina at least try to like her? What was it with women and their competitive, cat-like nature?

Maybe it turned some men on, but the way Georgina was carrying on lately had really gotten his back up. So much so that he'd feigned exhaustion since last weekend, preferring to return to his childhood box room, giving Alice some space at the campsite too. It wasn't as if he hadn't given The Love Shack a go. But for him it no longer worked, his libido frozen, locked in a time warp since the move to Aunt Sheba's. No matter how much Georgina tried to resurrect it, the inescapable fact remained that Alice was in the same 'house' now. It changed everything, mainly because it felt inexplicably natural to be living with Alice. And try as he might, he couldn't keep those visions of bare-footed children – *their children* – running around a marshmallow-toasting campfire at bay, much less the nagging sensation that he was cheating on her under their very own roof.

And then last night Alice had rung on the doorbell at his mum's, completely taking him by surprise to return a batch of his old CDs, many of which he'd clean forgotten he'd lent her eight summers ago in Berlin when they'd toured around Europe. It was unbelievable to think she'd prioritised them in her rather limited L.A. to London luggage. But with Heather away at her convention which had now dropped in on the lucky destination of Avebury, he more than welcomed not only the company but the surprisingly successful, and moreish filo pastry stuffed with feta, chickpeas, green olives and bell peppers that Alice rustled them up for supper; giving him the opportunity to knock up a kick-ass Kaffir Lime Sour; cocktail pairing perfection. It opened his eyes to a brand new side of Alice, a dimension that he'd never had chance to get to know. They chatted for hours about their very individual experiences with the band, awestruck at how different their two perspectives had been, despite their physical proximity both onstage and off it. And then he began to understand the real reason she'd fled from Avalonia, something which sparked a rage within that went beyond the level in the hotel reception, taking him to a brand new threshold he didn't even realise was possible.

"I know it sounds like the very stereotypical claim of a very stereotypical woman," she said.

"Lennie."

She remained silent.

"I might have guessed it. Please tell me he hasn't—"

"Not exactly, no." She switched from her cocktail to water, as if detoxing herself of every trace of bad memories.

"Look, I believe you already. You don't need to explain anything to me, or go into details if it's too lecherous to repeat." She laid her head on his shoulder and he wrapped her in a warm but big brotherly embrace. They stayed like that a while, comfortable in the stillness of conversation, the beats of *Portishead* taking the edge off the desire to scratch at the itch until the track faded and River got up to change the CD.

"I wish you'd been there the day we filmed the drinks commercial, you know… in Guadalajara." She sighed. "That's when it all started getting a little too out of hand."

"Go on." His stomach tightened into one of those unending sailor's knots. He'd kind of hoped that would be the last of the lowlife's name pervading the house.

She sat upright, clutching at her glass, baggy cardigan sleeves covering her hands like a pair of mittens. How childlike she looked. How he wished he had been there to protect her.

"I mean it didn't exactly begin then, he'd been knocking on my door at night for several weeks… and then I guess if I'm really honest about it, ever since day one when Bear and Alex invited us up to Soho to meet him in the recording studio, he'd always had his eye on me… in a slightly unsavoury way. There was this one time when the three of you were late for rehearsals, and he'd propositioned me, you know, kind of like Robert Redford did in that film to Demi Moore… I forget the name of it, but our age gap would have been similar. Anyway, it wasn't quite a million dollars on the table, but a couple of hundred thousand." She laughed morosely.

River's head began to spin and now he wasn't sure which part of his anatomy felt worse.

"He'd clearly no idea of my roots," Alice continued, "that I'd come to inherit ten times that amount one day… well, that I always thought I'd come to inherit ten times that amount. I didn't take him up on his offer, of course. Just ridiculed him, and so did he, but it left me in no doubt that if I'd have given an inch he'd had taken a mile. That should have started the ringing of the alarm bells, shouldn't it?" She put her fingers to her temple. "If ever there was a time to get out and run back to the countryside and equestrian life, it was then. How could I have been so stupid?"

"I need a cigarette." River cradled his head. This was all getting way too much.

"I thought you'd given—?"

"Yeah, I had quit, but just for tonight," he stood, "just for one night," and grabbed his coat. "I will literally be five minutes, that's all. The corner shop at the end of the street should still be open."

Alice curled herself up like a cat, her soft features highlighted by the flickers of the candle on the wooden trunk which served as their dining table. He stole a glimpse of her as he left the room; his hands seemed to stroke the frame of the door in the same way he wanted to caress her body right then. Yes, it was definitely time for fresh air and nicotine before stupidity had its way with him.

***

He lit up his cigarette, parkoured over the bench outside the shop – forgetting his age – and sat there awhile, letting the rush fill his lungs, so bad but so good. A total one off, he promised himself. The streetlights flickered, as if displaying their disapproval, but he puffed on heavily anyway, as if that might somehow help him make sense of his lack of intuition. How could he have been so in tune with Mercedes and the blessed bottle, and yet at the same time, so out of the vibrational range of his friend, the one who needed him to protect her?

He couldn't believe what he was hearing, or what Lennie was making him do to his body after two years smoke-free. Heather would go bananas. Just as well she was away levitating, or meditating around ancient stones and painting mandalas, as bananas as that was anyway. And then he shook his head at the cheek of his ego.

Hypocrite!

Were they ever so very different after all when here he was, infusing drinks with unknown substances: One Chosen One down and two more to go?

***

"There's more," Alice started and then paused, deep in thought, when he returned to see her seated, suddenly looking more awake, more radiant than ever. He noticed she'd opened the bottle of red that she'd brought as a sorry-for-hoarding-your-music present, and now she was gesturing to his glass, clearly unsure as to whether she should carry on with her next revelation.

"Fill me up then, why not?" he said. He wouldn't normally dream of being so uncouth as to mix cocktails with wine, especially considering the headiness of an oaky red after the citrusy punch of their recent tipple, but he knew now wasn't the time for being uppity. "I thought you implied earlier that he hadn't touched you physically?"

"No, he didn't," she said, passing him his glass which he shunned momentarily to the mahogany chest. "He would have taken his chances one of these days I'm sure, but thankfully I wizened up to it. Anyway, that's not what I'm talking about." She tore her eyes from him, took a gulp of her drink and then returned her attention to him again. "What I mean is I'll give you the backstory later, but it's water under the bridge now anyway, I escaped. This is a totally different subject."

River sat on the futon, his second cigarette in one hand, shaking slightly, and Heather's favourite artisanal lavender-stuffed beaded cushion in the other, if only that might shield him from what was to come.

"God, I don't even know how to break this to you and the chances are it's complete and utter nonsense but he claims to be," she took a deep breath and moved next to him, placing an arm around his neck as if that might offer some comfort, "he says he's your father."

133

River felt his body numb then from head to toe, a trickle at first and then an overall state of momentary paralysis. Finally he broke away from Alice, stood very slowly, both hands covering his face at the very suggestion, hair flopping forward, desperately in need of a cut.

"I know, I know," she said. "How could that possibly be? I'm just telling you because I think you have a right to know the kind of poison that's inside his head."

"Shit," said River finally, flicking the wavy strands out of his eyes. "Shit... that explains everything. How could I have been so blind to it; the constant referral to me as 'son'? And the other night when he was chatting with Mum through the... and she slammed it down... and then, oh, hell no..."

Lennie, in three very different ways, had tricked them all like the sweet vermouth in a well-made Cheshire Cat. But in actual fact, he was a Gypsy's Warning. Why, oh why, had it taken River this long to suss him out, and more to the point, why had Heather kept this dark secret hidden from him his entire life?

Chapter Twenty-One
ALICE

She was appalled with herself for letting it slip out like that, the zesty cocktail and heady wine only speeding up the lightning bolt of a prophecy. And yet she had reached the stage where she could no longer keep such a secret from River, the man she was desperately trying not to fall in love with.

She wasn't really one for The Royals, despite her very privileged upbringing, but there was something so tragically Wills and Kate about the pair of them. And his return to Heather's to give her some space – space Alice hadn't even requested; space she had no desire for – felt about as wrong as the future king and his wife's infamous temporary separation. Just about the only thing keeping her going right now was the sweet realisation that they did reunite, quickly coming to their senses, and in time she hoped she and River would back each other into inevitability's corner too, a destination with no escape.

The past week had been a roller coaster of emotion, as clichéd and *X-Factor* journeyed as it was to admit it.

"Shit." River had finally spoken after she'd told him Lennie strongly suspected he was his son, a 'confidence' he'd revealed to her too many weeks ago now, after Heather had slung the crockery and biscuits at him and they'd scarpered back to the RV and then pegged it to London, before flying back to L.A. "Shit… that explains everything," he'd continued.

Alice had never been through these kinds of dramas growing up. Life had been a continuous flow of ease and abundance, birthright and immunity, an incessant collection of money and passing 'Go'. Old Kent Road struggle,

EastEnders-like strife, they simply hadn't existed in her bubble. Now, for the very first time, she was beginning to see the world that had been masked to her. Sure, there was nothing to like about it. And yet the chaos of it, the grapple for something better, the paths and the obstacles to be overcome, all of these things shone brightly like the stars. How much more fulfilling a life when there was something to fight for, when you didn't have it all served up on a platinum plate.

Little did she know that he'd come back to sit by her side, that *Portishead* would change to *Massive Attack*, and that the fast-paced African-inspired vibrations of *Angel* would mutate into the indecipherable, ethereal lilt of *Teardrop*. Both had instinctively turned to the other, thirsty for some tenderness, edging closer, ever closer, until her body's tingles merged with his, lips upon lips, skin on skin, arms nowhere and everywhere all at once, taking in every piece of each other in a frenzy.

He pulled away first, just as the moment was coming to its natural end, courtesy of the song releasing them, changing tempo again to something with the potential to take them in a very different direction. But there was no awkwardness. Nobody blushed or ran off to confession with a priest. It was exactly what it was, two people, the music their vehicle for an outpouring. They slept on opposite couches that night, and he drove her back to the campsite the next morning, chatting, laughing, just good friends, not a question to answer.

No rush, she reminded herself as she stole that kiss from her memory again.

Que sera, sera.

So much wisdom in those Spanish words. Every time she meditated – and she was making a point of doing so regularly lately, through the splashes of indigo as she came closer to perfect alignment with that ever sought after third eye chakra, a mysterious voice, the voice of a woman, would whisper over and over in Spanish, the kind of Spanish accentuation that came only from Latin America, that: *Que sera, sera.*

And then Alice would hunt for the finer detail, trying to match that kiss up with the snog that they'd shared in Blake's tent all those years ago, but this felt too shiny and new, too

136

wondrous to compare with what would have undoubtedly been a wrangle with a washing machine. At least that's how she remembered most of those juvenile brushes.

When she backtracked to Georgina's recent overnight stay, a place she didn't plan to reside in for very long at all in her head, she couldn't help but pick up on the tension between them. She'd minded her own business, of course, as River and Georgina had propped themselves up at the small kitchen worktop eating Sweet and Sour Pork, trying to disguise her revulsion at the thought of the poor animal who'd been slaughtered, as well as her revulsion at Georgina for pretending she didn't exist, as she took her sushi from the fridge and went to eat it outside in the deckchair with her Kindle – once again – for company.

She missed *his* company, who was she kidding? The weekend was a drag, Aunt Sheba – and it was hilarious to think of the pleasure she derived from referring to her as her Aunt, too – couldn't have been more welcoming though, checking up on her several times a day, inviting her into the main house for dinner so she wouldn't have to eat alone. And wasn't that a blessing in disguise? She had to laugh at the two very different images she'd been broadcasting to River: Alice the Michelin starred chef, with her Feta Bake Fantastique, and more accurately, Alice the Flaming Disaster in the Kitchen, unable to scramble even an egg without almost setting the place alight. For the former she had craftily purchased from Zara's bakery.

One night the inevitable did happen. Sheba had proffered a reading of her cards and Alice had found she was unable to resist:

"I'm not going to do your tarot reading though, Alice. Oh no... we'll use the angel cards instead – did you know I created this set myself?"

Sheba's smile had been full of pride as she'd pulled a small satin drawstring bag from the sideboard behind her and opened it, gently tipping the pack of cards into her palm. The top illustration was exquisite, causing even Alice to feel a brief twinge of jealousy that River had always been surrounded by

137

such creativity, as opposed to the horsey, empirical world of her own family.

"For that is the way I perceive you." Sheba went on to study her face with the kind of intent one reserved for reading an exam notice board, and then smiled kindly. "Far be it from me to suggest it, but just like an angel, you my dear, were put on River's path for good reason."

"Golly no," Alice protested. "We've been friends since we were knee high to grasshoppers. There's nothing likely to go on romantically between your nephew and me, not now, not ever. And I'm hardly the goodie-two-shoes you make me out to be either."

She laughed nervously as Sheba laid down a pale lemon square of silk on the table, and added to that a cherubic looking figurine, presumably some part of the ritual as well as a useful anchor. Such a fuss for something Alice wasn't even sure she believed in, but no harm in going along with it now. She could certainly use the guidance.

"Beg to differ."

Sheba finally settled herself into her chair, lowered her head, and raised her eyes to make it clear she wasn't buying the blatant lie. She formed an excellent double chin as she began to shuffle the deck of cards.

"Aren't you meant to be impartial if you're cutting my cards?"

"Technically yes, but you're the one choosing them, with the help of your angels, of course. They'll always have you pick out what you need to have reaffirmed. No danger of me brainwashing you, don't worry."

"So they're surrounding me... right now?"

"Always, Alice, always." Sheba closed her eyes, drew in a breath, held it some seconds and then exhaled, opening her eyes again to look endearingly into Alice's. "Okay, so, have a question ready in your head... no need to divulge it to me, and then take the card you feel most drawn to. We'll repeat this three times as a kind of past, present, future spread."

Alice's heart began to race excitedly, her fingers felt an inexplicable magnetic pull drawing them dead centre of the

138

fanned out pack, and she carefully pulled a card out and lay it face up on the table, without even taking a prior peek herself.

"Ha, The Angel of Displacement," said Sheba. "Does that resonate at all?"

"I was kind of expecting you to do the talking." Alice was none-the-wiser.

"This magnificent being is telling you that you've been living a life that's, well, not been too true to your higher self for quite some time. Seeing as you left the band and Hollywood behind to return to your hometown, that's some pretty accurate picking, Alice."

"Let's see how the present follows it up then, shall we?"

Alice shifted her posture, upright, eager, ready to see what The Now had to say for itself – despite the fact this was all complete nonsense. Nothing more than beginner's luck, even if Sheba's knowing smile as she extended the fan across the table yet again, said otherwise.

Alice's fingers weren't so sure what to do this time, hovering back and forth as if she were a kid in one of those modern handmade ice cream parlours, dithering over Cookies and Cream, Mint Choc Chip and Bubble Gum. Finally, intuition had her reaching for the penultimate card on the far left. She didn't dare tempt fate with an alternative procedure, and gently placed it face up on the silky table top once again without looking.

"Oh, looky-looky, what have we here?" Sheba couldn't contain her excitement. "It's only The Angel of Push and Pull."

"I had no idea there were so many different types of angels."

"Oh there are, you'd be surprised. Many are the commercial angel card packs who keep it all nice and romantic and spiritual with their phrasing, but a lot of the more practical angels that surround you are forgotten about. Take the Parking Angel for example. How many times have you called on him to help you find a car parking space? Exactly."

Words escaped Alice and so she sat there, mute, wondering what the Angel of Push and Pull could possibly have to reveal

139

to her.

"Any idea as to how you'd interpret this one in your current situation, Alice?"

It was all Alice could do in response to bite her lip and shake her head sideways.

"My instinct tells me this angel speaks of the drama centred round a man... I see him being pushed and pulled in two different directions... by two different females, as it happens, a bit like a tug of war. Except she who wins his heart will give up the resistance, let it be."

Sheba pushed her half-moon glasses closer to her eyes and directed them at Alice, waiting for a response.

"Oh, okay," Alice mumbled. Still, this could all be coincidental, she tried to convince herself. "Let's just get on with this now, shall we? It's late after all. I should be letting you get to sleep. I should be getting my own beauty sleep."

"My darling, you could go a hundred years without needing *that*. I don't think I've ever had such a celestial being stay in one of my caravans," she laughed, and then got serious again. "Now then: focus, breathe in and out. That was your present; we're on to your all-important future next."

"No pressure then."

Alice made it snappier this time, almost tugging a whole cluster of cards in the process.

"Steady on, you are one eager beaver, aren't you? If I have to take the whole of that heap into consideration, we'll be here all night."

She pushed the cards that 'didn't speak' to her back into the pack, laid the final card upright once again and breathed deeply, her heart almost in her mouth as to the news she was about to witness.

"Will you just look at that, now isn't this all quite something?" Sheba was a mathematician who'd finally sussed out the Riemann Hypothesis. "And here it ends... or shall we say begins... with the Angel of Twin Hearts."

"Meaning?" Alice had taken to biting her nails.

"Meaning, my dear, the one who takes up space in yours is your true twin, your soul mate. Though another may attempt to come between you, love conquers evil, always. Maybe it won't happen today, and maybe not tomorrow either, but from the one you are supposed to be with, you can never stay long apart."

How uncanny was that? Sheba knew nothing of Georgina, well, at least Alice presumed not.

All of which pointed to that wonderful, wonderful mixology course. London couldn't call for Georgina quickly enough.

Chapter Twenty-Two
GEORGINA

He sat there like a flump before Hyde Park's bandstand, head down, cigarette balancing between his crinkled, unappealing lips, feeling about his leather jacket for a lighter – she guessed that's what he was looking for, anyway. As she walked closer to him, and the amateur trombonists began to practice their tooting, while a bigger throng of Sunday afternoon strollers deposited themselves on stripy Victorian repro deckchairs, Lennie located a shiny silver rectangle, unclipped it, lit his fuse and drew in a large puff.

She'd suggested they meet here for purely selfish reasons – collaboration aside; it was a shorter distance from The Esmeralda and its world of pomposity, saving another taxi fare and Georgina's legs. Yes, she should have returned immediately after her lunch break to complete the final quarter of the poncy weekend 'Brunswick Mixology Course', but the opportunity to meet with Lennie was now or never. The Hooray Henry running the show was sure to understand when she explained she'd "been mugged, had had to call in to the local police station..." and then of course he'd probably feel sorry for her, lend her a few notes which she'd 'forget' to reimburse... or River could just put it down on expenses.

The thing was, in a couple of days Lennie would be back in Los Angeles, his touting for new band members in London had been a full-blown disaster, he'd admitted via his text message, with Bear and Alex loafing about in Camden's bars and pubs as opposed to putting any feelers out. All of which had only bolstered Georgina's confidence, further loading a weapon whose trigger Lennie would surely be only too obliging to pull.

Plus the fact, there was only so much exhibitionism anyone could take from that pair of Manchester-band-hair-cut plonkers from Up North, who thought they were God's Gift at everything and, seemingly delighted in showing her up at any and every opportunity at the training bar. It had hit her for six, this shocking revelation that she wasn't quite hip enough for this city and the idiots it attracted when they'd pulled out the ultimate trump card: sniggering at her attempt to serve them Cosmopolitans during the role play exercise, causing her to spill the contents of the tray all over the hotel's pristinely cream carpeted floor, regardless of the fact she could normally handle such a trivial part of her job day in and day out with ease in Glastonbury. Here she was a small fish in a very large pond, and the moment when she could hop aboard that coach headed for Somerset at six-thirty pm could not come quickly enough.

"Georgina, sweetheart, you're looking ravishing… if I may say so, my dear, how lovely to see you again."

Lennie dive-bombed in for a highly unsophisticated kiss – thankfully on just the one cheek – as the French horn hit a bottom F, and the stench of stale tobacco, fresh smoke and last night's booze joined in. Any brownie points for using her full name went straight out the window and into the Thames.

"Hello again, Lennie." She accepted his offer to occupy the deckchair next to him, grateful for the breathing space and narrow passage of air. They were right at the front of the semicircle, hence him standing out like the Great Wall of China. A traditional ice cream cart trundled past them, peddling its wares, flattening Georgina's carefully pre-planned choice of words with its squeaky wheels, igniting a momentary panic.

"Got rum n raisin?" Lennie shouted as the vendor whizzed past.

Surely he couldn't be serious, food and a fag in the same mouthful? His vulgarity strangely soothed her immediately; she could more than handle a man like this.

"And for you, princess?" He turned to look at her with tender eyes, whose fake intensity made her snatched *Subway* baguette of half an hour ago do a loop the loop in her stomach.

"No… thank you, not for me." She hoped, in both senses of her reply, that he'd read between the confectionery lines there.

"So then, what can I do for you?" he asked as he dropped his coins in the vendor's open hand.

"Two things," she said, determined to keep this business-like. "Just two things: your time and your money."

Lennie took a lengthy drag on his *Malboro*, exhaled at a leisurely pace, and then switched to the ice, his mouth sucking the top off as would an over-eager child, making for quite a revolting sight. Any minute now she was sure he'd go in for the kill; chomp the end off of the cornet, tilt his head back and let the juices dribble.

"My time *and* my money, she says, hmm…" He returned to his glow stick, as if that might help him decide if he was in for the ride. "Yeah, all right, I'm listening, doll. Talk to Uncle Len."

***

Hours later, as the coach was finally able to put the miles between the fume-filled capital and Georgina, Windsor Castle popping up and back down again in the distance like a Jack in a box tormenting the working classes, she ran over the outlines of the plan in her head.

October.

Although any day but the thirty-first. Even she wasn't cruel enough to take things that far. Lennie would need picking up from Castle Cary train station. Well, that was easily sorted; Blake could do the honours courtesy of Dad's car. The Guinevere would make the perfect 'HQ' for the before and after party, River and Airhead Alice (her new nickname, well, she was a blonde, she'd asked for it) never likely to set foot inside again. Zara had also confirmed that October was perfect for her, just before the Christmas cake orders and mince pies piled up. As for the skills and the resources, the cover up; those things could be organised nearer the time.

And then the coach driver made a surprise announcement over the tannoy system.

"Right… um ladies and gentleman: can I just have your attention please? A bit of an urgent situation has come up and we'll be making a very brief detour to the next service station…" He broke up for several seconds as the passengers exchanged puzzled glances with one another, and a murmur which threatened to become a ruckus briefly took over the slow lane of the M4.

The coach driver let out a hearty cough and then resumed his patter.

"Nothing to be concerned about, folks, the coach isn't about to break down or anything… I promise." And now he substituted words for a string of unconvincing chuckles, "just an unscheduled mini-break to pass on a message to my… err… to my colleague."

The murmur and confusion reduced to a simmer and soon the driver pulled over to the coach bays of Reading services, where a racing green Bentley was somewhat cheekily hogging two entire parking spaces. Georgina watched, amused, as its driver with her concave Miss Piggy-style snout, and her lengthy frame, emerged from behind the wheel. She slammed the door shut, designer looking clutch bag in her posh piano-fingered hands, and then appeared to climb up the steps to talk to him. But this was no cardboard cut-out of your bog standard coach driving colleague. Maybe she ran the entire fleet?

"Thank you, thank you so very much," her Queen's speech filtered down the aisle to where Georgina and her bags occupied the left hand side of row fourteen. The woman then turned to stride brusquely, proprietorially, eyes locking with Georgina, who began to shift uncomfortably in her seat, no idea what was going on.

"This is for you, darling." She produced an envelope which blatantly looked like it carried a wodge of bank notes inside it, pressed it into Georgina's palms and whispered, "from Lennie, via *moi*, for the uh… well, let's just call it Operation Payback, shall we?"

Chapter Twenty-Three
RIVER

When you are raised in a town like Glastonbury you are different, marked with an indelible ink, somehow more spiritually tuned in and turned on. Well, unless you are Blake – or Georgina, as River was realising more and more with the passing days. And that's why the news of Lennie's potential promotion to father hardly surprised him.

River was waiting in the living-room for Heather, perching like a canary on the window sill, feet resting on the coffee table trunk when she walked back through the door after her convention.

"Bit late, aren't you?" he remarked.

"Hi Riv, how's the bar?" She barely looked at him, wrapped up in raincoat and bags as she was. "And what are you doing here anyway? Oh, do watch you don't infringe on the spacing of my set of Buddhas on the ledge there, won't you? I thought you and Alice were still staying at The Guinevere? Ooh, have you found a house? How exciting... sorry, yes, I got side-tracked with Terry. He's going to be staying tonight, you know, as in... in my room... in my bed... under my duv—"

"I'm pleased for you, Mum, really, that's great. But I think it's about time you filled me in on the past before you get carried away with the future."

"What do you mean?" Heather stopped for the first time to study her son properly, she appeared genuinely confused.

"What I mean is this: is there a distinct possibility that my former band manager could be my father, in your esteemed opinion?" He lifted the smallest of the Buddhas and cradled it in his palm, transferring it from hand to hand as if weighing up

146

Heather's possible responses.

"So you know."

The colour drained from her face then and she crumpled onto the futon, dropping her Tibetan and hemp holdalls at her feet. How she'd hemmed everything into them as opposed to a suitcase for her gargantuan excursion, River had no idea.

"It wasn't exactly hard to put two and two together," he chirped, setting the figure back down again with its spiritual friends.

"Look," she sighed, her initial breeziness long since gone, "I never said anything that night when he paid you a visit, because although he's undoubtedly the guy I had a one night stand with at the festival thirty-five summers ago—"

"He's wh... hang on... are you saying you *slept with him*... at... at *Glastonbury*?"

What was it with the freakin' festival's ability to make everyone forget themselves? But then River realised this was the most ridiculous of questions.

"I'm afraid I was a complete mess at that time," her head wobbled at the recollection, "searching for myself... all too often in the arms of a stranger. The thing is: your real father could be any one of three men as it... as it turns out." She tempted a peek at her son, her face a picture of regret.

River felt like one of those ten pound diving bricks the swimming instructor used to lob in the pool, sinking slowly in a giant chlorine vat devoid of air; that and the girl from the *Mamma Mia* film. Although unfortunately for him, there was no wedding to Alice reeling in the other two male contenders for father, for a knees-up the evening before a ceremony atop a pretty Greek island hill.

Actually, make that fortunately. If ever anything permanently romantic happened between them, after the rigidity of their 'contractual' obligations with the band, he was sure they'd both had their fill of rules and regulations. Partners-for-however-long-they-stayed-happy-together would be marital status enough. But it was as good as wishful thinking anyway. He couldn't even begin to compete with the type of men from her past, and as for that kiss which had sprung forth from nowhere on the very futon he was also now parking his backside on, well, as meaningful as he'd wanted it to be on Alice's part, he gaged it came only from her pity; which was a fact that had him don an immediate iron veneer, impenetrable to feelings, for however long he could keep up the act.

"I'm as sure now as sure can be," Heather reminded him his thoughts were leading him astray yet again, "I always knew the guy's name began with 'L'. It's hard to forget a face when you've been—"

"La-la-la-la-la, all right, Mum, I get the picture, no need to go into the finer points." River childishly stuck his fingers in his ears.

"Much as you despise him," Heather shouted to make herself heard, "the music in his blood has clearly been passed down to you. And you're each as stubborn as the other."

"That's as may be," he said, elbows on thighs, hands now curled up into tight balls and resting on his chin, "but fortunately I didn't inherit his sleaziness... if indeed he is my pops after all. And what about the other two, any clue of their whereabouts, any photos of your time together so I can hunt for traces of myself in their long lost faces?"

"I'm sorry, River." Heather began to shake and then tears streamed quickly down her cheeks. "You had a right to know and I should have told you a very long time ago. I always said I would when you turned thirteen. But the truth is I was a right harlot back then, a lost soul, constantly looking for reassurance from a male, I was embarrassed to let you in on that. What kind of a role model would you have thought me?"

"It's okay, Mum. Come here." He hugged her close to him, astounded at his ability to accept such a major fuck up. "Maybe I'm a freak of nature... and that would be a very literal description if he is my dad, but family are the ones you choose to spend your time with. You have been Mum *and* Dad to me. And that's always been enough. It's been more than enough, because you've always been there, always supported me, no matter what I've done. It's like when I look at you and compare you to Alice's parents... and I know, *I know*, 'we don't do judgmental in this household'," he did his habitual fingers around his head thing, to highlight the importance of Heather's wisdom, "but just for today, let's… for sixty seconds anyway. What I'm trying to say is: you're poles apart. Alice may have had both of them around as she grew up, and bags of money to boot. But all of that is worthless when it isn't coming from here."

He put his hand over the left side of his chest and wondered if in another life he ought perhaps to have been a vicar.

Heather sniffed and then smiled. "You know my theory on these things from the stories I've told you about my own upbringing."

He knew what was coming next and bit his tongue.

"We choose our parents, River. We don't always take the easiest path because where's the spiritual lesson in that, how would our souls grow otherwise? But we do choose them."

"Yeah, I know." He felt a smattering of guilt then at the tales Heather had passed on to him about the way her father – his grandfather, who he'd fortunately never met – had beaten her as a child, his grandmother besides. When he looked at it like that, he supposed he could have chosen more extreme parents. Although, try as he might, the idea of him floating about on a cloud looking at a giant TV screen with potential mums and dads lined up on it – as Heather had so often tried to put the idea into context when he was a young child and he'd frequently questioned her as to the whereabouts of his daddy – seemed ludicrous. Surely, if he had spotted Lennie – a younger, trimmer version, or not, he'd still have wanted to avoid the creep at all costs.

"I think we could both do with a nice pot of catnip. What do you say?"

"Just this once then, I'll put it on and you put your feet up." He took that as her hint that he should move now to the kitchen, and he reluctantly left the traces of Alice's touch behind him. "But I didn't just come here to confront you, Mum. There's something else you should know."

"You're going to be a father. Oh-em-gee. I've suddenly

come over all dizzy, see if there are any ginger biscuits in the freezer that you could pop in the microwave for a quick defrosting… radioactivity, I know… but needs must."

"No, Mother! I am absolutely not going to be a father… and as for those flipping biscuits, can't you take a little of your own advice and know that all grounding comes from within, not some outside object?"

Heather looked thoughtful, before her face shone with admiration for her son.

"What I was trying to tell you is, I've, we've – that's Alice and me – moved into one of Aunt Sheba's *large* caravans down at the campsite. Listen, I know you'll be far from enthralled, but I had to think fast, he, my father," River was back to his customary bracket fingers either side of his ears again, a habit so middle-aged it petrified him, but it was something akin to a tube of *Pringles* – once you started, you just couldn't stop.

"Well," he carried on with his story, "he was camped out himself… in the reception of The Guinevere, would you believe it. The receptionist had given him a tipoff. Anyway, we're safe down there at the campsite. We have more space, more private space… each of us, that is, not more *private* space."

"Good. It's about time you two got your act together. The caravan park will throw Georgina off your scent for once and for all, much as Terry is a good friend and I probably shouldn't be talking about his daughter like that."

"From what I gather he's a little more than that."

"I'll come clean when you do."

"Touché," said River, immediately despising himself for regurgitating Georgina's favourite catchphrase. "Anyway, are you… are you telling me you're okay about us staying at your sister's?"

"River, darling, as you very well know, I'd hold my arms wide open to let Sheba back into my life tomorrow. It's she who's playing stubborn. All over a man who is quite happily married to the lovely Trudie Styler, and all when she has a husband of her own. I'm sure your Uncle Tony doesn't know the half of it."

***

"I've a very special ceremonious task to request of you, Mr J."

Cassandra dazzled River with a smile straight out of The Rocky Horror Show as she leaned over the bar almost toppling over his straw jar, whispering like they were members of some secret society.

"Oh?" he feigned surprise.

"My cat sanctuary, it's all been officially approved by the authorities, given the royal seal and whatnot. Will you open it? Oh, do say yes, River, please."

"I—," River had no doubt this was the work of the recent cocktail, especially since Cassandra's friends at book club night had left him under no illusion as to how messy her house really was. It had sounded like the last place to be given the thumbs up for anything.

"Since the birth of this wondrous bar, I cannot even begin to tell you about all of the equally wondrous incidents that have woven their way into the fabric of my life, him for starters." She span and pointed her index Twiglet at a boho-waistcoated guy with a banjo balanced on his lap, sat with the rest of her regular group. He couldn't have been a day over twenty-five. "It's no coincidence, I'm sure, never mind that 'Magical Mañana', you're the true magician in all of this."

River's eyes were transfixed at the implication of Cassandra's toy boy. Surely he couldn't be genuine? The age gap had to be at least forty years. Then again, Mercedes had promised magic. If only Cassandra knew how lopsided her words were.

"That's—"

"Will you? Well?"

"Of… of course I will. I'd be honoured."

Well, what choice did he have? Plus it could prove good PR for the bar.

"That's settled then. Eleven am Saturday, be there or be

square... no really... *do* be there, or otherwise Madam over there," she gestured at Lady Rigby-Chandler, who was taking advantage of her second Peach Bellini of the night, "will try to steal your thunder."

"Oh, Mr Jackson," Her Ladyship signalled to him in a Mary Poppins singsong, as if she were suddenly telepathic, "I'll have a third please."

Bitch... publicly road testing his rules.

"Now what is the deal there with our Dear Friend?" asked Cassandra conspiratorially. "It hasn't escaped my attention that she seems to be part of the furniture... and as for her husband... I've seen John Prescott looking more lively."

"You could say that," River snapped. "It's definitely not through choice."

"Alice! Alice darling, how simply wonderful to see you," said Lady Rigby-Chandler for the entire bar to hear, an action River hoped in vain would make her forget about the Bellini. "You're not working here though, surely?"

He watched the painful scene from afar as Lady Rigby-Chandler rose to look Alice up and down taking in the vision of enchantress clad in crisp white shirt and black pencil skirt, her mouth twisting and contorting as if she'd just bitten into a sour lemon.

"Indeed I am, Lady Rigby-Chandler." Alice bustled over to air kiss her. "And my, you're looking wonderful, in fact I swear you get younger the every couple of years we do bump into each other, and always outside of the village. It must be a super place for you to escape to, here in River's glamorous bar."

"It's not a patch on The Savoy, sweetheart, you must know that."

Cow, she was certainly drinking enough of the profits.

"It's a little piece of paradise for all of us Glastonians. And I'm happy to play a small part in its success." Alice threw a smile over her shoulder to River and he gratefully caught it.

"That's it, I vow to talk to your mother... get you out of this dreadful place. If only I'd known about this sooner, why I'd soon have talked her out of her childish siding with Tamara over that what's his name? Glenn Luke Sherringham, the wooden actor you used to cavort with?"

"But if it's so very dire, prey tell why are you drinking here?" Alice replied un-frazzled as River swallowed his temporary envy over the mention of that total jerk.

"Yes," River echoed between gritted teeth. "Perhaps you'd care to enlighten us, my Ladyship?"

"Well, where else is there, darling? Believe me, I'd hotfoot it up to London in a jiffy if only I'd had the gumption to take driving lessons back in the heyday… word of advice, Alice, for thou art worldly-wise, well-travelled and all that. Never hitch up with a man who owns vast quantities of land in the West Country."

"Do you know what? Not so very long ago and I might have agreed with you… but now I can't think of anything more appealing." She dazzled River with her smile and they both turned their backs.

"My Bellini, Jackson: you're forgetting my Peach Bellini," Lady Rigby-Chandler retorted and returned to her seat and her dozing husband.

River sighed, begrudgingly thankful this would lower his pulse which Alice's statement had just rendered uncontrollable, and even began to feel sorry for Lady Rigby-Chandler for a few seconds; something was very amiss in her seemingly upper-crust life. Surely she and her husband should be inundated with appointments and invites to stately manors and creaking castles far and wide, as opposed to being holed up in – an upmarket and trendy, admittedly – cocktail bar?

Terry walked in with Heather then, taking River's mind off the incessant beck and call of those sapphire-spangled snapping fingers. He obediently pureed her peaches anyway, a quick wave to the smiley couple as they took up the last table on the floor.

"I think we're going to have to open the upstairs tonight," he said excitedly to Georgina as she made for the dishwasher to fill it up with empties.

"Have you heard back from the Brunswick yet… about my certificate? It's not fair to keep me pacing the floor like a

153

skivvy when I should be round here with you, impressing the clients."

"That would be *customers* and not yet, no," said River, annoyed that she hadn't taken the rather large hint to ensure upstairs was shipshape and ready for business, equally surprised the Brunswick hadn't awarded her a grade yet. "Can you put the vacuum cleaner round on the first floor for me please? The next *customers* in here are going to have to be seated upstairs... unless the Rigby-Chandlers make a sharp exit, or anybody else leaves in the next half hour, all of which is looking highly unlikely."

"Why should I?" she back chatted him like an eight-year-old in the playground.

"Um, that'll be because I asked you to... nicely. Why are we even having this conversation?"

"Why can't *Trash* there do it?"

"Excuse me... are you talking to me?"

Alice's eyes became saucers. Saucers River wanted to dive into, lapping every inch of her up. It unnerved him for a second or two. His groin panged with desire. He wasn't sure if that came from her unusual Maid Marion act of defiance, or the many weeks he'd spent in a sexual desert. Either way, he needed to mask it quickly.

"You must be mistaken," Georgina cut through his thoughts with the serrated blade of her tongue. "I said, after I've taken *out* the trash. The bins need emptying too, you see. It's a good thing some of us are on the ball."

And with that she marched off.

"River, look, I know it's not my right to say this," said Alice, "and it's your bar, you employ who you choose. But how can you possibly stand for that attitude?"

"And how on Earth can I let her go now Mum's shacked up with Terry?" he heard himself snap back unfairly, lamely, unable to hide his emotion.

"They're hardly at wedding bells stage yet. Nip it in the bud. Not because I'm some jealous friend, as she'd have you believe, but because she's up to something. Why can't you see it?"

154

Alice picked up her tray of mixed orders and left him to his thoughts. But she had a point, more than a point. Georgina was stripping him of his dignity, a locust swooping down on a field of crops and soon there would be nothing left.

Terry came to the bar then, sensing everybody was a little overworked.

"How's it going tonight, pal? Busy one it seems." He sniffed at the air as if it encapsulated the presence of a crowded house. "You've even pulled in The Queers." He tutted, eyes wide, and shook his head from side to side.

"We're rushed off our feet here, Terry," River was not about to get into an argument, but made a mental note to drop several hundred hints to Heather about the bigoted views of the man he thought was becoming the increasing tonic to his mother's life, "but always time for regulars. What can I get you… and Mum? Let me guess—"

"Your mother will have her usual, you're right there," he laughed. "But I'm gonna be brave and step out of me comfort zone tonight. Now we've been wondering about it for ages, like… why's th'ick there 'Magical Manyanerr' – is that how you pronounce it – on a page all of its very own? Little bit strong is it? Little bit special?"

Goosebumps pinged all over River's forearms. It was all he could do to not tug at his sleeves. Terry must have noticed them too, dotting his skin with the appearance of a plucked chicken.

"Oh that," he laughed a little too nervously. "Stupid printers, they mucked up, not sure how it happened, but well, next time I redo the menu, everything will all be squashed back together again."

"I rather think that's a shame, makes a drink look more intriguing when it stands out." Terry sniffed at the air again as if considering his options.

"True, true." River nodded, wondering how he was going to potentially dart to the skittle alley without anybody noticing on such a busy night – that was if Terry did take the plunge.

"I'm not saying I'm a convert to these drinks. God rest my father's soul, he'd turn in his grave if he could see me now, call me a right old poof." River cringed for the second time, hoping Terry would quickly get to the point, either settle his nerves or fire them into action. "But there is a certain finesse that I quite enjoy when it comes to a cocktail. And fair play, not just anyone can throw 'em together. That's why I'm so proud of our George for seeing that course through." River flashed a strained and pearly white smile at Terry, furious with himself now for letting both Georgina and her father pin her future financial and professional life on him.

"She never finished that BTEC at college," Terry was on a roll though, "despite all her interest in business, and the job she had waiting for her if she'd only just knuckle down. T'were the boys, you see. Always is – that and her impatience for a bit of pocket money... and those owners in the organic café in town who made her feel like they couldn't run the show without her. But she's come good in the end. And I can't thank you enough, my man, for the part you've played in that."

"Hey, don't mention it, Tel," River punched the air playfully with a fist. And although he knew the moment had no choice but to present itself soon enough, right now he didn't have the heart to remove the golden halo Terry had placed upon his daughter's rebellious head, nipping proceedings firmly in the bud as Alice had so sensibly suggested.

"Anyways, what will I have? Hmm..." he flicked through the pages quickly, like a child entranced by one of those books full of 'moving illustrations', an early attempt at a cartoon. Who did that with a menu? "A Magical *one of them*... or something else?" he questioned himself.

River could never have imagined such a quick succession of willing participants, but it appeared that no sooner had Cassandra made herself volunteer number one, than Terry was stepping forward to take up second place.

"Nope, can't think of anything better. I like Tequila – just a little mind, I like me Sherry too, and an OJ a day, well I reckon that's what keeps the doctor away, never mind the apple."

So that was that then: two down, only one more to go.

Chapter Twenty-Four
GEORGINA

It was now or it was never. There was no time for rationale, the devil inside her head had spoken, and she'd succumbed to his brainwashing within seconds.

"I'm sorry." Alice, about to start the vacuuming on account of Georgina's delay, dropped plug and cable to the floor, somewhat stunned as Georgina held out her hand to shake her love rival's. Georgina grimaced inwardly at the emptiness of her words as Alice accepted her hand and then outstretched those stick thin, model-like arms for a full-on hug. How could she forgive so easily?

Weirdo.

"I think that we both needed one of these," she said and Georgina nodded, a weak smile upturning her lips as their union broke apart again.

Oh just turn that friggin' white noise on, woman, and drone this conversation out of me already – that and the short snappy warmth of the arms of another, a potential *one of them*, a *friend*.

But now she had started there was no going back. The words, etched in her mind like a tombstone would be the perfect beginning of Alice's end.

Georgina proceeded to slump herself on a chair, head cupped in her hands as if it were a weight she could no longer support with her shoulders alone, realising she may as well go the whole hog with the dramatics. She began to sniff and snort, gradually releasing her hand to tug at her shirt sleeve where a ragged tissue poked out, so she brought it to her eyes, dabbing pathetically at the tear ducts.

"Oh, Georgina, what's up?"

157

Alice was poised beside her, where she began to rub her shoulders. It felt undeniably good, yet once again she tried to ignore the warmth, the fact that in this moment, right now, she could change the course of fate by saying something, just about anything else than these treacherous words.

"I can't say," she sniffed. "I'm just too scared... sc...scared of what people will think, what he will do."

"Has somebody been hurting you?"

Oh, the concern in Alice's voice was crippling. How could she be such a bitch to her? Of all the things she had ever done, surely this was one step too far.

Pushover! The devil inside her took over. Do you want her out of his life and yours? Blake's besides, or not?

"I'm pregnant."

There, she'd said it.

And actually, technically, she really could have been, for she was a day overdue – not that this was anything unusual, her cycle never having been regular as clockwork. That fact alone made her feel a little more justified, easing her into the act she had slipped on like a well-fitting cloak.

"Oh my, right I... um... I see," Alice sat down next to her now, those rubs lessening in meaning and intensity. "It's River's I suppose."

She got a childish kick out of noting Alice couldn't bring herself to say the B word.

"Well, I definitely haven't been with anybody else... so... yeah, the baby is River's."

She couldn't resist but to give proper reference to the new life that almost certainly wasn't within, careful as she had always been with contraceptives, because who in their right mind fancied the prospect of being lumbered with the 'me-me-me-ness' that was a child? Still, she let the very utterance of 'baby' promote her to a level above and beyond whatever it was that was taking shape between Alice and River. How could anybody compete with the status of Mother of his unborn son or daughter, carrier of his genes; his precious bundle of joy?

The atmosphere between them hung heavy and uncertain,

Alice undoubtedly adding the months forward and back in her mind in an attempt to pinpoint the where and when, the changes this invisible child would bring into his life, the sacrifice she was going to have to make so that two had a clear path to become one again... and now three, heck, possibly even four.

"Have you told anybody else?"

"I can't."

"How many weeks do you think you are?"

"Ten or so."

Too many for the deed not to have taken place after our apparent cooling-off period, Allie, sweetheart; oh Gee, she mocked herself silently, you are a bloody legend and a half.

The stairs creaked then and River appeared, looking from one to the other of them, evidently puzzled by the scene.

"Guys, I was kind of hoping we'd be ready to rock up here. None of the customers are clearing off downstairs and I can only keep the next ones at the bar for so long with complimentary Japanese rice crackers. Any chance you could get a shifty on?"

"I'll see to it," said Alice. "Georgina isn't feeling too good, isn't that right, honey?"

"Honey?" he questioned her, as if completely out of her mind. "But a moment ago you two were at each other's—"

Georgina lifted her hand from her sodden cheek then and clocked River's mystified expression for herself.

"Since when did you become best friends? Wait, you're crying too? Oh for bleep's sake, of all the nights. What's wrong with her?" He looked to Alice for an answer.

Georgina stood slowly, straightened herself up and took a deep breath.

"Does it need any more explanation?" Alice barked, back at the vacuum cleaner already and looping the extension cord between her fingers as if that might help untangle the mess. River looked seriously affronted.

This was working a treat, Georgina stifled a smile.

"Well, yes, ideally, I'm trying to run a bar here and it's seriously busy down there, we might even fill the top half tonight the way things are carrying on, so I really need all hands on the deck."

"And like I said, she doesn't feel too special. Let her have the weekend off."

Georgina could only look at the floor. Her deceit knew no limits; it was enough to send her into one of her Cruella De Ville laughter fits. And yet a tiny part of her felt sorry for Alice. Clearly she was in love with him, her heart shattering in a million pieces in front of Georgina's eyes.

"Right... well... whatever. I'll have to ask Mum for a hand, if she's not too merry after two Ginger Rabbits, that is. Georgina," he looked at her as would a boss, not a lover, all traces of their union erased. Her stomach churned, making her wonder if she really was with child, "take the weekend off, Alice is obviously clued up as to what's wrong. Get yourself better and we'll see you next week."

And with that he ran back down the stairs two at a time.

"Thanks, Alice, I... I couldn't seem to find the words." Georgina took a couple of very tentative steps towards her, but Alice was a young fawn now, ears sharpened, senses heightened, the drawbridge of friendship well and truly up. "I guess that's why I've been so moody with everyone, so snappy and unpredictable."

"Not today you couldn't tell him... perhaps... but you *will* find those words and you'll find them very soon. You can't keep him in the dark like this. It would be like history repeating itself." Alice's words were hard and stony. She switched on the vacuum cleaner and Georgina took this as her cue to leave.

She too took the stairs two by two, but only once she was clear of Alice's line of vision, ever mindful of the fact she needed to keep up the Expectant Mother Act. She saw her moment to sneak behind the bar for her bag, and she left the building, echoes of her dad and Heather chuckling in the background at something undoubtedly highly inconsequential, echoes of River enjoying banter with a group of tourists, echoes of Alice and her threat as she continued to scrape those floors with the *Dyson*.

160

Chapter Twenty-Five
RIVER

River fixed himself a Frisky Bison, anything to take the edge off Alice's sudden and nonplussed stance with him. What was all of that about upstairs? Georgina looked perfectly fine to him, if she was at death's door then how come she'd taken the rubbish out? Despite being brought up solely by one, he still found the Venusians impossible to work out at times. Add to that the almost melancholic fact that his mission was nearing well and truly accomplished, and a cheeky sip at a tipple on the job was pretty much excusable.

"What's in that then?" Lee quizzed him. "And shouldn't you yourself be staying dry when you're behind the bar?"

"Liquid alcohol apple pie… and normally, yes, but this is something I'm sampling as a potential newbie to the menu… and I haven't got time to do it during the week."

"Not convinced, about either."

"Always good to break out of your taste buds' comfort zone, Lee; if it wasn't for innovation the only cocktail being served up anywhere would be the monotonous Mojito."

"The idea of drinking pie is one thing. What I'm talking about is your stress levels; they're visibly through the roof, mate. What's up?"

"Just some staffing issues, that's all. Nothing I can't handle."

"You know, I never thought I'd say this and don't you dare repeat it to a soul… but I could *almost* see myself doing something like this in a couple of years," Lee cupped his hand to the side of his mouth to whisper then, "something like you are."

"What, drinking on the job, or you running a bar?"

"I meant the latter, and why in the hell not? Take it as a compliment, bud. You've opened up my eyes to new possibilities. I was even saying about it to Jonie the other day. This cocktail malarkey is growing on me... embarrassingly... or perhaps not embarrassingly, nothing wrong with being in touch with your feminine side nowadays, most blokes are at it."

"See, that's what makes me laugh." River shook his head as if to add to the education he was about to bestow on his friend. "The cocktail, in many of its guises, and especially if not respected, if downed like a succession of wine glasses, well, it's the strongest alcoholic drink you'll ever encounter. The dressing it up with umbrellas and fruit thing is simply a ploy... might make it come across as all innocent, pretty and feminine, but if you don't know what you're doing you'll soon figure out it's a wolf in sheep's clothing."

"Are you going to take my order at some point this evening or give me a history lecture?" snapped Lee.

"All right, keep your shirt on. So what's it to be then?"

"Well, there's one little attraction in your menu that's got me totally stumped... and that's this one... now, where is it again?" Lee flipped open the menu with such showmanship that River grabbed it off him. "Hey, why'd you go do that?"

"I know the one you mean and I haven't got the ingredients," River began to panic, realising what an idiot he was making of himself but more than mindful of the fact that other customers were too close for comfort. If Lee was going down Magical Mañana Street as well tonight, he'd have to remove the cocktail from the menu immediately thereafter. So the last thing he wanted was for the trail of drinkers behind him to follow in his footsteps and plump for the same thing. And wasn't that just the way everyone behaved when they saw the puddings deposited at the neighbouring table in a restaurant? A cocktail bar, as River had more than witnessed over the years, was no different. It rendered people option-less once the seed of another's choice had been planted.

"River? Are you alright?" Lee looked flabbergasted.

"Yeah, yeah, it's cool. Just chill, Lee." River caught his

162

breath again and realised he was the only one needing to chill, as well as coming up with something sensible to say – and fast. "What I mean is," he began to whisper now, "don't say the drink out loud else you'll give everyone else the same idea... and I don't have enough ingredients to make more than one!"

"Sounds like you could use a stocktaker. Blimey. I've seen some right sights at the supermarket over the years, frustrates the hell out of me. It doesn't take a genius to figure out the basic model of ye olde supply versus demand though." He shook his head pitifully.

"Thanks for the advice. I'll keep your CV on file."

"Perhaps you'd better. Right, well, I best get back to Jonie before somebody thinks they can muscle their way in with a cheesy chat-up line. Looking forward to my drink... oh and a Sea Breeze for the missus... I mean, the lady."

"Coming right up," River jeered through a forced smile.

He fixed up the new arrivals' orders first: Everything from Coco Fizzes to Little Tickles, and thankfully not the remotest loiter of a fingertip mid-menu, he asked Alice to mind the bar so he could 'replenish some stock', and then he ran, as fast as his legs would carry him to the skittle alley, for the second time that night, creating a brand spanking new character for the Roger Hargreaves collection in the process – Mr Undercover Dodgy Barman.

Two hours later, after last orders had been taken, two sets of ten globules had safely been deposited in two glasses, and Alice had mysteriously insisted upon walking home on her own – something River was loath to let her do, and so had called his Aunt Sheba, who needed no convincing that she should 'just happen' to be passing by in her car, so would Alice like a lift – and River was on his second Frisky Bison. It had definitely won a place on the menu, conveniently replacing the Magical Mañana, which he was now tearing from the saddle stitched seams, along with a mountain of blank pages, relegating hope to history in the paper bin.

He sat cross-legged on his favourite couch, taking in his surroundings anew, each sip seemingly heightening his awareness of his achievement. It was the only way he could round off what had been the most perplexing day of trading since he'd officially opened the bar. If only he'd finished his degree in Psychology, then perhaps he could delve into the minds of those around him, understand what was going on. He mentally listed the people who surrounded him, each one an enigma of their own making:

Terry – he'd start off with Lover Boy because he'd royally turned River's perception on its head. What was his problem with same sex relationships? He wouldn't be tolerating any more of that kind of inequality in this establishment – under hushed tones or not. What was it with half the population of this supposedly free-loving town not getting with the times and embracing one and all?

Blake – and where in the hell had he disappeared? First his sister started working here; then his father took to drinking here… not to mention sucking the face off Heather, an act which was beginning to turn River's stomach now too, in light of the evening's revelations. Lest he forget Lee's growing intrigue for all things spirit based, something that had to surely be akin to poking a large grizzly with a stick. And yet Blake was completely off the radar, something which made zero sense. A fact which implied something shady was about to reveal itself. How could it not? A bear with a sore head only hibernated for so long.

Georgina – she seemed to be getting the message that hadn't yet been spoken: their unofficial entanglement was in the deep freeze of the cooling off period. And as for the period pains, she'd need to man up or get out; a thought which more than rattled his cage as its very sexist undertone was probably proof enough he was the son of one Lennie. But he couldn't get conned into letting her take time off every four weeks, the bar was gaining in popularity now, they all needed to muck in and carry that momentum forward.

Lennie – there was another bear with a sore head whose imminent presence wouldn't let River relax, whether indeed this one turned out to be Daddy Bear or not.

Heather – okay, finally (with the exception of the evening's

164

unwanted news about Terry's belief system) she seemed to be levelling out now, the mystery of her involvement with Lennie unearthed; she'd even quit whipping up her weekly Root Ginger biscuits. River never thought he'd see the day, but the appearance of Linseed Flapjacks and Cardamom Prune Scones was looking promising.

Aunt Sheba – how much longer could this ridiculous feud with his mum go on?

And now there was Alice. Like the inventory needed to get any longer!

Before he knew it his ringtone was waiting for Lee's voice to answer, somehow he had to get him back in the bar tonight, just for a nightcap, just for some reassurance that normality could be found in this place he was desperately trying to call home again.

***

"Okay. So there's something you should know: the Magical Mañana is kind of different to the rest of the cocktails on the list, and that's why it's embedded deep in the menu."

What was River thinking? He quickly cast his mind back to Mexico, Mercedes hadn't exactly said he couldn't tell anyone, in fact she hadn't said that at all. He'd only tell Lee though, he promised himself now he'd started. That was it, line drawn.

"Only three people are ever meant to drink it," he continued, taking a gulp of his own drink to quell his nerves. "You, my man, were one of the chosen few; in fact, not just one, but the very last of the chosen few."

Thirty-seven minutes and sixteen seconds after his phone call, River and Lee had made themselves at home on the bar stools, River on his third Frisky Bison, and all the more open for it – they were going down a little too well. And Lee had finally been persuaded that liquid alcohol apple pie was indeed a very good thing.

"What on Earth are you chirping on about?" Lee smacked his lips after another giant suck on his straw.

"It's a long story. A very long story and one you'll no doubt

165

scoff at," River replied.

"I'll take the compliment. Carry on."

"I'm serious." River scratched his head as if that might trigger his brain to locate the best words. "But if I'd told you before you drank it, the magic wouldn't have worked. Plus for sure you'd have got all suspicious, thought I was poisoning you."

Lee's eyes darted from left to right as the colour drained rapidly from his face. He pushed his current glass aside and hopped off the stool, hands frozen mid-air, as if they might need to grab it on reflex to fend off what was to come.

"Oh, it's nothing to worry about, I promise. It's all good actually, very good. But first you might want to take a seat?"

Lee eyed him suspiciously, relinquishing the invite at first. But as River recounted his adventures en-route to Tequila that day, the blood slowly returned to his lips and cheeks, until he was back on the stool and almost toppling off of it, clutching at his stomach, howling with laughter in a way that made River wonder if they'd been transported back to their teens and had just shared a super strong joint.

"I've heard some questionable patter from you before, Jackson, but this is just ludicrous," he said finally.

"Well, the proof will be in the pudding, Mercedes assured me."

River nodded his head to back up his statement, despondency written all over his face. If Lee was going to play ungrateful, indifferent, he may as well have taken his place.

"I'll go put two pounds on the lottery now then," Lee teased, torment flashing in his eyes.

"You probably should," said River.

"Daft bugger, Blake was right. You clearly did take one too many pills on the road."

166

Chapter Twenty-Six
ALICE

There was no undoing the damage that had been done. A fuse had been lit behind Alice, propelling her involuntarily to a land far, far away, neither home nor L.A., the city she'd left behind. She was a circus cannonball now with not a horizon in sight – let alone a horizontal net.

The shock smarted. For as she totted up the weeks in her head, it was clear their mutual affection for River had dovetailed, at precisely the time he'd assured her – hell, she'd even assured herself – that the-thing-that-was-never-a-thing-with-Georgina – was well and truly over.

She had to get away and she had to get away fast, before he suspected a thing, before her heart attempted to sweet talk her into the kind of oblivion that would physically break it in the end. How wrong she had got it coming back to Glastonbury. You couldn't run away from your problems. Maybe in one guise, but they'd only show up again in another.

She'd continued to clean the upstairs in Georgina's absence, continued to lavish her false smile on the customers, continued to transport Great Gatsbys and Coco Fizzes, Sea Breezes and Little Tickles, Tors In The Mist, Avalon Ambers and a solitary Magical Mañana, all the while wondering how she'd got her life so very, very wrong. Most people started off with the rough ride, striving for betterment, fuelled by the kind of desire that only comes from the contrast of knowing hardship like a big brother. By the standards of Alice's upbringing she should be married to Prince bloody Harry by now. Which wasn't far off the grand plans Mummy had had for her.

Instead she was stuffing her few and increasingly

threadbare belongings into her case, hoping against hope that River wouldn't stir next door in his bedroom, and that his Uncle Tony's snores would drown out the trundle of her suitcase wheels as it snaked its way out of the campsite, so that Aunt Sheba wouldn't be on her proverbial case. Three am seemed a pretty safe bet, even if – as Heather had recently informed her – there was markedly less *prana* in the atmosphere at said hour, hence the increased risk of a heart attack.

Some twenty minutes later and she had somehow managed to pull it off, nobody any the wiser until sunrise. The taxi greeted her at the top of the driveway and she breathed a sigh of relief to see the driver was a woman: one less thing to worry about in the dead of the night.

"Am I right in thinking you're wanting me to take you to Bath station?" the driver quizzed her.

It was all Alice could do to nod. If she spoke, the tears would match her word for word.

"But it's pitch black, well, more like morning really," the driver pressed her again for her reassurance, adding one of those annoying Australian question marks which really needn't hang in the air as decoration.

"Yes please, I've got an early train to catch."

"The first of the day by my reckoning," the driver said as she mirror-signal-manoeuvred, loop-the-looped and headed back into the town. "We'll go the scenic route."

Great – in other words one last glimpse of The Cocktail Bar, one last pang of the stomach as they passed by all that she was leaving behind.

They drove in silence initially until the driver asked her if she'd mind a little music.

"No, no, you go ahead, be my guest."

"Well, technically you're mine, so I don't want to play something that might assault your ears. What with you being a musician and all…"

"Oh, so you recognise me."

"It's hard not to with Avalonia being one of my favourite bands." She let out a strange snigger. "But I promise not to get star struck, Alice – *may I call your Alice?* – I'm kinda used to ferrying the big names about. I've had Björk and her tatty hair knots, that Heather Small from M People, Ana Matronic out of the Scissor Sisters… her real name's Ana Lynch, did you know? Then, who else, let me see… Ant and Dec… even old Kanye in the back of my cab over the years. So no biggie when it comes to discretion, I won't be tipping off the press."

"Thanks, that's good to know."

"De nada, love."

"Ant and Dec though, really?"

"Oh yeah, well they needed a trip to the supermarket, were glamping it up in the VIP fields at the festival, like."

"Oh right, yes. I suppose the festival attracts all sorts."

"Certainly does."

"Stop!"

"But we're not quite in Bath yet, pet."

"Please, sorry, stop here, just a short while. I need to write a note. I can't leave it like this. Not after all he's done to help me."

"Whatever you say, nothing to do with me. You see to your business." The driver pulled the vehicle over to the side of the road and tugged at the handbrake. "I can't stop the metre running though no more than I can stop the Earth spinning, just so's you're aware."

"No, it's all right, it's all right. This won't take long. But do you have some paper, a pen?" Alice felt herself getting more flustered by the second, hardly helped by the random tidbits of gossip being involuntarily thrown her way, as if she were some kind of starved seagull.

"Course… here you go." The driver twisted her bulky frame awkwardly, showing off an impressive neck tattoo, as well as an array of gold hoop earrings straight out of an *Argos* catalogue, proportionately decreasing in size as they ran down her earlobe. She handed Alice a notepad and pen.

Alice scribbled the first words that came into her head, hardly poetic at this time of the morning, but better than vanishing without a trace of an explanation.

"I'll be fifty-nine seconds, literally," she said, tearing the paper with its taxi details off the pad and opening the door.

"No probs, but how about some music? I'll get the CD ready while you're doing your thing."

This woman was seriously something else at three forty-five am.

"I dunno... um... err... what about some Sting?"

Hardly her favourite, despite singing his praises to Heather, but bizarrely he was the first artist to pop into her head.

"Your luck's in."

Alice smiled wanly at the back of her head as the driver lunged at the glove box compartment and busied herself rifling through her musical collection. She stepped onto the kerb and walked the few metres behind her, past the organic bakery, to River's bar, took a deep breath and then slid the paper under the door, immediately berating herself thereafter that Georgina might well return to work within hours, the first to place her grubby mitts on it.

She ran back to the cab only to be welcomed by the beats of The Police and *Every Breath You Take,* which serenaded her in an irritatingly timely fashion. The driver began to whistle along and Alice closed her eyes, trying in vain to focus on the woman in front of her and her tragic middle-aged impediment, as opposed to Georgina and her growing stomach. In any other circumstances this would definitely not be preferable.

Somehow it must have worked though, because when she opened her eyes it was to the site of the lush green hills of Peasedown St John, basked in a pretty pink sunrise, and not long after, the trickle of Georgian terraced houses and Bed & Breakfasts, witnessing her arrival into the glorious city of Bath.

"Almost there. I must say, I for one can't wait – gonna treat myself to a fry-up in one of the city cafs before I head back to Glasters."

"Sounds great," Alice lied and again she tried to focus on anything but the kind of subject which threatened to evict the contents of her stomach.

"Now are you one hundred percent sure you're doing the right thing?"

"I beg your pardon?" Alice wasn't sure how much more of the driver's tiresome quirks she could take.

"Look, far be it for me to interfere, and what is spoken in this taxi, stays in this taxi. From Dec to Kanye, Ana Matronic to Alice, Joe Bloggs to The Queen... should I ever be lucky enough to have her grace my behind."

For almost five am this was beyond painful.

"What I'm trying to establish, love, is are you sure you won't change your mind about running away from him?"

"How did you... I mean, running away from who? I'm not even running away!" Alice tried in vain to reassure the both of them, completely overlooking her giveaway high pitched voice, now on the brink of a screech.

"Okay, fair dos, I see the subject's off limits." The driver held her chubby hands up and shook her head in defeat. "All the best to you, I'll be seeing you around."

"Yeah, thanks, same to you... no don't bother, it's okay, I've got this." Alice held up her own hand to stop her chauffeur from heaving her weight out of the seat to help her with her luggage, and went to the boot to do the honours solo.

A round of completely unnecessary *bon voyage* beeps later and the mysterious woman, whose name had never been revealed, was presumably off for her Full English Breakfast in a greasy spoon, leaving Alice to feel equally full – of paranoia, fear, guilt, regret, and just about every other lower spectrum emotion one could conjure up besides, as she made her way to platform one.

Chapter Twenty-Seven
GEORGINA

Georgina treated herself to two days off work, just enough for Alice to slip out of the picture, as she'd cleverly predicted. Of course River had dressed up her disappearance with the announcement that His Beloved was taking a weekend break to visit her sister in London.

Oh, the irony! As if.

Little did he know Georgina had already had her own introduction to that grotesque specimen of a Society Darling, courtesy of their mutual swift mini break at one Reading Services. Georgina rather thought River would find that Alice was in fact flunked out on a sunbed at Glenn Luke Sherringham's mansion in Bel-Air, attempting to revive his affection in a barely-there bikini and a string of diamonds dancing around her neck. She was more than welcome to stay there.

It was almost like wiping the slate clean: just the two of them running the bar. And with the ever-increasing chance of Alice's eclipse really being for ever and ever Amen, it was also something of a relief that Georgina wouldn't need to start desperately stuffing cushions up her jumpers like some child playing Mummies and Daddies in a Wendy house. She'd already started experimenting with socks in her bras, realising quickly that it would have been a desperately hard act to keep up.

Depleted stock brought them to the local supermarket. River had left the wholesale order too late for the delivery to arrive on time and had instead called Georgina in early, seemingly eager to encourage her to make up for those lost hours of the last weekend.

Loser Lee was strutting his stuff on the shop floor, biro tucked behind his ear as if he'd suddenly shot up to management level. River spotted him and left Georgina to bag up the fruit, passing her an extensive shopping list behind him.

"Pineapples, lemons and limes in first, don't squash the peaches whatever you do."

"Blimey, I must be going up in the world," she said to his back which was now halfway down the aisle to bestow Lee with a handshake.

"Coincidence?"

River couldn't seem to help but tease him about *something*, and Georgina couldn't help but overhear. With River's focus firmly on his friend, she couldn't resist but to wheel the trolley closer, eyeing the pineapples' handy location, just to the right of their dialogue and on special offer. Because who exactly *did* buy pineapple in a town like Glastonbury?

"It's nowt to do with your outlandish theory. They had a vacancy, I fit it. Simple as," Lee replied, and Georgina found herself raising her eyebrows and listening in more intently.

"Wonder why it's never happened before in... how many? Thirteen years of service for the same supermarket?"

"Because I wasn't ready, obviously, but now I am," Lee replied in a funny kind of yodel, more than hinting at his uncertainty regarding this apparent twist of fate.

"Exactly," said River, and then promptly turned, visibly more than a little stunned with the realisation that Georgina had been all too obviously eavesdropping. She dived onto the pineapples like an amateur actor, grabbing the two closest to hand and carefully deposited them upright in the front section of the trolley where they made the perfect likeness of twin babies in the child seat, wild new born hair in spikes, not all that dissimilar to River's – or her own on a windswept morning on Glastonbury Tor. She couldn't help but let out a giggle at the synchronicity given her recent cunning plan, upon which River eyed her, curiously.

"What was all that about then?" she asked, averting him from her childish behaviour.

"Leeroy's only been promoted to Assistant Manager."

"He's what?"

"Lee, he's *going up in the world*."

That was an all too obvious dig at her earlier comment which she'd sarcastically assumed he hadn't heard. She'd have to be more careful around him, she was starting to realise he wasn't quite as naïve as she'd previously thought, although quite how he'd still not twigged she'd pilfered the Spanish letter, was anybody's guess.

"But Blake's been working here eighteen months longer than Lee, how's that for dedication?" she snapped back as he burdened her with a heavy netted bag full of Seville oranges. "Ever since he's stopped doing the night shift and got together with that short-arse Jonie, it's like he thinks he's a cut above or something. He's lucky Blake is still working nights. There's no way he'd stand for taking orders from *that*."

"Oh for crying out loud, Georgina, why can't you just be happy for him? He's had an opportunity and he's taken it, that's all," said River, flinging a bag of limes into the trolley, grinning bizarrely like the Cheshire Cat in an undeniable attempt to blind Lee with the flash of his teeth even from afar.

She wanted to loathe him for that remark.

Yet these weeks without him wouldn't allow hatred to completely consume her heart. And that's because she was in love with him, the bastard. Why couldn't he trade that pony tail for a man bun and make things easier for her?

She'd been as sure as hell that she'd built a fortress around the word 'emotion' when she'd entered those tween years, but it was becoming more apparent by the day that she hadn't tended to the cracks. She'd let her guard down big time and he'd turned her into that pathetic teenage tomboy again, the one who masks her insecurities by clothing like the unassuming girl with the pudding basin haircut; the one who simultaneously embraces the masculinity *and* convenient hiding place of the shell part of shell suit, the one who gazes adoringly at those cult *Athena* posters of the man and the baby, and the *Smash Hits* pull outs of Robbie Williams, with Mark and Howard vying for second place, Gary coming in third at a push; all safe bets, as good as fictional characters in a story book. Apart from Jason, who never got a look in, *poor Jason*. But it was easier on the heart that way. When your own mother abandons you as a child, never again will you be foolish enough to let anybody else get close to you.

Love and hate; a potent mix when they strike at the same time, and, like a desperate teenager, clinging to a rock of nothingness, now that she truly knew Blake's anguish over Alice, she also knew she was ready.

Chapter Twenty-Eight
RIVER

"Oh my God, you won't believe what's happened!"

River, bogged down with sterilising his worktops before bar opening time, inventing a plausible excuse not to open Cassandra's cattery, as well as the mild depression that was already taking hold over Alice, had long forgotten to look out for the latest signs of improvement in Lee's life.

"What's up? Traffic jam on the High Street because my mum and Dawn Brierley are doing another of their peace marches?"

"No, no, no, nothing like that, are you going to listen, or not? This is crazy, absolutely bat shit crazy." Lee paced the length of the bar and back again as would a soldier outside Buckingham Palace. "But I'm telling you, it's true. I don't know how, or why, and I'm not about to put it down to that blessed cocktail… but on the other hand maybe it actually—"

River stopped his circular scrubbing motions. It was working. It really was working. Mercedes was right. His intuition to trust her, no matter how out of his head that made him feel, was right. Lee didn't have to say anything. He could feel it. This new energy that surrounded him was palpable. River might not have been able to detect auras and weird things like that, much to Heather's dismay, but he could feel Lee's vibration, raised up several notches, inexplicable, wonderful and mesmerising all at once.

"You had me at hello," said River, throwing his cloths into the sink and then seizing the bar's edge as if he were about to play a little Mozart to heighten the drama of the moment. "I'm listening."

"So," said Lee, seated now, swivelling round and round on

the bar stool, as impatient as a child in an old-fashioned sweet shop waiting for his quarter of Rhubarb and Custards to be weighed and bagged up. "Jonie proposed to me last night."

River, speechless at first, slowly began to jump up and down, and then before he knew it he was fist pumping, too, in that pathetic 'Get In' way that all modern footballers seem to have to sign contracts to do the very moment a camera pans into their line of vision.

"Hey, congratulations, mate." He finally stopped moving and found some words. "Let me fix you up a little something on the house to celebrate. Although, I suppose you're obliged to ask Blake to be Best Man—"

"Pff, I've not got that far in the planning. But yeah... do crack open a bottle, I'm gonna need at least two of something strong before I leave here and make a decision. Couldn't you bend the rules to three cocktails though... pretty please, just for me, seeing's I'm an old friend and all?"

"You're a current friend as much as an old one and you damn well know the answer to that already. But what do you mean, make a decision? What's to think about? It's a no-brainer, surely? She's a lovely girl and you're smitten with her, sail off into the sunset and enjoy your happily ever after, how many of us get the chance?"

He cursed himself quietly for letting his head swim with Alice all over again.

"No, I don't mean Jonie. Of course I said yes, didn't flinch to hesitate. Was even starting to dream up scenarios of me asking her myself. But I'm glad she beat me to it, I'd have been my usual car crash of a nervous wreck unable to get my words out. In the end she asked me going down on one knee in the fruit and veg aisle."

"Romantic. That's um, well, it's original."

"See, that's what I love about her. She's one of a kind, my Jonie, and that aisle means everything to us. It's where she first asked me out, after two days of flirting when we were reducing the prices of the corn on the cobs."

"Nice."

"What I mean is... this."

177

Lee looked this way and that over each shoulder, before slowly, with very measured actions, producing something that looked uncannily like a lottery ticket.

"I kid you not... I've only gone and won the weekend's jackpot."

"What?" River almost toppled backwards.

"Yeah," Lee frowned. "All six numbers, been playing every Saturday since I was old enough and finally me numbers came up. So that's it now, destiny ruined by a dumb piece of paper."

"H...h...h...how so?"

River's language struggled to make it out as a stuttered whisper now. This sudden news was unbelievable; things were happening for Lee dizzyingly fast, River could barely register the latest revelation. First a gargantuan promotion, then a proposal and now a mammoth lottery win, all in the space of a couple of weeks.

"Magic catches like that, it's wildfire," Mercedes whispered from nowhere, so that River was forced to examine Lee's face to see if he'd heard her too – apparently, fortunately, not.

"Just shy of two point five million, that's my share. According to the bloke I spoke with on the phone at HQ anyway. There were only two of us that hit it last week, me and some other poor unsuspecting sod. Why did I bother playing? Now I've got a meeting with him and some other *Lotto* official, plus a financial advisor. They lay all this stuff on and give you a chat and some tips as to how to deal with the queue of scroungers you can expect to attract, not to mention the likes of the red-topped papers poking their noses in."

Lee sighed, right fist supporting his out-turned bottom lip, just like he used to during those hot, sticky GCSE exams in the school gym when he evidently hadn't a clue what was being asked of him.

Huh, like he'd ever needed that shiny string of A-C grades anyway.

"I mean, who really and truly stops to think through the impact this kind of money is going to have on their life?" Lee continued. "Nah, instead we just blindly put our two quid on, week in week out, oblivious to the catastrophe we're inviting to happen. But I want this marriage to be built on a stronger foundation… and now this has come along and just swiped that away from me in a heartbeat. There's always charity I s'pose… but the chances are, any donation I make in this gossip crazy town, will soon become public… and then Jonie will up and leave me because I gave all our money away to a donkey sanctuary."

Sanctuary.

Did he have to mention that word? River didn't need any more reminders today that he still hadn't found his get out clause for Saturday's date with Jane Austen and her furry friends.

Two men were engulfed in silence. One sitting, one standing, until River knew it was his turn to offer up some advice.

"Want me to let you into a little secret?" He coughed in a bid to calm himself down again, like that might also help him locate his voice.

"Well yeah, okay," said Lee, still looking as glum as could be. "Shoot for the stars but I doubt it'll make any difference."

"Give or take a few hundred thousand, you and I have a rather similar looking net worth."

"Geez Louise. You're joking, right?"

"No, I am not." River moved his head from side to side to further reassure.

"Well then what did *you* squander it on? And more to the point, why are you still driving around in that hideous excuse for a motor?"

"I've been a bit boring, true; a tad sensible. But I'm proof that you can come into money – and mine also came in pretty thick and fast…" He turned, suddenly regaining his composure to gather a selection of bottles, since a stiff drink could not come soon enough for the both of them. "Put it this way," he continued, "I never really had chance to spend it, that's how quickly it was piling up. What I mean to say is you can be a multimillionaire without it running your life; you can do it in such a way as to enhance what you have. It's all about staying grounded. That's it. Find the thing you're passionate about, and follow it. Refuse to get entrapped by life's falsities."

"Can I ask you something?" River plonked the bottles down and carried on with his interrogation anyway. "Would you still have said yes if Jonie had popped the question after your balls had been picked?"

"Such a way with words, Riv... such a way with words."

"Well, are you going to answer my question?"

"Yes. Not a doubt about it."

"There then. That tells you all you need to know... but also that you owe *me* a big fat drink as a thank you for having the inspiration to walk to Tequila that day."

"I'm still not convinced about that story, you know."

"You will be soon. Things are only warming up."

***

River faltered, paper in hand; one last look at Alice's hastily penned words before he decided if this gave him permission to investigate.

"*...weekend break in the city... maybe longer, really not sure. Not sure about anything anymore to tell you the truth. Something's come up, got to get my head together. Don't want to hold you back. Will love you forever for all you have done for me. Alice xx*"

Autopilot – and the Black Russian he'd shared with Lee half an hour earlier – took over his logical mind. The next thing he knew, he was calling the number at the top of the taxi company's headed paper receipt, and then waiting, nervously, for somebody to pick up the receiver.

"I've been expecting this... to be honest, like." The woman on the other end of the call let out a deep breath, and, if he wasn't mistaken, appeared to be simultaneously munching on a packet of crisps. "I'll call into the bar, gimme five." And with that she'd hung up on him before he'd even had chance to protest.

"I didn't mean right now," River said to the four walls.

He walked over to the door, twisted the sign to 'closed', and waited at the nearest table so the driver wouldn't escape his notice when she did arrive, fingers drumming in anticipation. How had he been so bloody jejune as to take Alice's erratic words at face value? He stared at them again, suddenly realising they were nothing but a lie laced with anger, fear and upset. There was clearly more to all of this than met the eye and had he only been more tuned in from the start, she'd still be here now, helping him prep for the evening, spoon feeding him with jokes, coming out with long forgotten snippets about the past, further cementing their bond.

No way was she in London. Yet if she'd got a taxi all the way to either one of the two closest cities to Glastonbury, who did she know in Bristol, or Bath?

An excitable shadow blocked the stream of daylight which would usually illuminate the bar through the sheer glass door at this time of day. Intuition told him it wouldn't be long before this woman spilled some seriously helpful beans, and so he let her in with a welcome smile, and the offer of a strong drink.

***

"Well this is like one of them deja-vus," said the woman matter-of-factly, adding a quite non-essential snort. She'd thanked River for his cocktail offer, opted for a non-alcoholic Mexican Limeade and then insisted upon taking him to Bath Spa train station immediately, not before outstretching her hand for a business deal kind of a shake. "I'm Hayley by the way, never did introduce myself to your... to Alice."

"Are you sure about this?" he'd asked. "It's more than hospitable, and I'm more than happy to drive – the both of us – if you think you can help sniff out some clues."

"And miss the opportunity to give a lift to the original frontman of Avalonia? Not a snowflake's chance in hell."

Somehow he didn't dare challenge her.

"I'll have to get your autograph before the day's out, mind."

Hayley snapped him back to the present and the fact that they were approaching the nearest car park to the station.

"I'll have to park her up here, else there'll be every man and his dog trying to get me to ferry them about in Jane Austen Ville if I chance it for a local taxi rank."

The bust of Cassandra tilted her head back and laughed at the way she'd weaseled her way into his life for the third time that day, until he blinked her ferociously away.

"Good idea." River nodded as if he knew all about the logistics of cab parking. "And thank you, Hayley, once again. This is over and above the call of duty."

"You're most welcome, Sir. No... sit... I insist... it's my prerogative to open your door for you."

River had gathered by now that it was easiest at all times to agree with this lady.

"I'm not sure what I think I'm after here," he said, as they crossed the road moments later and entered the main building. "But I guess there could be a notice board, or maybe we could ask the station master if there's some way they can give us access to camera footage?"

"Hardly likely, total invasion of privacy." Hayley frowned at the suggestion and River berated himself immediately for his ridiculous and very desperate clutch at straws.

"What does she mean to you: Alice?"

"Hey? Where did that come from?"

"Well, I get the feeling you're both dodging each other politely, when what you're really wanting is to just *get it on*. You might have spared yourself all of this bother if you hadn't insisted on playing silly games. What is it with men and freakin' dating games? Don't even get me started on my last boyfriend's constant messing me about like we were on a Snakes and Ladders board."

"All right, all right calm down!" River was stunned at Hayley's impetuous words; to an outsider she must have looked like his bolshy big sister. "You sure you don't want to take a seat and let me see if I can find you a shrink while we're here?"

"I'm right though, aren't I?" she ignored him.

"In a way... yes... perhaps," he conceded.

"See, I've seen enough of this over the years, in and out of the cab, as well as my own private life, should have a degree in Psychology, me."

That threw River back once again to the degree he himself had walked out on. Perhaps if he had followed it through things wouldn't be the catastrophe they were revealing themselves to be before his very eyes – oh, and he might have some kind of a light bulb moment as to where Alice would take herself next.

In the end it was Hayley who provided that, River having unsuccessfully scoured the station's entrance, while she strolled the platform, authoritatively hunting for clues.

"Now she did go on about her love of horses briefly... for the short amount of time I could get any small talk out of her on the journey, at any rate."

"And?"

Hayley breathed in through her nose as would a matriarchal dragon, rankled by its slow-to-catch-on young. Just as she pointed at a notice board at the doorway leading on to platform one; the doorway River had failed to as much as notice, Mercedes' voice whispered lightly in his ear: "Yes."

River walked, half-possessed by the murmur which had already vanished, until he reached the notice board. And there it was, clear as day.

"Strawberry pickers wanted; additional expertise with horses preferable. Live-in summer job, small wage, great benefits."

All of which sounded like the epitome of cons, a magnet for anybody down on their luck, and a quaint little disguise for modern day slavery, all rolled into one. But still, he was in no doubt that this was the detour Alice had taken. He ripped the notice down, at which point a steely-eyed station official began to march forward, mouth open to say something equally stern, until Hayley made herself Piggy in the Middle, hands on hips, glare unbending, putting paid to any attempt of reprimand. The worker retreated Michael Jackson style in an unusual moonwalk, best left to drunken uncles in white patent

183

loafers on wedding dance floors. And Hayley took River under the bingo wing of her arm, a quick peek at the address on the notice, as they paced back to the taxi.

***

They didn't have to look far once they'd sped past the rural clotted cream fudge factory on the city's outskirts, and on into the village beyond it. Alice was sitting atop a wobbly stone wall, sandwich in hand, chatting to a girl, both of them presumably taking an afternoon tea break.

"Well that's something, they can't be quite as harsh as these slave drivers you read about in the papers if they're keeping them fed and watered. But still, your Alice wants to put several stone on, let alone pounds. She's got to weigh a quarter of me," said Hayley, as she rustled in the sweet bag nestled dangerously close to her handbrake and popped a handful of *Jelly Babies* into her mouth.

"Al, what's happened? Please come back," River's words jumped out of the taxi before him, and he walked after them, carefully towards the woman he loved, fearful that if he came on too strong, she might scurry off like a field mouse.

Alice looked plain startled. She muttered something that sounded decidedly French to the younger girl, evidently a worker in her checked shirt and dirty jeans, and then swung her own body over the back of the border and into the strawberry field.

"You! I trusted you... all your sworn secrecy with your chitchat about the stars and their confidentiality. What a crock of shit that was!"

Alice pressed her palms down on the wall now, sandwich discarded to a cranny of its stonework; she was a gymnast about to vault over the horse, an angry gymnast at that. Alice's friend headed back to the farmhouse alone, looking back over her shoulder uncertainly.

Don't you dare have any grand plans to call any rifle-toting farmers down! With any luck, River would get Alice to come to her senses in minutes, even if that came to some serious

184

financial bargaining with the landowner.

"You gave yourself away, me number was on the taxi receipt, sweetheart. What man wasn't going to call it to try and find you?"

Hayley popped her head out the window to add her pearls of wisdom. Magically, this seemed to soften things.

"I actually wished you'd come sooner... it sucks here, Riv."

Alice put her head in her strawberry-stained hands, slunk down against the jagged wall and began to cry. Huge fat tears. River was all a dither.

"Are you happy to wait here a bit?" he shouted back to Hayley.

"All in a day's work, I've got my *Jelly Babies*... might have to call into that fudge factory's shop on the way home, mind... that'll keep me energised 'till supper."

He leapt over the wall. "Christ, she's a case, that one... bet you enjoyed the journey to the station."

They both laughed then and Alice spurted out the entire backstory. From start to finish, not a middle bit of Georgina's declaration left out.

"Why that twisted little... just you wait until I see her."

"River, no: you're not like that, you've never been like that, and you're not going to start being like that now."

He looked to Alice, only to see it wasn't her who had uttered those words.

Chapter Twenty-Nine
GEORGINA

"George: outside, this instant."

Holy moly! What now?

Just when everything was nice and cushy; okay, so even though she had him all to herself, romance had unofficially died, and she was all out of ideas as to how she could reignite that again. The short skirts and occasional flash of her backside when she bent over – which was with an embarrassing frequency, her desperation for some flirting forcing her to throw napkins, straws and spoons in all directions – making no odds at all to the frustrating secret loyalty of River's eyes.

"I've got a bone to pick with you. Alice claims you told her that you're pregnant, and that's what that whole episode upstairs was about the other weekend."

That rotten cow! How dare she resume contact?

Georgina smiled sweetly and quickly, her brain sharp enough to realise he wouldn't believe a lie, not like this, so she'd change the story slightly.

"I had," she paused to inhale deeply, "a miscarriage, actually, River… if you must know. Not that my private life is any concern of yours nowadays. Happy now?" She lowered her head for effect.

Oh, the magic of her zippy calculating mind to have this wrapped up in seconds as per usual.

"So you're suggesting that Alice has a hearing problem?"

He was unbelievable. Georgina was stunned that this hadn't silenced him, let alone not had his conscience firing off questions as to his potential involvement.

"I'm suggesting," she brought her head up now, eyes

flitting between his and her stomach which she covered protectively, "that you take a very large hint and ask me no further questions. You've no idea what I've been going through, no idea at all."

"I don't know what to think any more, really I don't." He bit his lip, shook his head and then stopped to sweep a hand through his hair. "If it wasn't for your dad and my mum, I'd have asked you to kindly move on already. You're not a team player, George. I took you on in good faith… albeit under regrettably sordid circumstances… circumstances which suited the both of us at the time. But things are different now. We've had our fun, we're colleagues and the bar is growing. Al's back on board for as long as it takes to find her a decent job elsewhere. You're just going to have to accept that and frankly muck in or check out."

"Well that's just charming! Do you talk to all your staff like that when they've lost a baby, *your* baby… as if I needed to make it any clearer, to spell all the letters out for—"

"I've heard enough, Georgina!"

River cut in, hand in the air now as if to halt any remaining flurry of words.

"*If* that's the truth then I'm sorry, for my part in it, really I am. But firstly, you assured me you were taking the pill… and you… well, you're just something else altogether, aren't you? I mean never mind the boy who cried wolf…" he paused to take a breath, to gather his next flurry of words. "In any case, it's over now, and this dialogue totally redundant. A child, between the two of us, just no… as insensitive as this is going to sound, I'm going to say it: what life would it have had?"

She couldn't believe what she was hearing, had she truly been pregnant, oh, how those words would have stung. But more than anything, she couldn't believe that an annoying little waif had more front than she herself did, straying just a little while to fool her, but now here she was back again from Cali-flippin-fornia, presumably, for Round Two. Well, you know what, 'Al' – *and since when had he started calling her Al?* – bring it on. And bring it on with bells on, the jinglier the better.

187

And as for that love rat who had made her fall in love with him, well, he was taking absolute liberties now in every sense of the word. Whereas most when they were in trouble would cringe deeply at the mention of their full name, Georgina felt her buttons pushed when anybody dared to shorten it; it was like they'd cut off her significance or something, diminished her universal existence with the chop of a knife through a particular arrangement of the alphabet. River Jackson had not only dared to do it.

But he'd dared to do it twice.

All of which seemed to be the natural conclusion to the end of their affair, and goddammit, she was the one who terminated the contracts in that department; which was precisely why Operation Payback would officially start that very night.

Chapter Thirty
ALICE

You can be sure there's something quite genuine about a man whose weekend priority is opening a cat sanctuary. A few days after Hayley and River had rescued Alice from the hell that was fruit picking with the offer of a very occasional horse riding session at a discounted rate; a discounted rate which happened to be give or take a day's wages, she found herself beaming in a rather sedated crowd as Glastonbury's Hero cut the white satin ribbon to officially open Cassandra's Cat Sanctuary.

Then the throng cheered, ramping the festivities up several notches, Alice included.

And he was a hero. What other way was there to describe River? Once again, he had come to her rescue, stopping at nothing, even paying Hayley quadruple the fare to rope her into rescuing Jocelyne, the French student too, transporting her back to the safety of Dover where she boarded the last ferry of the day over to Calais as a foot passenger, vowing to return to the parents who were worried sick about her when she'd fled her village home as a teenage Goth and made off for Paris.

"You wanna keep hold of that one." Hayley nudged her out of her daydream, quite from nowhere, almost knocking her down like a skittle. But Alice had warmed to her now, how could she not?

"Definitely," she replied. "But one step at a time, I feel like a hamster on a wheel at the moment, at least let me step off and take a breather before romance fills the air."

"Romance has an agenda of its own, I think you'll find," said Hayley, looking sentimentally into the distance. "You couldn't stop it if you tried."

189

Alice watched with curiosity as Hayley sniffed the air, evidently picking out the cocktail sausages, and cheese and pineapples on sticks which she made an immediate beeline for; hideously, unbelievably, all were being served up on the same platter. She definitely wouldn't be partaking.

The Rigby-Chandlers began to march towards her then, and as the waiter dilly-dallied behind Alice with a most timely tray of champagne flutes, she grabbed two swiftly, thankful for the diversion they'd provide during this imminent exchange. If River wasn't done with his mingling soon enough, she'd drink his as well, anything to ease the pain of the next however many minutes; it wasn't like there was anybody else nearby – at least not anybody she knew, who could spare her.

"Alice, sweetie," Lady Rigby-Chandler air kissed her, standing back to look her up and down in a way that either would or would not meet with her approval. "Do you realise just how worried your poor papa has been about you? Where in God's name did you disappear?" she said through the customary twist of her mouth.

"Probably back into the arms of that double-barrelled what's-his-name from Beverly Hills." Lord Rigby-Chandler broke his habitual second in command silence and let out a gargantuan chortle.

"He comes from Bel-Air actually, your Lordship," Alice couldn't help but courtesy, the Ps and Qs of her noble upbringing overbearing as ever in the face of a couple of fellow toffs, a label which hung to her own clothing by the dangle of a very thin thread nowadays. "And it's not a double-barrelled name, but the typical American trait of using one's Christian and middle name... which would appear to make one more prominent in the film industry... think Jamie Lee Curtis, for example."

"Ew, I'd really rather he did not!" Lady Rigby-Chandler retorted. "What a hussy that woman was in *A Fish Called Wanda*. Lord R-C and I had to abandon the theatre when we went to watch that most common, alarmingly cheesy portrayal of a heist on a rainy Tuesday afternoon in the eighties. Never again."

"Cinema, my Lady, cinema."

"Theatre, my Lord, theatre. And anyway, that's by the by. Your father, as I mentioned, has been most perturbed by your vanishing act."

"Mummy less so, I gather."

"Well, can you blame her, dear? How many years have you spent out of her keep? Not even a postcard or a telegram to inform her of your whereabouts."

Alice didn't have the patience or inclination to recount the tale of her mother slamming the door in her face just a few weeks ago, an act which made it perfectly clear she preferred the company of de-crusted cucumber sandwiches to that of her own daughter.

"A telegram?"

"Oh, you know full well what I mean, Alice, a whatsit... an email... same thing, same thing."

Poor Lady R-C, she was positively marooned in the sixties with its debutant's balls, pomp and ceremony, order and regalia, Stepford Wives in twinsets and pearls, sweet nostalgic Victorian Christmas cards handwritten with quills. Please somebody shoot Alice if she ever clung so tightly to her youth. Life was change and change was life.

"I was on the outskirts of Bath, if you must know, picking fruit with foreign workers... mucking out horses and living on bread and water."

"Why, how absolutely frightful for you, my dear... whatever possessed you, Alice? And how could that so-called *friend* of yours allow it?"

"Awlright?"

Hayley sandwiched her way between the small gathering now and Alice couldn't have loved her more for it. "Oh, you saved me one, Al, how very kind." She swiped at the spare flute in Alice's left hand and began to swig hastily, blissfully unaware of the double entendre in her words.

"My goodness," said Lady Rigby-Chandler. "It really does take all sorts. First I'm declined by my dear friend, Cassandra, who would rather have a pony-tailed, bearded ex rocker to open up her home for moggies... not to mention that carrot-

191

topped commoner over there…" she circled her hand as would The Queen waving from her jewel-encrusted horse and carriage, in the direction of a smooching couple, who Alice instantly recognised as Jonie and Lee, both resting cosily against his recently upgraded car on the waste ground to the left of Cassandra's house.

Alice raised her eyebrows, at a loss as to why anybody could be disenchanted by Lee's presence, social act of passion aside, on that note she had to agree with her ladyship: get a room or go to the seventh *arrondissement*.

"Didn't you know?" Lady Rigby-Chandler continued, "Apparently he's footing the champagne and canapé bill. With what exactly, one can only hazard a guess, but it certainly can't be his poxy salary from that banal excuse for a supermarket that no doubt pays in shirt buttons…"

"Is he really?"

Alice could hardly believe it herself, far be it for her to stereotype, but that was one grandiose act of generosity. Sure, River was opening the sanctuary, but that hardly put him out of pocket, only added to the bar's popularity really.

"Well, what a lovely fella," Hayley interrupted again without having introduced herself, or as much as been granted the chance for Alice to do so – to be fair, Lady Rigby-Chandler would insist on hogging the conversation. "For he's a jolly good fella… for he's a jolly good feller," she began to sing.

"Next," Lady Rigby-Chandler cut her up, "I'm witnessing the mixing of not so much upper class with middle class, but nigh on aristocracy with the scrapings of the barrel of working class suburbia… and a token cat's choir – whatever next?" she carried on, unmoved by anybody's endorsement of Lee. "I bid you good day." She looked solely at Alice and pivoted to commence a prompt high-heeled march across the undulating meadow.

"Blimey, who rattled her cage?" said Hayley, with one of her hallmark snorts of indifference.

"I rather think you'll find that was me, the moment I married her," said Lord Rigby-Chandler, as he saluted Alice and Hayley to signal his presence here was very much over and out, and scurried to keep up with his wife who had by now randomly fled to join Heather and Terry up near the main house.

Evidently *their* social status had somehow mysteriously just gone up several notches.

Chapter Thirty-One
RIVER

"How about some pudding?"

Terry rubbed his hands together with the intensity of Ray Mears about to start up a bush fire.

"Not for me, thanks, Dad," said Georgina.

"Why what's up with you, my love? That's not like you at all. They've got chocolate brownie, your favourite. And you've not touched more than a drop of your wine since River poured it."

"I'm just not feeling my usual self, that's all."

Fear wrangled with River's stomach then, not that he had much of a sweet tooth either himself, but he certainly wouldn't be doing anything that gave Terry chance to insinuate that he and his daughter were like two peas in a pod. But then he remembered she'd had a miscarriage. If indeed that was even true – since it was highly likely she'd faked the entire idea of a pregnancy. So then she was simply feeling a little drained, that was all; in which case surely the most sensible thing would have been to stay at home.

"Well, I'm having the lemon cheesecake," River announced, "Al, are you joining me?"

"Don't you go telling me you're dieting too, Alice," said Terry. "You're skin and bone as it is."

River could sense the red mist that was the inevitable envy in Georgina's frown without even needing to look at it for validation.

"Okay, why not, it's been years since I've had a cheesecake," Alice replied.

"Oh my God, Al, do you remember the size of that slice we had after Lennie took us all ice skating at The Rockefeller

Center in New York that December?"

"For heaven's sakes, don't let it be that colossal!"

Alice laughed and River joined her, the chemistry between them fizzing and popping across the table, until Heather, Terry and Georgina, the rest of the diners besides, could have been spectators of a merry-go-round, one they were unable to hop onto to join them, their curious faces blurring at the edges while the figures at the centre fell ever deeper into love's inescapable centrifuge.

"Are you ready to place your orders now?" The waiter semi-snapped them out of it.

"What… what… um… what about you, Heather?"

River's heart skipped a beat as Alice leaned in closer to his mum, her eyes unable to leave his.

Was this it, her reciprocation that she was equally smitten; her invitation to permanently be that little bit more than just good friends?

He felt a twinge of shame as he remembered Georgina was also sitting at the table, but wild horses couldn't have broken this public interchange. How were they going to contain themselves when they got back to the caravan tonight? God, he didn't want them to contain themselves! He wanted all of Alice, now, every inch of her body. Why of all the inconvenient bloody moments in time did she have to make it clear to him she wanted him too, sat in a country pub surrounded by villagers and tourists and well-meaning 'family' and waiters taking orders for cheesecake whose indigestible morsels would cloy at the throat because frankly, some people had very different things on their minds?

"I think I'll go for the steamed ginger pudding, no custard though… well, unless you have lactose-free, organic in the kitchen?"

"Sorry, we don't." The waiter's eyes were scrunched up now, mouth resembling an exasperated bullfrog.

"Typical, any pub remotely outside of Glastonbury and the words 'allergy' and 'organic' are received as if I were speaking in tongues," said Heather. "It's okay, I've brought my own supply." And she bent then to rather embarrassingly retrieve a

195

small ethnically-printed carton from her bag. "No point in me checking if you've subbed sugar for stevia in the pudding," she continued, "then again, I'm pretty sure your chef wouldn't dream of baking ginger with a white refined sugar... oh well, if it's muscovado or golden granulated, it's hardly going to kill me, just this once I suppose."

"I'll join her," said Terry, adding an apologetic facial expression to the waiter. "So that's two steamed ginger puddings, just to be clear. Good old regular custard for me though."

The waiter disappeared with a sigh, and Georgina pushed her chair backwards then, too.

"Sorry... got to run to the ladies," she announced, standing quickly with one hand pressed over her stomach.

Thankfully, Alice hadn't noticed. Something about her had changed this afternoon. She was dazzling, not that her beauty ever escaped her for a moment, even when she was sobbing into strawberry-stained hands; those irises had the power to captivate, overruling the puffy red rims of her eyes. In fact he would go as far as to say she'd changed so much, that if he wasn't completely mistaken, her now un-booted foot was travelling the length of his thigh, caressing it sensually, sending a lightning bolt up his denim-clad legs, through his boxer shorts and beyond.

Oh hell.

This was good, it was very good; it boded well for the kind of future he had recently thought he could only dream of. But at this precise moment in time, it was hardly convenient, and it was all he could do not to develop a sudden ingenious code language which would see them wink conspiratorially to find their individual excuses to leave the table – in exchange for one of those giant, bouncy looking haystacks in the field beyond.

If she was this naughty now, what was she going to do to him later?

He had to play hard to get, just for a short while. But moments later, he too had freed foot from shoe, and, whilst trying desperately not to think about the stink of his socks – or the fact that Georgina would be reunited with them at any moment, not to mention the dreaded challenge of eating a heavy slice of cheesecake – he slid his foot slowly, sexily, from the tip of her toe to the length of her thigh. Alice let out a gasp, a gasp which was timed to perfection: the waiter appeared with their dessert, and in the distance, an unusually pale-faced, sweaty Georgina trundled behind.

"Right then," said Terry, as soon as he'd hacked away the tough recycled cardboard corner from Heather's special custard carton, and everyone – except Georgina – was digging in. "I've got an announcement to make."

Could the meal get any more eventful? But please, not a marriage proposal. River wasn't ready to walk his mother up the aisle. Playing Best Man to Lee was marital excitement enough for one year – unless of course Alice cared to flirt with that idea – and now he placed his foot back onto her shin, rubbing seductively, well, as seductively as one could when they were faced with a breaking news story and half a pound of cream cheese.

Faces turned expectantly to Terry. River braced himself for the inevitable, somehow resisting the urge to check up on Alice's facial expression.

"So… the other day, when I was propped up against the bar, having a good old gas with Jacob and Ryan… this were up at The Pear Tree though… sorry River, hope you don't think I'm being disloyal, but sometimes I do miss my cider," – hang on, did he just say what River thought he said… that he was chatting… like a normal, *accepting* human being… to the very gay couple he was spitting feathers at for their sexuality just weeks ago? – "a certain somebody approached me."

Here we go: Mum, ever the goddess, had gone and popped Terry the question. He knew it.

"This certain somebody happened to be a TV exec… producer… thingummyjig, whatever you call them nowadays. Well, any rate, he's working on a brand new show – this is strictly confidential mind, you lot, you've gotta promise me you won't say a word… well," Terry looked to Heather, "I know you won't, my love."

"Get to the point, Dad, so we can get the bill and get out of here," said Georgina, hand glued to her glass of water which she seemed to be constantly draining.

"All right, love, don't rain on me parade."

"Your daughter has got a point though," said Heather, "I'm not sure I've ever met anybody with such a tendency to waffle… much as I love you."

Georgina could have rolled the cloth from the table with her eyeballs.

Heather snuggled closer to Terry anyway, putting River in mind of a baby animal. He shook his head, somehow simultaneously ensuring his foot was still doing its thing, and Terry went on:

"Okay, okay, so, the TV bloke, well, he's in the area filming, like. Works for one of them companies that go around doing up posh houses… and he's looking for people – tradespeople – to star in the show."

Georgina rolled her eyes again. "Please don't tell me you've put yourself forward—"

"As a matter of fact, George, yes, I have."

She tutted.

"And, why shouldn't he?" Alice couldn't seem to help but grill her.

"Just butt out," Georgina slammed down her water glass, "you know naff all about my family."

"Georgina!" That was Heather.

"Oh, so what is this now? Daggers at Georgina day? Am I now not allowed to have an opinion? Do none of you realise I know my own dad better than all of you put together."

"That's as maybe, but you don't know me better than I know myself."

"Fine, tell your dumb story, I'm going out to wait by the car." She snatched at her bag and stormed out of the pub, leaving the muttering diners to guess at the roots of her problem behind her.

River instinctively returned his foot to his shoe then sensing things would be winding up here quickly enough.

"I'm sorry," Terry shook his head. "I just don't know

what's got into her lately."

"Anyway, where was I? Oh yes, so myself and Jacob and Ryan, we're all chatting at the bar and this bloke comes to join us. Course, Jacob is a dab hand at plastering, Ryan runs his own fancy doing up houses business—"

"I think you mean he's an Interior Designer, Terry," Heather chimed in, nodding at the details of the story as they replayed themselves for what must have been the umpteenth time.

"Yes, yes, one of them, that's what I meant. But the funniest thing of all is," Terry slapped his hand down on the table, laughter creasing the corners of his eyes, "they're only looking to film and renovate The Rigby-Chandlers' palace!"

"No way."

River was astounded, forgetting initially that Terry had drunk the Magical Mañana, that he should already have been able to see the very clear path this story was taking him on.

Like yesterday.

"Yes way, River," he replied. "But there's more… there's more." Terry simmered to a half-whisper now, suddenly plugged in to the attention of the neighbouring table. He leaned in and encouraged River, Alice and Heather to bring their upper halves forward to almost touch the bread basket too. "After chatting with us three at the bar for the best part of an hour, he only went and offered us contracts to appear on the show. How's that for a turnout? We're doing up The Rigby-Chandler's house… and we're gonna be on the telly!"

It beat a marriage proposal to his mum that was for sure. What were the chances of any of this sequence of events happening had Terry not had the cocktail? A TV Exec, no matter their pecking order in the hierarchical chain, would hardly choose The Pear Tree as their first port of call under normal circumstances.

The bottle was definitely weaving its wonder. And all of this proved his own past thoughts about the aristocrats' freeloading right; something was clearly afoot in his Lady and Lordship's lives. No wonder they'd found a reason to bribe him for free drinks and had then clung onto it for dear life.

Their regular jaunts to The Cocktail Bar were quite possibly the only thing keeping them going. And now, presumably, they were going to get paid for their appearance as well, not to mention the great publicity the very public renovation would bring. Next thing the world knew, they'd be seeing Lady R-C gracing the screens of *I'm A Celebrity Get Me Out Of Here*.

River excused himself amidst the bubbling enthusiasm of the table, went to the toilets, and was briefly consumed by a bizarre white powdery trail. It seemed to lead into the Ladies; on first glance it resembled talc – the heavily perfumed stuff old ladies use, and for some reason, here it was decorating the busily patterned and carpeted floor. On second glance, he'd convinced himself it was cocaine.

Blimey!

Who'd have thought it, out here in the safe, timid countryside? It was true what they said, as much as Glastonbury was the pigeon-holed drugs capital of the entire nation, in actual fact all that assumption really did was act as a cover-up for what was really going on in the most unassuming of locations.

He walked on into the gents, lifted the seat of the toilet and peed into its rim, more than aware of someone chatting in the car park outside, so he squinted through the small gap where the porthole of a window sat above the cistern, eyes taking in the figure of Georgina, all fired up and talking to *someone* on her mobile phone.

He finished his business, pulled the flush, and waited several seconds for the silence which ensued. Call it instinct but something told him to hover by that window pane.

"Okay, Ara, yeah, everything's in place my side. Chat soon, babe."

Ara?

Frustratingly he missed the beginning part of the name Georgina mentioned – oh, it was definitely a name. Was she out there talking to Tamara on her phone? And then he shook his head and laughed at his crazily warped imagination. Georgina couldn't possibly know Tamara... Of course, who else? It had to be Zara.

To hell with her anyway.

Yes, they may still work together at the moment, but she'd get the message soon enough once romance started heating up with Alice, as only it could.

Chapter Thirty-Two
ALICE

"Did you just hear that?" Alice said loudly, grabbing at the corner of her thin duvet and pressing it against her body to cover her modesty – just about; damn she should have slept in her pyjamas, but it was one of those hot and sticky, unsuspecting Indian monsoon nights, and who expected a visitor at this hour?

She jumped out of bed with a start and fumbled for the light switch, heaving the bedding behind her.

"Hmm?" said River, eyes not quite with the world, so that she wasn't altogether sure if he was in fact, sleepwalking. He reached out for her instinctively as he emerged from his own bedroom and they met in the middle in the caravan's kitchen.

"Stop it, Riv!" she said with a laugh as he moved in for a cheeky embrace, but she was too high on that very unique kind of lust that only comes with love to be able to censor its opaque translation. "I've told you before I can't just jump into bed with you like that... even despite my promiscuity at lunchtime. It was risqué, I know, and perhaps I shouldn't have encouraged you, but I want to take things slowly, to get it right this time."

To be the absolute opposite of Georgina.

"I'm sure it's just your rather excitable imagination," he teased again, eyes very much open now and drinking all of her in, so much so that when she took in the size of his erection through his boxer shorts, she couldn't deny that she too wasn't just a little bit tempted to break her draconic self-imposed rules.

"I'll go see anyway," she said, stealing her eyes away from his groin before he had chance to register their interest.

"Maybe it's Blossom clawing at the door again." Aunt Sheba's cat was treating the caravan as her second home of late. Alice was sure Sheba would highly disapprove of the second helpings she was clandestinely feeding her, but Blossom had the loyalty of a dog, the most irresistible little face.

"Probably… that cat's eating us out of house and bloody home," said River, evidently more than a little miffed he'd been spurned after the tease of the foreplay she'd given him that lunchtime.

But she had to be sure. Sure that *he* was sure more than anything else. It wouldn't do him any harm to serve his apprenticeship, for both of them to truly get to know one another's domestic habits, to decide if they really could tolerate the dirty socks thrown on the floor, the toilet seat that was never put down, the dirty crockery piled up in the sink, the post cocktail snoring, oh, and her badly cooked eggs.

Alice trailed the quilt behind her and made for the door, as if she were trying out her wedding dress for the very first time. Mummy would definitely approve of the Princess Diana-esque length, a little less though if that were sweeping the floor in any kind of nuptials involving River, who paced the short length of the caravan to the left of her, no doubt trying in vain to get everything back under control down below.

Alice turned the key, just about able to make out the silhouette of a woman. Perhaps it was Sheba? The frosted glass made it impossible to pinpoint the figure's facial features and so she opened the door cautiously, taking a couple of steps back as she peered into the darkness, fear now coursing her veins. Why hadn't she let River deal with this? Admittedly, she wasn't one for sexism in the twenty-first century, and she'd more than hedged her bets taking taxis alone and walking back to hotels in strange lands, usually just to defy Lennie who would insist that he accompany Cinderella after the ball. But there was no need to carry on like that now.

She froze to see she had opened the door to Georgina instead of a cat. And at that very same moment, River, evidently to satisfy his own agenda, re-appeared in the kitchen and began to wrap his arms protectively around Alice's waist.

But she was too stunned; too half-asleep herself to protest as she wished to, despite being all too aware she was painting the ultimate portrait of Man Snatcher.

"Well, well, well, isn't this nice and cosy?"

"It's not what it looks like," said Alice defensively.

"It is what it looks like," said River.

"One of you get your story straight, why don't you? Just good friends, hey, Riv? Wasn't that the lie you sold me?" If looks could have killed, River would be taking his last breath about now.

Alice freed herself from his arms, frustrated at River's totally unnecessary knee jerk reaction – which only served to make matters far worse than they needed to be – as well as the unbelievably chilly air which nipped angrily at her décolletage screaming out Somerset's brief summer's end. Just as well too, caravan life, as much as she was grateful for it, was beginning to feel more like being holed up in a greenhouse.

She walked to the kettle, took it to the sink and filled it slowly with water, letting the tap's trickle soothe her momentarily, leaving the two of them to battle this out alone. After all of this, the last thing she wanted was to be caught back up in a ménage a trois. If that was what he'd lured her back to, she may as well be plucking berries from bushes and filling up baskets. If nothing else that storyline was predictable.

"What the frick are you doing here? It's half past one in the morning," snapped River behind her, still guarding the door.

"I left something here so I came back to get it."

"Not at this unsociable hour you don't." Alice turned to see River's arms were folded now in defiance.

"You didn't used to find one-thirty unsociable… or two-thirty… or three, as I recall."

River said nothing. As comebacks went it was a pretty good quip, Alice had to grant Georgina that much.

She sighed deeply instead, flicked the switch down on the kettle, reached for three mugs from the cupboard, threw a tea bag into each of them, and began to walk back to her bedroom, like that might also help to erase the succession of images

204

Georgina had just unhelpfully conjured up.

And then she changed her mind.

"Do you know what?" she said, her words directing her back to the kitchen, where she pushed past River and his cruddy attempt at imitating a bodyguard. "We *are* going to resolve this situation here and now tonight, the three of us, like grown adults, even if that does take until the dawn flipping chorus. I for one have had enough of this. Georgina, come in, you'll catch your death out there. Take a seat, have a drink and then take whatever it is you've left behind—"

"Big hint: it's not me," spat River, his eyes wide with disbelief at her audacity.

"Hilarious." Georgina pushed past him and parked herself onto a seat at the kitchen table as she'd been instructed.

"River?" Alice continued, "Don't just stand there, take up the opposite pew until the kettle's boiled and then get pouring. I'm going to put some clothes on now. No, if you must know," she looked to Georgina now, "your instinct doesn't serve you right; we haven't just had full blown sex, when I'm feeling hot, I always sleep naked."

"With a body like yours, I know I would too." River raised his eyebrows.

"River!" Alice reprimanded him, unable to completely hide the secret pleasure that was all hers.

Oh, how those words swirled in her stomach though. It was all she could do not to lead him to his bed, her bed, any bed behind a very closed door.

Instead she walked with the kind of authority one has when they know not only erotica, but love too, is reciprocated, the deal sealed; back to the bedroom, re-dressing herself in the very clothes he'd wanted to strip her naked from, the clothes from the meal Georgina's father had footed the bill for, and re-emerged to a very awkward atmosphere. River had fixed everybody with their mugs of tea, and Georgina was staring angrily into hers, her silver teaspoon stirring and then poised, stirring and then poised until Alice could take no more.

"For God's sake will you stop making that irritating noise and just fish the tea bag out; here." She pushed forward a saucer inviting its deposit.

Unbelievably, once more, Georgina did as she was told. And then she removed her coat, as if it were her trump card and she'd been waiting for the optimum moment to reveal a pair of breasts nestled in a ridiculously low-cut, skin-clinging top, breasts that had evidently grown an entire cup-size in recent weeks. How had Alice not noticed them at work, at the pub that very afternoon? What exactly was this statement trying to imply? That she'd lied about the miscarriage... something Alice refused to mention. It was obvious Georgina had rehearsed this move a hundred times before coming here in the middle of the night. Sadly for her though, the episode was wasted on River.

And Alice had yo-yoed back and forth for long enough now herself. If this so-called loss had been a lie and this child really was a 'thing' – immediately she felt rather dreadful for silently referring to anybody's unborn baby in that way, but in this case, needs must – the fact remained that not even the poor soul's presence could dim the light that was them: River and Alice. The love of *her life* shoehorning himself back into Georgina's, should a baby indeed turn out to be the course of events, would be cruel, unfair to the infant. And it would never last, not now, anyway. It was too late to rewind, to step back over that fine line.

"Now then, what have you left behind? Because it's not, as River has already made it very clear, him." She turned to Georgina again, her voice awash with sudden pity for this girl who had obviously had the shoddiest of childhoods to turn out quite as precipitated as this.

"Just some toiletries... as well as... uh... the pill... well actually... a whole pack of pills."

"And what's that supposed to mean?" said River.

"That she's left some deodorant behind, some shower gel, some medication too," Alice's hands flailed about wildly. "Could it be any clearer? Okay, Georgina, then drink your tea, get whatever else it is you've got on your chest, well and truly off it, pick up your things and please leave us be. We'll see you in the bar."

Alice more than sensed that all of this was red rag to a bull, a bull who was evidently playing some kind of game, but as she'd realised mere moments ago, she really had now passed the point of caring. Frankly, she'd dealt with bigger things in the band, and in L.A. What threat could a lost twenty-something seriously pose? Sure, she could tip off the media as to their whereabouts, but months had passed now since Avalonia had split, they were yesterday's news and tomorrow's fish and chip papers. And who really cared enough about C-list-now-off-the-list people and their pastimes anyway? Not when there was an endless *pot pourri* of Pippa Middletons and Taylor Swifts to delight the camera's lens and the media's thirst for an exclusive story. And grassing Alice or River up to the paparazzi would hardly score her any of her beloved brownie points.

Speaking of which, it did seem more than a little strange that Georgina wouldn't indulge in one yesterday afternoon in the pub. And then there was the avoidance of the wine. Before she knew it, Alice had let her thoughts come full circle on her once again. That was it. She couldn't bear to look at Georgina for a minute longer.

"Call Hayley to take her home, River, I'll cover the fare. Georgina, you come with me… and take this…" She went to the drawer and pulled out a plastic bag. "Fill it with your things, make sure you take them *all* this time… and I'll say it one final time: consider this your very last chance… to say whatever it is you have also come here to say."

But it couldn't be that she was pregnant, after all. It was ludicrous, impossible, and besides, River had assured her that even if she ever had been, prior to this new twist in the story that she'd 'miscarried', there was absolutely no way on Earth it was his. She desperately wanted to believe him, and despite the odds which were increasingly stacking against her, Alice decided that was exactly what she was going to *make* herself do.

Eighteen minutes and thirty-one seconds later, she breathed a sigh of relief as Hayley buzzed her message through to River's mobile:

"I'm here at the entrance to the park, like," River announced, reading the nondescript text aloud.

Georgina walked slowly, carrier bag in hand, playing her moment out, evidently enjoying her final chance to string them both along, and then she stepped out into the cool evening air from whence she had come, so that Alice could release the breath she'd been holding, once again. But then Georgina turned unexpectedly, opened her mouth like a ventriloquist's doll and stood there for several seconds, almost causing Alice to hyperventilate at the suspense. And yet at the same time she could sense the workings of her mind, the movie screen flashing and projecting the combinations of the possible future outcomes of her potential actions while her eyes glazed over, insulted to the core at the very sight of the couple who were yet to officially come out.

Finally, her head drooped in defeat and she started to walk the long dark path to Hayley and her ride home.

"I'll message the driver to let you know you're on your way. We'll see you at work tomorrow," said River loudly, voice awash with a badly disguised relief.

But she didn't turn back. Still they stood there awhile, watching her form as it became smaller, ever more insignificant; maleficence morphing to mischief, morphing to meaningless. River shut the door and locked it. Twice.

Alice, overcome with a neediness she had never known, turned behind her to bury her head in the warmth of his chest, lifted her head to meet his and then smiled knowingly, possessively, one finger tracing the outline of River's shoulder, running slowly, seductively down to his elbow, before making its way to his hand, which she took in hers, leading him back into his bedroom.

Chapter Thirty-Three
GEORGINA

"Da-da-da-da-da-da-da-da-da-da-da-da," sang Lennie. "This reminds me of *The Great Escape* for some reason."

Blake scowled. Georgina frowned and held her hand out to receive the tools Lennie was passing her. Zara just carried on with her pastry, metres away in the open-plan kitchen area; rolling, dredging more flour, tossing and fastidiously patting it one side and then again the other. She had met them at the designated time in the bakery and let them through to the secret passage which led to the cocktail bar's skittle alley. But that was only the beginning. It was impossible to calculate the tunnelling that lay ahead and how the hell were they going to complete it in just a few hours. Georgina didn't trust an outsider though, so they'd have to somehow do the job between them, the males having the least clue about anything when it came to hammers and nails.

"So, you're the lady who provides my weekly dietary intake of organic Cornish pasties then; I'm Blake." She could hear her brother chatting up Zara as opposed to getting his hands dirty.

Which would be about right; it was always Georgina who'd had to plunge the toilet when he'd pitched an unsavoury loaf, or take care of the crane fly that had 'invaded' his bedroom, or change the light bulb, or flick the trip switch in the pitch black dark of a power cut – the utter wuss.

"It's Zara, and it's a pleasure to meet you at last. Georgina's told me all about you."

"Only the good bits, I hope," his voice was dripping with flirtation.

Great 'first date' material, Blakey Boy, part of a gang

chiselling out a hole in the wall under the pretence of being a victim, like some kind of modern day Tim Robbins from that prison film. Yep, as far as first impressions went, this was pretty epic.

"Less of the chat, guys." She found herself getting narky with the banality of their conversation when she was doing all the hard grafting. "There'll be plenty of time to get to know one another later. Pass me the chuck key, Lennie, Blake, anyone. The drill bit seems to have come loose from the drill."

"And what does one of them look like when they're at home?" That was Lennie. And Blake was still stuck somewhere under a hypnotist's spell.

"Forget it. I'll do it myself. No wonder they call it DIY. Clearly Dad passed his genes on to me and not you," she hissed over her shoulder.

She turned to the day-old toolbox resting on the day-old workbench. Tamara's wodge of cash gifted to Zara on the National Express coach that day had kitted them out with state of the art this, that and everything. Lennie, living up entirely to the penny pinching portrait River had painted of him, had made a swift call to Alice's sister mere minutes after his date with Georgina in the park. Tamara had needed little convincing to fund the whole thing, and had then tracked down the National Express bound for Glastonbury, racing down the motorway in her Bentley. Handy of course that one of the nannies should be in the passenger seat, able to stick the succession of purple crayoned signs up to the coach driver as they overtook him, requesting he kindly *"Pull over at Reading Services, please. One of your passengers has left urgent medication at their hotel, matter of life or death!"*

This contrast in sibling loyalty was nothing short of a shocker. Georgina wouldn't have traded her council house upbringing ever, not if that was what money did to you. Yes, Maggie Thatcher may well have afforded her family the opportunity to buy their own place – well, until they lost it and then had to start all over again in the nineties – but the sudden addition of the word 'mortgage' to their vocabulary had never inferred they were above tribal. You looked out for one another, with the exception of your cheating mother; that's just what you did.

She finally fitted the hammer drill with its bit to loosen the first couple of bricks in the wall, and everybody stood back to witness her handiwork – courtesy of any number of *YouTube* tutorials watched back-to-back over the past few weeks, that and the impressive power of a twenty-nine year old woman, heart set on revenge, bra getting tighter by the minute, already wearing leggings a size too big and one of those floaty tunic things to disguise her bump at home.

Next she took a lump hammer to knock the bricks out to make a hole that was big enough to climb through. But after ten minutes of sweat and toil, it was clear that even revenge wouldn't provide enough momentum for her to go this part of the job alone, and so Blake took over, listening carefully as Georgina instructed him – breathless after her own efforts – as to how to hold and swing for maximum effect. Fifteen minutes later and Lennie had been dragged into the charade too.

"My time and my money, that's all you said you wanted, Georgina."

"Yeah well, you rather wormed your way out of the capital, time to roll your sleeves up and put some elbow grease in like the rest of us, *Uncle Len.*"

The irony being, despite his unwillingness, he was really rather good once he got going, the betrayal of two of his band members, which had encouraged the idleness and lack of response from the remaining 'employees', evidently fuelling him with the kind of focus and precision which could just as easily gather the components for a brand new group of rock wannabes. Until Georgina felt her own desire to blast the wall to smithereens take over anew, and a red faced, sweat covered Lennie was only too happy to oblige.

"You always were good at Craft Design Technology at school, George. Remember that doorbell you made us for the front door?" Blake was back chatting to Zara again now, although ever mindful of the dust getting into her pastry, she was keeping him at arm's length.

"The one *she* rang on her fourth return from Benidorm...

when she was 'back for good'?" said Georgina, as she rubbed her dusty hands into the loose cotton garment that was surprisingly comfy actually. "Yeah, I definitely remember ripping it out with pliers after that."

Georgina knew she'd stepped over the threshold of trading places then. At a metaphorical crossroads and now there was no going back. Not only had she taken on Blake's venom, but her own was thickening too, with no antidote in sight, ready to spit at River and Alice. It was something straight out of a Shakespearean tragedy, all right. Brother and sister in love with one half of the same couple, a love that was unrequited. And she wasn't born yesterday; it was pretty obvious where all this was going, even if the starry-eyed duo were dragging it out.

Which was why she'd revel in this power trip; even if she knew deep down inside that the bitch that was karma would get her eventually. It always evened out the odds, even to those playing Angry Entitled Stepmother, those whose cause went above ethics to snatch at the revenge that felt justified.

***

Strangely, River hadn't been down to the skittle alley in weeks. That's why Georgina was confident that they'd pull this off unscathed, undetected. It was quite the weirdest thing when she thought about it: just what had stopped his visits?

This past string of weeks had been nothing short of a nightmare, especially when she considered her changing shape – and the Amazon delivery guy's crap timing when it came to signing for the parcels she thought it prudent to order in already to accommodate it. But she'd turned up to work like a horse with its blinkers on anyway, honing and perfecting those actor skills of civility; to River, to Alice, to the customers. She was punctual, efficient, in short the model employee.

There had been zero promotion to mixologist behind the bar, and she couldn't deny that this fact alone hadn't peeved her completely, only adding to her desire to settle the score. In fact, that lanky idiot, Lee, had seemingly been trying his hand

212

in that department. Wasn't it enough for him to be promoted down at the supermarket? Now here he was swiping her job title too. Okay, admittedly, this bizarre twist of events only seemed to take place once a week, River teaching him to build and construct, refine and perfect simple concoctions. But still, she was the only one in that bar who'd received any official training and it should be her stood behind it. Her looks alone would have the cash till ringing with more vigour than the bells at St John's Church up the road. Besides, how long did a certificate take to process?

But she didn't dare ask him, and anyway, her mind was elsewhere most days. There had been much to learn; a team to manage, tools to buy, and, just like an athlete will play a movie reel over and over in their head until they know the event like the back of their hand, Georgina had become a bit of an expert at doing the same. A fact which made her positively buzz. Ha, she was basking in a radiance far greater than even pregnancy. She'd only gone and done it, conducted a team of blithering idiots to tunnel a hole through a very thick wall with admirable precision. Did it really matter that this had taken a little over a day, that they hadn't quite hit the jackpot on October 30th?

No, not at all, in fact it was better this way. She'd been too kind from the outset. River Jackson deserved nothing less than to have his precious bottle taken from him on the *Dia de los Muertos*, the Mexican Day of the Dead.

Once they'd taken stock of their achievement, they wasted no time at all in breaking into the cupboard. It couldn't have been simpler. Blake came into his own then, he'd learned to pick locks in his early twenties, supplementing his part-time hours at the supermarket with a little petty cash from minor car theft – well, he only took cash and cards… no actual vehicles were harmed in the process. And of course, River being River, he was hardly going to go in for the most technologically advanced of security systems.

"Stand back, this is my moment," said Georgina. She felt around the door frame for the cupboard light switch once Blake had put her kirby hair grips to good use and bust open the lock.

The others did as they were told, but despite her shifting and shuffling of paint and tools, rummaging in cardboard boxes and scavenging under the shelves, she could find nothing to fit the bill of a mysterious bottled elixir.

"Noooo!" she screamed, bringing her hands to her face and then falling into a heap on the floor. "It was here, I know it was here, the numpty's moved it... there's no other explanation... all this work... for nothing... for nothing!"

"I hate to point out the obvious, Georgina," said Lennie, "but um, you kind of missed checking under those chequered blankets there."

Georgina was Charlie Bucket.

This was her last shot at the golden ticket, the visit to the chocolate factory, the wrongs being put to rights, justice, and all things being fair in love as well as war. She peeped through the cracks of her trembling fingers, irked by the disloyalty of her emotions, and sure enough, there sat a cosy pile of tartan blankets on a shelf. My they looked guilty. How had she missed them? Was she colourblind or what?

Blake helped her to her feet and for once she didn't shrug off another's assistance in turn for her own independence, and besides, she was expecting now, she had to get used to this. The cupboard fell silent, and another kind of expectation shrouded the air, as she inched herself forward, slowly, hardly daring to believe her luck could truly be in, after all. She slid her hand between two of the heavy weaves, felt to the left, felt to the right and then wedged her arm in further, and there it was, the beautiful, quite unmistakable shape of a bottle.

"Quick, guys, help me separate the blankets. I think I've got her!"

Lennie and Blake shuffled forward, one holding the top blanket up, the other pulling the bottom blanket down, and Georgina carefully slid a bottle full of opaque liquid out of its snug hiding place, holding it gently aloft to the light bulb as if that might give them all a clue as to its contents. But there was no label, and there were no distinguishing features. It was simply a bottle containing fluid that was so clear you could literally hold the original Spanish handwritten message the other side of it, and read every word it had to say.

"Now what?" said Blake.

"Back to The Guinevere for Part Two, of course," said Lennie, cramming the blankets back onto the shelf.

"Can Zara come too?"

Georgina looked at Lennie to gauge his response. "How much have you told her?" he said.

"I've not quite gone into the rest of the details."

"No is your answer then, Blake. You've gotta pace yourself, lad, with the ladies; in any case, never a good idea to chase."

But then Georgina smiled, clutching the bottle to her wonderfully full breast.

"Oh, I think we can make an exception… just this once. Tamara couldn't get down for the occasion and it would be rather nice to even things out with another female."

Literal translation: at last, after all these months, hell, after all these years, he's taking an interest in another woman, somebody other than Alice! It was like she'd always convinced herself; had Alice stayed around, had River not lured her off to stardom and bright lights, she'd have become almost mundane to him, a teenage crush fading into local obscurity with an equally low-profile hubby, round mumsy hips, a sensible beige Nissan Qashqai and a golden retriever.

And then the novelty of Georgina's realisation wore off, for it quickly became apparent that she was now the sole holder of the grudge.

Chapter Thirty-Four
RIVER

River and Alice flew over to surprise the travel group in Prague, mainly because River had no intention of tempting fate by opening the bar on carnival night.

"But it's the perfect time to be trading," Alice had said when he'd first run the idea of the much needed mini-break past her. "We'd easily fill up the top floor with customers at long last, besides, Lee could probably get the time off to help us cope with the extra demand now he's learned the Martini and Piña Colada basics with you for that bar he's had installed. Jonie was telling me all about it – where *is* he getting all this money from by the way? First he's funding the drinks and nibbles at the cat sanctuary's opening, even the Rigby-Chandlers were put out about that… funny as it was, then he's whisking Jonie off on a cruise around the Med; he's updated the car, they've got a wedding to pay for, I'm guessing a honeymoon too—"

"Some people are just better at saving than others, I guess."

River had blatantly ignored her questioning over his decision not to open up that Saturday, equally keen not to blow Lee's cover. He'd only just told Jonie about his win during said boating around the Mediterranean, was keen to keep his secret closely guarded for as long as he could to the outside world.

Still, what *was* notable was the way Alice was changing. Not so long ago in the band and she'd have felt entitled to all of life's little trappings, and whilst her prying into Lee's finances might have come across as nosey to an outsider, it was as sure a sign as any of her descent from noblesse to ordinariness. Not that she could ever be ordinary if she tried.

But it boded well for the kind of grounded life he was keen to live, preferably always with her by his side.

And in a funny kind of way it felt terrible not to be sharing Lee's Lotto windfall with Alice. Despite that incredible evening in the caravan weeks ago, they'd sat down at the kitchen table as two responsible adults the very next morning, agreeing to take things slowly by officially dating – regardless of the inescapable fact they were already cohabiting – with all the movies and dinners and takeaways and beachy Weston-Super-Mare style strolls that entailed; sex, for the moment, frustratingly on hold. So far, so good; they'd stuck to *Alice's* principles. But their relationship felt all the more authentic for it, he had to admit it.

"But I haven't seen a live carnival here for so many years," Alice had continued that day in the bar when he'd sprung the idea of a zip trip to Prague to surprise everyone upon her, "imagine how cool it would be to watch it out the top window... and to be able to drop coins for charity into those long pole collection thingys that the people in fancy dress carry up and down the High Street."

"It's a recipe for disaster, a Jägermeister bomb waiting to explode."

River shook his head, genuinely surprised at the way she'd glossed over her childhood memories of the really quite terrifying faces of some of the town folk dressed as clowns – and other creations he couldn't always put a name to – but also genuinely reluctant to upset her. He knew all too well the truth behind his reasoning. Plus the fact, Lee wouldn't be able to get the time off just like that. The supermarket would be heaving. It would be all systems go in every retail outlet within a ten mile radius of Glastonbury's epicentre: this was the second prime weekend in the year for shoplifting, the festival aside.

He couldn't help but smile though at the journey his friendship with Lee had taken. It was the most curious of things. Just at the beginning of this year they were sworn enemies, well, at least sworn token enemies, it was clear with whom the real hatred lay, and now they'd become such good friends that not only had Lee officially asked River to be Best

Man at his nuptials which were just around the corner, River had also approached Lee with a proposition of his own. But that was something he wasn't quite ready to tell Alice about, not just yet, anyway. Amazingly, neither she nor Georgina had questioned his recent disappearance on 'business' last Wednesday and Thursday.

It certainly felt like life really was falling into place, those unaccounted jigsaw pieces fitting into their rightful abode. He no longer had to sweat it out worrying over the bottle, secure as it would be, quite literally under wraps – at least until the call he was waiting for came in, and depending of course upon that call's revelation. Until then, there it would stay, beneath the cosy tartan. Georgina had calmed down of late too, and whilst River still hadn't managed to find a reason to eject her from the bar and truly wondered what he'd ever seen in her, at least he had regained enough trust to let her manage it while they were away in Prague – with the exception of its definite closure on carnival Saturday.

She'd seemed genuinely thrilled at the prospect when he'd put it forward. He'd hired a mixologist from Newquay for three nights and everything, putting him up at The Guinevere and paying him well for his time. Lee was going to step in as well, at least to partner up with Georgina on the service front, but only for the three nights which fell either side of the actual carnival – a feast for the senses in every sense of the word, taking place as it did every year at the end of November. All in all, he was confident he'd left things in very safe hands.

"But we're off to Prague… as tourists this time! It's gonna be so much more fun than watching a bunch of tractors and sweat-drenched *X-Factor* hopefuls singing and dancing on neon light bulb studded floats. We can do that any year, but there will only ever be one inaugural travel group visit to the Prague Christmas market," he'd reminded her.

"True," she'd said. "I *am* looking forward to it, I promise, I can practically sniff the mulled wine in the air, and I'm especially curious as to how Terry is going to get on with all that driving."

They both laughed at that.

The travel group had decided, during one of its many get-togethers in The Cocktail Bar, to hire a mini bus and drive all the way to the Czech Republic's capital, that way they'd have more room for their goodies and could fit in more countries en-route, ticking the boxes on all of their club requirements. Nobody had been more relieved than Terry, as he'd never set foot on a plane.

**

"Are you absolutely sure this is the same boat hotel they're staying in?"

Alice quizzed River as the silent and melancholic Czech taxi driver pulled over to the quay and pointed at the fare on his screen, a couple of weeks later. It made a refreshing change from the incessant dialogue and munching they'd become all too acquainted with courtesy of one Hayley, who'd more than become their personal chauffeur since the summer, taking them here, there and everywhere at discount rates in return for guaranteed pole position as chief taxi driver for The Cocktail Bar – even if she too would be a recipient of their Cilla Black style shenanigans later.

Fare paid, soon they found themselves inside the boat, heading up the short queue for check in, where River also found himself the recipient of a surprise of his own: resorting to having to use his C list past to help secure what would normally be top secret information.

"But I really shouldn't be revealing the dining plans of fellow guests, Sir," said the male receptionist, whose name badge with its Dutch flag told them his name was Piet.

"Would you do it for a signed CD then? A signed *Avalonia* CD?"

"I haven't a clue who Avalonia are, and no, it's against company rules to disclose this kind of information." He threw in a string of tuts to make that extra clear.

"But what's stopping me as a guest from knocking on all the doors in the hotel and finding them that way?" said River, his voice desperately trying to shroud his irritation. "This is my mum we're talking about—"

"Our friends besides," added Alice, removing her shades and propping them up on her head so her curls fell enticingly over her face and it was all River could do not to sweep them away, or attempt to nuzzle them as they swayed to and fro. "Surely you wouldn't begrudge them our company tonight?"

He'd always swore that he'd never be one of those sickeningly sweet men who refer to their partner with a pet name, or adopt childlike habits in the bedroom, lest he lose his dignity completely. But Alice had him hook, line and sinker and there wasn't a damned thing he could do about it if he tried.

And then he felt a little justified, having taken in the come-hither smile of the designer-stubbled 'Piet'. It wasn't just River after all.

"On this occasion, I suppose I could overlook that conformity," Piet replied, gazing solely at Alice, "In return for *your* signature on one of those CDs."

River delved, overenthusiastically into his suitcase's thin outer pocket, his large hand straining, mimicking a duck webbed foot until he finally fished out a spare CD. He handed it to Alice. "You're in luck," he told Piet, whose eyes remained permanently fixed on their new object of desire.

"Pen?"

Alice challenged him, unperturbed by such public sleaze. Piet opened the drawer beneath the desk, still unable to break out of his trance. "The travel group have made a booking for a restaurant called '*Nejen Vepřové a Knedlíky*' this evening. This loosely translates as 'Not only Pork and Dumplings', in case you are interested. It is geographically located near the castle across the Charles Bridge," Piet said, with all the automation of a robot, as if he had always known this would be a part of their check-in drill.

"Thank you," said Alice. "We got there eventually... and um," the intensity of his gaze was starting to wear a little thin now, clearly knocking her confidence, "would you be able to add us to this reservation... as well as um... as well as kindly booking us a separate taxi, for an hour later... please?"

"Why of course, Madam… and Sir," Piet finally snapped out of it. "That would be my pleasure, and thank you again for the CD. I look forward to playing it… very, very soon indeed. Yes, very soon indeed." He held it close to his chest and River could feel Piet's eyes burning his back as they wheeled their cases to the antiquated looking lifts which would apparently take them to the penthouse suite on the upper deck.

They squeezed themselves inside, River suddenly regretting the garlic croutons he'd unnecessarily sprinkled on his budget airline soup at 38,000 feet a couple of hours prior to their current jigsaw puzzle of a conundrum – although, the way they'd equally been squashed together on that flight had hardly afforded them that many extra inches than their latest dilemma.

"You push yours into your corner first then wedge yourself up against it, and I'll just have to sit on mine and curl into a very small ball in my corner," said Alice. "And please God, nobody else attempt to join us or I think I might die."

River craned his neck awkwardly to press the button to their floor, the doors shut, the mechanics creaked ominously, and finally there was upward movement. Just for a little while anyway. Seconds later the lift stopped with a rather abrupt clunk.

"Holy shit! What did you do?" Alice shrieked. Her eyes were wild and terrified, bouncing back at him through the mirrored glass. "We should have stayed home and opened the bar, I knew it. Never mind that Jägermeister bomb you referred to, this is like drinking Ernest Hemingway's Death in the Afternoon, quite literally."

"But I did press the right button, floor three we're on… I swear I hit the right one," River said cringing at his bleary reflection as it steamed up the mirrored glass, and wanting but not daring, to smile at the fabulous way mixology jargon had started to creep into Alice's vocabulary.

Before either of them could further process the horror that was, or search for the alarm button, a familiar voice came through the loudspeaker, though curiously it was quiet as a mouse.

221

"Sit tight. This always happens when there are two in a lift. I will just go to the technical room to hoist you back down. Then one of you must take the stairs."

"I think we'll both be taking the stairs, mate!"

"Bloody hell, I need that mulled wine and I need it now," screamed Alice.

***

"Oh," said Alice minutes later. "I thought we'd booked two singles."

"I'll behave if you will," said River with a wink, secretly delighted at the rather snug double bed Alice was flinging her case on, practically unzipping it mid-air such was her enthusiasm for catching the Christmas market before dinner, as well as generally exiting the hotel.

"You know how important my rules are to me and now you're just making them a mockery." She stopped her unpacking suddenly and fell in a frazzled heap on the bed. He couldn't blame her. The early start, the entrapment in the lift and now the let-down that was a poo brown hued room dubbed a penthouse, had put him in a sour mood himself.

"Let's just make the best of this," he said, sitting beside her on the hideous seventies inspired duvet complete with its giant moths perched on sunflowers. "This was a last minute decision anyway, so I take full responsibility for the current balls up. Next time you are in charge, and we'll go wherever you like, promise. In any case, this trip was simply to surprise our friends and family, to feel proud of what we've both helped a bunch of people who previously didn't get out much, to achieve."

"You make them sound like they've never left Somerset."

"Well in Terry and Hayley's cases, that couldn't be more accurate."

"She did drive us down to Dover."

"Yeah but only with the lure of a four times mark up on the fare… plus two service station stops for a snack both on the way there and on the way back."

Alice was all smiles again. "Ohemgee, her head's going to be positively spinning at all the Czech dumplings and sweet pastries in the markets. I can hardly wait myself."

"Well then, let's take a quick tour of the erm… hotel… boat… whatever it markets itself as, and get going."

They hugged and Alice walked over to the massive window to draw back the curtain linings and drink in the view.

"Actually, River, furnishings aside, it's pretty damn impressive. Just look at this."

He crossed the epically large room; that was the curious thing, in terms of space they were practically inhabiting a palace; it was just a shame the décor hadn't caught up with the modern world, and put his hand around her waist, in awe of the beauty in front of him, as well as the beauty beside him. He slid the sheer glass double doors wide open so they could step out onto their own personal balcony and enjoy it even more. The water twinkled, dappled here and there, reflecting sunbeams in other spots as the light hit its surface, a barge tugged with the grace of a swan to the right of them, its cargo headed for who knew where, canoeists hugged the Vltava's outer banks, canary yellow and populated with bobbing heads, the bridges of Prague hung elegantly over the river like strings of pearls as far as the eye could see, the castle overseeing all of this in its top hat Gothic grandeur. And music floated from one of the lower decks. It sounded suspiciously like banjo music, which hardly went hand in hand with the distinctly wintery climate or the city's architecture.

"Banjo Boy, it's gotta be," said River.

"Well, he is here with the group after all, and I must admit, I'm wondering how Cassandra is keeping him so *entertained*, shall we say, twenty-four-seven." Alice folded her arms and took to jogging lightly on the spot in a bid to warm up.

"If he's down below then the others are sure to be floating about too."

"Ha, and hopefully not in the literal sense," said Alice.

"Perhaps she's getting ready to go out and he's sat at one of the cafés on the lower decks, passing the time," River continued. "In other words, let's get ourselves out of here now and head for the market, before they spot us."

His words were a click of the fingers, transporting Alice into ultimate city break mode. She skipped around the room like a character out of a Disney movie gathering scarf, coat, gloves and ear warmers.

"Let's do this. I'm so pumped! I think it's just the novelty of being free, no ulterior motive for being here – surprise aside. We're on holiday, a real holiday, a holiday without the constant fear of the snail trail of the media... sorry, I, erm, the last thing I wanted to do was hark back to the *vaycays* of my last relationship. But you know what I mean."

"Hey, this is me, Al. If this is it now, you and me... possibly... hopefully, for ever and ever, then I don't want you walking on eggshells. We're always going to let the odd thing slip out when it comes to the past," irritatingly, Georgina sprang to mind, "and if you can't be you around me and I can't be me around you, then none of this is going anywhere."

He held his arms out wide, inviting her in for a tender embrace, ever hopeful that this shiny and new, carefree mood would carry its sentiment into an equally carefree evening. It was time. They were almost entering a brand new year, after all. And he had plans for the both of them, plans he couldn't keep to himself for much longer. It wasn't that a certain kind of intimacy was a prerequisite to his future announcement, rather that he couldn't help but feel Alice was holding part of herself back from him, out of protection maybe, or some similar kind of self-deprivation to the way she would frequently refrain from partaking in calorific food perhaps, some unnecessary trace of guilt for winning his heart over and above the infatuation of Georgina? He couldn't quite put his finger on it, but something wasn't right.

Still, it made no odds because the only thing he did know was *she* was right.

The One.

It was crazy really that it had taken them both so long to see it.

They left the room, gingerly, it had to be said, River taking Alice by the hand and leading the way along the hideous transcendentally-carpeted corridor to the stairs. Once back down on the ground floor the passageway looked safe, remarkably so given the increased volume of the banjo strumming, whose chords seem to bounce off the tread of what appeared to be a very freshly laid carpet, another seventies creation, this time in buttercup yellow.

"Oh no! It's Cassandra and friends—"

Alice almost hyperventilated, an over-excitable child in one mammoth game of hide-and-seek.

"Quick, shunt yourself up against the wall next to me." River had already transformed himself into *Flat Stanley*. "We've come too far to let them see us now." He pulled her closer to him and they held their breath against the side of a rather expensive looking grandfather clock, conveniently lining the corridor.

Cassandra and her groupies marched past, giggling, intoxicated in the kind of glee that only a girls' holiday among ladies of a certain age, can manufacture.

River chanced a peep around the edge of the highly polished heirloom to see them walk through the inner part of the hotel's café and out onto the deck beyond, presumably to take custody of Cassandra's lover, chaperoning him en-masse for today's pre-planned excursion, whatever that entailed. One of these days he *would* find out Banjo Boy's name.

"The coast is as clear as it's ever going to be," he whispered to Alice behind him, "after three, yeah?"

"One, two, three," they counted together and then sprinted, past Piet and his second daze of the day, and out onto the quayside.

***

A remarkably short stroll later – short because they'd absolutely pegged the distance from the boat to Prague's infamous Wenceslas Square, hardly daring look over their shoulders – and they were in what could only be described as utopia. To look at Alice in that moment was to regard a Victorian doll in one of those cute snowstorm globes, the old-

225

fashioned beauties with rosy cheeks and cascades of curls, wearing Santa-red muffs on their wrists, elegantly cast out before them with traditional intent as they skate the vast perimeter of the ice rink. Indeed the only thing that was missing was the snow.

"I'm in love," said Alice, "in love with life, in love with Prague, in love with you."

"I can't even," River wanted so badly to reciprocate those words but the crowd had grown thick now and so he linked his arm in hers, leading them to somewhere, anywhere for a little privacy. "I can't even begin to tell you—"

"Look, *mulled wine!*"

She dragged him back into the cheery throng and he knew then that the moment had decidedly passed but that was fine because he didn't actually want to tell her what she'd told him, in some kind of pathetically whimsical 'me too, babe' half-hearted effort of a retort – what she'd only just gone and flipping well told him… *that she loved him!* He'd find his own moment sure enough.

And talking of moments, this was another time capsule of absolute enchantment – once Alice had weaved them both through the dawdlers and gawpers with their precariously balanced hot toddies, anyway. Quaint little market stalls stood proudly, exhibiting their handmade wares, and draped in the most promising of red, the red of all his childhood Christmases parcelled together with a giant satin bow. Heather may not have celebrated many conventional English traditions, but unlike Halloween, she always made an exception at Yuletide, so River didn't feel completely left out compared to his friends. Being here, totally enveloped in this festive spirit, it was to be a boy again, to catch the scent of cinnamon and clove on the air, then emanating from the old-fashioned Aga and the (spelt flour) Christmas cookies Heather used to bake, now from the vapour trail of the mulled wine the stall holder was gently ladling into two cups.

"Here," said Alice. "Get this down you."

She passed him a cup and he knew immediately this baby of a punch was going on the special Christmas menu. They

226

were soon planning to throw an end of year party, to thank all the locals for their support over the past few months, and a River-style twist on mulled wine was going to be a must. He tentatively began to sip, almost burning his mouth at the sudden intrusion behind them.

"Well, well, well, fancy bumping into you two lovebirds here," said a woman's voice, snapping him immediately out of his creative daydream. She looked remarkably like Hayley, holding aloft several slithers of the juiciest looking ham in one hand and a *trdelnik* pastry in the other, reminding River that he himself hadn't eaten in hours. His heart thudded, first through the short sharp shock of being caught red-handed, second with utter disappointment.

"You haven't seen us!" said Alice, almost choking on her drink.

"And you haven't seen the half of this yet, you wanna get on down to Old Town Square, guys. That's where the real buzz is. Flippin 'heck, the Christmas tree is summit else. What are you two even doing here, anyway? Who's looking after the bar? It's carnival weekend, are you mad?"

"I could ask the same of you," said River. "Think of all the money you could be making."

"Tsk," said Hayley, in-between her sampling, "I never operate over the carnival weekend, oh no Siree, not since the year Burnham-on-Sea's entry of a float broke down halfway up the High Street and Muggins here ended up having to jump start the bleedin' tractor."

"Gosh," said Alice. "That would be enough to put you off."

"Anyway," said Hayley, "three's a crowd and I'm beginning to feel like a strawberry."

"Don't you mean gooseberry?" River corrected her.

"I think I know the rumblings of my own stomach better than you, River Jackson. *Jahodový Řez*, says that wooden sign over yonder." Hayley pointed to a traditionally painted sign which could have been written in Japanese, for all of River's linguistic capabilities.

He shrugged his shoulders at Alice as she continued to down the fragrant magic with somewhat shaky hands.

"Czech Strawberry cake," said Hayley. "Oh my days, I'm glad one of us did our culinary homework prior to coming over here, like."

"Oh yeah, that… Czech Strawberry cake, of course… heard loads about it," he lied.

"Laters!"

Hayley had somehow finished her various collections of morsels already, as well as the unexpected conversation, and was beginning to walk, very briskly, in the direction of the stall she had pointed to.

"Hey, Hayley, wait up, just a minute," River called after her. "Not a word to the others, please… we're here to surprise them."

But she was already a speck in the crowd.

"Well… that went well," said Alice, eyes glazing over from lack of food and sudden consumption of alcohol. She looked dreamy, ethereal, but despite the devil of temptation perched on River's shoulder, he was categorically not going to take advantage of that.

"I guess we ought to Czech out – geddit? – the Old Town Square then." River paused for a laugh, met only by the kind of face one pulls *a propos* a Bruce Forsyth gag.

"River Jackson, tipsy I may be, but that was the corniest thing that has ever flown out of your mouth. If you're trying to impress me… to build things up to a dirty weekend of pure unadulterated sex, you're going to have to try a helluva lot harder than that."

***

Czech folk music greeted them as they were led through the foyer of the restaurant by an elderly waiter. River began to feel nervous, transferring his irrational fear to Alice through the energy centre of his hand which she squeezed gently to reassure him.

"Are you alright?"

"Yeah, course," he replied, clearing his throat.

It wasn't so much that he was about to potentially give his

mum a heart attack, rather that he'd built his hopes up high for tonight, and now he was wondering if he'd taken things too far, like the architects who'd designed Dubai's Burj Khalifa, when frankly the Burj Al Arab had sufficed. He'd even snuck off to ask Piet to scatter rose petals on the bed while they were out – this whilst Alice was blissfully unaware and taking a tepid bath. It was probably the most ludicrous and potentially risky request anyone could make, Piet evidently having become completely smitten with the love of River's life, and totally spooking him out when on arrival in reception, Avalonia's one and only love song, 'And Then My Eyes Found You,' from the recently gifted album, blasted out as the latest arrivals checked in, but he wanted things to be perfect.

"Guess who?"

River was back in the present, blindfolding Heather's eyes moments later with a napkin, and Terry was almost spitting out his goulash.

"Woop woop," said Cassandra. "Oh heavens above, what a wondrous thing to do. Well, I always said magic follows this man wherever he goes, but now it seems that very magic is here at our table."

All this before Heather had even stabbed a guess at the person who was letting her veggie dumplings get cold. Much as he'd warmed to Cassandra in recent weeks, why couldn't she just keep a lid on it, show some decorum?

"Ha," added Hayley, "I've had to keep schtum all afternoon after bumping into Riv and Al down in Wenceslas Square, now the secret's out at last and I can breathe a sigh of relief, the number of times I've almost let the cat out the—"

"Well, cheers for that, Hayley. I might as well uncover this now then, hadn't I?"

River released his grip on the napkin, thoroughly pissed off at the lack of discretion. Then again, going by the growing collection of empty wine bottles, clearly this lot had been knocking back the glasses for a couple of hours already.

"River? No… I don't believe it!"

Heather was practically shaking, somehow only catching up with the revelations of the others once she'd laid eyes on the boy for herself. "Oh, the pair of you," she looked around for Alice now as well, and pulled them both in for a hug, "this is just amazing... oh, what a day we've had." She turned to her right to squeeze Terry's hand, happy tears in her eyes. "And we've only just arrived as well... this is all just so exciting. It had been too long since I'd visited another land, Stonehenge and Avebury aside... way too long."

"Hey, you're not wrong there... and this is just the beginning," said Terry, raising his glass to prompt another toast from everybody at the table. "The 'ole globe sure is our oyster now."

"Am I missing something? What is this significant other thing that's happened today?" River said with an expectant smile. He could already tell what was coming.

Banjo Boy began to pat his instrument, sat as usual, protectively in his lap, to signal some kind of a build-up to a public announcement. The pat became the hard beat of a drum and soon he couldn't resist leaving the table to try his luck with the Czech musicians at the restaurant's entrance, who had little choice but to accept him – just for one song, which admittedly, he did a pretty decent job of providing a strangely haunting melody to.

"What a day it's been, as I was saying," cried Heather again as the musicians finally called it a day and began to pack up their instruments. "Terry's only asked me to move in with him... permanently, on the Charles Bridge."

"The... did you just say on the Charles Bridge?"

His question was met with a round of hearty giggles.

"She doesn't mean I'm gonna knock up bricks and mortar on the bridge, River. No, course not. Plus the fact, I'm a man in demand these days, soon to brighten up all of your television sets... Nicholas Knowles eat your heart out."

Terry's index finger scanned the guests at the table then, as if it might find the traitor, the one who had always secretly had the *DIY SOS* front man geek crush but was too embarrassed to admit it.

"She means when we get back to Glastonbury, we're going to shack up together permanently, your mother and I. Well, I can hardly kick out Blake and George – mind you, I'd probably be doing them the biggest favour if I did, so we're going to pool our resources together, love, aren't we?"

He paused briefly to look lovingly into Heather's eyes, and despite the genuine sentiment, River almost had to clutch at his stomach, as would have Georgina, had she not been serving up trays of heady mixers right now. "Because actually, there is a little bit more to tell you about this TV show I'm appearing in right now where we're filming the stately home improvements at the Rigby-Chandlers—"

"Sounds fascinating," said River, pulling up a spare seat for himself and Alice, figuring that any story emanating from Terry after wine, and now the *slivovic* which the waiter threatened to uncork, was going to be akin to a reading straight out of War and Peace – but also, that they couldn't hover behind Heather for ever and a day, making her strain her neck this way and that.

"I'm only flippin' well earning more than I've done," Terry broke off momentarily to switch to a whisper now, suspicion washing over his face at the sight of the waiter and his huddle of shot glasses, "in a bloomin' decade," he added, eyebrows tall as skyscrapers, head nodding affirmatively.

"Well that's brilliant, Terry," said Alice encouragingly.

"And there's more," Terry rubbed his hands together. "Please don't think me greedy... and only God above knows how this has come about, 'cos stuff like this never happens to a run of the mill kind of Joe Bloggs like me... but they really are tipping me to be a bit of a future Somerset celeb, like."

River couldn't help but smirk inwardly at this little nugget. How Terry would scoff at his own hand in all of this; at his unknown link to Mexico, and the gratitude a little woman with wonky teeth living in a shack in an agave field so deserved for the way she had personally seen to it that lives would be changed.

"Gosh, never mind River and me giving people autographs." Alice quite unnecessarily forced River to imagine Piet snooping around their room now, a vision he was keen to entrench in drink before he arrived at the sniffing at her underwear part. "It sounds like you'll be doing that soon enough. But if I may say so myself, hasn't your luck changed since you've started visiting the cocktail bar?"

"He's worked hard all his life and when opportunity knocks at our age, you really do have to grab it," said Heather.

"Here, here," echoed Hayley.

"Our sentiments exactly." Cassandra raised her slivovic in a toast to Terry, for the drink had now made its merry way around the table. "I must echo Alice's words though, there's something about the tall, handsome, bearded, pony-tailed hunk of a mixologist sat beside her... well surely you've all noticed it?"

River swallowed down his fear at having been sussed out as Cassandra got to her feet now, her little thimble of potency undulating left and right.

"Sorry we're late!"

River had to do a double take, a double take of sheer relief but a double take nonetheless. Lady Rigby-Chandler was only rushing over to join them all in an outfit straight out of *Dynasty*; shoulders wide as plane wings, pearls layered heavily around her neck as if she'd been scooped off a seabed. She turned to click for her tortoise-like husband and as if by magic, Lord Rigby-Chandler began to scuttle a little faster in their direction too.

The group became silent.

"Now," said Terry, "be friendly one and all... that was the part I was rather trying to get to... but as usual, my tangents stopped me in my tracks. Lord and Lady R-C, *Rigby-Chandler*, I mean, Rigby-Chandler..." He bowed down low to the aristocrats who stood wide-eyed and expectant at the head of the table, so low it was a wonder he didn't set fire to his few remaining sprigs of hair on the Gothic candelabra. "M'lady and his lordship... well, they wanted to come over to Prague as well. They've sort of taken to the idea of the travel group in recent weeks, you see, as per my relaying of the trip's details whilst they've been overseeing my plastering above their drawing room fire place."

Lord Rigby-Chandler removed his bowler hat to signal his

agreement.

"Um, well, let's all make them feel welcome then."

Alice jumped to her feet, helped herself to a couple of chairs from another table, prompting everybody to bunch up together to make room for their unexpected guests. Cassandra panned the restaurant for the dregs of her now forgotten conversation and resigned herself to her own chair.

***

"You're off the hook, River, and I can only apologise, I've been a snob of the first order," said Lady Rigby-Chandler halfway into her first glass of wine.

River pinched himself behind the screen of the lace tablecloth; sure he'd wake up from this kaleidoscopic dream any minute. Even Mercedes couldn't have made this shit up.

"So," he mustered up a smile, "this means you're going to stop threatening to grass me up to the local papers… for things I haven't even done?"

"Yes, yes… as well as to start paying for our drinks. We've behaved quite monstrously, with myself taking the lead… it's just… it's just…" She shook her head then and drew in her top lip, presumably to prevent the bottom one from wobbling. "Just between you and me," she turned to look at River with glassy eyes, "our castle was starting to resemble more of an Abbey Ruins than a stately home. The place was dilapidated, ceilings caving in, more damp and mould and rot than an episode of that frightful excuse for light television entertainment, *Coronation Street*. That's when we applied to feature in one of those programmes, out of desperation, we'd become charity. Terry has been a godsend. Yes, he's awfully common, but it's that delicious contrast between us and him, him and us, which is going to save our house, transforming it into its former glory—"

"*Breathing new life into the saddest and darkest of corners*," Mercedes' voice seemed to cut in then with her reminder.

"Opening it back up to the public, fuelling their aspirations

233

and filling our coffers, just like the good old days. I couldn't be more grateful if I tried." Lady Rigby-Chandler retained control.

River knocked back his second slivovic, letting the fermented plum burn his throat, and preferably his voice box too while it was at it. Because what could he say to that? He might still semi-loathe the very blue blood of these silver-spooned idiots, but essentially, Lady Rigby-Chandler was showering him with the very evidence that he craved, the proof that his task had been worth it, that he wasn't simply enriching the lives of three random customers in his cocktail bar... but a whole world beyond it.

Never underestimate the power of three. It's a magic number. The ripples of joy this chosen trio will generate is going to envelope your town – and beyond – in something never seen before.

Isn't that what Mercedes had predicted?

Chapter Thirty-Five
ALICE

"I still think Georgina's pregnant... you know... that the baby is yours. What would you do if it was? Wouldn't you be tempted to go back to her? After your own childhood being brought up by just one parent... doesn't... doesn't," Alice faltered and then drew a deep breath, it was now or never, despite the copious amounts of alcohol she had imbibed, despite the fact she wasn't even sure if she could string together a half logical sentence, "doesn't the presence of a child, regardless of who its mother is, change everything between us?"

"What on Earth has brought this on?" River flopped back onto the bed, nursing his head. "We had... such an awesome time... tonight, why ruin it?" He too was hardly coherent, and now she wasn't even sure if he was truly taking in any of what she thought she had said.

"I just can't do this. I'm head over heels in love with you," she cried, "but it's the thought that she is carrying your child... it's doing my head in, River... and in all honesty, that scattering of twigs and leaves all over the bed when we walked in tonight, well, it's hardly helped to keep me in my previously passionate mood. I mean, who does that?"

"And I... I... told you," River sat up now briefly, reaching for the water bottle standing on his bedside table and gulping at it greedily, "I will be having... more than a word with this hotel's... management about it... I asked for... for rose petals," his words slurred and swirled, "red rose petals... at that... not flaming weeds."

He put his head in his hands, sloshing the remains of his bottle all over the bed, and she wondered for a moment

235

whether he'd laugh or cry.

"I'm sorry, but I just can't stop thinking about it," Alice steered the conversation back on her track. "And surely, River, *surely* you've noticed her titillating bust which is only getting larger by the minute, her ever-growing paunch which definitely can't just be passed off as eating one too many of Zara's pies; the way she declines alcohol at every given opportunity, no longer partaking in a new cocktail when you whip one up for us to sample, the pale face, the permanent parking of her hand on her back, the emerging from the bathroom with a beaded brow, the collection of her pills from our caravan – pills she'd evidently been neglecting to take. Want me to go on?"

Alice was shouting now but found she couldn't stop, such was her anger at Georgina's hell bent plans to ruin their relationship. And anyway, the dialogue flowed better this way.

"Let's move away… for a fresh start."

River's face was serious now, as if implying it was something he had already been looking into, whether drunk or not. But to Alice this felt like nothing more than diversion.

"It's not the answer… besides, the caravan is so homely now… and I've only just put up the tinsel."

"It's only November, we can put it up somewhere else."

"But… but… but… why are we even having a discussion about tinsel? You're evading me, avoiding my question, which leads me to believe that if this baby is yours… because make no mistake about it, there is a bun in that oven… in truth, you've absolutely no idea whether you'd run to her side or stay by mine."

"Alice! There's no bun and there's no baby, okay. This is just your imagination… and even if there was, in which case I am positive it isn't mine… but even if there was a miniscule chance I was this phantom child's father, then no, I assure you, I would not go running back to her."

"You're just saying this now, I know it. You have to remember, River, your own dad didn't stick around, men change when they become fathers and they've lived through that absence as children. They know the pain, the suffering,

236

the loss, *the void*. The love for a child outweighs everything, even going above and beyond the way we feel about a partner, the way you profess to feel about me. Grown men stay with women they *detest* simply to give a child the bond they deserve, some stability so they don't let history repeat itself when they themselves have been deserted in their childhood."

His tired eyes appeared to follow the words she had expelled. She watched him, quite voyeuristically, trying to capture them as they circled the air, invisible to all but the two of them and this moment; a moment which would quite possibly redefine everything they thought they were working towards.

A moment which also meant that Georgina had, once again, won the tug of war that Alice vowed she would never partake in.

***

Whilst the threads of that inebriated conversation could only be clutched at, Alice was sure enough by the next morning that she had heard as much as she'd needed to hear. Sometimes drink will out the truth like that.

No, River undoubtedly didn't have a smidgen of a feeling for Georgina, she could see it in his eyes; the hatred, the bitterness for the way this Man Eater had taken advantage of his kinder side, propelled as she would have been by her ego and greed. Not that River's malice was to be encouraged in any shape or form, but under the circumstances, it was useful to know. And yet as she had always feared, the word 'baby' had become not so much an elephant in a room, but an elephant in a caravan, tipping his world, and their small world, upside down with it.

But Alice was tired of running away.

Sometimes you just had to stay put and accept things. What use had it been last time anyway? He'd only come to find her once more. And so, as she would insist upon sleeping on the couch – for the Czech penthouse was furnished with a burnt orange one, draped in those distastefully embroidered arm

237

covers – equally she would insist upon exploring Prague alone, by day and by night. This causing quite the height of speculation within the travel group no doubt, but she had three days to get her head together, to resign herself to a life of Just Good Friends all over again in the caravan, until the New Year when she would hatch out a new plan and a new start.

On the final morning they waited for their taxi to the airport, to fly back to Bristol in quite the anti-climax of the mood they'd taken off with, and the others were preparing for their epic drive back across Europe, with Hayley taking the helm at the wheel this time.

"No offence, Tel," Hayley said, as she helped Terry board his luggage and Christmas market purchases into the trailer which was hitched onto the rear end of the mini bus.

"None taken, Hayley. To be honest, you've done me a favour. How am I ever going to fill in Cassandra's Eye Spy scrapbook with photos and snippets from the journey if I'm constantly staring at cats eyes and road signs? There's a prize for the best recorded memories of the trip when we reconvene next week in the bar: drinks on the house courtesy of Cassie herself... for a whole year!"

"Now you tell me," said Hayley with her very best disgruntled look. "There's no way I'd have volunteered to drive you all home if I'd known that."

Banjo Boy appeared then from the boat, instrument tucked under his wing. Somehow he'd transformed during this trip from chick to fully grown sparrow. Cassandra left the group for a moment and went over to hug him, their words inaudible as they bid their adieus. She turned back to wave at him one more time, only to be lunged at by River as she climbed on board the minibus.

"But I thought you two were—"

"Oh never mind about him, River," said Cassandra. "Don't you dare feel sorry for me, just because he's decided to stay here and run off with that charming folk band; I've got a whole queue of young models waiting back home."

For the one and only time in her life, Alice wished she was Cassandra.

Chapter Thirty-Six
RIVER

River opened up the bar early. He had a sneaking suspicion it would become something of his man cave now they were back. Prague had been a triumph on so many fronts, and yet nothing short of a disaster when it came to his own.

Where had he gone wrong? Why was everyone else enjoying life and getting all the 'lucky breaks'? Talk about the universe taking the mickey when he was the one who'd got off his backside, walked miles along a baking hot road in Latin America, risked sunstroke and a succession of muggings; taken chances above and beyond what any half intelligent person would have done, all to smuggle a bottle containing Lord only knew what, into the UK. And all to have the love of his life shun him one final time, except on this occasion, she'd banged the nails into the coffin and he couldn't see any way out.

Georgina was not pregnant. And that was all there was to it.

Admittedly, he was no longer the least bit turned on by anything about her appearance, that alone was reason enough not to let his eyes rest on her for a second longer than was strictly necessary. But even so, he wished Alice would give him some credit, quit labelling him as one of those typical men who wouldn't even notice if a woman had got her hair cut.

But then Georgina did walk into the bar, earlier than early for her shift which began at two that afternoon.

"Hi," she said, as if they had never fallen out precisely half a dozen times. "How was Prague? Did it bring you any inspiration for new drinks? You must tell me all about it."

She unbuttoned her navy trench coat and hung up her red

polka dot umbrella, droplets of water danced across the floor and River couldn't help but be drawn to the new and peculiar curves of her body; the soft rounded stomach which had previously been toned, easily fitting into a pencil skirt, now clinging to the edges of something suspiciously elasticated and unflattering, the bust which seemed to spill out above the rest of her, creating a sudden and indisputable muffin top.

"Yeah," he heard himself reply, feeling quite as if he'd left his body. "It was good, great, fun, lots of fun, I'm sure your dad told you all about it."

"So lovely he and your mum are moving in together, isn't it?" A Georgina far friendlier than even the slightly more chilled out version he had left behind to run the bar replied.

"Hmm?" said River, eyes not only glued, but super glued to Georgina's contours.

"Are you okay?" she asked, unable to mask her worry as her voice warbled, or was that just the ringing in his ears as he decided he needed to lay, very quickly, upon his favourite bar couch? "River? You've gone a slightly whiter shade of pale."

***

The last thing River Jackson recalled before his head hit the pile of cushions was a fuzzy weeble-like person standing over him, a strange figurine brimming with concern. And she was the first thing his eyes regained their focus on when he did come around.

"I've called in Lee," she echoed, as he attempted to sit up and then thought better of it. "You just stay there. I didn't know what else to do. You fainted, River! You poor thing," Georgina moved towards him with a cold dishcloth from the sink.

"Not one of those, health and safety," he muttered. But she was already dousing his forehead with it and he could only succumb to the relief.

What a lightweight he was. He guessed the stress had done it, followed by the shock of Georgina's changing shape, the realisation that Alice was right; the growing likelihood that he was, in fact, soon to become a dad.

Dad. Daddy. Father. Pops.

The words reverberated through his skull then, bouncing off the edges, vibrating north, south, east and west, until Lee arrived with a small amber bottle of something which he appeared to wave under River's nose, causing his body to contort as the assault to his nasal passage caught up with his brain.

River sat up immediately, coughing and spluttering, clutching at a fluffy cream cushion which he used as armour to ward off the intruder from his face.

"Oh man! Why did you have to do that? That smell is mental, like ammonia or something."

"Spot on," said Lee, "my nan's smelling salts."

"Yeah? Well next time just make me a Frisky Bison or something."

"You sound like you could do with one," Lee laughed. "But at least your colour's coming back." He raised his brow as if that would give River a clue as to his former shading. "I don't think we need to call in an ambulance after all. Let's see if something purely medicinal will help. Georgina, can you prop him up against some pillows, watch your bump of course."

Watch her bump?

So Lee was in on this sudden pregnancy? Well in that case, Terry must be too – and Heather. Then why had none of them said *anything*? River was motionless, cushion still very much in his grip. If he held onto it tightly enough perhaps it would take him right back to his own childhood, a time and a place of zero responsibility.

"Right then," Lee shouted behind him, "I'll see if I can remember how to make it."

River eyed him curiously as he went about his business; he was a natural though, carrying himself in a stance of complete confidence as he measured mixers and spirits, pausing to select the most appropriate glass, tasting his concoction discreetly as he went along. And though River may have felt like the literary Alice suspended in some kind of trippy wonderland, he knew now was almost the time to propose.

***

Somehow River made it through until closing time, but trade had been light, thank God for Tuesdays. And somehow he had managed to sweep Georgina's physique under the carpet. It was the only way, after all. He wasn't going to confront her, and when he thought back to her promiscuity that day on the Tor – then sending his erogenous zones haywire, now filling him with the kind of nausea that was enough to have him wondering if he was some freak of nature carrying a joey in his own pouch – it would hardly surprise him to hear there had been a string of potential candidates for fatherhood since he'd given her the cold shoulder. Case closed as far as he was concerned, and surely that had to be why Terry had never aired his soon to be status as grandfather in public. He was ashamed. His daughter hadn't the faintest idea as to who the father of her child actually was.

The rush of the cocktail had worked wonders though and he began to go through the paperwork for the weekend that had just passed, sorting out the cash and receipts, tallying up the proceeds of the pre and post carnival trading. Yet for some unfathomable reason, his figures kept falling short. In the end he resorted to good old fashioned pen and the local newspaper which lay unread on the bar.

He ordered one every week just as a café might stock the papers, not that he'd go as far as to start buying the sensationalist tabloids; he'd rather put a bullet to his head. But such an innocent regional rag would have enticed him immediately as a teen, full as it was with pictures of his friends and their various sporting victories, snippets about local bands and festivals, the wall of fame – and equally – the wall of shame that was the high schools' and colleges' exam results. Old habits soon had him leafing through the paper, until there on page fifteen his hand froze, and then began to shake with rage.

It was Georgina.

Unmistakably Georgina, leaning out of the top window of *his* cocktail bar, with a couple of male 'friends', putting money – and he didn't need to second guess where her charitable offering had come from – down one of the collection poles, held aloft as it typically was by a *Pierrot* clown complete with freaky black teardrop. Words failed him. Action didn't. He downed the remainder of his second Frisky Bison, letting the liquid alcohol do its thing and hollered out her name.

Georgina waddled forth, already bearing more than a striking resemblance to a penguin doing an impersonation of Tina Turner, but River wouldn't let himself get distracted this time. Business was business and she was about to be sacked from his. Lee watched on nervously in the background, much as his personality had had a transplant, some things never changed when it came to confrontation.

"Yes, River, did you want me?" she said through the innocence of her smile.

Lee began to edge himself over to the most distant table in the bar, sensing the sparks that were about to fly, one ear cocked out should his intervention be required. River was only too glad he was there to support him.

"What the hell do you think you've been playing at?"

He slammed the paper down in front of Georgina as she stood at the customers' side of the bar, sensing immediately that she clearly hadn't had chance to flip through her father's edition this week.

"Man gets rescued from slurry pit on farm... that's nice," she said, her voice laced with fear for the first time since their paths had re-crossed, "not really sure what it's got to do with me though."

"Not the farmer... this," he pointed to the photograph which framed her jubilant act of benevolence as two thugs claimed possession of her, cocktail glasses – *his* cocktail glasses, probably full of beer or something equally uncouth – in hand, balancing on either side of her shoulders.

"Oh... well... you know, it was just a couple of mates, they had nowhere else to watch the parade... and since you'd decided to shut shop... and I had a key... there was no harm done though, honest."

"I think that's a little beside the point, don't you?" he yelled, unable for the moment to find any further words, thankful to Lee for stumbling forward.

"I knew Jonie and me should have watched the carnival down this end of the High Street so we could have kept an eye on the premises for you, mate. I knew it... I did try to convince her, but her Aunt lives in Chilkwell Street, had put on a mammoth spread of food and everything, kind of like a family tradition. Jonie couldn't let her down. But now I'm sorry, 'cos I've been and let *you* down."

"Course you haven't," said River, dismissing the very idea on the spot. "But she has." He pointed at Georgina. "And it's one step too far this time."

"But we tidied up after ourselves... you have to admit, there's not a trace of us having been here."

"How many of you were there? Did Blake get in on the fun and games too? The cat goes away... the mice will play, huh?"

"I'm sorry, really I am. It won't happen again."

"Damn right it won't."

"You sound like you're going to fire me."

"Clever girl."

"I hardly think you have the grounds to," she snuffled and brought a timely tissue to her nose, like that might attract his pity, "over a simple misunderstanding. All you ever said to me before you went away was we weren't to open up to the public Saturday night. That didn't exactly cover a small private get-together with friends."

"It's not your bar... and these so-called friends of yours have been having a little fiddle with the takings as far as I can see. Look at this."

River pushed the calculations under her nose. Lee took a deep breath and gave himself permission to come across now too, to bear witness, shaking his head at the chunk of missing money that was circled in red pen.

"Five hundred quid unaccounted for, did you think I wouldn't notice, just because I'm semi-wealthy, does that make it all right?"

Georgina lowered her head.

"Here," said Lee, reaching into his back pocket for his wallet, "let me chip in to cover it. It's the least I can do for not second guessing something like this would happen."

"And why should you have to cover her tracks?" said River. "A couple of weeks and you're walking down the aisle with Jonie, why should you spend the honeymoon period of your life babysitting grown women who can't keep their fingers off other people's property?"

"It must have been the Rigby-Chandlers who stole the money," said Georgina, matter of fact, looking River straight in the eye. But oh how she'd have failed a lie detector test.

"You've had it in for them since the official opening night," said River, desperately trying to keep his cool now.

"Yeah, well, perhaps there's good reason they haven't been paying for their drinks and Mrs High and Mighty carried out that threat. The perfect cover up. They're broke, just like the aristocrats you see on the TV documentaries with their pleas and the background violin playing because, poor things, they live in those crumbling stately homes that we have to fund with our taxes; how simply awful for them."

River began to clap slowly, sarcastically, increasing his hand movements with speed.

"You really are too bright for this place, you know that? I'll concede: your suspicions are one hundred percent correct when it comes to their former financial situation... perhaps have a chat with your dad though who will fill you in on the current turn in their luck... but the thing is there's just a slight problem with that theory when it comes to the carnival weekend, George. You see, it seems *Lord Pervert* and his wife decided to go to Prague themselves to join in with the fun."

"I... I... told you they were scroungers, beneath the Trilbies and... and the emeralds, they're brassic... broke, inviting themselves along to everything."

"But that still doesn't explain how the float and takings don't tally for the weekend *when they were in Prague*... when they were in a whole other country, a fact that you are completely overlooking!"

245

Georgina began to bite her nails, as if that might help her come up with something more convincing.

"Well, I'm waiting for a proper explanation, it's that or your P45."

"So that's it?" she said after a lengthy silence. She rubbed her stomach in a manner that was getting über predictable already, and treated him to one of her atypical smiles, game face back on, kindly disguise of hours ago, ancient history. "First you cool things off with me... not long after shacking up with her in a caravan."

"Alice has a name and yes, we are very much together... and happy, extremely happy."

How he wished that were the truth.

"And now you are sacking me, after I nursed you this afternoon as well? I didn't have to do that, you know."

"That's about the size of it, yes."

"You are unbelievable, and as for this place, I hope it goes to the dogs."

"Once upon a time, Georgina, not all that long ago, we could have had something meaningful, you and I. There was a seed, a spark, a call-it-whatever-you-will, and I'm not going to deny it. But you abused my trust, took me for a fool, and even those of us who are a little slower off the mark," he didn't dare look at Lee then, much as he would have made the perfect illustration for his point, "we get there in the end, see through the wool women like you pull over our eyes. Will that close my heart up if another relationship comes along... be that with Al, be that with anyone? No, because unlike yours, mine isn't made of stone. I don't hold a vendetta against the world. And yes, for the record, I am more than in love with Alice, I've loved her all my life, it's just a shame it's taken me until now to realise it. So thank you, *thank you* for pushing me further away from you and closer in her direction. You've been more of a Guardian Angel than you'll ever know. I want to grow old with her, have her babies and live happily ever after. There. You satisfied now?"

Georgina held her stomach with both hands now, her eyes boring into him with an intensity that spoke its own language:

River Jackson, father of one.

"Okay, good bye, River," she said, "you've more than made your point."

She walked to the hat stand by the door, melancholy shrouding her, and slowly put on her trench coat. She unhooked the umbrella which had been hanging beneath it. River and Lee could only stand motionless as she reached for the door handle. River couldn't wait to pour them both the nearest excuse for alcohol to hand. He couldn't do this alone anymore, had to halve the problem by sharing it with a friend.

Georgina was midway out the door when she turned back to them, as if she'd forgotten something.

"Oh, what now?" sighed River.

She began to laugh a small laugh, making it heartier, ever more staged and deliberate, and then stopped, without warning, letting the peels of her joy linger in the doorway.

"Did you *honestly* think I'd walk away just like that?" she said finally. "I'm a pregnant woman, babe: you're about to become a daddy." She chuckled again, sadistically this time. "How's that going to look when you want custody? Not to mention the fact that the dismissal of a woman in my position," she stopped then to nod her head and purse her lips for added effect, "is just a wee little bit of a faux-pas in this day and age. So, it looks very much like I will be seeing you tomorrow."

And with that, the door slammed on River's life as he knew it.

Chapter Thirty-Seven
GEORGINA

The real reason Georgina decided to use the bar for her private carnival party that night was that she was angry. Several weeks of her life had been spent learning how to bore a hole through a wall, a discretionary act which had been completely unnecessary. He'd entrusted her with a bunch of keys that weekend in late November, and that bunch of keys would have made for a far easier journey to a skittle alley cupboard and its cloak-and-dagger bottle. Revenge was essential every step of the way. Who wouldn't invite two of the semi-fit male employees from the local DIY store where she'd purchased said tools for the job, for a little weekend flirtation – pregnant or not?

But she hadn't returned to work because she wanted to keep River on his toes. Remarkably, her weekly wages kept being paid into her account, a sure sign that she had him right where she wanted him, at her beck and at her call. And yet it wasn't enough. The more you had, the more you wanted.

Desire was a diva like that.

Lennie may well have run off with the bottle, Blake may well have found his second chance of lurve in the arms of Zara – the so-called friend who had ditched Georgina with all the haste with which one of her bakers would bin a weevil-infested bag of flour, and her father may well have decided to take things one step beyond with Heather. Happiness may have abounded for *them*, but all it did for Georgina was leave her with a very bitter pill to swallow. Because it was one thing to watch your former lover run into the arms of another, but it was quite another to see this gut churning happiness do the rounds like a Mexican sodding wave.

And now it seemed it was Lee's turn, the wedding to that pint-sized excuse for a woman of his was only taking place on the weekend, and Georgina was fuming that she hadn't been invited, but it was her fury over Blake's lack of an invitation which really pushed her imagination over the edge. They'd been friends since the water and sandpit of primary school. Wherever Blake went, Lee, like Mary's little lamb, would go.

Shoelace undone? No worries, Lee would stoop to tie the bow again; Mummy forgot for the gazillionth time to put a bag of *Walkers* crisps in his lunchbox? Like a disciple, Lee was there with the supermarket branded back-up supplies; scolded for something Blake kind-of-did-but-kind-of-didn't-do… a little *Tippex* illustration added to the classroom geek's blazer, the Valentine's card stuffed unimaginatively in Alice's rucksack as they crunched the gravel up the back lane while the peels of the school bell trilled in the hinterland? Legendary Lee would come to the rescue.

Friends didn't abandon one another like that, and whilst Blake may have been floating on a cloud shaped like a number nine, Georgina was only too happy to turn his weakness to her advantage.

Chapter Thirty-Eight
ALICE

It was do-able, just about.

Hell, who was she trying to convince? It was terrible, the days stretching out painfully before her, a long straight road of nothingness separating a desolate Australian bush, somehow turning into weeks of civility, pleasantries and the odd furtive glance. She was in a catch twenty-two which she'd pretty much brought upon herself in one way and yet hadn't in another.

She got by at work. That was the easy part, particularly since Georgina had apparently left, paving the way for Lee and his increasing appearances, as well as his genuine kindness which offered a most welcome buffer between herself and River. And then of course there were the customers – and heaps of them these days, making for welcome opportunities for banter and general busyness, sweeping her along from daylight to sundown.

But there was no escaping the fact that she had to start making a Plan B, and whilst she was no longer prepared to keep running away, knowing full well her problems only trailed behind her like the wedding dress she'd now probably never wear, she was also no longer prepared to keep living in limbo. The dream was to get back to her beloved horses, no matter how low down in the pecking order that might place her. Sure, she had rich contacts from the past, buddies living in Cheltenham and its bordering villages who could give her green card to the upper echelons of the racing world. But she wanted to do things by merit this time, privilege having turned out not to be all that it was billed as.

And so her evenings were spent in her bedroom in the

caravan, putting green biro loops around interesting classifieds in horsey magazines, making phone calls, adding up finances; a trot here, a canter there in the right direction of her new calling. But it would have to be February, and of course any day but a certain Saint's. Her last January departure for pastures new hadn't exactly gone to plan, so February had a better feel to it. And for some inexplicable reason she was strangely feeling drawn to the toe of the kingdom.

Cornwall, why not?

There was something refreshing about the Cornish, after all; their other-worldliness, their strength of character, their up-keeping of tradition, and their pride in their Celtic roots. Glastonbury would always be home. But alas, she had lost her sparkle as a nest. Rather she'd been a wellspring, a fountain, a cauldron of fresh ideas and inspiration; a metaphor in many ways for the magical things that were happening to the customers of River's bar – in other words, everybody else except Alice.

Yes, that's what coming back had taught her. Phase one of being Alice was to experience Wonderland. Phase two was to give back for the riches she'd received, to work *on* the land.

Chapter Thirty-Nine
RIVER

The big day arrived and Alice couldn't have looked prettier, careful not to upstage the bride, she was dressed in a simple mint tunic with cream leggings, hair in one of those elegant French baguette buns – and not of the edible kind, a matching cream clutch bag in the hand of her pearl-spangled right arm, all finished off with a pair of mint kitten heels which looked sleek enough to adorn a cocktail.

Maybe when you were a mixologist you just had to go into overkill with the descriptions. Yet none of Alice's classicism could steal the show from Jonie, and heaven only knew how much that dress cost. But a pavlova she'd always dreamt of – according to Lee, anyway – and a pavlova was what she steered herself down the aisle in, for to all intents and purposes, she really was the epitome of a hovercraft.

But none of this mattered when you were in love. And now River's two, arguably most loyal customers, stood side by side at the altar of St John's Church, halfway up Glastonbury High Street, ready to declare that very undying love to an impressive gathering, many of whom could just as easily be quaffing Pimm's or Manhattans a few doors away in the bar. In fact, River had offered the use of his premises as the reception, but Lee had declined. Jonie had long ago had her heart set on a wedding breakfast in a windmill – not that Somerset could exactly take her pick of those, or was in any way twinned with a small town whose population wore clogs, but miraculously, a small windmill on the banks of the Brue in a village not a million miles away, did have a couple of willing and fairly broke owners, and so a windmill was what Jonie was going to get. Albeit the Top Table only would be dining

252

inside the miniscule monument, everybody else would be spilling onto the river's banks – but hopefully not into the water.

River brought his attention back to the all-important present moment; the exchanging of the vows – and rings – he felt the small circular piece of platinum embedded safely in the satin lining of his trouser pocket and gave a very private sigh of relief.

"We are joined here today in holy matrimony to..." began the vicar.

It was at this point that against his better judgment, River decided to steal a look back at Alice. Unbelievably, her eyes had been locked on his back all the time, but they fell to her lap immediately when he returned her gaze, and that's when the emotion hit him and he thought he might just cry in the kind of vast quantities that only his namesake could hold. He would never get to experience any of this with her and that was too bad.

Of course, he had always assumed that she wouldn't be up for the contractual thing, and he was pretty sure that neither of them would be up for inviting God to witness the joining of their hands either. But all of those protests aside – isn't that what anybody who wasn't quite sure of their partner's commitment found themselves saying these days? Wasn't it just easier to spout out 'oh, you know, it's just a piece of paper... it doesn't change the way we feel about each other... we don't see the need, besides, if ever we did, it would be a beach wedding in the Dominican Republic, just the two of us and a witness... blah, blah, blah.'?

If River was honest, he could think of nothing less tragic. For a wedding was a celebration and the bigger the better. A real man should have the balls to stand up in front of a happy crowd and declare his feelings for, and commitment to, the woman in his life. Yes, Heather would practically disown him if *he* ever declared this newfound thought aloud. But there was something wonderfully knightly about the way Lee had the bravado to do this here, on King Arthur's land, not even shifting his weight from side to side as he might once have done.

Mind you, the hypnosis sessions he'd been paying the guru friend of Heather's for, may have set him back a small fortune at such short notice, but they'd undeniably done the trick. River had never seen his friend so calm. It was like watching a millpond. Even if he skimmed a pebble at Lee, he doubted he'd flinch.

"Is there anyone here present, who knows of any lawful impediment, why this man and this woman may not be joined in—?"

The church door slammed shut then, casting the holy building in a most eerie silence. River hardly dared look around, not least because he didn't wish to see himself publicly rejected courtesy of Alice's body language once more. But also because he couldn't believe how late these guests were. Talk about crap timing just as the vicar was questioning the appropriateness of the wedding.

But nobody took their seat discreetly in the rear pews. Instead, all that could be heard by the congregation – who had now strangely grown necks like giraffes, the majority most rudely with their mobile phones in hand, ready to record some kind of evidence – was a commotion. The shuffling of feet seemed to be coming from a salt and pepper-haired man in his mid-thirties, who was being thrust forward by a woman donning a giant black fascinator better suited to Ascot atop her head, clip-clopping in stilettos as she projected him mid-aisle:

"*He* does!"

The silence became a bubbling of hushed whispers. Somebody tittered, as folk do when they bear witness to a situation which is about as far removed from funny as the climax of a crime novel. Elsewhere in the assembly, somebody began to wail. It was an awful version of anybody's attempt at crying, and he could only hope Lady Rigby-Chandler was not its proprietor, seated as she would have been somewhere towards the middle to back.

"Then…uh…" the vicar broke off to clear his throat, "then kindly step forward and do show us your face," he continued, with a look of total surprise on his own, for clearly it had been some time since this unwanted predicament had occurred, despite him having been the one to publicly put the question to the floor in the first place.

"Go on," said the woman behind the man causing the furore. But the figure said nothing and so the female continued to be his mouthpiece.

"He's the traitor of traitors, the lowest of the low!"

Her voice thundered down the aisle, bouncing off the church's arches, so that anybody who didn't catch her words the first time, certainly wouldn't miss them the second, or third.

It was at this point that the light streaming in through the stained glass window ceased to blind River, casting a spotlight instead on a man who looked the spit of Blake, shielding a visibly pregnant woman behind him, dressed from head to foot in jet black.

Oh dear God, no. Why of all days today? This was Lee's wedding, Jonie's big day; her chance to be the centre of attention for once in her run-of-the-mill life. Not that it would ever be remotely mundane after her groom pocketing the jackpot, but still.

"Man alive… this is Lee's wedding, Jonie's big day—"

River started to yell uncontrollably, hoping his lips' movement would come to a grinding halt before they had their way with his musings about Jonie's golden moment as centrepiece.

He needn't have worried.

A weighty figure rose from the pew – once more it was difficult to make out precise details, the bright stream of light having moved again now so that River suspected he wasn't the only one to wish he'd brought sunglasses – she… and it was definitely a she, well, he guessed that much anyway since the figure was clad in a purple skirt, lunged at Blake in an angular fashion. Which was precisely when the bride screeched out: "Oh my God!" and the vicar signalled his apologies heavenward for the unexpected blasphemy that had occurred, "it's only Hayley taking Blake out!"

And indeed it was.

Georgina had vanished into thin air while Hayley followed up her lunge by using her left arm as a blade, cutting into Blake's right shoulder, preventing his futile attempts to grab at her leg. Round and around they shuffled for a while mid-aisle, a couple doing the do-si-do on the Wells Cathedral green in the annual country dance competition. Except Hayley was too smart for her partner: with her left hand she cupped the left side of his head, with her right hand she covered his right temple and eye, effectively cranking his neck – so much so, the congregation began to audibly wince – until finally, she managed to disrupt his balance completely, and a couple of nearby male guests stepped in to take Blake away.

Hayley rubbed her hands together as if she'd just taken out the dustbins, granted herself a bow, everybody returned to their seats, the vicar signed the cross skywards once again, before crouching to remove a hip flask of something – and River was pretty sure it wasn't holy water – from his sock, until now covered by his robe, and took a rather lengthy and shaky swig.

"Well," he said, pulling out a handkerchief to pat his lips dry, "now that the annual recreation of *Four Weddings and a Funeral* is over and done with; let's get on with the show."

***

"You never cease to amaze me," said River, arm in arm – to keep his teeth from chattering above all else – with one of the most incredible women he thought he would ever meet.

"It's pretty much physics," said Hayley, pulling away from him to pluck at the long grassy blades which fringed the River Brue, running her fingers along the length of their pale seed displays and scattering husks onto the water's surface to mingle with the pond skating insects, "wherever the head moves the body follows."

"Come again?"

"Krav maga, mate. You never do know when it's gonna come in useful, like. I've had to resort to using it more times than I've had hot dinners with some of me passengers over the years. All's I can say is I'm mighty glad to have befriended the bride and groom courtesy of your bar over the course of this year… looks like I well and truly saved the wedding day."

Hayley stopped to adjust her faux fur stole, an accessory which put River in mind of the Egg Nogs circuiting the after party, something he'd be happy to down immediately, should a waiter care to pass this way.

Alice appeared from the windmill's doorway then, a glass of Eggnog in her mittened-hands.

"Why the wistful look? Surely you two haven't had a ding-dong again?"

"It's not her, it's me."

"Oh don't feed me that line. If there ever was a sentence that needs to be deleted from the male bleedin' vocabulary, it's that; drives me up the wall."

"Well, in my case it's true. She's perfect, I'm an idiot. There's nothing more to say. I had my chance, I blew it."

"But what did you do this time?"

River's brain began to weigh up the pros and cons of going into full blown details, and then Terry made the decision for him.

"Ladies and gents, hope you're enjoying the day… well done Hayley for earlier and rest assured I shall be having words with… with… it pains me to say it, my kids."

"The pleasure was mine, Tel. And *who* is this?"

Hayley turned to the unconventional, yet somehow dashing guy who was accompanying Terry. River definitely hadn't spotted him earlier in the church.

"The name's Bob." The mystery man held out his hand to take Hayley's for a rather corny kiss. River was stunned to see her oblige.

"Yeah, this here is the one and only Bob, aka the geezer who's turned my life around."

Aha, TV Exec Dude.

Well, little did Bob know he wouldn't be standing here now losing himself in the eyes of this lady had River not followed his instinct and penchant for a shot of Tequila, but that was the best thing about all of this, having this amazing

257

secret and not being tempted to tell a soul about it. Okay, with the exception of Lee that one time. But it hardly counted, and besides, he hadn't believed a word of it anyway.

River and Terry gave each other The Mutual Nod and peeled off in their separate directions, each instinctively aware their presence was no longer required. Unsure quite where he was heading, River began to whistle, like most men inexplicably seem to do, as if to put in a little premature practice for the big 4-0. It worked a charm to attract the attention of a waiter, even if the Eggnog was 'temporarily on hold'. A mulled wine was no bad substitute. He took a sip and closed his eyes, resurrecting their Prague Christmas bauble of a bubble. Oh, to go back there, to say the three words he should have spouted back at Alice, to personally see to the depositing of red rose petals on a seventies bedspread himself, to deck Piet and throw him into the Vltava.

When he opened his eyes he saw his opportunity to catch Alice alone instead, as she stood serenely in a chocolate box pose, elbows propped against the gates of the orchards flanking the river. He knocked back his mulled wine so fast it almost winded him, recovered; straightened up his tie, and soon his legs appeared to be transporting him to her, despite the lack of an invite.

"It wasn't so long ago that we were jumping over these with a fleet of bulls' horns at our backsides."

He climbed on top of the gate, wincing at his dreadful attempt to break the ice, and looked down on her golden halo with a smile. It still looked like she'd 'just stepped out of a salon', to quote one shampoo advert. She'd definitely picked up far more style tips along the way than he had.

"Don't remind me." She allowed herself a more modest curl of the lips, before reverting to the seriousness with which she'd greeted him once more.

"Are you getting the first coach back, or staying on a little?"

Talk about a mawkish chat-up, River. Is that the best you can do after all these weeks of purely platonic behaviour?

"I hear they're going to have thirty outdoor heaters

tonight," he heard himself plough on. "The mind only boggles at the bill, but then again, Lee can certainly afford—"

Damned alcohol and lack of nourishment! Please don't put two and two together, Al, please.

Her eyes flickered, as if registering this remark about Lee's newfound abundance, but if she'd made the financial connections, she certainly wasn't letting on. Thank God for that. It wasn't that he'd never planned to tell her, and it certainly wasn't that he didn't trust her, but it was Lee's secret, and hardly your bog standard one at that.

"I think we both know it would be best not to tempt fate… I'll take the first coach, you must stay on and celebrate, it's your duty as Best Man, you can't not fulfil it. Who knows, perhaps Georgina will show up again, a few drinks… you, I mean, not her… in her condition… and suddenly life with a ready-made family will look a lot rosier."

"Just stop this, Alice, stop it!"

Silence, until in a distant field a cow mooed. It seemed to be telling him to tell her something, anything, even if his words were to spew out in a pile of utter drivel.

"I'm out of my mind, life's been so tough that at times – and I can hardly believe I am saying this… but at times I have been ever so slightly close to understanding just how a man could take his life."

Now she looked at him, eyes reluctant to let themselves become shiny, it was a trait of hers he knew too well.

"I love you, Alice Goldsmith… I wanted to tell you that day in the market in Prague, but you'd only have said I was returning the compliment, matching your words… and besides, I loved you too much to keep you away from your beloved mulled wine for a second longer."

Alice climbed to sit next to him on the gate, keeping a safe distance apart. It was a start of sorts. He somehow stifled the urge to smile and he definitely didn't dare inch closer. She was still a wild animal, wilder than she'd been that day when he'd rescued her from the strawberry fields. And yet as they sat there in the rural Somerset Levels' silence, watching herons stoop low to take their fill from the water; watching waiters annoyingly deposit the last of the Eggnogs before the claxon called for one and all to huddle to graze on caviar... and Alice a gourmet slice of nut roast; watching Hayley and one TV Executive called Bob enjoying a thoroughly cheeky snog beneath the sails of a quaint windmill, River knew that he and Alice had turned a corner.

Somehow destiny had brought them back together. And now, much like the millers who had ground their crops for long enough, he wasn't so much determined to make hay while the sun was shining, as flour – preferably of the self-raising variety, of course. Which was quite the corniest of puns given their location, yet somehow there was no better way of summing things up.

Soon it would be *their* time.

Chapter Forty
RIVER

A few days before the Christmas party at the one and only cocktail bar on Glastonbury's High Street, the one and only cocktail bar in Glastonbury, and Somerset's cocktail bar of the year, Lee had not only worked his notice at the supermarket, but was made manager of River's establishment, in a move which raised more than a few local eyebrows. And stock control had never known a swifter way of life.

But of course none of this came as a surprise to River. In fact, it had all been part of his master plan, concocted fairly recently, all things considered, but since when did a plan require a four year BA Honours degree to be a good one? Lee's love of cocktails couldn't have been plainer for all to see, he had certainly been frequenting the bar with all the gusto of a zebra visiting a watering hole, he'd learnt every process and procedure of every fusion on the menu under River's steely gaze – admittedly only for home recreational purposes, but still, those skills were transferable. The Magical Mañana had worked its regional magic, and so had River. It was time to move on, and what better send off than a Yuletide bash?

The party was in full swing already, despite the doors only having opened half an hour ago. The book club had started a little too early on the cracker pulling, fifty pound notes hitting the floor like confetti – Lee had secretly funded those, no more tacky plastic festivities for anything *he* linked his name to, being more or less his precise choice of words when River had caught him tying gold and silver bows around their middles. The travel agents were bopping away in a corner whilst intermittently supping on Lee's delectable Homemade Irish

Cream, their actions slightly less frantic than they had been during their first visit to the bar, their garments slightly more in keeping with the fashion too. And the Rigby-Chandlers had not only insisted on paying for their own drinks, but standing outside the door gifting the Christmas shoppers with free champagne cocktails, causing River to rub his eyes more than a dozen times.

River and Alice had gathered everybody back inside so he could make a thank you speech, before things got too chaotic, the crowd of well-wishers had clapped and whistled – many with momentary tears in their eyes for it was the first they'd heard of River and Alice's departure – soon dissipating once they learned Lee and Jonie would be the new faces behind the bar.

And then in breezed Aunt Sheba.

It wasn't that River hadn't invited her, rather he hadn't expected her to put herself in the way of forgiveness's temptation, and after all the recent drama in his own life, he'd rather she stayed at home if there was even a smidgen of a chance of round two of the dreaded Sting Thing.

"Well, it is the season of goodwill to all men and women," said Aunt Sheba, removing her spruce green fingerless gloves. "And I want to spend as much time with you both as I can now you're off on a new adventure… wherever that may be, although, I can't deny the thought of having my roomiest caravan back to advertise online for anybody wishing to purchase a late Christmas break at high season prices, doesn't delight."

"Don't ask me where we're headed," said Alice with a grin. "I swear your nephew's brainwashed me, but I'm learning to go with it, I guess it was always going to happen with a mother like his… I mean your sister… I mean—"

"Come on, that's enough waffle, group snog under the mistletoe," Aunt Sheba insisted in an elaborate ploy to change the conversation.

River and Alice found themselves cocooned in her henna tattooed bosom beneath one of the scant sprigs in the bar. Thankfully Lee hadn't gone to town on the flora, much as he'd threatened.

Aunt Sheba released them at River's insistence they'd be back for the holidays, upon which he made his escape to the bar to admire the gathering, to take some discreet and un-staged snaps of the partygoers for old time's sake.

"You did good in this place, I only hope I can be a fraction as successful," said Lee, as River clicked away, angling his iPad this way and that, intent on capturing not just the people but the bar's every nook and cranny. "Who'd have thought it though, hey, me... a cocktail bar manager, with my gorgeous wife by my side? If you'd told me that this time last year I'd have spurted my pint of cider all over you."

"You and me both," River laughed, and then, quite without warning, his laissez-faire attitude of the past couple of months caught up with him. "I'm just heading down to the skittle alley, something I need to check up on... keep doing your thing." He double clucked his tongue and winked at Lee in the manner of a vexing uncle.

Once outside in the snappy air, River ran, careful to avoid skidding along the slippery path in his tread-free party shoes. He panned the horizon as usual, unlocked the skittle alley door and let himself in, creeping, quite unnecessarily, in the air with which he'd grown accustomed, over to the cupboard in the corner.

"Shit, no!" he almost screamed.

Everything looked as it always had done, except for one very minor but important detail; the lock was on back to front. He'd never have hung it like that. Somebody had been in there, or at least made an attempt. He took the small key from his pocket, opened the padlock and cursed himself, this time with every expletive under the sun. At first everything seemed perfectly normal, but a quick scan confirmed his suspicions: The tartan blankets were in a different order. And he knew this because the top one should have been Bruce Modern, which in red tartan terms was a pattern with sizeable squares. But instead he was looking at Heather's Cochrane Modern blanket, its tartan pattern made up of smaller lines and squares. Only someone with the attention to detail of a cocktail bartender would notice this, but to River it spelt one word.

Trouble.

All of which led to the inescapable fact that he'd been robbed of the bottle, as well as the world's greatest idiot for not having bothered to check up on its status and condition since Terry had knocked back his Magical Mañana. River removed the top blanket anyway, heart thudding, rendering him queasy, dizzy at the thought of the elixir being in the wrong hands.

Who could have done it? He'd been meticulous with the keys. The only possible explanation had to be the picking of a lock. As with the missing translation, naturally his mind was rife with accusations for Georgina, and yet he couldn't quite find the facts to stack up. She'd never shown a single sign of knowing what he was up to, her only venture into the backyard being to park her rear on a deckchair to read trashy magazines.

Then perhaps somebody had followed him from Mexico, had been on his case ever since day one? It was the only feasible answer.

Great.

So he was like the guy in *The Celestine Prophecy* now... or Tom Hanks in *The Da Vinci Code*, with the perpetrator always too many steps ahead of him.

"It is true, you've been a little... hmm... shall we say 'haphazard' this time, but then you are still serving your apprenticeship."

"Mercedes?"

River stepped back from the cupboard and spun around several times, head flitting up and down, around and around, in a bid to locate her elusive voice. For he swore he wasn't imagining that trickle of words, whatever it was coming from.

"Get back in the bar, get ready to leave and trust me. All will come good in the end; all will become clear very quickly. Rights wronged in moments. But for goodness sake, mi chiquito, tell Alice this time and let her be in charge of the bottle's hiding place."

"But the bottle's gone, someone's stolen it."

"Did you miss the first part of my instruction? Get back in

the bar, get ready to leave and trust me."

"Okay, okay." River held his hands up like a criminal turning himself in. "I trust you, I'll do it, I'm going."

He knew the drill by now, much as any normal person would have locked him up months ago. And so he marched up the path, on tiptoes, dodging the icy bits, eager to see how this mystery would play out. It was pretty clear that Mercedes knew something he didn't, something that was soon to reveal itself. So far her track record had been accurate enough, so what other option was there but to put his faith in her once again?

"I'm back," he almost sing-songed to Lee.

"About time, what was that all about? Forget to put something on the inventory?"

"No, no, everything's good. I just wanted to... y'know, have a moment."

"You are sure about this, starting over so quickly, leaving me here to steer the ship?"

"As sure as I'll ever be... you, me, the bashing up of the bar... it was written in the stars that day."

They both smiled, River simultaneously cringing at himself for nabbing Mercedes' quote, but under the current circumstances, it was wholly appropriate. And then Lee surprised him completely by going in for a semi-man hug which didn't quite take off in the way man hugs were intended but ended up as several slaps on the back.

"All right, calm down!"

They stood there awhile like that; a silent metaphor for out with the old and in with the new, a friendship restored to something even better than its former glory. Lee's eyes were ablaze with joy and fixed on his wife, River's were transfixed by Alice, wondering where life would take them, relinquishing the very thought of worrying about the current location of one bottle, lest Mercedes boom out over the loudspeaker next, scaring them all out of their wits. He let his eyes move over to his Aunt Sheba as he took a drink of his final cocktail in this bar – damn that Frisky Bison for making its way into his glass again – but he'd allow himself approximately a third of its goodness, he was driving soon, after all. Aunt Sheba stood a distance from Heather and Terry, the spirituous apples danced on his tongue, and Sting's *'Free'* began to blast out on the sound system.

"Right, that's it. If that isn't a flippin' sign, I don't know *what* is," he overheard a voice sounding very much like Heather's declare. And sure enough as his head followed its direction, there she was, abandoning her Ginger Rabbit on a table like an exclamation mark, walking over to grab her long lost sister, rigid crab-like pincers held out before her, the kind that would not take no for an answer.

River swore his jaw was about to hit the floor. This was unbelievable, a decades-long feud on the brink of becoming history, all because of a song. But then someone made a grab for him, and it didn't take him long to work out that it wasn't Alice, whose arms were otherwise engaged as she topped up trays of Irish Cream at the far side of the bar. The two spindly hands continued, threatening to tickle his chest through his thin white shirt:

Cassandra.

Ooh, that woman. Forever creeping up behind him when he least expected it.

"I'm starting up a travelling library service again for the local villages," she said, letting him go at last and spinning him around as if they were about to take to the floor on *Strictly*, which she could flaming well forget, he'd played the charming Anton du Beke with her for long enough.

Tonight he was Alice's. All Alice's, and in many ways their 'going away car' moment, a piece of cinema he had endlessly visualised over the past couple of weeks, couldn't not put his beloved in mind of one of those vintage after-the-wedding-reception cars, a move he thought portended well for their new life together. Of course, there was the slight issue that he still insisted upon driving a mustard rust bucket. Some things, reassuringly, never changed.

"And I just wanted to let you know," Cassandra continued, bringing him right back down to Earth as she'd clearly intended, "that actually, it's with the help of Lord and Lady

Rigby-Chandler. You see, they don't know that I know that they know that this little charitable, do-good PR stunt of theirs is going to help more visitors tune into the TV to see their castle in ruins appearing on that documentary soon with your future stepfather, but if you can't scratch one another's backs from time to—"

"Oh absolutely, Cassie, I couldn't agree more, what a wonderful idea."

And it was, though he was loath to admit it. But never mind that, who in God's name had he left in charge of the music?

Just as Sting morphed into Mariah Carey, who began to croon out about all she wanted for the festive season, the door to the bar opened with an almighty bang. Lee welded himself to the far corner of the bar, an act that told River all he needed to know – in both senses of the word.

"Very *high-gurr* this is; isn't it?" said the outsider.

River was sure Blake was trying to say 'hygge', the Danish word for 'cosy' as he set foot inside The Cocktail Bar for the second time since River had made it his. Behind him, Georgina revealed herself, clad in a cranberry-red coat, her hand clutching at her swollen stomach – its shape now an ever-expanding figgy pudding.

Here we go again.

But then he remembered Mercedes' reassuring words and a strange but welcome calm descended upon him.

Everyone else fell quiet then too, except River. Because unlike the last time Blake took issue with his right as a human being to be, do and have what he wanted; to live his life, River was no longer scared.

"So… you found out I made Lee a manager, and now you're here to let us know about it. Let's give him a round of applause everybody."

All around him people slowly began to clap, faces looking from one to the other, clearly unsure where any of this was going; all excluding Terry who just looked utterly miffed at the audacity of his grown children to keep throwing not so much spanners, but entire toolkits in the works.

267

"You're sounding a bit surer of yourself than last time, Jackson. But what did I tell you? Should've taken heed of my warning: I'm the mallet, you're the mole, remember?"

"Then go ahead and do your best." River stepped forward, a willing volunteer.

"Yeah," Lee echoed confidently all of a sudden, un-gripping his limbs from the bar's counter, "I'm not your puppet anymore. Bring. It. On. Hopkins."

"Oh yeah... back for round two are we? Some people never learn, do they?"

A thunder that was unmistakably Hayley's threatened to take down not so much Blake but the entire bar as well. But River wasn't about to let her play Wonder Woman today. Blake and his sister were *his* excess baggage and if they'd chosen to set the scene here, he was more than prepared to deal with it.

"Do *his* best? Do *our* best, I think you'll find... oh yes, there have been any number of us involved in this little Operation dubbed 'Payback'," yelled Georgina, fire crackling in her eyes as she attempted to woo the crowd. "How's about this then ladies and gents, will this do you?"

She opened her coat to reveal not just another layer swaddling her rotund stomach, but a bottle; River's bottle, strapped to her side with a belt. She yanked it free and held it up high as if she were in a courtroom defending her brother: "River Jackson here... the town's beloved former indie swooner... he's only been contaminating your drinks."

River knew it was crucial to keep his cool now despite the inevitable shockwave of this image. Somehow he had to keep hold of Mercedes' assurance; somehow this was all going to blow over in moments.

He hoped.

Voices chirped and gasps rang out around the room. Alice looked to her love for an answer, he couldn't give her one. Heather looked downright ashamed taking him right back to the teenage time when he'd furtively added dope to her vegan brownies, getting all of her kundalini yoga class completely off their heads. Everybody else just merged into one single

268

being, reeling at the way he had let them all down. And Georgina began to open her mouth to carry on, at which point those former chirps and gasps became loud 'oohs' and 'ahhs' and 'did you just *see* thats?' – with a whole range of colourful expletives thrown into the mix besides.

In the slowest of motion, her bump – or more precisely, the expandable, flesh-coloured stage prop that had been posing as her pregnancy all this time – slipped down her maternity trousers and fell in a heap on the floor, circling her feet.

The bar was engulfed in the kind of silence that only sudden shock can provide.

River was a Punch and Judy puppet, minus the helping hand, gulping at air like the oxygen might convert to words, offering up some kind of sense to put to this diabolical scene from the Callous Crocodile. But out of his mouth came nothing.

It had been Georgina all along. She was a schemer and a liar, an evil, ridiculous piece of work. Even Blake raised his eyebrows then, began to step back from his poisonous sister and her latest ludicrous scam.

"Georgina Hopkins!" Terry burst out, almost on the verge of tears, "I think I could just about disown you for this."

But then in a moment seemingly more choreographed than pro-wrestling, Lennie burst into the bar before anybody else could even think to add their two pennies worth.

"Sorry I'm late, guys," he fell about, coughing, spluttering and panting all at once. "It was…" he just couldn't seem to get his words out, laughter consuming him now, giant exuberant guffaws, the annoyance that is a private joke the recipient refuses to share, yet refuses to stop cackling at either.

"I say it was… it was water!"

"You say what?" said Georgina.

"Could it ever have been anything else?" He started up again with his ghastly noise. "He's a River… and he's been serving you all up water."

No wonder it had been tasteless when River had asked Mercedes for a little. His mouth remained agape, unable to process what he thought he had just heard Lennie declare. And how did *he* know anyway? He'd never even met Georgina.

"Give me that flaming lab report." Georgina yanked it from his hand, pregnancy bump still framing her matching cranberry-red high heels, showing her up as her own unmistakable piece of evidence. "You've got to be lying out of your giant backside, fat use you've been to me since day one."

"Now, now, I rather think that's a little uncalled for, darling. It has been my absolute pleasure to double cross you." He handed her over a piece of paper as would a gentleman. "Why else do you think I jumped at the chance to get involved? As soon as I twigged I might be River's daddy; that was it, everything changed. See, the real reason I came back to try and patch things up, Son—"

"Do not... call me... that word," said River. "You have absolutely zero proof."

"You're right there, of course you are. Call it a sixth sense though, your mother and I... you might want to cover your ears at this point," Lennie advised Terry, whose iron grip had positioned itself either side of Heather and Aunt Sheba, "well, it was a one-nighter, Glasto summer of eighty-three if I recall correctly. I'm not going to insist we do a test on you and me though, like we did with the bottle. I can feel it in my bones: I'm your father for sure, why else would you have such a love of music? I'm here if you want me... always... you've only to knock at my—"

"That's enough," snapped River. "Thanks, but no thanks."

Everybody's eyes naturally returned to Georgina now as she studied the document, her own eyes glossed over in denial.

"Composition breakdown – H20," she read aloud, all her previously put-on decorum a thing of the very distant past. "It can't be... you've rigged it... I knew I should have taken care of that part myself."

"Too greedy, love, weren't you... That's why I had to call in Tamara, get an injection of cash to meet your demands."

"Tamara, as in my sister?" shouted Alice, unable to disguise her contempt.

"Yes, Alice, and I'm sorry by the way, for hounding you as well... especially now I know my true relationship with my former lead singer—"

"Oh, I am not your anything, quit while you're ahead, Lennie," River pitched in.

"As I was saying, now I know the true nature of our relationship," Lennie continued unfazed, directing his words between River and Alice, "you have my solemn vow that I will leave you alone, the both of you… you make a jolly good couple by the way… especially seeing's you make that tart," he swivelled to point to Georgina, who unbelievably had the nerve to still be standing there with the stage prop at her feet, hand now diva-like on hip, "green with envy."

Georgina looked to Blake for back-up, it wasn't forthcoming.

"I fail to see why any of this is remotely funny."

Lady Rigby-Chandler scraped her seat across the floor making a sound akin to fingernails running down a blackboard, and all fell quiet again.

Except for Aunt Sheba.

"You're damned right there. What a heartless, twisted little madam you are. Who fakes a pregnancy? Have you any idea how many of us have baby stories, *real* baby stories about our cherished infants who never got to set foot on this Earth. You should be locked up, young lady in my humble opinion. And I'll tell you what: I hope you never do get to experience the joys of having a child. Why in God's name should you when you make a mockery of a heaven sent gift not all of us got to see to fruition?"

Heather took Aunt Sheba in her arms. Terry's face was ablaze. In fact, everywhere River looked – despite his own undeniable relief not to be fathering any baby of Georgina's – folk were outraged, disgusted, dismayed, seething. What an incredible anti-climax to what was supposed to be the event of the year in this place that had known nothing but his heart and his soul.

Lady Rigby-Chandler stepped forward then and River hoped against hope that somehow order would now prevail. She snatched the report – and the bottle – from the statue that was Georgina, passed River back his property, and surveyed the document for herself.

"Why yes, it is water. Not quite as velvety as *Evian*. But pretty soft on the palate all the same. And why shouldn't a mixologist add a little water to his creations? Who else here is qualified enough to tell me otherwise?"

Georgina went to open her mouth.

"Now, Gee, you know that's not true," River found himself stepping forward too. "From what I hear, you missed most of the final quarter of the course I invested hundreds of pounds to send you on."

Georgina bowed her head, finally moving out of her circle of shame which she picked up and tucked under one arm, as if she might put it back in the wardrobe, bringing it out again for a rainy day.

"The head of the Brunswick wrote to tell me he couldn't issue your certificate, after all," River went on, "so it wasn't just the missing money from the till... or you and your gentlemen friends' gate crashing the premises which led to my decision to turf you out."

"I'm embarrassed, George," said Terry, shaking his head helplessly, wiping his eyes with his frayed brown handkerchief. "What's it come to, eh? I didn't bring you up a liar, a grasser-upper or a stitcher-upper besides. River's a good kid, well... man. You had your chance with him; you had your chance of a really great career in this here bar too. But you went and blew both, nobody but yourself to blame. And that's why River and Alice, you have my blessing."

"And mine," said Heather, "woo hoo, I'd been rooting for you two lovebirds to make a nest all along."

"Oh gawd."

River put his hands behind his head, a somewhat pointless coping mechanism, and Alice's eyes grew to the size of flying saucers, as was usually the case when she knew not what to say. They'd dealt with more focus upon them in their past lives, true, but nothing quite compared to the focus of your nearest and dearest – a couple of foes besides – topping your never-in-your-wildest-dreams-wedding-cake with a big fat cherry.

River wondered who'd spark up the next piece of dialogue. Lennie soon answered his question.

"I'm sorry, Alice, about your sister's involvement in all of this." Lennie bowed his head as if worshipping a deity. "But the fact of the matter is, there was no way I was prepared to pay for anything myself, that would have felt plain wrong, I merely stepped in to ensure River was protected… in the end that was relatively easy."

"And what about this weird mystical translation?"

Georgina scrabbled about in her bag, finally revealing a very crumpled piece of paper.

"I think we're done now, George," said River. "You must think I was born yesterday… but I knew all along it was you stealing snippets from my cocktail bible… talk about scraping the barrel."

Which was an outright lie and he knew it.

"She paid me too," Lennie cut through everybody all over again, visibly wanting to continue to offload his shame. "And the truth is," he paused then to suck in air as if it were a substitute fag, not before pulling one of those vile E-cigarette things out of his jacket pocket, "the truth is, it was a pretty penny too."

"Jesus Christ, does everything have to be about money with you?" River cut in.

"Come on, guys, see this from my point of view. I've lost a lot. Gigs cancelled, new album postponed, bills to pay, expenses going out on auditions for new recruits, not to mention covering for Bear's Priory bill. That all adds up."

"So she was happy to fund you as opposed to lend some money to her sister. Lovely," said Alice.

"That you are, sweetheart," said Lennie, treating her to his habitual eyelash flutter. "It's just like Snow White and the wicked Stepmother." He enjoyed another drag on his black shiny stick.

"The only wicked Stepmother in this place is her," said Georgina, pointing at Heather.

It was unbelievable how much lower she was prepared to go, but once the final remnants of your dignity had deserted you, River supposed there were no limits to how far you could exceed yourself.

"I hope you're not talking about River's mother like that," said Alice.

River didn't dare clock Terry's expression, could practically feel the steam emanating from his ears.

"Yeah," said Hayley.

River had been wondering how long his third favourite woman in the world would be able to stay out of this.

"Your dad deserves a little happiness now… and if that's with *his* mother," she gave River a mutual nod as if to confirm his mutual ranking in *her* world, "so be it. Anyways Lady Muck, from what I've been told, you were the one to come up with the idea of a travel group. You shot yourself in the foot there if you didn't want Terry mixing with the women." She threw in a laugh accompanied, of course, by a snort.

"The lady's right, you can't eternally blame your parents for the way life's turned out."

A man seated towards the back of the gathering, until now hidden completely from River's line of vision, and, going by the look of glee on Hayley's face, hers too, stood then.

"Everybody has a shovel load of crap to deal with at some point in their childhood," TV Exec Bob went on. "I'm living proof of that, and look what I've achieved, all despite one of the most working class, broken family beginnings you could imagine."

"He's right." River took over the imaginary baton he felt had been handed to him. "And at least you started out with both parents around; at least you and Blake had each other."

Blake half-raised an eyebrow at that; sort of conceding River might have a small point.

"Look at me. I've probably got any number of half siblings roaming around the planet, and I'm lumbered with a father who up and left before my goddess of a mother had even popped me out – a father who, as it turns out was probably my flaming band manager, unbeknownst to either of us for over a decade, a father who could give your beloved Lord Pervert a run for his money," the latter slipping out of River's mouth before he could stop it, but fortunately nobody was any the wiser and so he carried on. "But what would you know, I'm actually relatively unscathed... even after all that."

"Speaking of numbers," Terry interrupted, "what she's not told you is she's had *any number* of invites out to sunny Spain from her mother. I've told her she should go, learn the lingo, stay a season or two, put the past behind her, and see where the wind takes her."

"And as for him," Terry nodded at his son, "he's got possibilities that could turn into permanent commitments back here if he gets his act together."

"What's that supposed to mean, Da—?"

Terry walked to the door then, heads following him as if he were the tennis ball in a Wimbledon final, he ignored his son's question and moments later called in a young boy, a young boy who turned out to be Blake's son. Blake's ex-wife trailed, protectively, not far behind him, she stood at the door with arms folded, looking on unconvinced. Ethan ran across to his dad and Blake began to sob.

It was a magical moment, all traces of anger at River's former friend, dissolving in a heartbeat. Hurt people hurt people, and that was all there was to it.

"I'm sorry... I will sort my head out now, no more letting you down anymore, I promise... I promise you and your mum. I really will be a proper dad to you from now on."

"Don't get too used to this, it's early days, and I am categorically not part of the plan," said Blake's ex.

"I wouldn't worry about that, love." Georgina just had to pipe up again, one last time. "He's got himself a Zara now, pop next door if you want to check out the competition... might have to wait until the morning though: shop's shut at the moment."

"The only thing that should be shut now is your mouth!" shouted Blake, his eyes finally seeing through the malice of his sibling. "I'm sorry... I didn't mean to come out with it like that... I'm just fed up with her butting into my life all the time. Dad's right, Sis, best thing you can do for yourself now, best thing you can do for all of us is to fly out to Benidorm...

tonight. Here." He released Ethan from his embrace and walked over to Georgina, handing her a bundle of notes. "Take what you need and come back when you've got your head straight, but I'm inclined to say preferably never. There's nothing for you here, all you seem to do is cause everyone grief."

Georgina accepted the cash in her right hand, and, with the mock bump still tucked under her wing, she turned on her heel, walked out the door, and didn't look back.

"Pain's me to say it," said Terry, "but I'm kind of hoping that's the last I'll see of my daughter for some years, until she's matured, got her head screwed back on, made a life for herself. All of which is highly unlikely under the influence of the mother who had umpteen affairs when our George was a wee nipper, but still, one lives in hope."

"You did your best, Terry," said Heather, looping her arm in his.

"Yes, you did, Dad, you did a stellar job. I, for one, am thankful, it can't have been easy."

"Nothing worthwhile ever is, Son."

"Ha, don't think *you're* off the hook already. You have a lot to prove," Blake's ex-wife retorted again, still reluctant to desert the frontline of the bar. "Until I'm persuaded otherwise, until the courts are too, everything's gonna be *through* and *with* your dad, Blake. I don't trust you without Terry. You've got a lot of winning back in that department to do, before I grant you any time alone with our child."

Blake smiled, acknowledging the truth in her decision. Clearly there was a lot that both had, and hadn't, gone on behind closed doors in their relationship. He genuinely hoped Blake would make amends, turn his life around now he had been given the chance.

Gradually, with nothing further to publicly announce, individual conversations started to spring up until they became fountains of fun. The travel agents – although only merry – had begun a worm-ish Conga, grabbing at people to join them as they wended their way around the bar, ever hopeful it would grow into a snake; Lee and Jonie were clearing away glasses, providing the last of the Irish Creams to the most recent arrivals, Blake had departed with Terry, Ethan and his ex-wife, unbelievably giving River a Hitler style salute, and perhaps more unbelievably still, not batting an eyelid at Alice, whose magic had inexplicably worn off.

Perhaps Zara really was the woman who had achieved the impossible? He'd choose to believe that anyway, just as he'd choose to interpret Blake's extremist parting gesture as an olive branch of sorts. Heather hovered a short way behind them at the doorway, waving them off, more radiant than River remembered her ever being in any of the outlandish outfits she had donned for her processions and conventions.

Could anybody be leaving this bar on a better potential happily ever after? New beginnings called for each and every person who'd celebrated and deliberated that particular evening in December 2017. Of course, this was in no small part thanks to one group of very special Toltex Indians, in no small part thanks to one marvellously mystical woman named Mercedes – who River quickly realised shared joint third place on his Favourite Females in the World list.

Yet all of this was also, in no small part, thanks to himself for having the belief to listen to his inner voice that day almost a year ago, when it led him deep into the Mexican *campo*. Despite the twists and turns that inner knowing had led to, it had proven just about the best life lesson: to think with his heart, not his head. And now, for however many years he had left on this planet, he vowed to remember it. Well, as much as was humanly possible, anyway.

Belief is everything.

Wasn't that what Felix had said when he'd dropped him off at his hotel? It had been a placebo all along, nothing more than a bottle of water – on paper at least. Except River chose to think otherwise; this was no ordinary water. This wasn't even water from the town's Chalice Well, or nearby Bath's Roman Spa. This was 'a little bit special' in the words of one Terry. It was water with one super powerful blessing, all right.

***

River squeezed Alice's hand. He took a deep breath and started up the ignition.

"So… where are we driving to now, James?"

"God, you are starting to sound Somerset again."

They both giggled at that, the relief enveloping the Citroën and themselves in a warmth that suggested the craziest, biggest bridge they would ever come to know in their relationship, had been crossed now. Those Three Billy Goats Gruff; Lennie, Blake, Georgina – four he supposed if you counted Tamara and her handiwork, far behind them.

"Actually, that might come in handy… Somerset… Cornish, they're kind of the same."

"I'm not so sure anybody from Cornwall would agree with you there," said Alice.

"We could always put it to the test, what do you say?"

"We *are* going to Cornwall? Do you mean to say that was the surprise?"

"One of the surprises... I hear there might be a pub up for sale in that general kind of direction… a pub in need of a little cocktail bar conversion… which might just happen to be in the same village as some buildings commonly referred to as stables… with a gert lush farmhouse attached to them besides."

"Now you're going all Bristolian on me… and no, no, you aren't serious… Oh, River, I—" Alice's eyes filled up with tears.

"I think we've both been holed up in that caravan too long, and we've both put other people's happiness first for too long." Of the latter, River was surer than he'd ever been about anything in his life. "Time to treat ourselves now, I can't promise I'm going to be the lucky bidder, but I'm sure as hell going to give it my best shot… kind of helps knowing your dad has offered to counterbid, should the offers exceed my retainer."

"Daddy's what?"

"He's popping down next week… your mother's blissfully unaware though… so Mum really is the word."

"Ha," said Alice with a smile. "That'll be easy on my

part… I'm just delighted to think he's finally making contact, even if it is behind her back. Sometimes I wish it had been Mummy and Tamara in one house, Daddy and me in another. Family dynamics would have been a whole lot better that way."

"If there's one thing I know for sure, it's that we don't choose our families… well," Heather's reminder flashed before him, "at least not when we're in this physical incarnation."

"*Que sera sera.* Let's look to the future now." Alice's grin grew wider at the very idea.

And it was no ordinary grin, but that legendary spellbinder of hers, the one that had broken Blake's heart, the one that had broken too many wooden jerks of an actor's hearts, but the one that hopefully wouldn't do the same to River's.

She couldn't have sounded more like Mercedes when she said that, and that had to stand his vulnerability in good stead, at the very least – the rest he'd make up as he went along. Yet those three simple Spanish words were as true in his life and Alice's, as they were in anybody else's, be it a question of labour or love, Blake or Georgina, the world's most off-the-wall-and-all-the-more-beautiful-for-it taxi driver, or heck, even the Rigby-Chandlers.

Except in English they translate to five words: what will be, will be.

River Jackson would take it one step further than that though: when we want something so badly that we're scared it might consume our very soul, and then we surrender to that soul's dark night; when we get out of our own way and stay there just a little while, finally, one morning we rise to see that the universe had our back all along, the dark clouds have parted, the sun is shining, and we have arrived at that perfect place.

THE END

Tor In The Mist – created by Vanessa Couchman
Ingredients:
Somerset Apple Brandy
Somerset Apple Juice
Mint sprigs arranged to look like trees
1 pellet of dry ice (frozen CO2) to make it fog
One of the most dazzling creations in River Jackson's bar, no visit to Glastonbury is complete until you have sampled a Tor In The Mist. This liquid sensation is guaranteed to take Instagram, and the Glastonbury Festival foodie stands by storm, in the year that is 2018.
Dry ice should never be handled directly, but picked up with tongs! The pellet drops to the bottom of the glass and dissolves before the drinker can get to it (unless they are a very thirsty drinker…).

Avalon Amber – created by Ailsa Abraham
Ingredients:
Somerset Apple Juice
Gingerbread Spice Cordial
This non-alcoholic cocktail (the only teetotal brew to be found in The Cocktail Bar), is a simple yet complex concoction comprising of locally grown Somerset apples, with a tot of gingerbread spice cordial for that wickedly subtle hint of spells!
It tastes sublime and is best supped on a cold winter's afternoon in front of a roaring log fire, preferably accompanied by a book about ley lines or crystals or shamanism.

The Magical Mañana – created by Isabella May (with a little help from River Jackson)
Ingredients:
1 measure Tequila
1 measure Sherry
Freshly squeezed Orange Juice to taste
10 globules of high quality Spring Water… and a belief in magic
Muddle everything together and wait for miracles to happen!

Fantastic Books
Great Authors

CROOKED
CAT

Meet our authors and discover
our exciting range:

- Gripping Thrillers
- Cosy Mysteries
- Romantic Chick-Lit
- Fascinating Historicals
- Exciting Fantasy
- Young Adult and Children's
  Adventures
- Non-Fiction

Visit us at:
www.crookedcatbooks.com

Join us on facebook:
www.facebook.com/crookedcatbooks

Made in the USA
Columbia, SC
07 April 2018